# PRAISE FOR JERUSHA AGEN

"Fast-paced, explosive thriller. I couldn't turn the pages fast enough."

CARRIE STUART PARKS, AWARD-WINNING,
BESTSELLING AUTHOR OF *RELATIVE SILENCE* ON
*RISING DANGER*

*"Rising Danger* grabbed me from the first chapter and never let go. Don't miss this edge-of-your-seat story of suspense and romance."

– PATRICIA BRADLEY, AWARD-WINNING AUTHOR
OF THE *LOGAN POINT* AND *MEMPHIS COLD CASE*
*SERIES*

# COVERT DANGER

# BOOKS BY JERUSHA AGEN

## GUARDIANS UNLEASHED SERIES

*Rising Danger* (Prequel)

*Hidden Danger*

*Covert Danger*

*Unseen Danger* (2023)

*Falling Danger* (2023)

Untitled Book Five (2024)

## SISTERS REDEEMED SERIES

*If You Dance with Me*

*If You Light My Way*

*If You Rescue Me*

# COVERT DANGER

GUARDIANS UNLEASHED  BOOK TWO

# JERUSHA AGEN

 SDG Words, LLC

© 2022 by Jerusha Agen
Published by SDG Words, LLC
www.JerushaAgen.com

Library of Congress Control Number: 2022914968

ISBN 978-1-956683-18-9

Scripture quotations are from The ESV® Bible (The Holy Bible, English Standard Version®), copyright © 2001 by Crossway, a publishing ministry of Good News Publishers. Used by permission. All rights reserved.

This book is a work of fiction. Names, characters, places, and incidents are the product of the author's imagination or are used fictitiously. Any resemblance to actual events, locales, or persons, living or dead, is coincidental.

# ACKNOWLEDGMENTS

The process of writing and publishing *Covert Danger* proved, once again, that publishing is not a solo effort. I'm grateful for those who came alongside to support my work, who contributed knowledge and information, and who simply asked me how the writing was going.

This is my chance to thank a few of you specifically who made a big impact.

The enthusiastic readers of the Guardians Unleashed Series—your excitement and impatience for this book provided the motivation and inspiration I needed to see it to completion. I hope you enjoy the results!

Marcela Charles, you are one of the coolest people I know and the inspiration for this book's heroine in many ways. Thank you for helping me get the Spanish right and for giving me a glimpse into Colombian culture.

Federal Special Agent Judy Adams, one of the most thrilling sequences in this book was made possible by your willingness to share your wealth of knowledge and experience in law enforcement. I'm so thankful God brought you to my inbox when He did and that you were willing to help add more realism to the lives of the ladies and canines at the Phoenix K-9 Security and Detection Agency.

Allie Kirsteatter and Leah Kirsteatter, thank you for your friendship and enthusiastic encouragement for every step of writing, editing, and publishing *Covert Danger*. Your excitement for this project and interest in all the details were bright spots of hope and joy for my (sometimes weary) writer's soul.

To Stephanie M. Gammon, Julie Grace, and Natalya

Lakhno, I give my thanks for taking the time to read the earliest copy of this work, for catching errors, and for giving the story your hearty approval to be launched into the world.

Angelique Daley, thank you for lending your sharp eyes to catch the remaining final typos that hide from everyone but you.

To Mom, my best friend, greatest supporter, and brilliant brainstorming partner—thank you for reminding me of the truth and believing in me when I lose sight of my purpose and certain hope. I couldn't do this without you.

*To my Savior Jesus Christ*
*—the Way, the Truth, and the Life*

*Soli Deo Gloria*

*And we know that the Son of God has come and has given us understanding, so that we may know him who is true; and we are in him who is true, in his Son Jesus Christ. He is the true God and eternal life.*

1 John 5:20

# ONE

*Colombia – Three years ago*

The CIA had trained her to withstand interrogation and torture, but they'd never prepared her for a stench like this one. The putrid scent greeted Marita Gomez as she opened her eyes and immediately assessed what she could see and feel.

She lay on her side, facing a cement wall. Where the wall met the floor, dark blotches of rotting food attracted a gathering of cockroaches.

Her hands and feet were tied in front of her body with thick rope that chafed her skin.

She tried not to inhale more of the foul odor than necessary as she used her elbow to push off the cold floor and tensed her ab muscles enough to sit up.

Her vision blurred, and she swayed. The blow she'd taken from behind when fighting off the rebels had apparently been hard enough to knock her out and leave her with concussion symptoms. In this windowless room, she couldn't tell how long she'd been unconscious.

She must be in the ERC terrorists' bunker. If she could

believe what her source Ramone Benito had told her about its location, she at least knew where she was geographically.

She blinked until her eyes began to clear, then scanned the room.

Small, almost square, and dimly lit with one bulb that dangled from the dark ceiling.

The only apparent exit was the door six feet away from her. A heavy steel door that was sure to be locked.

*"Jacob says you're CIA."* The rebel leader's accusation pounded in her brain, adding punch to her growing headache.

The meeting should have gone smoothly. Twice before, she had met with the leader, Martinez, and other members of the group for recorded interviews, using her nonofficial cover as a documentary filmmaker friendly to the rebels' cause. But this time, the meeting had been an ambush.

Thanks to the one weakness she didn't know she had.

Hot fury surged through her body, combating the dampness that seeped through her jeans from the hard floor.

Jacob. Fellow CIA agent. Her fiancé.

And rebel conspirator.

How could she have trusted a man who would help terrorists? A traitor to the United States' interests?

Even worse, he had exposed her cover, told the rebels she was a CIA operative. He knew betraying that secret would be signing her death warrant.

Had he ever loved her at all?

She shouldn't feel the pain that squeezed her heart. The hurt. Her instructor at The Farm six years ago had told her she'd better do something about her soft heart, or she would never survive the Central Intelligence Agency. She had tried to harden herself ever since—a task made easier by every killer she faced, death she witnessed, and lethal action she had to perform.

Her heart was like an impenetrable rock now.

Except for the hidden pocket where she'd let Jacob in. Where she'd loved him. Become involved enough that the agency wanted them to get engaged and told them to marry as soon as this assignment was completed so they wouldn't pose a security risk.

It should have been safe to trust a fellow CIA agent.

But she'd forgotten he was as good at deception as she was. He'd been trained in the art of it, too.

A clang cut through her thoughts and jerked her gaze to the door as it began to open.

*Idiot*. She should have been breaking free from her bindings, not psychoanalyzing the worst mistake of her life.

A man in his late seventies entered the room, his movements slow but elegant.

Ramone.

She let out a breath as her asset within the ERC came closer under the bulb, the light casting shadows in the wells of his thin face. But her muscles didn't release their tension.

Her trust in Ramone hadn't backfired yet. As the founding leader of the ERC, his dismay at the terrorism the group was embracing had only grown stronger during the months she'd known him. Still, one could never be entirely sure of a source within the enemy's camp.

"*Que está pasando?*"

He shook his head. "English. In case we are heard."

They better not be overheard, or Ramone would be killed, former leader or not.

"You know why you are here?"

She nodded, hiding a wince as the movement shot more pain to the front of her head. "Jacob turned on me."

Ramone stepped closer, looking down at her as the wrinkles that crossed his forehead deepened. "I'm sorry. I not know before today."

"I believe you."

"Martinez pay him to find assassin. Verdugo."

The unidentifiable assassin the CIA had been trying to catch for years? His penchant for skilled disguises was nearly all they knew about him. That and his genius for never being tied to any killings. The man was ruthless and a sought-after commodity for all types of assassinations, from political to personal. If the price was right, he'd do the job and do it better than most.

Ramone squatted in front of her as easily as if he were ten years younger. "Maybe Jacob think you get in his way."

And apparently loved money a lot more than she'd thought. At least that explained why he'd risked blowing his own cover when he exposed her. He'd already worked out a deal that would keep him safe. And get her killed. "Who is Verdugo supposed to take out?"

"*Senador* Hernandez."

Not surprising. The ERC had already made several attempts to halt the senator's presidential campaign. But Senator Hernandez was the favored candidate of the U. S. because of the democracy, peace, and freedom he would bring to Colombia if elected. It was the very reason Marita and Jacob were here.

The CIA had assigned Jacob to go undercover as an assistant to the U. S. ambassador who facilitated financial and political support for Senator Hernandez. Marita was supposed to work the rebel side, tracking their movements and attack plans through Ramone and her interviews as a friendly film-maker who wanted to make them famous heroes of Colombia.

Should have been a perfect plan. If she'd seen through Jacob's lies. If she'd known he would use his assignment to kill the very person he was supposed to help.

"When?"

"Soon." Ramone looked at his watch. "One hour. There is a meeting for his supporters and members of his party at the villa of Senador Cabrera. Verdugo must kill Hernandez in a way that seems he is killed by his *amigo*, a man of his party."

That explained why the ERC was shelling out the funds to hire a professional. If they pulled it off, Hernandez wouldn't just be dead—the whole political party would be compromised and could disintegrate into suspicions and accusations. "How long does it take to get to Cabrera's villa from here?"

"More than *uno* hour."

"Then you have to get out of here now so I can stop the assassination."

Ramone tilted his head, confusion clouding his eyes as he looked at the ropes that cinched her wrists. He checked over his shoulder. "I can free you."

She shook her head, ignoring the resulting pang behind her eyes. "I won't risk your life. You're far too valuable to us here. I never told Jacob about you, so you should be safe." Thanks to the fact she couldn't see Jacob while on this assignment without compromising their cover.

"I know. They kill me already if they know." Ramone slowly stood, a bit of stiffness betraying his age. "They keep you alive for hope of ransom. For now."

"Don't worry. That won't be an issue."

Ramone's salt and pepper eyebrows reached for his hairline.

"Trust me. Just go out there and make sure you have an alibi for my escape."

A small smile angled his closed lips as he reached in the pocket of his pants. "You will want this." He pulled out her cell phone and set it on the floor beside her leg.

He went to the door. Paused. Turned back. "Will I see you again?"

"They'll send you a new handler."

"*Cuídate*, Marita."

She met his gaze. Nodded. Taking care of herself would be her top priority.

He opened the door and closed it behind him.

She ducked her head and used her teeth to peel off the sticky, skin-colored covering secured to the inside of her upper arm. The small blade she had hidden beneath the adhesive stuck to the covering that dangled from her mouth. She grabbed the blade with her fingers and leaned forward to prop the getaway tool upright between her feet.

The rope that bound her wrists didn't last long with quick

sawing motions across the blade. As soon as the binding dropped from her wrists, she untied her ankles.

Just as the clang of the steel door opening resounded in the room.

Perfect.

She leaped to her feet and bolted to concealment behind the door.

The barrel of a rebel's shotgun proceeded him into the room.

She grabbed the easy target, yanked the weapon away, and pulled him past the door. She dropped the shotgun and jumped on his back in one swift move, slipping a chokehold around his neck.

He crumpled to the floor as quickly and quietly as she'd hoped.

She grabbed her phone and rapidly tapped through the sequence to access the backdoor messaging portal to headquarters.

*Assassin Verdugo to kill Sen Hernandez at 1800. Jacob turned. Will attempt to stop Verdugo.*

To her knowledge, she and Jacob were the only operatives in this sector.

Only her now.

Her captors must've taken her wristwatch, but she caught the time on her phone's screen. She'd have to make the drive to the villa in fifty-five minutes or less. Which meant she only had a few minutes to escape the bunker.

She pocketed her phone and took the semi-automatic shotgun in both hands. Thanks to the rebel who'd donated his weapon, that wouldn't be a problem.

Marita tried to explain to the armed security guard at the villa entrance that she was a member of the press. But the list of approved attendees was his law, and she wasn't on it.

She could force her way past him, but the ensuing

commotion would only help the assassin. The pistol she'd swiped from the ERC bunker on her way out rubbed against her back as she stepped away to scout another entry point into the sprawling villa.

Past the tall guard's bulk, she spotted Senator Hernandez. He stood in front of the huge fountain at the center of the courtyard that was surrounded by ornate balconies.

Balconies that were perfect for a sniper.

But she hadn't seen Verdugo or anyone behind the pillared railings when she'd stood closer to the guard.

Her phone buzzed in her pocket, and she whipped it out. Message from HQS.

*Go to airport. Booked on Flight 1113 home.*

Not the response she'd expected. Suspicion crept into her mind. Did they think she was a traitor, too?

She tabled the question. Right now, she had an assassination to stop. She moved toward her car so the guard wouldn't get suspicious. From there, she would park a short distance away and double back, approaching from the rear of the house.

Two shots rang out.

The guards left their post and rushed into the courtyard.

She darted through the entry into the chaos where politicians and supporters ducked and scattered, yelling, screaming.

Several men bent over the fallen senator by the fountain.

She checked the balcony.

A man rested a high-powered rifle on the railing. A man she recognized. Santiago Diaz, a member of the senator's party and one of his closest friends.

Shots pierced her ears as the guards returned fire.

Marita sprinted to the stairway she deduced led to the balcony. She rushed up the stone steps, gaze ahead and weapon ready.

She paused at the top of the staircase, back to the wall at the corner. Cleared the angles she could. She swung around the corner, pistol aimed.

A man lay next to the railing.

She hopped her gaze beyond and back to the unmoving man as she approached. She crouched behind the thick pillars that supported the railing so the guards wouldn't start shooting again. The rest of the balcony appeared empty.

She glanced down.

Diaz lay still, shot in the head. A pistol lay by his body near his hand, as if he had killed himself after shooting the senator. The rifle had been set down by the railing.

She scanned the rest of the balcony to check for surprises, then crouched to search for a pulse, not expecting to find one.

His skin was still warm, the blood moist.

Verdugo must have disguised himself to look like Diaz, whom he'd kidnapped and brought here. The assassin had likely killed Diaz as soon as the security guards returned fire.

It was a perfect crime. If she hadn't known Verdugo was here, she might have believed Diaz had done the shooting.

But the assassin would still have to get away.

And so would Jacob. He was supposed to attend this event. Perhaps he still had, even if only to deliver the balance of Verdugo's payment.

Verdugo must have taken the staircase on the opposite side of the balcony to escape without passing her on the way up.

She hurried to follow his probable exit, concealing herself behind pillars and other decorative objects on the way. She took the first exit out of the house and emerged behind the villa where a narrow road curved around the property's green lawn.

A small red car waited on the road. A getaway car?

Someone sat in the driver's seat.

Marita dropped and rolled to the left, though the driver likely would've shot at her already if he or she intended to.

Marita crouched as she approached from an angle outside the driver's peripheral vision. She knew not to hope this could be the assassin. Verdugo wouldn't make capture so easy.

She crept along the back door, nearing the driver's window with her pistol aimed. "Put your hands where I can see them."

No movement. No sound.

She repeated the command in Spanish.

Did that silhouette look like…?

Her step hitched for half a second. Then she pulled away from the car and swung her weapon on the driver.

Jacob.

His head was propped straight but supported by the headrest so he would stay that way. Because he couldn't hold his head up on his own. The single bullet wound in his skull made that obvious.

She scanned 180 degrees, weapon ready, in case Verdugo tried to finish her off, too.

The call of birds amplified the silence.

Until it was broken by a wailing shout inside. The senator must have died.

And so had Jacob. A victim of his own plan.

Deductions clicked into place as Marita lowered her weapon.

Verdugo had probably told Jacob to meet him here with the other half of the payment, since the assassin always wanted half up front and half after the job was done. Perhaps Verdugo even told Jacob he would be his getaway driver.

Greed must have blinded Jacob to the danger.

Just as love and foolish trust had blinded her.

A vibration shook her pocket, and she snatched her phone. Maybe HQS would offer a more helpful response this time.

But the text was from Johnson. The CIA operative whose life she'd saved two years ago in Somalia. He was posted at the home office now, moving up the ranks higher than Marita.

*You're suspected as traitor. Come in at your own risk. Now we're even. Destroy this message. Don't try to contact me.*

The news slugged Marita in the chest, stealing her wind. A traitor?

She swallowed. *Breathe.*

Air returned to her lungs as she forced her mind to override the horror that squeezed her throat. *Think.*

Of course they'd suspect her because of her personal relationship with Jacob. And because she had the inside track with the rebels who hired the assassin. It looked bad.

She had no evidence to the contrary. Nothing she could show the CIA that would make them believe her. If Jacob were alive, she might have a chance if he confessed and told them she wasn't involved. Even then, they might not have believed him. But he was dead, and there was nothing she could do to clear herself.

She couldn't go in. If she were tried and branded a traitor, it could make the news. If her parents found out, it would kill them. Patriotism meant everything to them.

And there was no way she was going to spend the rest of her life in prison.

She'd have to hide.

Wouldn't be hard. She'd been living with false identities for six years.

She looked at Jacob one last time.

And she didn't feel a thing.

Finally. She had the impenetrable heart of a perfect CIA agent.

Just in time to run.

# TWO

*St. Paul, Minnesota – Today*

Something was about to go wrong. The honed instincts that had saved Amalia Pérez's life more than once pulsed energy to her fingertips and prepped her for danger as she crossed the marble floor of the mansion's entry room. Her gaze didn't stop moving as she took in the minimalist décor, the empty spaces.

Raksa walked at her side, the German shepherd's nails clipping against the marble floor. His big, erect ears angled forward toward the figure standing thirty feet ahead. But the K-9's relaxed body language signaled he had determined the FBI agent wasn't a threat.

Amalia nodded to the agent who guarded the two hallways that split in opposite directions. Following the floorplan she'd stored in her head, she turned left into one of the oversized halls.

A woman and a black Labrador retriever headed Amalia's way at the other end of the hallway. Bristol Jones and Toby.

Amalia smiled at her co-worker from Phoenix K-9 Security and Detection. "Hey, Bris."

The brunette grinned as they moved closer, her explosives

detection K-9 skimming his nose over the floor and along the edges of the walls. "Raksa's looking very handsome today."

"Sure, admire the dog not the girl. Everybody does."

Bristol laughed. "Toby, release."

The women met in the middle of the hallway and let the dogs greet each other. The boys had been best buddies since Bristol and Toby had crashed at Amalia's house last year when a terrorist bomber was targeting the former explosives technician. The only challenge now was to keep the dogs from playing every time they saw each other.

"Can you believe this estate?" Bristol glanced at the marble walls and cast her gaze upward to the unnecessarily high ceiling.

"The FBI scored big when they got possession."

Bristol nodded, returning her gaze to Amalia. "I heard it belonged to an embezzler. Works pretty well as a luxury safe house."

Amalia shrugged. She understood why the Federal Bureau of Investigation wanted to use the mansion to house all three witnesses who were to testify against alleged arms trafficker, Leland Rottier. The mansion was isolated from the city in a suburb, settled on ten fenced acres. The FBI controlled access with gates and a security system. Should be a cinch to keep secure. "I'm with Phoenix. It could backfire."

"Yeah." Bristol glanced at the dogs as they settled beside their handlers instead of trying to play. "I'm sure the security is cheaper and easier for the FBI with only one location to protect, but..."

Amalia knew exactly what Bristol meant. "It makes a pretty tempting and obvious target." If Rottier decided to eliminate the witnesses before they could testify, as the FBI anticipated, he might not be able to resist the chance to take them all out at once. "I'm glad you and Toby are searching for bombs. That should rule out the easiest method of killing all the witnesses in one blow."

Bristol smiled. "Pun intended?"

"Of course." Amalia winked.

Bristol chuckled. "Then you and Raksa better take care of the other threats. I mean, we can't do everything."

Amalia laughed. "No worries, girl. We got your back. But I guess that means we'd better get to it. We're on duty in five."

"Right. I saw Nevaeh and Alvarez outside at the west end a few minutes ago. Catch you later." Bristol looked down at her K-9. "Toby, search."

He launched into action, and Raksa wagged his tail as he watched his friend leave.

"Come on, boy. We've got someone to see before we start our patrol this morning."

Amalia rounded the corner to another hallway as her sense of foreboding returned. Due to her security concerns. Couldn't have anything to do with the fact she was about to see Michael Barrett for the first time in twelve years.

Though maybe her instincts knew her encounter with him wouldn't go well. But it couldn't be avoided. She needed to see him alone to prevent him from blurting her name and other compromising information in front of anyone.

She reached the room he'd been assigned to, and Raksa stopped at her side. She checked her radio earpiece to be sure it was still switched off. Technically, she wasn't on duty for another fifteen minutes, and she couldn't risk anyone hearing this exchange.

Rapping her knuckles firmly on the carved wooden door, she spoke the password of the day. "Security, four nine three."

"Hold on." A strong, male voice powered the words. Deeper than she remembered.

She slammed a mental door on any emotions that might try to emerge from her vault. She was Amalia Pérez now. She had no emotions connected to Michael Barrett.

The door opened, and a man she didn't recognize stood in front of her.

This wasn't the lanky eighteen-year-old she'd left to return to college. This man filled out even his relaxed, light blue button-down shirt and jeans with a mature, buff physique Michael never had. Intentional stubble contoured the jaw she hadn't remembered being so chiseled, and the head he'd always kept shaved now sported brown hair parted down the middle, falling on both sides in waves that teased his ears.

He looked like some hunky actor or model, not Michael.

He seemed to be just as taken aback at the sight of her. His widened gaze scanned her, then dropped to Raksa, probably noticing the vest that identified him as a protection dog with Phoenix K-9. Michael pushed a tanned hand through his hair as he raised his head, lifting the brown thickness away from where it had fallen into his face.

His attention landed on Amalia, soft blue eyes targeting her gaze.

There. There was the Michael she knew.

"Sofia?" His one-word question was heavy with shock.

It jolted her back to the present. To the reality that she'd almost felt something. Unacceptable.

She checked to her left and right, verifying the hall was empty. She shouldn't have let him get out that word.

"Hi, I'm Amalia Pérez." She flashed a big smile and pushed him inside by moving into his space with Raksa.

He backed into the large room with an incredulous expression that was pure Michael.

The old Michael. She had no idea what he was like now, and she'd better remember that. He wouldn't have stayed the same. She certainly hadn't.

She scanned the room behind him for surprise witnesses or danger. A sitting area with a sofa and armchairs, wet bar in one corner, king-sized bed, and a short hallway that led to a private bath. The room belonged in a luxury hotel more than a house.

"Are you serious? You think I wouldn't recognize you?" A note of hurt touched his tone.

She reached back to shut the door. "For reasons of my own, I'm Amalia Pérez now." She kept her voice light, casual.

"I need you to promise not to mention my former identity to anyone or call me by that name at any time."

"Your *former* identity?" His straight brown eyebrows squeezed toward each other. "I don't get it. What are you doing here?" He glanced at Raksa again.

The dog stood, relaxed and panting at her side, wagging his tail as he watched Michael. At least Raksa's approval was a positive sign Michael might still be one of the good guys.

"I'm working in security and rescue services with the Phoenix K-9 Security and Detection agency. I'm part of the protection detail hired to patrol this property."

"That's not what I mean." Those blue eyes roved her face. "I can't believe you're here." The last words took on a breathless quality.

Was that a hint of moisture glistening in his eyes? Exactly the kind of emotional response she'd hoped to avoid.

"It's just part of my job, Mr. Barrett." The formal address might have been a bit much, but it did the trick.

His mouth sloped in a frown that made him look half-child and half-man as her memories of the boy collided with the man before her. "Your last email, the one you sent *six months ago*, said you were in Guatemala. Technologies consulting."

So, he did read the emails she sent to her parents. Necessary to keep them from thinking she was dead or in trouble, which could prompt them to search for her. But maybe he didn't read the emails himself. Her parents may have told him what she'd written if he didn't live at their house anymore. She kept her smile without a problem. "Six months is a long time."

"Are you saying you didn't lie about it? Because from where I'm standing, it's looking like you lied. To your parents." He took a step closer.

She put her hands on her hips to deter more forward motion.

He crossed his arms, corded muscles he didn't use to have tightening along his tan forearms beneath the sleeves rolled at his elbows. "No wonder I couldn't find you in Guatemala when I searched online. Or anywhere else you said you were. Why would you lie about where you were, what you were doing?"

She let her smile fade but kept her tone casual. "If I wanted them to know more, I would've said more. All you need to know is I'm Amalia Pérez, and I need you to call me Pérez or Amalia. Whatever makes you happy."

"Is there another option? Because I'm not happy. I'm disgusted." He turned away from her, walked a few steps to the large glass-topped desk along the wall where a notebook computer sat open.

He swung back. "I don't know why you lied to them and why you're lying now, but you know better than anyone I won't lie. For you or anyone else."

An odd sensation pinged her chest. As if he'd shot an arrow that bounced off the rock of her heart. She mentally brushed away the laughable image and returned to her objective—persuading an uncooperative protected witness not to blow her cover.

"There's a lot at stake in your cooperation, though I can't tell you what it is." The words, *You'll have to trust me*, died before they came out. She wouldn't go that far. Not with Michael. She didn't even trust herself, and she was the last person he would trust.

"I understand you don't want to lie." She held the breath she wanted to exhale. It'd be a tell that suggested compromise, giving up ground. "You don't need to lie about knowing me or keep our history a secret if you're asked directly. All I'm asking is that you call me by my right name and don't reveal my former identity to anyone. I am Amalia Pérez now, so you won't be lying. The person you knew no longer exists."

He walked farther away from her and stopped at the end of the large bed, looking out the glass patio doors eight feet in front of him. "Okay."

Amalia relaxed her grip on Raksa's leash. Another successful negotiation.

"But on one condition." He turned toward her, sunlight from the window behind him backlighting his strong frame. "That you tell me what happened to Sofia."

She nodded. A non-binding gesture. "I could do that."

Why hadn't she just straight-out lied and said she would? Some strange instinct made her pick the evasive phrasing that kept her from having to actually lie. She'd been able to abandon that avoidance tactic years ago, when she'd reached the point where any identity she chose to assume became real and allowed her to lie with authenticity in a way most people couldn't. Lying to Michael shouldn't be any different than—

A vibration in her back pocket saved her from having to answer her own question. She pulled out the cell phone.

Ramone.

Calling her? Two years ago, when she had moved to Minneapolis where she knew her asset from the Colombian rebel group planned to retire, she hadn't intended to contact him. But working for Phoenix K-9 meant she could use a source with a pulse on criminal and underground activities in the Twin Cities. She'd opened up communications with Ramone, and he'd proved useful again. Especially when the intel he'd provided helped them catch the bomber terrorizing the Cities last year.

But though he had Amalia's number, he'd only ever texted. A phone call had to mean this was something he wanted to guarantee she, and no one else, received.

"I have to take this." She turned toward the oversized armoire in the corner. "Hello?"

"*Quien es este?*"

She'd hoped to avoid saying another of her names with Michael in the room, but Ramone was being cautious, wanting to verify who she was. "Marita." Speaking only the name shouldn't make Michael assume *she* was Marita.

"Verdugo is here."

17

Amalia's grip tightened on the phone. "Are you sure?"

"*Si.* I confirmed with more than one of my people. Someone hired him for job in the Cities."

"What job?"

"I don't know."

Scenarios pulsed through Amalia's mind. Would the arms trafficker have brought in an assassin as high-caliber and expensive as Verdugo? It would be a smart move. Then again, there could be any number of criminals in the Twin Cities who might have contracted him for a different job. "Who hired him?"

"This I don't know, also. But I want to tell you he is here."

"Thanks. Keep me posted if you hear anything else."

"Si. Be careful, Marita."

"Trouble?" Michael's voice, different but familiar at the same time, beckoned her to turn around.

She could leave now. She'd accomplished what she needed to. Activating her radio earpiece, she smiled as she moved toward the door. "Patrol duty."

Raksa emitted a low rumble.

She jerked toward the K-9.

He stared at the patio doors, his erect ears trained forward.

"Is he growling at me?" Michael watched the dog with raised eyebrows.

"What is it, boy?"

A bark burst from Raksa's deep chest, and he lunged toward the doors, hit the end of the leash. He barked and snarled as he pulled hard.

"Get down!" She released the leash, sprinted for Michael. Threw herself into his torso.

A suppressed shot sounded.

Glass splintered as they crashed to the floor beside the bed.

She rolled off Michael. Crouched to use the bed as cover while she drew her Glock from the holster in her waistband.

18

She peered around the corner of the bed, weapon aimed to return fire. She depressed the button for the coms radio. "FBI Team Leader, this is PT2. Active shooter. Backyard pool area."

Raksa snarled and barked, mostly drowning out the response from FBI Special Agent Katherine Nguyen.

"Raksa, here."

He ran to Amalia at her command but whirled to face the patio doors again, still vocalizing.

"Was that a bullet?"

She barely heard Michael's question over Raksa's loud barks.

A bullet puncture, positioned where Michael's head would have been, created a spiderweb circle of small broken pieces in the tempered glass.

The pool and patio beyond appeared empty, undisturbed. But the sniper likely lurked behind the row of manicured bushes that bordered the patio.

"Stay here." She held her crouch as she rotated to see Michael.

He kneeled inches away, his blue eyes locking with hers.

She cleared the sudden dryness from her throat and nodded past his shoulder. "Move to the wall. Wait here until I come back."

She turned away and picked up Raksa's leash. The dog stayed with her as she bent low and darted from sofa to desk, using the furniture as concealment on the way to the hallway.

Once in the hall, she burst into a sprint that Raksa easily matched.

As she reached the tall pillars that flanked the opening to the backyard patio, she slowed her pace. "Raksa, wait."

The shepherd let out a low rumble but stayed by her side.

She checked around the nearest pillar.

Something moved by the bushes on the far side of the pool.

A man walked onto the patio, Glock drawn. FBI cap on his head.

Amalia lowered her weapon.

A woman followed him. Agent Nguyen, the FBI agent in charge of protecting the witnesses.

Amalia stepped out onto the patio.

Raksa growled again. Was the sniper still close?

"Agent Nguyen!" The shout sounded in a male voice from behind the row of bushes. Nguyen swung back.

"Find it."

Raksa lurched forward at Amalia's command to look for the culprit. He jogged with her around the pool and onto the stone path that led to the other side of the bushes.

Nguyen and two other FBI agents surrounded a man lying on the ground. One of the agents checked him for a pulse.

Looked like Paul Bischoff, one of the wits the FBI was protecting. Or supposed to be. Didn't look like he'd need protection anymore.

Leaving the victim to the agents, she unclipped Raksa's leash and let him run ahead of her. She jogged after him, following the path that curved through the landscaped garden.

She scanned the map of the property in her mind, checking for quick escape routes. This garden led to a tennis court and then more gardens, all surrounded by a fence at the edge of the property. A road followed the distant border, but the back gate was guarded by the FBI just like the front gate.

Raksa slowed his run to a walk, then paused at a tree and looked back at her.

Maybe the shooter hadn't gone this way at all. Or Raksa wasn't sure who the shooter was.

Verdugo.

The hairs on the back of Amalia's neck pricked.

If the sniper was the skilled assassin, he likely would have used a disguise. Something to make him invisible in his surroundings. To make him look like he belonged there.

Like an FBI agent.

"Raksa, here."

The German shepherd hurried to her, his tongue dangling in the increasing heat of the summer day.

She could take Raksa past all the FBI agents to check them out, but most were strangers to him and all carried weapons. The K-9 was able to pick up on evil intent, but Verdugo, if that's who they were dealing with, wouldn't risk getting anywhere near the dog at this point. He'd keep his distance from Raksa but without being obvious.

The assassin could have already left, slipped away by behaving like an FBI agent checking the grounds.

Or he could be inside the house, attempting to kill the other wits.

Agent Nguyen had likely sent agents to secure the remaining witnesses, but what if Verdugo was one of those agents?

Amalia picked up her speed as she returned to the patio area.

An FBI agent took pictures of the body by the bushes.

Agent Nguyen stood nearby, talking to Michael. Who was supposed to be concealed in his room right now. He never had followed Amalia's instructions very well.

Nguyen looked at Amalia as she approached. "Anything?"

"No." Amalia focused on the agent but knew Michael watched her. "What was the witness doing outside?"

"Probably smoking."

She swung her gaze to Michael at his response.

His eyes were cloudy, mouth pulled into a pained frown. "I talked to him just a little while ago. He was planning to step outside. Said he needed some fresh air. I think he wanted a smoke. He was trying to quit, but the stress was getting to him."

"Didn't you remind him all witnesses were supposed to stay inside?"

He met Amalia's question with a hardening stare. "Yes. But he was making his own choice. That makes it okay, right?"

A low blow, perfectly executed. Maybe Michael had

21

changed just as much as she had. But he'd never be able to phase her with such tactics. She flashed an amused smile, then looked at Agent Nguyen. "Was he shot?"

The agent shook her head. "Not a mark on him. We're not sure how he was killed yet."

Not a mark. A Verdugo specialty when he needed to kill silently.

Amalia tucked her weapon into her IWB holster. "I have reason to believe the shooter may have been disguised as an FBI agent. I suggest you do an in-person roll call immediately to check that all the agents here are who you think they are." A personnel check might force Verdugo to leave if he had planned to continue masquerading as an agent while he killed the other witnesses.

One of Nguyen's eyebrows arched. "Care to explain why?"

"From the sound and damage to the door, I'm sure the shooter used a long-range sniper rifle with a suppressor. He would've had to set up a straight-on shot to hit the target through the tempered glass with one bullet. To make that shot without being seen, the shooter had to be here in the bushes." Amalia pointed to the row of dark green plants. "To get that close, he'd need to look like FBI."

Agent Nguyen placed her hands on her hips, one resting above her holstered weapon. "He obviously got in somehow, but not as FBI. The agents on this team all know each other, and there's the check-in process to get through the gates and into the house. It'd take a whole lot more than a fake badge and FBI cap to just waltz in."

"I think we're dealing with someone capable of much more than a simple disguise."

"Like in the movies?" The agent's mouth slanted in a disbelieving line.

Or covert operations. But Amalia stuck with a less revealing response. "Something like that, yeah."

"I'll need more to go on to pull them all in. Right now, I

need every agent available searching the grounds for the shooter."

Amalia couldn't reveal her source or her background to explain. She'd have to go through Phoenix to let Nguyen know about Verdugo. "At least let me check on the other witness with Raksa now."

"Of course."

Amalia glanced at Michael before she turned to leave.

He stared at the dead body, his features contorted with pain or dismay. She couldn't tell which.

He may never have seen the body of a crime victim before. First time was hard for most people.

Amalia pulled out her smartphone as she returned to the patio and veered around the pool to go inside. She selected the programmed number for Phoenix, who picked up before the first ring ended.

"Katherine filled me in." Wonderfully efficient as always, Phoenix didn't waste a moment on greetings. "I'll be there in ten."

Amalia wasn't surprised Agent Nguyen had already called Phoenix. Amalia's boss was the only person she knew who was close enough to the agent to use her first name.

"I think I know who did it." Amalia watched Raksa's body language as they entered the house again.

His tail and posture were relaxed, as if the threat had passed. But Raksa was only working moment by moment. Amalia had information he didn't. "If I'm right, this protection job just got a whole lot more complicated." Impossible for Amalia.

She filled Phoenix in on what she knew about Verdugo's reputation and tactics, sharing that she'd received a tip he was here and had dealt with him previously at the CIA.

She kept to herself what the assassin's arrival meant for her.

If the CIA was homing in on Verdugo, they would come to the Twin Cities. And find her.

Time to run again.

Thirty minutes. Michael sat silently in the passenger seat of the car for all that time while Sofia—*Amalia*—drove him to a different FBI safe house. This was the first time he'd seen his best friend in twelve years, but neither of them had said a word the entire drive. The questions that had clamored to be voiced when he'd first seen her seemed to pale in importance after they'd found Paul Bischoff. Dead.

But the killing didn't appear to bother his childhood buddy at all. He glanced at her profile, this woman who wanted to be called Amalia and who seemed to have become as different as her new name. The details of her features were the same, down to the small mole two inches below her eye on her left cheek. Yet time had changed her appearance somehow.

Now her high cheekbones seemed more prominent, transforming her face with dramatic angles and lines that accentuated her full lips and dark brown eyes in a way he'd never noticed before. Her complexion reminded him of a light brown topaz, smooth and mesmerizing.

Her hair was shorter than the waist-length she'd had when he'd last seen her. But it still cascaded well past her shoulders in thick, black waves that added to the womanly, attractive essence she'd never had when they were young. Or maybe their closeness then hadn't let him see it.

Her small hands relaxed on the wheel as she handled the car with ease on the freeway packed with traffic. Her gaze kept moving, checking the rearview mirror and everywhere else.

She oozed confidence, as she had from his earliest memories after their meeting as three-year-olds to the worst day of his life, when they'd fought, and she'd left. But her confidence then had been fueled by passion, by the emotional volcano harbored inside her that often erupted in torrents of fury, compassion, sadness, or love.

There was something glacial about her now, as if the volcano had frozen over.

"What happened to you?" The question came out before he decided to ask it.

She glanced at him with a smile and light laugh, her eyebrows lifted. "I don't think we have time for a twelve-year history."

"I'm not asking for that." At least not at the moment. "I just want to know what happened to the Sofia I knew."

Her gaze went to the side mirror, and she checked over her shoulder before switching to the right lane of the freeway. "You'll have to be more specific."

"Okay." Michael angled toward her as she signaled to take an exit ramp. "You used to cry if I killed a fly. Remember that?"

She didn't look at him.

"A man was killed today, and you didn't bat an eyelash."

She turned the car onto a four-lane street as he watched her for a response. "It's not the first time I've seen a dead body."

Wasn't his first either, and she knew it. She'd gone to the funeral home with him and attended the viewing and service for his mother. Since then, he had seen several other bodies in open coffins on such occasions. But he'd never seen someone he had talked to twenty minutes earlier murdered.

It was horrible. The senselessness, the injustice and cruelty of the killing churned his stomach with revulsion and anger. Some people would stop at nothing to silence the truth. "This was murder. Doesn't that bother you? Or have you really become that cold?"

"I protect and rescue people for a living." She waited at a light to take a left turn. "Sensitivity and emotion keep me from doing my job well."

"So you've what—stopped feeling?"

Her gaze landed on him, the dark caverns of her eyes so different from Sofia's that he couldn't begin to guess what she was thinking. "How did you end up in this mess? Become a witness worth killing?"

Deflection questions. He and Sofia had used the technique in their lying game when they were kids.

Amalia only asked the questions now to keep him from grilling her. But he'd play along, for the moment, if it got her to talk to him.

"I'm an investigative reporter."

"So I heard. Not all reporters get protection from the FBI." She checked the mirrors again as they drove past small businesses on a two-lane road.

"I was investigating arms trafficking at the Texas-Mexico border, and the trail of some major, frequent shipments led me to Rottier Furnishings."

"How did you find that connection when they're here in Minnesota?"

"Their headquarters are in Minneapolis, but they also have a factory and warehouses in Texas. I discovered Leland Rottier was behind the arms trafficking, using his company as cover to ship arms illegally. My articles in the Houston Chronicle drew the attention of the FBI. When they saw the evidence I'd gathered, they launched an investigation of their own and decided to prosecute."

"Ah." She scanned the other vehicles as they reached a four-way stop. "And did you persuade the other witnesses to talk?"

"Most of the sources I approached weren't eager to talk to an investigative journalist. The FBI had more success recruiting Brenda Nixon to testify. But Paul was different." Michael looked out the passenger window, watching houses that replaced the businesses as they moved into a residential neighborhood.

"He'd been the Houston branch location's bookkeeper for ten years. He was tired of living with the guilt from keeping quiet about what was happening there." A lump clogged Michael's throat. Paul had agreed to testify in court, even though he knew what Rottier could do.

Michael cleared his throat. "He was vital in helping me get the evidence I needed to make a case against Rottier. And his testimony in court as a firsthand witness would have had a big impact in the trial."

Now Paul had given his life for that effort. *Lord, please comfort his family.* He had a wife and two adult children who would mourn his passing.

But Michael would see to it that Paul's sacrifice was not in vain. He wouldn't rest until Rottier and whomever he'd hired to kill Paul were exposed and brought to justice.

The woman who sat beside him seemed to have answers that could help with that. She'd instructed Agent Nguyen on what to do after the killing, clearly based on information she had that the FBI didn't. But she probably wouldn't tell him what she knew about the shooter. They were strangers now. That much was clear.

Then again, he'd never let fear of a *no* keep him from asking a question. "You know who killed Paul, don't you?"

She yanked the car into a hard turn.

He gripped the armrest as she gunned the engine. "What are you doing?"

"We've got company."

# THREE

Michael checked the passenger side mirror, taking in the three cars behind them that shrunk as she sped to the next intersection. "Where? I don't see—"

Amalia jerked into another swerve onto a different road.

His stomach lurched as she veered in front of oncoming traffic to pass an SUV.

A semi barreled toward them. Close enough for him to read the license plate. That was about to be imprinted on his forehead.

She darted back into the proper lane, and the semi passed by without smashing into them on the way.

"What are you doing?"

She flashed a smile that was positively gleeful. "Raksa and I like to open her up now and then."

He glanced to the back where the dog lay on the floor, snug and relaxed as he panted behind the front seats as if his owner was a race car driver.

The car turned again, and Michael's stomach swirled. Looking backward probably wasn't the best move at the moment. He straightened in the seat and stared out the windshield.

Not much better at the speed she took turns and passed

cars. "Seriously, I think I'm going to be sick. Can you slow down?"

"Sure."

The car instantly slowed, and he dared to look at his kamikaze chauffeur.

She watched something intently through the windshield, giving him the impression her sudden slowdown had nothing to do with his request.

"What are you looking at?"

"Our tail."

"In front of us?"

"I doubled back. Got around him."

"Oh." Michael looked at the vehicle in front of them. The shooter drove a minivan? "How did you know that would work?"

"He couldn't speed up without giving himself away." She kept her gaze locked ahead. "There he goes."

The minivan stayed in the lane in front of them. Movement farther up caught Michael's gaze, just in time for him to see the trunk end of a black car turn unto a different street. The vehicle had been about six cars up—too far to see the plates. How had she known their tail was there?

Michael braced himself for her to gun it again and race to catch the car. But she drove under the speed limit as they passed the side street where the car had turned. She barely glanced that direction.

He leaned past her to see.

A solitary red car drove past houses on the otherwise empty road.

"Shouldn't we try to follow him? Maybe we could catch him."

A quick smile showed off her white teeth. "Not with a protected wit in my car. My job is to get you to the safe house without a trace."

"I don't mind. That was the shooter, right? We should go after him."

She shook her head and laughed, a loud and hearty sound only vaguely reminiscent of Sofia's.

Even her laugh was different?

"I don't think you have the stomach for it." She tossed her unfamiliar grin his way and laughed again. She pulled her phone from the cupholder between them and held it close as she tapped the screen.

"Who are you calling?"

"Agent Nguyen." She pressed the phone to her ear. "Pérez here. We picked up a tail. Black sedan. I lost him." She paused, probably listening to a response. "Yes, I'm sure. We're still twenty minutes from the location, so it shouldn't be compromised. But it's your call."

Another pause.

"Right. You'll tell your people to watch as they come in?" She listened a moment longer, then lowered the phone. She gave him her big smile. "Sounds like you still have a place to stay."

"Who was following us? The same person who killed Paul and shot at me?"

"Another K-9 protection team is meeting us at the house. Nevaeh and Alvarez."

Avoiding his questions again. He opened his mouth to call her on it—

"I'll introduce you to them before I leave."

Leave? Michael swallowed the urge to admit he'd thought she was going to stay awhile, to say she couldn't leave until he got answers. About where she'd been, why she had changed. Why she had never come home. Her parents deserved answers.

"The FBI will post a couple agents at the house, too."

Panic started to close his throat. He'd just found Sofia after twelve years of hoping, wondering, and searching. He couldn't let her go without making sure he'd see her again. "You'll be back later?"

"My next shift starts at eleven tonight."

Another lying game technique they'd used as kids. The

art of appearing to answer a question without actually answering it.

She didn't say she would be back later. She only stated the time of her next shift.

A sinking feeling traveled from his chest to his stomach.

She wasn't coming back.

---

Goodbye Amalia Pérez, hello Brandi Henderson. Amalia stuffed the new fake driver's license she would use from now on inside the pink purse that belonged with the new identity. She would cut her hair short for this one, but she could do that after she finished packing and stripping the house of all evidence she'd ever been there.

The timing of her escape couldn't be more perfect. With Phoenix wanting her and Raksa to cut their shift short to rest and recoup after the morning shooting, Amalia could get away long before the CIA followed Verdugo and found her here. And before anyone from Phoenix K-9 noticed she was missing.

Snapping on nitrile gloves, she went to work on the stock photos she had hung in the hallway of her Minneapolis house. She took them off the wall one by one and wiped them down with a microfiber cloth to eliminate fingerprints.

Her huge chocolate Newfoundland, Gaston, lay at the start of the hallway, requiring her to step over him each time she carried a picture to the cardboard box she would use to transport her props to a garbage dump outside the Cities.

She looked at the photo that ended up on top of the stack. A picture of a happy couple sitting in a sun-bathed wheat field with two smiling children. Amalia's sister, brother-in-law, niece, and nephew. Such idyllic relatives she had, frozen in a photo for all time. A perfect family for a fake person.

She would find new ones to flesh out the realism of Brandi Henderson and her existence. Maybe a nice photo of a gray-haired couple that could be Brandi's adoptive parents from Los Angeles.

Raksa broke the silence with a bark. He jogged past her to the front door.

A single firm knock followed his warning.

Amalia's gaze locked on the navy blue door. The only visitors she ever had were her coworkers from Phoenix K-9, and they always called first.

Suspicion heightened her senses as she let Raksa keep barking. Gaston added his deeper *woof* and lumbered to his feet to join Raksa, dwarfing the German shepherd.

Amalia went to the curtained picture window near the door and drew her Glock from her holster.

She pulled the far edge of the curtain a micro inch away from the glass.

A woman wearing a gray baseball cap, black windbreaker, and jeans stared at Amalia. A tan dog sat at her side.

Phoenix and her K-9 Dagian.

What was Amalia's boss doing here? She'd never visited before. And why didn't she call or text first?

Talk about rotten timing for a sudden drop-in.

Amalia let the curtain fall into place, grabbed the box of pictures, and hustled to hide it in her room. She'd already stripped the living room and kitchen of decorative knick-knacks, but maybe Phoenix would assume she was a minimalist rather than deduce she was leaving.

Amalia rushed back to the door, whipping off her gloves and stuffing them behind a sofa cushion on the way. "Enough, boys. It's just Phoenix." She'd delayed too long to have the dogs sit before she opened the door, so she grabbed the knob and flashed a bright smile. "Phoenix. This is a surprise."

The dogs pressed into the doorway, eager to greet their trainer.

Phoenix petted both dogs and spoke to them in her deep, soothing tone that instantly calmed them. Her only answer for Amalia was an indecipherable glance.

The usually enjoyable challenge of trying to read her mysterious boss wasn't so appealing right now. Amalia needed to get out of here. The faster the better, without any scenes or explanations. She manufactured another smile. "Not an unwelcome surprise, of course. Want to come in?" Amalia stepped back from the door.

"For a minute."

The dogs followed Phoenix as she walked inside, but they were careful not to crowd Dagian, who was practically glued to her leg as usual. She stopped in the middle of the living room and scanned the undecorated space. "I wanted to catch you before you left."

Amalia's senses went on high alert, but she allowed only lighthearted puzzlement on her face. "My shift isn't until eleven, right? Or did you want me earlier?"

Phoenix went to the cleared-off mantle above the fireplace and stared at it. Her back was to Amalia, her long, honey brown braid dangling against her windbreaker.

Then she walked to the end table next to the sofa. She trailed her fingertip through the light coat of dust into the clear circle that marked where a decorative vase had sat until Amalia removed it moments ago.

She turned and pinned Amalia with another stare. No accusatory or knowing expression accompanied the look. Her face was inscrutable as always.

But it was obvious the game was up. "How did you know I was leaving?"

"The sniper today—he was the assassin who blew your assignment in Colombia." Phoenix didn't ask, just stated. Facts Amalia had no idea her boss knew.

Their history meant Phoenix knew Amalia was from the CIA, since they'd first met six years ago when Phoenix consulted on a joint investigation between the CIA and FBI involving a serial killer. Before that investigation had ended, Phoenix had invited Amalia to look her up in the Twin Cities if she ever wanted a change in her line of work.

But when she showed up to accept Phoenix's job offer

four years later, Amalia had told Phoenix only that she'd decided to leave the CIA.

Amalia chose her words just as carefully now and kept her growing unease hidden. "I know you have impressive sources, Phoenix, but you got some bad intel this time."

Phoenix didn't blink. "See if this sounds familiar. You were involved with another agent who went into business for himself, hired Verdugo, and made the CIA think you were a traitor. You didn't have evidence to clear your name, so you ran." Phoenix went to the sofa and sat, returning her attention to Amalia while Dag lay at her feet. "You've been running ever since. Until you came here."

Amalia's mind raced for explanations as to how Phoenix could know any of that. Had she known the whole time, ever since Amalia came to the Twin Cities?

"You want to leave now because Verdugo's presence here could draw the CIA. They've been trying to catch him for years. And you don't want them to catch you at the same time."

Amalia slowly sat on the far edge of the coffee table, angled halfway toward Phoenix.

Gaston pressed his head onto her lap, and she stroked his soft ears.

"You don't have to admit any of this. But you do need to stop running."

Amalia watched Raksa as he sniffed Dag's tail before walking a few feet away to lie on the carpeting.

"If you don't, you'll be running the rest of your life."

Was Phoenix right? Amalia had never intended to stay here for two years. She'd planned to leave after six months, tops. But the work was rewarding and exciting. Her coworkers were terrific, women she would trust if she could trust anyone. And Phoenix...

Amalia met the steady gaze of her boss. Phoenix had proven to be the most fascinating and skilled yet mysterious and secretive person she'd ever met. But, somehow, Amalia was tempted to trust her more than anyone she had known since leaving home.

Tempted. But even if Phoenix was the one person in the world she could trust, and even if Amalia's coworkers sometimes seemed like a family she'd like to be part of, that didn't mean staying would be smart. "It's been an honor to work for you, Phoenix. I'm grateful you brought me on board. But I have to leave."

Amalia got to her feet, prompting Gaston to back up in front of her. "I've stayed too long already." Even if Verdugo hadn't shown up, the CIA could have found her because she'd lingered so long in one location. She should've moved on after six months.

"Not so fast." Phoenix stood, and Dag instantly popped up beside her. "You were on the job today, as were Bristol and Nevaeh before you arrived. Phoenix K-9's reputation needs to be repaired after what happened."

Phoenix's change of tactics brought a smile to Amalia's lips. She wondered, not for the first time, if Phoenix had CIA training. Her interrogation and persuasive techniques were stellar.

"The agency hasn't been damaged." Amalia slid her hands into her jeans pockets. "It wasn't our fault. The FBI will get the blame. We were only on patrol, not witness protection."

Phoenix slowly shook her head, jaw firmly set. "We were an active part of the security detail. Our name and reputation are attached to this job. And a witness died."

"The witness went outside when—"

"You're part of our team, Amalia." Phoenix's stare turned implacable. "This happened on our watch. And now we have a bigger responsibility. Katherine wants us to join the security detail for the witnesses themselves. A protection assignment, not just patrol this time."

Protecting Michael more directly? No way.

She wasn't afraid of him. Amalia Pérez had nothing to do with him. But why put herself in a situation where she'd have to deal with suspicions and personal questions all the time? And what if he decided to tell her parents she was here?

"We need you to help redeem our reputation." Phoenix's words interrupted Amalia's racing thoughts. She paused, holding Amalia's gaze for a moment. "You do this, and I'll help you redeem yours."

With the CIA? Could Phoenix do that?

Could be a bluff. Amalia searched Phoenix's gaze, but couldn't read anything, as usual. What she did know about her boss—her dedication to saving others, whether human or K-9, no matter the cost to herself—said Phoenix could be trusted despite her secrecy.

Amalia flashed a smile. "Okay." She offered her hand to Phoenix. "I'll stay until the witnesses are able to testify. But one whiff of the CIA, I'm gone."

"And I'll make sure they miss you." Phoenix shook Amalia's hand with a strong grip. "But by that time, you might not have a reason to run." She ended the handshake abruptly while Amalia processed the promise in those words.

Something that felt like hope warmed her torso. She cooled the feeling with a quick dose of reality. Phoenix likely couldn't do a thing to clear Amalia's name with the CIA. She was probably only using that possibility as leverage to get Amalia to do what she wanted. After all, Phoenix would be down a K-9 protection team to guard the two remaining witnesses if Amalia left.

"I'll let you and Raksa get some rest." Phoenix gave her a look that, while it betrayed nothing, still made Amalia feel as if her boss knew the suspicious thoughts that had just run through her mind.

Phoenix moved to leave, Dag following at her side while Raksa and Gaston hurried to catch her. She paused at the door and looked back. "What were you going to do about Raksa and Gaston? Were you taking them with you?"

She left without waiting for an answer.

Without waiting to see Amalia sink to the sofa as her heart squeezed, paining her for the first time in three years.

The two dogs in question vied for her attention, pushing her hands with their soft muzzles and cold noses.

She hadn't thought of them. Not once as she was packing up and beginning to execute her exit strategy.

She couldn't take them with her. The dogs would make her too easy to trace and wouldn't allow her to blend in or disappear.

But as she buried her hand in Gaston's warm fur and scratched behind Raksa's upright ears, the truth cut her to the quick.

She couldn't leave them behind.

---

Michael read through the email from Detective Rawlings with Dallas PD. The message confirmed what Michael had suspected—there was a connection between the Dallas prostitution racket he was investigating and human trafficking. But he still hadn't been able to find all the links in the chain of evidence to expose the person he believed was behind it. Hard to gather evidence when he was more than a thousand miles away.

He sighed and looked up from the screen of the notebook computer he held in his lap on the sofa.

His protectors of the moment, Nevaeh and her rottweiler mix, Alvarez, had returned a few minutes ago from checking every room of the house. Nevaeh now sat in the armchair in the living room while Alvarez lay on the floor, resting his dark head on her foot. Every half hour, they patrolled the outdoor property, and they were about as quiet when they were inside as when they were gone. The FBI agent in the house was just as taciturn as he sat beyond them at the table in the dining room.

Michael had attempted small talk with Nevaeh, but she was a tough nut to crack. Maybe that was a job requirement for employees at Phoenix K-9. Judging from their boss, whom he'd only met once, he could see why toughness rather than friendliness might be the agency's business model. Probably made sense for their line of work.

But he had interviewed harder subjects. "So how long have you known Amalia?"

Nevaeh's head jerked toward him, a bounty of afro curls framing her oval face.

He'd found people who didn't want to talk about themselves would sometimes talk about others. It was worth a shot.

"Since she joined the agency."

Could be a deliberately evasive answer. He'd try again. "Oh, that's cool. How long ago was that?"

Her big eyes narrowed. "Why do you want to know?"

He shrugged and smiled, hoping to put her defenses into park. "I haven't seen her in a long time, so I'm just curious what she's been up to."

"You know her?"

There. Interest sparked in Nevaeh's dark brown eyes as she leaned slightly forward, her bulletproof vest stiffening her movement.

"Used to. We grew up together. We were next door neighbors as kids."

"Nice. Did you keep in touch?"

"We sort of drifted apart when we went to college." Especially when he didn't return to college with her.

"Oh."

"I wished we'd been able to keep in touch better. Do you know what she did before she came here?"

Nevaeh glanced away and pressed her lips together. "Not really. But I wouldn't tell you if I did. Her business is her business."

"Of course." He nodded politely. Message received.

Looked like he'd have to use his trusty internet sources to find out more. He had searched for Sofia several times over the last twelve years, but she'd seemed to disappear after graduating from college.

He would've been concerned she had been kidnapped, or

worse, if not for the phone calls to her parents that became more sporadic with time. Then they'd stopped all together, replaced by an occasional email that said she was working in some foreign country as a technologies consultant. Supposedly.

The gun-toting woman he'd met now made him suspect she'd never been in the technologies field at all. What had she been doing?

She'd never written to him during those years. Never wanted to talk to him when she used to call, though she knew he was living with her parents. But he didn't search for information about her for his own sake.

Her parents put on a good front, thrilled every time they got one of her emails. But he knew Sofia's disappearing act pained them deeply.

He still couldn't believe the Sofia he knew would do that to her loving parents, even with what had happened between Michael and her. She didn't even feel guilty about her part in the tragedy. So why would she never have come home again?

He needed answers. For her parents. And now that he knew she'd changed her name, he might be able to find those answers.

He opened a search box on his computer and typed in *Amalia Pérez*.

The house went black, a beep piercing his ears as the lights went out.

Alvarez growled, a deep rumble that unnerved Michael more than the power outage.

"Get down." Nevaeh's voice, suddenly commanding, punched the darkness.

He set his computer aside and slid off the sofa, lowering to his hands and knees on the carpet. "What's going on?" He looked for Nevaeh and Alvarez. Couldn't see anything but darkness.

"Macey, cover the back door. I've got the target." Nevaeh spoke quietly to the FBI agents through her radio earpiece.

Macey, the agent inside the house, must have moved to the rear of the house.

"Barrett," her voice dropped to just above a whisper, "whatever happens, stay with me and Alvarez. We'll keep you safe."

*Whatever happens?* Did she mean the assassin was coming? His breath hitched. "Couldn't someone have just hit a power line?" He whispered the rational question, trying to diffuse the tension that seized his muscles.

"Roger that." Nevaeh must be answering someone on the radio again. "Change of plan. Amalia's here. She's going to get you out."

He barely heard Nevaeh's last statement as his mind locked on the first one. Sofia—Amalia—had come back? His pulse picked up speed. Only because of what it would mean to her parents. He could finally get the answers they needed.

"Move." Nevaeh's hiss made him start. "Front door."

He stood as she did and aimed for the slips of moonlight that cut around the inner door of the enclosed front entry.

"Hurry." Nevaeh's voice came from behind, nearly on top of him.

He opened the door and stepped through.

"We'll wait here." Nevaeh and Alvarez slipped into the narrow entryway with him. She shut the door behind her.

"Shouldn't we go outside?"

Nevaeh bent her elbow, holding a gun upward in a ready position. "The assassin's probably going to raid us from the back. But if we're wrong, he could pick you off when you go outside. We'll wait for Amal—

*Pop-pop-pop.*

Michael jumped at the sound just as Alvarez launched a series of barks, stinging Michael's ears in the small space. "Was that shooting? In the house?"

Nevaeh turned away from the moonlight that streaked through the window of the front door and fixed her gaze on the entryway's inner door—their only shield for bullets. She pressed closer to the wall, away from Michael. Maybe trying to give him more space in the cramped pocket between doors. Did her fingers tremble against the gun she gripped? He must've imagined it in the dimness. "Amalia's driving up to the front. Tell me when you see her."

He peered out the window.

Moonlight cast a blue tone over the lawn and concrete path that led from the short staircase to the street.

"There's no driveway in front."

Nevaeh snorted. "Don't think she cares."

A black sedan that looked like Amalia's appeared on the road.

"I think—" The words froze in his throat when the car swung toward the lawn, screeched over the curb, and blazed across the grass to the house. "She's here." The car nearly crashed into the steps as it slid to a halt.

More pops jerked his gaze to the inner door past Nevaeh.

Alvarez snarled and launched a string of deafening, ferocious barks.

Nevaeh aimed her gun at the closed door. "Go. Now."

He spun away and escaped into cool night air.

A crash made him look over his shoulder.

"Keep going!" Nevaeh rushed behind him with her dog.

"Get in!" Amalia's yell yanked his attention to the car. She'd dropped out and squatted next to the open driver's door, her gun aimed at the house.

Could this really be happening? He ran down the steps and pulled open the passenger door.

Something shattered as he dove into the car, his elbow scraping against the upholstered seat.

Shots punctured the night. He ducked.

Amalia returned fire. "Nevaeh, you better get in!"

Michael dared to peer out the bottom of the windshield as Nevaeh and Alvarez sprinted to the car.

A shooter, hidden somewhere behind the few remaining shards of the front door's broken window, fired again.

Alvarez jumped onto the back seat.

Amalia answered the attack, her bullets splintering the

wood of the door as she aimed low, apparently trying to hit the shooter's body. Or make him back off.

She darted into the car. Jerked to check the back seat. "Nevaeh!"

She hadn't gotten in? Michael pushed his door open and looked behind.

Nevaeh was on the ground, attempting to climb into the car. Was she injured?

He dropped out.

"Michael, don't!"

He ignored Amalia's shout as he lifted the slim woman and helped her into the back.

Amalia fired more rounds.

Michael lunged onto the passenger seat. Slammed his door.

"Get down." Amalia's glare was as sharp as her tone as she jerked the car in gear and tore away from the house.

As the tires hit pavement, her eyes flashed. "What were you thinking? We're risking our lives to protect you. We don't need you pulling stupid stunts like that."

Michael's heart pounded, his body surging with adrenaline as rolling emotion tumbled through him. "We take care of each other. Remember?" He stared at her, willing her to show some sign that the old Sofia was still there.

She looked away and gave the rearview mirror the force of her glare. "Nevaeh, you okay?"

"I..." Her voice weakened.

Michael looked back.

"Don't..."

"Nevaeh?" Amalia glanced over her shoulder.

He scanned the woman for an injury. Couldn't see much in the dark.

But her hands went to her chest as her shoulders hunched, and she grimaced.

"I think she's been shot."

# FOUR

"Nevaeh, are you all right?" Cora Isaksson held open the back door to Phoenix K-9 headquarters, concern drawing lines across her forehead.

Michael went inside first, following Amalia's instructions for once, though she could tell he'd wanted to get the door for them.

Amalia helped Nevaeh inside, keeping her arm around Nevaeh's waist and her shoulders under the taller woman's outstretched arm.

Amalia let Raksa and Alvarez stay in the fenced yard at the back of the building for now. Parking at the rear inside the fence should insure no one would've seen Michael arrive at headquarters. Though it was unlikely anyone was watching the place. Only the FBI and maybe the U. S. Attorney's office should know Phoenix K-9 was involved in protecting the witnesses.

"You're not even talking. That's bad." Cora's hands went to her pearl-toned cheeks as her golden retriever, Jana, circled the new arrivals with her tail wagging. "Where are you hurt?"

"I'm fine." Nevaeh cut her grimace short and slid her arm off Amalia's shoulders.

Amalia took the hint and slowly released her hold on

43

Neveah's waist, watching to be sure she remained steady.

"Are you sure she shouldn't have gone directly to the hospital?" Cora's big, blue eyes were filled with worry as she looked at Amalia.

"She—"

"No hospitals." Nevaeh's hiss cut Amalia short.

"That's what the woman said." Amalia grinned.

"Vest caught the bullet."

Amalia could see why Cora was worried.

Nevaeh usually would've dished out a snappy comeback with a grin. But she was too busy trying to hold back a wince as she held a hand to her side.

"Even so, I should take a look. You could have broken ribs." The medical training Cora was undergoing through classes and study on her own seemed to have given the PK-9 technologies specialist a new confidence in medical emergencies.

"Bruised." Nevaeh breathed out a sigh that carried a whiff of humor. "Two bruised ribs."

"Oh." Cora cast a glance at Amalia.

She shrugged.

"Well, I defer to your greater knowledge as a former EMT." Cora gave Nevaeh a gentle smile and stepped closer to put a hand on her shoulder. "Will you at least come into the breakroom and sit down for a bit?"

"Love to." Nevaeh pushed out the reply through gritted teeth that almost looked like a grin.

Good. Her classic Nevaeh humor was returning. She'd be all right.

The thought loosened some undefined tension in Amalia's chest as Nevaeh proceeded Cora through the door that led to a small room and then the hallway. Only because PK-9 wouldn't be down a protection team. Nevaeh was great, but Amalia hadn't allowed herself to become attached to her or any of the PK-9 team. Bad enough to realize she'd somehow started to feel something for her dogs. But at least dogs could be trusted.

"Hey, everyone else okay?" Bristol paused in the open doorway Cora and Nevaeh had disappeared through.

Amalia jerked a nod.

Bristol's gray-blue gaze shifted to Michael. "I don't believe we've officially met." She stepped forward to shake his hand. "I'm Bristol Bachmman, explosives detection."

"Nice to—"

Toby reached up to shove his no-doubt wet nose into their hands, his black tail a wagging blur.

Michael laughed as he released Bristol's hand and petted the eager greeter.

"And this is Toby." Bristol chuckled, but the sound of Michael's laughter was still ringing in Amalia's ears. Sounded just like it used to but deeper and rougher around the edges. Like it was a little worn from being used for more years.

"Phoenix told me to give you the tour of the place and show you the security features you need to know about."

Michael glanced up from Toby to give Bristol a quizzical look. "I need to know about your security features?"

"The safe room." Amalia was sure that's what Phoenix most wanted Michael to see and know how to reach it quickly.

"Safe room?" He swung his gaze to her. Was he deliberately parroting everything, or was he nervous? Most civilians would be traumatized by what he'd just been through. She'd have to send him to Cora for some coddling if that was the case.

"It's not at all likely anyone saw you arrive here with the precautions we've taken." Bristol gave him a smile. "But our boss, Phoenix, likes to cover all contingencies." Like calling Bristol to headquarters in the middle of the night so they'd have another gun. Though she didn't have a protection K-9, Bristol's years as a cop with the Minneapolis Police Department made her a security force to be reckoned with.

"I've never actually seen a safe room in real life." Michael's lips angled in a smile just before he returned his attention to Bristol. "I'm all yours."

"Okay, then. Follow me." Bristol paused at the doorway and looked back at Amalia. "Phoenix is in the breakroom."

Amalia nodded. She opened the back door first and called the dogs inside. Raksa and Alvarez trotted alongside her as she passed through the small office and walked up the gray-carpeted hallway. Just before reaching Cora's desk in the lobby, she veered off into the breakroom on the left.

Phoenix lowered her cell phone from her ear as Amalia entered.

Alvarez rushed ahead, making a beeline for Nevaeh. He rested his slurpy mouth on her leg, drawing her head up from where it had slumped against the back of the sofa. Her brown skin that usually had warm bronze undertones still looked pale. But she managed to smile as she stroked the dog's black and tan head.

"Status?" Phoenix's deep voice pulled Amalia's attention to her boss who stood about six feet away, her arms crossed over her gray T-shirt and open black windbreaker.

"Barrett's with Bristol. No injuries. We came in clean. No tails. Parked in back like you directed."

Phoenix watched her, expressionless. "Katherine called after you phoned. She wants us to take Barrett to another safe house." Phoenix glanced at Cora as the blonde stopped hovering over Nevaeh and moved to pick up her notebook computer from the coffee table.

"You'll take him there, but we're going to debrief first. The team needs to be prepared for the threat." Phoenix's unreadable gaze still sent a message Amalia understood. And Phoenix was right. Knowledge of Verdugo and his tactics was the only way the team could hope to defend against him. "Cora, status?"

Cora looked up from the computer she held in her lap as she sat on the loveseat opposite the sofa where Nevaeh rested. The coffee table between them held their mugs of the team's favorite hot beverage. "Security system is armed, and all the cameras show nothing suspicious."

"Keep watch during our meeting." Phoenix walked behind

the sofa to reach the armchair she always sat in, facing the entryway to the room. Dag matched her pace and settled on the floor next to her.

"Of course." Cora nodded solemnly while Jana sat close to her in front of the loveseat.

Amalia moved around the other sofa and sank onto the cushion at the end, which left the middle open between herself and Nevaeh.

Raksa trotted past the sofa and chairs, making a beeline for the coveted air-conditioning vent.

Toby burst into the breakroom, and the black lab wriggled his whole body as he jogged by everyone to reach his buddy Raksa.

Bristol and then Michael followed at a slower pace and stopped just inside the room. Was that a blush coloring Bristol's ivory cheeks?

Michael nodded to Phoenix. "Quite a setup you have here, Ms. Gray."

Amalia smirked. Didn't hear that often. Everyone called her Phoenix. Amalia looked at Phoenix to see if she'd correct Michael.

She just watched him with her usual indecipherable gaze.

He grinned. "Though I thought you were an all-female agency."

Bristol chuckled. "He met Rem out front at Cora's desk."

Amalia shifted in her seat. "Rem is here?" That explained the blush. Bristol and Rem still acted like newlyweds, which made sense for a couple that had only been married a month.

Still, Michael sure seemed to bring out Bristol's light-hearted side—something she didn't let everyone see. At least she didn't use to. She had become cheerier in the last year. Especially since she'd married Remington Jones.

"Yeah, we were on a stakeout together tonight, so we came right from there. Rem is getting some work done on his laptop and watching the front."

"The romantic life of a P. I.'s wife." Nevaeh let out a breath of a laugh that ended in a wince.

Amalia remembered that pain from her assignment in Venezuela. Though her ribs had been broken, not bruised, that time.

"It's the best." Bristol smiled.

"Mr. Barrett." Cora approached Michael, Jana walking alongside her. "I'm afraid I was so distracted by my concern for Nevaeh that I didn't welcome you properly when you arrived."

He smiled in return and held out his hand. "Call me Michael. And you are?"

"Cora Isaksson, technologies specialist and office manager for Phoenix K-9." And already engaged, if Michael was getting any ideas about the attractive blonde. Cora ended their brief handshake. "And this is Jana." She laughed lightly as she looked down at the golden retriever who sat in front of Michael, staring at his face as she swished her feathered tail along the carpet. "Narcotics detection K-9."

"Hey, Jana." Michael smoothed the golden's head with his palm.

"I just wanted to say how much I've been wanting to meet you since I learned you're the reporter who broke the case against Devereux last year. I followed that investigation with great interest."

"What investigation?" Bristol raised her eyebrows.

Cora glanced at her. "Wayne Devereux, the founder and CEO of Devereux Industries, the Fortune 500 company."

"Oh, that's right. He was using his business as a front for money laundering." Bristol's gaze swung to Michael, respect glinting in her gaze. "That made national news. I didn't realize you were the journalist who did that. You really nailed him. Impressive work."

Amalia rolled her eyes as she unfastened the Velcro of her armored vest and slipped it off. "Looks like we've got a Michael Barrett fan club at PK-9." She'd never heard of Wayne Devereux or any such investigation. Though she would've been off the grid at the time.

Nevaeh snickered, then pressed a hand to her ribs with a smile-covered grimace.

Bristol chuckled and Cora shook her head as Michael glanced at Amalia, shoving his hands into his jeans pockets. "I just shine a light on the truth. In Devereux's case, that revealed some pretty dirty secrets."

The truth and secrets. So that was it. The reason he'd become a journalist. Guilt. Just because they'd told some lies for a good reason and—

"Should we join the meeting or..." Bristol looked at Phoenix.

Their boss nodded.

Amalia leaned forward. No way. Michael couldn't hear all of this. "We're going to be discussing privileged information."

"Knowledge is power. Michael is the target. The more he knows, the more likely he'll be to survive."

Michael's eyes widened slightly at Phoenix's blunt statement.

He better get used to it if he was really going to stay for what should be a private debrief meeting. And he better not try to sit by Amalia in the middle cushion. Nevaeh would not like having a man so near. Close spaces with men could trigger a post-traumatic stress disorder episode, Phoenix had informed Amalia when they started this protection job. Nevaeh's troubles were her own, but Phoenix had shared that much only so Amalia would know what to watch out for during this security assignment that involved close quarters with the principal and FBI agents.

Michael went to the open armchair kitty-corner to Nevaeh and sat, glancing Amalia's direction.

Her muscles relaxed as she looked away.

"What about Jazz?" Nevaeh pushed out the question. Not surprising she was keeping track of their missing team member even while injured. Nevaeh and Jazz always seemed to look out for each other. The story was they'd been friends since they were kids.

49

"She'll finish her shift with the other witness in case the attacker goes there." Phoenix looked at Nevaeh. At least it appeared that was the direction of her stare beneath the shadow cast by the bill of her cap. "We'll fill her in later." Her head angled toward Amalia. "The attacker tonight and at the estate might be more of a challenge than we've had to face up till now."

Phoenix's pause indicated Amalia should take over.

"The shooter has all the marks of Verdugo, an international assassin who's eluded capture for ten years or more."

"How do you know that?" Michael's deep voice resonated in the room usually filled only with female tones.

And grated across her nerves. No one asked that question here. She shifted her gaze his way, about to tell him to keep his questions to himself, but he was already looking at Phoenix.

She leveled one of her silent stares at him.

"Sorry." Michael pressed his lips together.

This is what they got for inviting an investigative reporter to their meeting. Phoenix had better make him sign a non-disclosure before he left here. He might make exposing the truth at PK-9 his next mission. She wasn't the only one on the team who wouldn't want all their secrets out in the open.

Amalia wasn't the only one hiding something at Phoenix K-9. The mysterious aura the boss of the operation sported like a weapon begged Michael to search out her secrets and discover why she tried so hard to be an unsolvable mystery. What was she hiding?

But he had a bigger problem at the moment. Amalia. She clearly hadn't wanted him to stay at the meeting, but was that to keep more information hidden from him or just a Phoenix K-9 security protocol? One thing Amalia seemed to have in common with Sofia was not being much of a rule follower. So if he were a betting man, he'd put his money on the explanation that she didn't want him present because of what he could find out—because of the secrets she wanted to keep.

The stare Phoenix had given him meant questions were out. Even if he wanted to know what the PK-9 boss was hiding, he wasn't about to get on her bad side if he didn't have to. The woman was even more intimidating than she was mysterious.

Listening and observing were his next best options for picking up on whatever Amalia didn't want him to know. He tuned back in to hear what she was saying about the assassin.

"He often employs disguises. Part of the reason no one has ever been able to identify him."

"Any consistent type of disguises?" Bristol asked the question from the short sofa she shared with Cora. The woman packed a gun in a hip holster and an abundance of laidback confidence. What was her history? Law enforcement background?

"No." Amalia's flashy smile was missing as she turned her dark eyes on Bristol. So this new persona could be serious sometimes. "From what we know, he usually sticks with male disguises, since women are nearly impossible for a guy to pull off. But he's been suspected to impersonate a full range of ethnicities, ages, builds, and economic statuses. He's so detailed with his disguises that they can withstand closer proximity to people than normal ones. Allows him to blend in, never be suspected until it's too late."

*From what we know.* Who was the *we* she was talking about? Phoenix K-9 or a different organization?

"That requires planning." Cora looked up from her computer screen. "Does he always plan out his attacks in advance?"

"Seems to prefer it. But he can ad-lib better than most assassins."

"Like today." Bristol's eyebrows drew together as she

looked at Nevaeh.

"Don't worry about me, girl." Nevaeh grinned. "The bullet just gave me a couple bruises. Another ten minutes, I'll be ready to go." She braced her fists on the cushion and shoved herself up to sit straighter, prompting Alvarez to raise up and let his tongue hang from his mouth. "Besides, our wit's safe and sound. This Verdugo dude's gonna have to try harder if he wants to beat us."

"If he wants Barrett, he'll keep going until he gets him." Amalia delivered the ominous words without blinking.

So Michael was *Barrett* to Sofia—*Amalia*—now?

"Verdugo's used to getting his mark on the first try and moving on. He's not going to like this."

A new feeling quelled the frustration welling in Michael's chest and twisted his heart instead. Some super assassin was after him. Which meant if Amalia kept protecting him, she'd be in harm's way. She already could've been the one to get shot today, maybe even…killed.

His gut clenched as he remembered the sight of her, trading bullets with an assassin by the car. He'd just found her. Sure, it was her job to protect him. And from what he'd seen today in two different attacks, there was no doubt she was incredibly good at it. Almost frighteningly so. But he couldn't let Sofia, even if she was almost unrecognizable now, risk her life for him. Could he?

"Why do you think his plan failed this time?" Bristol watched Amalia intently.

"Besides the fact we're awesome?" Nevaeh grinned, resting her hand on Alvarez's large head.

Amalia's big smile showed off her perfect teeth. "Obviously." She swung her gaze to Bristol. "One word. Raksa."

The German shepherd lying next to Toby by the air conditioning unit lifted his head and stared at Amalia.

She grinned at the dog. "At the mansion, Verdugo had no way of knowing I'd be in the room at that moment with my K-9."

"That was amazing." Cora breathed out the words as if

they were carried by great relief. "How did you know to be there right then?"

Michael tensed. Would she admit she was in his room to tell him to lie about who she was?

"My gut was warning me something was off. Something about to happen. I wanted to make sure all the wits were safe. Started with Barrett."

He clenched his jaw. Blatant lies. Wow, she really hadn't learned from what they'd done. And she was a better liar now than when they were kids. Her skin didn't flush slightly like it used to when she'd first started to lie. She didn't have to avoid eye contact. She had no tell now, no hesitation. No conscience.

He should say something. Tell the others the truth.

"Then at the house, I'd just arrived for my shift." Amalia continued as if she hadn't just shot the truth full of holes and left it for dead. "Raksa growled as soon as we left the vehicle, warned me someone was there." The shepherd rose to his feet and headed for Amalia as she recounted the story. "I ducked back into the car and contacted Nevaeh on coms. Saw the power go out. Figured out what was happening. Verdugo might've picked me off if this guy hadn't given me the heads-up."

The German shepherd reached Amalia just in time for her to scratch behind his upright ears. He watched her face with what almost looked like a grin.

"Good work, Raksa." Cora smiled at the dog, as did the other women. Except Phoenix, who watched with an expression that was difficult to interpret. Cora glanced at Amalia. "So Verdugo didn't expect the difference the K-9s make?"

"Apparently not." Amalia looked up from petting Raksa. "But that won't stop him for long. He'll adjust. Find a way to beat the K-9s."

Nevaeh snorted. "I'd like to see that."

Amalia flashed that unfamiliar grin, challenge gleaming in her dark eyes. "So would I."

"Given the higher risk for the K-9s with this assassin in

the picture, Phoenix agreed we should take additional steps to keep them safe." As Cora spoke, her golden retriever approached and rested her head on Cora's lap. "I've ordered bulletproof vests for all the protection dogs."

"Whoa." Nevaeh's eyes widened.

"That's so generous, Cora." Bristol's eyebrows lifted as she looked at the woman next to her.

A faint pink flushed Cora's alabaster cheeks as she stared down at her dog's head and stroked the golden's fur. "It's overdue, really." She raised her gaze and gave her co-workers a soft smile. "But it seems this is a far more dangerous security assignment than we've had before, and I want to do everything we can to ensure our wonderful K-9s are protected."

A silence fell over the room as most of the women stared at Cora.

"Thanks, Cora."

The others nodded their agreement with Nevaeh.

That had to be expensive. Vests for four dogs, was it? Judging from everyone's reaction, Cora had bought them herself, rather than the agency. Cora must have a substantial source of income from somewhere. She wouldn't be likely to make that kind of money as an office manager and technologies specialist, even adding in the pay she must get for narcotics detection with her dog. What was her story?

"Weapons?" Phoenix's deep voice posed the question with a tone that left Michael feeling like she somehow already knew the answer. Though he had no idea what she was talking about.

"For long-range, he favors a bolt-action rifle."

Ah. Amalia's quick answer told Michael they were back to discussing the assassin.

"He goes for a variety of semi-automatics for close range." She rattled off a list of what he assumed were handguns that included several beyond the normal garden variety he was acquainted with. "Depends on the velocity he wants and what suits his disguise. I know of at least one time he used an AK-47, but as a situational control tactic, not to execute the hit."

The team members nodded, as if they knew all the weapons she'd mentioned. Michael knew some of them, but only because of his research for the articles he'd been writing on Rottier and his arms trafficking operation. Michael didn't imagine all security services, especially in the Midwestern Twin Cities, were quite so weapons-savvy and sophisticated.

Like the security setup Bristol had shown him on the tour. Some of the precautions and mechanisms at this building were like something out of a movie. Far from the standard of other security company offices he'd seen. Usually, they were just normal office buildings. The Phoenix K-9 base of operations was so greatly enhanced it seemed more like a fortress.

"Verdugo's best skills are marksmanship for long-range kills and close-range techniques for killing silently without leaving a mark on the body."

Michael watched Amalia as she continued sharing facts about the assassin. Where had she gotten all this information?

Clearly, the Phoenix K-9 Security and Detection Agency was exceptional. Is this where Amalia had spent the twelve years since she'd disappeared? She seemed comfortable with the other women, and they apparently knew her well. Or at least, they thought they did.

Wait a second. Someone asked Amalia a question, but Michael didn't catch it as a possibility lit his mind. Did they already know who she really was? Maybe they'd encouraged her to use a false identity for some reason.

But why would a respected security and detection agency that worked with the FBI and police want one of their members to live a lie? And why would Amalia have worked so hard to keep her location and occupation a secret from her parents and Michael?

Unless...the hairs on the back of his neck lifted off his skin. Maybe the Phoenix K-9 Agency wasn't all it seemed either. He'd seen it plenty of times before. A company that masqueraded as honest and above-board could fool a great many people while it secretly engaged in illegal activities.

"So asphyxiation then?" Cora's soft voice threatened to make Michael question his train of thought. But he'd seen plenty of criminals who seemed as innocent and sweet as the blond woman and turned out to be diabolical beneath the lies.

"Often. Quick, and without a sound or mark on the victim."

He fought the urge to narrow his eyes at Amalia as his suspicions grew. He'd have to keep his theories to himself until he could do some digging. If the Phoenix K-9 Agency was responsible for Sofia turning into Amalia, for her rejecting her parents to embrace a life of deceit and become this cold, unfeeling person he barely recognized, he wouldn't stop until he found the truth. And exposed it to the world. If he could do that, maybe he would not only find out what had happened to Sofia but would also be able to bring her back.

"One other thing." Amalia continued to relax against the sofa as if she wasn't spouting details about someone who murdered people for a living. Someone who had Michael as his target. "Verdugo kills anyone who interferes with his target. He doesn't just knock them out if they get in his way."

"So we have to watch the peripheries when we're protecting Michael." Nevaeh turned her head toward Amalia. "Guard against casualties, too."

Finally, someone used his name. Amalia had been making him feel like a bullseye on a dart board. Though it was ironic, given that Nevaeh hadn't even seemed to like him.

"We'll—" A blaring beep cut through the room, ending Phoenix's sentence.

"We have visitors." Cora grabbed her computer off the coffee table and leaned toward the screen.

Judging from the alarm that blasted from Cora's computer and the team members' tense expressions, the visitors weren't there for a friendly chat.

# FIVE

Adrenaline, mixed with the buzz of excitement, shot through Amalia's limbs as she stood and slipped on her vest.

"Six men, approaching in pairs from the east and the north." Cora studied the security feed on her computer screen. "They appear to be armed with semi-automatic handguns." She raised her gaze. "One also has an AR-15, and another is carrying an AK-47."

"Who are they?" To his credit, Michael's voice didn't even shake as he asked the question. Proved again that he hadn't lost the gutsiness he used to have.

"Foxtrot." Phoenix aimed the word at Cora.

The blonde nodded and stood. "Everyone know your positions?"

Amalia grinned. Loved the Foxtrot security response when they had drilled it. This was going to be fun.

Raksa shifted his weight and bumped into her leg, the same energy that pulsed through her probably making him itch for action, too.

"Want me to take Jazz's spot?" Nevaeh slowly got to her feet, the vest she'd laid on the sofa gripped in her hand.

Cora glanced at Phoenix, who gave her a look Amalia didn't know how to read. Cora nodded. Glanced at Nevaeh. "We'll keep you where you are. Sector three, inner failsafe.

Bristol, do you think Rem would be willing to take your position so you can fill in for Jazz?"

"Definitely." Bristol jerked a nod.

"Thank you. I don't think they'll try to come in the front, and it's well-protected, but we'd feel better knowing Rem was also there." Leave it to Cora to take the time to sound appreciative and sweet during an attack. "He brought his weapon?"

"Yep." Bristol unclipped the safety strap of the hip holster that held her Glock.

"Okay. Tell him the plan, please, and give him a coms earpiece and night vision goggles. Then take your post."

"Got it." Bristol took off, prompting Toby to jump up with a yip and scurry out of the room to catch her.

"Nevaeh," Cora turned to her as she finished securing her vest, "you'll see Michael to the safe room and then take your post?"

"Roger." Nevaeh grinned, no signs of pain in her eyes or on her face as she gave Cora a thumbs-up. One tough *chica*.

"Let's do this." Amalia flashed Nevaeh a smile and held up her closed hand for a fist bump.

"Are you sure I can't help somehow?" Michael's deep voice pulled everyone's attention his way.

"You're the target, Mr. Barrett." Phoenix's firm tone answered with the obvious.

"I just feel weird hiding when you're all putting your lives on the line for me." His blue eyes shifted to Amalia, something in them she didn't want to see.

"We're doing our jobs. Your cooperation will ensure our success." Phoenix looked at Nevaeh.

She took the hint and moved toward Michael, stopping six feet away. "Let's go."

He didn't budge. Just stared at Amalia like he was trying to communicate with her in that silent way he could with Sofia. When would he get it through his head Sofia was gone? He was slowing them down.

Amalia turned and stalked through the open doorway.

Paused against the wall outside the breakroom and listened to be sure he cooperated. A renegade witness would mean they'd have to adopt a different security strategy.

Raksa fidgeted as he waited with Amalia, looking up at her.

"Trust me." Nevaeh's voice carried outside the room. "With this team and the setup we've got here, nobody's even putting their lives on the line tonight. Well, just the thugs trying to get in."

Amalia grinned and pushed off the wall. She walked quickly up the hallway as she pulled her coms earpiece from her jeans pocket and slipped it in place. Nevaeh wasn't usually so friendly with guys, but Amalia would bet it was going to work with Michael.

Just what they needed. A witness refusing to cooperate because he was afraid the hired security agents were going to get hurt. Was it because they were women? Or because he couldn't get over her having once been the girl he knew. The look in his eyes when she'd walked out of the room answered her question.

A soft whine from Raksa interrupted the distracting thoughts she didn't need. "Excited, boy?" She grinned at the shepherd as he glanced up at her, matching her fast clip. "Me, too."

Her fingers twitched in anticipation of the takedowns she was about to execute. If all went according to Phoenix's plan. If not, they had backup plans they'd implement that would be equally enjoyable.

She stopped briefly at the supply closet, held her thumb against the print reader on the wall. The door unlatched, and she ducked inside, grabbed a pair of night vision goggles and moved on.

"Coms check." Cora's voice, undergirded with the firmness that only showed up when she was directing an operation, sounded in Amalia's ear. By now, Cora would've moved to the security center where she could monitor the team on larger screens that showed the camera feeds inside and outside the building. "Alpha Team?"

"Alpha Team, Roger. In position." Phoenix always did manage to be a few steps ahead of everyone else.

Amalia picked up her pace, turned right into a dark room. "Team 1?"

She reached the other side of the small space and opened the door. Raksa slipped through ahead of her into the darkness beyond. "Team 1, Roger. In position." She closed the door behind her and put on the NVGs. The room, laid out like a typical office with a desk, computer, and chair, checked out unoccupied through her green-tinted goggles.

"Team 2?"

"Team 2, Roger. Package secure." Nevaeh's voice sounded tighter than usual. "On my way to Sector Three." Being Amalia's backup outside this room should mean Nevaeh wouldn't have to face one of her triggers. No tight spaces with close proximity to any of these thugs, whoever they were. Not that they'd get past Amalia anyway.

At least Michael was stowed away in the safe room. Not that it interested her any more than the safety of any other witness. But it meant Amalia didn't have to keep track of him for once. Made her job easier.

"Team 3." Cora continued the coms check.

"Team 3, Roger." Bristol's tone was strong, solid. The ex-bomb technician had nerves almost as steely as Amalia's. "In position."

"Team 4?"

"Team 4, Roger. In position and ready. Thanks for letting me join in." Remington's smile carried across the coms.

Said a lot about how much Phoenix had come to trust Bristol's husband. First time Amalia had ever seen Phoenix let someone outside PK-9 fill in for a team member.

"Power termination in Sectors Three, Five, and Six. Ready in three, two, one."

Amalia's anticipation spiked with each number of Cora's countdown.

The air-conditioning unit groaned as it shut down with the power. Amalia grinned. None of the visitors would be able to see a thing, even if they found a light switch.

"Alpha Team, I have two men approaching Entry Four." Cora's words pulsed another shot of adrenaline through Amalia's veins. Her entry point. "Do you want one or two?" Phoenix would make the call.

"Base, this is Team Alpha. Take two."

Sweet. Taking down two would be so much more entertaining. Maybe even a bit of a challenge.

"Team 1, Roger. Team 2, be advised. Two subjects breaching Entry Four. Heading into mousetrap."

Amalia stared through her green-tinted goggles at the steel pocket door that was the cheese. And she and Raksa were the trap.

---

Who were these women? Michael stared at the monitor in the safe room as his disbelief grew.

The small screen that Bristol had shown him on the tour allowed him to observe everything the security cameras recorded inside and outside the building. He'd found through fiddling with the buttons that each one brought up a specific camera's image. He could also toggle through them and pause on any given view by pressing the button marked *Hold*.

But the cameras weren't showing what he'd expected to see. He'd thought Phoenix and the team would defend their headquarters by trying to keep the bad guys out of the building.

Wasn't the normal response to establish a perimeter or something until help from the FBI or police arrived? Though, come to think of it, no one had called for any backup, as far as he'd noticed. Hopefully, they had after he'd left with Nevaeh to go to the safe room.

He blinked at what he'd just seen with his own eyes. Two men had opened the gate at the back of the building as if it wasn't locked. But he'd watched Amalia secure it after she'd pulled her car in that way when they'd arrived.

And he knew there was a thumbprint scanner security lock at the rear door the men easily snuck through after that. Even the alarm system Cora had activated after Michael had come to the headquarters should've been blaring. Someone had to have turned it off.

The Phoenix K-9 team was letting the men in. On purpose. Without a fight.

How in the world could that be a good defense strategy?

The armed men looked big and tough. Like the muscle for a narcotics ring Michael had investigated in Dallas. They wouldn't be squeamish about knocking around women to get what they wanted.

Michael winced at the thought, his chest clenching. He should go out there. Unless the women were hiding and relying on the safe room to protect him.

Where was Amalia? He should at least try to find her and see if she was in danger. He could help, even if it meant leaving the safe room.

He switched through other camera views, hoping to find where she'd ended up. He hadn't been able to see her on a camera yet.

Wait. Was that...?

He squinted at the green-tinted view of what looked to be an office, judging from the eerie outline of a desk and chair.

A dark figure moved near a wall.

And a dog. A German shepherd? Raksa.

Amalia had to be the person with him.

A loud crack made Michael start. The camera apparently had sound.

Was that a gunshot? From someone off-screen?

He cycled through more camera views. Found one of two men in the green light he assumed must mean the camera was in night vision mode, and the room it showed was dark.

But their silhouettes were different than the men he'd seen enter through the back door. One of these wore a bandana tied over his head and the other had bushy, curly hair.

And both held guns.

The bandana guy lifted his gun and aimed at what looked like a door. Shot off three rounds.

The other guy kicked the door. It didn't budge.

Must be the door they'd come in by, now locked behind them?

Michael's lips twitched as he started to suspect what Phoenix could be up to. A trap?

The woman was either the most cunning he'd met or downright insane.

The bandana thug walked along the perimeter of the square room, running his hand along the walls. He stopped.

*Oh, man.*

Along the edge of the camera's view, something slid against the wall. Was that a short door that opened?

The guy looked back at his partner and hissed something Michael couldn't make out.

The bushy-haired man seemed to nod. He leveled his gun at the opening as the bandana thug ducked slightly and went through.

Michael's breath caught. The trap hadn't worked. They were escaping.

What was on the other side of that opening? He switched rapidly through the cameras.

Amalia. Where was she?

A flurry of action on the screen stopped his finger.

A dog—Raksa—crouched and barked, snarling at what looked like the bandana thug, just inside an opening that matched the one in the room Michael had just been watching. Hard to tell who he was for sure with the woman on top of him.

Amalia? Michael leaned forward. She'd taken him down to the ground and was on his back, her arms around his neck, from what Michael could make out.

His pulse pounded. Was she okay? What if the guy tried to punch her or shook her off and—

She stood, back to the camera as she let go of the man and stood beside him.

He didn't move.

She turned around, looked up at the camera, and flashed a gleeful smile.

Michael pulled back. Was that for him? He probably wasn't the only one seeing what was happening. Sounded like Cora maybe monitored everything.

He shook his head. Sofia had always been tough and strong, always ready to defend the weak. But she hadn't enjoyed it quite so much. Then again, her skill level hadn't been what it obviously was now either. Back then, her sheer fearlessness and wild fury in the face of evil had made much bigger kids respect her. That tactic wouldn't have helped her fell the guy who probably outweighed her by 100 pounds.

What about the intruder still in the other room? Looked like the opening the bandana guy had come through had closed at some point while Michael was watching Amalia's knockout.

Feeling a bit like a spectator at a mixed martial arts ring, he watched to see what she would do next. Whatever it was, he was getting the definite feeling she didn't need his help.

Amalia rolled the unconscious man away from the closed door and slid him into a corner, a remarkable feat for someone her size.

She spun to the camera and gave a thumbs-up as her mouth moved, probably saying something quietly into the coms earpiece Cora had referenced.

The sliding door moved again, disappearing into the wall like a remote-controlled pocket door as it created a five-foot high opening in the wall.

Amalia and Raksa pressed against the wall, close to the opening as she held her gun in her hand. "Your buddy's down." The camera picked up Amalia's shout so Michael could hear every word. "I have a trained attack K-9 with me."

She gave Raksa a hand signal, and he launched into snarling as if a criminal were standing in front of him. She waited a few seconds, then signaled him again. He stopped as quickly as hitting pause on a soundtrack and wagged his tail.

"I will send this K-9 in to retrieve you if you don't lay down your weapons in five seconds." Amalia braced her gun in both hands. Was she going to go in herself? "If you fancy keeping all your limbs, I suggest you don't make me count all the way to five."

She glanced up at the camera. Communicating with Cora? "Three. Two. Good call." She swung through the opening like she had knowledge Michael didn't.

He found the camera for the room holding the intruder quicker this time. Fast enough to see Amalia and Raksa move toward him.

The bushy-haired guy held his hands up, then moved them behind his head at Amalia's command. He dropped to his knees, staring at the K-9 who growled and held its position five feet away.

Amalia whipped something from her pocket. A zip tie? Hard to tell in the green lighting. Whatever it was, she cinched it around the man's wrists that he docilely crossed behind his back.

Michael let out a breath he didn't know he'd been holding. She was okay. And the guys who were after him had apparently been stopped.

But what about the two he'd seen go in the back of the building? They must've ended up in a different area. Had they been caught?

He flicked through cameras until movement caught his eye. A man, one of the original thugs he'd seen come in the rear, tried to shake off a dog. The tan one that was always with Phoenix.

Where was—

A blur of action made him lean into the monitor. A dark baseball cap, long braid dangling down her back. Phoenix.

The huge thug in front of her lunged and reached for her.

She spun to the side and smashed a flat hand upward into his nose, forcing his head back. She was suddenly behind him as he tilted off-balance, and she used both hands to pull his head backward. He crashed to the floor, his head landing hard. Looked unconscious.

She whirled toward her dog who still gripped the man's arm as he shouted and fought. "Out." She barked the order as she whipped out a gun. She aimed steadily at the man.

His injured arm trembled as he lifted it and the other one in the air.

"Knock, knock."

Michael jumped.

The female voice sounded as if it was in the safe room with him.

The intercom. Of course. He breathed again and pressed the button on the intercom attached to the wall by the door. "Nevaeh?"

"You're supposed to say a code, remember?" Humor lifted her tone.

"Sorry. Uh…'Remember the Alvarez?'" He'd had the feeling Nevaeh had made up that security code on the spot when she'd delivered him to the safe room.

"He's black and tan and scary to bad guys." Her laugh at the response she had told him she'd give cut off as she must have released the intercom button.

He pulled the lever on the wall, and the thick steel door released, allowing him to push it open.

Nevaeh's nearly black eyes gleamed with mirth in the shadows as she greeted him. "Safe and sound?"

Alvarez angled his square head up at Michael, tongue hanging from his mouth.

"Yeah. The light in there didn't even go out. It looked like everywhere else in the building was dark." He took in the beam shining from the flashlight she held low and the darkness of the hallway behind her. "Still is, I guess."

"Cora did a partial power outage to control the lighting better. She left on power to the safe room." The lights in the hallway flickered, then powered on, the air-conditioning making a whooshing noise as it kicked in. "There we go."

Sirens sounded, coming from somewhere outside the building.

"Did someone call the police?"

"Yeah. Must've heard the gunshots." Nevaeh switched off her flashlight as she rolled her eyes. "We could've caught 'em all otherwise. Had to stop with four. The other two left when the sirens started a few minutes ago."

"I'd have thought you would've wanted backup." Michael fell in step behind Nevaeh and Alvarez as she led him up the hallway.

She shrugged. "Phoenix likes the leeway to play by her own rules. We had it under control." She glanced at him over her shoulder. "She wants to see if you can ID the invaders."

"I can try. They didn't look familiar on the cameras, but it was pretty dark."

She chuckled. "Oh, yeah. What'd you think of the show?"

He tried to think of an answer. Some way to adequately explain how he'd felt watching his former best friend handle herself like a Jason Bourne assassin. How his suspicions that the Phoenix K-9 Agency was much more than it claimed to be had grown astronomically with what he'd just witnessed.

But he couldn't really mention any of that to Nevaeh, a dedicated employee of the Agency. "It was amazing."

So amazing, he couldn't for a moment believe Phoenix K-9 was an ordinary security and detection agency.

There had to be a reason Amalia was so determined to hide that she was here, working for Phoenix K-9. A reason that being with the Agency meant she had to deny her true identity and lie about everything.

He wouldn't stop until he discovered what those reasons were and, hopefully, found the real Sofia.

# SIX

Amalia stood over the four men lined up on the floor, hands bound behind them, their backs against the wall of the initial entry room at the rear of PK-9 headquarters. Three were still unconscious but one groaned as he started to stir.

"Theories on who they are?" Phoenix stood back about ten feet. Dag sat at her side as she crossed her toned arms over her gray T-shirt, the black windbreaker she wore even when it was hot momentarily discarded. Probably for the fight with the intruders. Never helped to have more material opponents could grab and use to disadvantage.

The police sirens grew louder outside. Sounded like they'd reached the building.

"I was hoping we'd have time to question them ourselves." Amalia rested her hand on her hip, closer to her weapon if needed for the bushy-haired thug who opened his eyes and peered at her through hooded lids.

"That was the plan." Phoenix's even tone didn't betray any frustration over it being thwarted. "Spencer was apparently working late tonight."

The co-owner of the electronics store next door occasionally stayed late. Probably playing video games rather than working. But his presence there tonight explained why the cops had been called in the commercial area when the intruder fired those shots at the door.

"Phoenix, the police are here." Bristol's voice came through the coms earpiece Amalia still wore. "Let them in?"

"Yes." Phoenix stepped closer to the men as she talked. "Hold them in the lobby until I come. Explain what you have to."

"Roger."

Phoenix stopped next to Amalia. Stared down at the intruders.

"We searched them." Amalia glanced at Phoenix, her boss's stoic expression inscrutable as always. "Nothing on them that links to Rottier. Standard driver's licenses. A gas card."

"Clear to enter?" Cora's voice came through the coms.

"Clear." Phoenix turned toward the door behind them as it opened.

Cora stepped inside and closed the door behind her as her blue gaze traveled to the men by the opposite wall. "Michael's here with Nevaeh for the identification."

Phoenix glanced at Amalia. "Make sure he's protected while he IDs them. Let me know the results." She walked toward Cora. "Katherine's on her way. We'll let her sort out the issues with the police. I'll handle them until she arrives."

Lines crossed Cora's forehead. "Do you think Rottier sent these men?"

"It's possible." Phoenix watched the blonde with that slight hint of affection she sometimes got around the eyes when she spoke with Cora. "If Barrett can't ID them, I want you to check with Thomson."

"Oh. I hadn't thought of that."

Neither had Amalia. Cora was in the middle of investigating another drug case with Kent Thomson, her fiancé at the Drug Enforcement Administration. Could be these men were here for Cora instead. Wouldn't be the first time thugs from a drug ring had been sent to finish Cora and her narcotics detection K-9.

"Take him to the new safe house as soon as he's done here." Phoenix glanced at Amalia as she opened the door and motioned with her hand for Nevaeh and Michael to enter. "Cora will give you the location."

Alvarez came through first, then Nevaeh, her gun in her hand as she stared at the men across the room.

Michael stepped through last. His gaze traveled from the thugs lined up against the wall to Amalia, where it halted on her face.

He looked a bit like the hostage she'd recovered in Somalia after a three-month stint in captivity. Shell-shocked.

Michael had no reason to be afraid or feel threatened in the safe room. Maybe he hadn't realized that.

"Are you okay?" Cora put her hand on his upper arm. "You don't have to do this if you're too upset."

Michael pulled his attention from Amalia. "No. I don't have a problem with doing this." Implying he had a problem with something else.

Amalia pressed her lips against the urge to ask him what, exactly, his problem was.

"Okay." Cora looked at the thugs. "Do you recognize them? We wondered if you could have seen them associated with Rottier or his operation."

Michael walked closer to the men.

"That's close enough." Nevaeh snipped out the warning from where she still stood near the entry, about eighteen feet from the men.

Michael glanced back at her, then rotated his head toward the thugs. He squatted down in front of them. If he'd been afraid of them before, he apparently wasn't now.

He studied each one for a minute. Stood. Turned to Cora instead of Amalia. "No. I've never seen them before."

Too bad. Would've been nice to know for sure who these characters belonged to.

"Sorry."

Cora smiled in response to his apology. "Don't be. These things are rarely that simple."

"Do you think they're from Rottier? Trying to kill me?" He didn't balk or flinch as he said the words. Maybe Amalia had misread the cause of his beleaguered condition.

Cora looked past him to Amalia, apparently checking for the answer she should give.

"Maybe." Amalia's response drew his gaze to her. "There are other factors we need to consider." Like the unlikelihood Rottier would hire Verdugo, one of the best elite assassins in the world, only to then bring in these amateurs as backup.

"Seems like overkill to hire a super assassin *and* these guys, doesn't it?" Michael's mouth angled in a closed-lip smile. "Pun not intended."

A shiver tracked up Amalia's spine. Couldn't be because of his smile. Had to be because of how close his thoughts had just come to hers. Unnerving. He didn't know who Amalia Pérez was, let alone how she thought.

"That's a very good point." Cora nodded at Michael.

A pretty obvious point. That's the only reason he'd thought of the same thing she had. Amalia took in a breath through her nose, relaxing the tension that narrowed her eyes.

"They could also have come because of a different case I'm working on." Cora looked at the men, a glint of concern in her eyes. Couldn't really blame her. She'd nearly lost her brother and her life the last time a narcotics ring had wanted her dead. But Michael didn't need to know about any of that or what the team was thinking now about these thugs.

"Time to move out." Amalia held out a hand and flicked her fingers toward Michael, indicating he should back away from the prisoners.

"Move out?" He didn't budge.

"New safe house."

"Safe house." He looked at her, suspicion pinching his eyes. "Right."

Now he suspected her of something? She flashed a smile. "Does that mean you'll go with me now?"

"Guess I might as well." He shoved his hands in his front jeans pockets as he sauntered away from the intruders.

"Terrific."

Amalia left Nevaeh on guard and went with Cora and Michael into the hallway, where Cora gave Amalia the safe house address.

Michael cooperated well enough as Amalia got him out of the building. Didn't say a word as he sat in her car, and they drove away with Raksa in the back seat.

She braced herself for a Q and A session on the drive to the safe house.

But Michael stayed quiet for once.

Was he angry? Scared? Maybe just tired.

The soft light of dusk cast shadows over his sun-kissed almond complexion and highlighted the dark circles under his eyes. The stubble on his face was darkening with additional growth that shaped his jaw. His tightly clenched jaw.

She'd go with angry. But she wasn't going to start a fight, if that's what he was waiting for.

They arrived at the safe house in silence. She slipped her earpiece into place and called the FBI agents on-site. One watched from the unmarked car on the street. The other two should be inside the house, front and back.

"FBI Team Leader, PT1 here with package."

The supervising agent inside the house responded and verified the locations of the other agents. Gave her clearance to enter.

"Let's go." She released Raksa from the back seat.

The shepherd dropped to the blacktop of the driveway and shook his whole body. He smelled the air, alert but not giving any signs of a threat.

She took Raksa to the passenger side of the car where Michael got out. "Stay in line with me." Her tone should make sure Michael obeyed without argument this time. She kept her gaze moving as she walked alongside him the six feet to the side door of the house.

The door instantly swung open. The FBI agent inside gave her a nod as she followed Michael into the house.

She glanced back to be sure the agent armed the security system again.

The system beeped, signaling it was ready.

And so was she. Even for Verdugo. Especially if she didn't have to deal with the distraction Michael was becoming. "I'd suggest you get some sleep while you can." She moved past him into the kitchen.

"You mean this safe house isn't any safer than the others?"

She paused at a cabinet door above the kitchen counter. Looked at him.

A little smirk rested on his mouth, surrounded by the dark stubble on his upper lip and chin.

She pulled her gaze back to the cabinet and grabbed a bowl from inside. She'd go back out and get her supplies for Raksa as soon as she ensured this place was secure enough for her to do so. But in the meantime, the K-9 looked too hot. She turned on the faucet and held the bowl underneath.

"You looked like you were having fun back there."

She kept filling the bowl, testing the water with her finger to make sure it was cold.

"Beating people up."

"Sure you don't mean keeping you alive?" She turned around and squatted to set the bowl in front of Raksa who started lapping the water like there'd be a drought tomorrow.

"Where'd you learn how to do that?"

She stood and gave Michael a smile. "Which part? The takedowns? Chokehold?"

"All of it." He crossed his arms over his chest, watching her with stormy blue eyes. "And especially the part where you love it. Where it isn't just normal for you, it's fun."

So that was it. He thought she liked violence, killing. "There's nothing wrong with enjoying my work." She kept her smile, even as her mind turned on itself.

What was she doing? Trying to defend herself on the basis of his view of right and wrong? She didn't need to do that. She didn't answer to him or anyone. She lived her life in the grays. He couldn't even begin to comprehend the necessity of people who could do that.

She didn't need to tell him she loved protecting others, loved the challenge and thrill of taking down bad guys and beating them at their own violent game. Of coming out on top. Better to let him think she was some kind of sociopath. It'd make him believe Sofia was gone forever.

"You're very good at it."

Why did she feel like that was a put down? "Lucky for you." She delivered the quip with a smile.

He didn't answer.

"Well, whether or not you want to get sleep, I have work to do. Gotta make sure this place is safe enough for you." She hit him with the verbal dig behind a grin as she brushed past him.

"Hey."

She paused at the opening that led from the kitchen to the hallway. Turned back.

He'd lowered his arms, his stance less confrontational. "Thank you."

She took in the tired lines on his face, the slump of his broad shoulders, the expression in his eyes—sincerity mixed with...disappointment?

Her throat swelled slightly. Impossible. Amalia Pérez never went soft. She swallowed. Instantly banished the hint of emotion. "Just doing my job."

He took a step toward her. Stopped. "You were right. I don't know who you are anymore."

Victory. Finally.

"After what I saw today, I have to wonder." He moved closer. "Am I safe with you, Amalia Pérez?"

For one unforgivable moment, she didn't know how to respond.

Even as he closed the gap between them. Leaned slightly toward her, blue eyes penetrating. "Goodnight." His deep voice warmed her ear as he brushed past and left the room.

She turned to track his progress as he went up the staircase she could see partially across the hall.

He watched her until his head lifted past the upper floor.

He was trouble. More trouble than she'd figured he'd be. She'd thought she would have the advantage. He didn't know her anymore, but she'd expected she knew him well enough to predict his every word and thought.

Unfortunately, the teenager she'd known in Texas had turned into some kind of persistent bulldog that kept surprising her.

*Expect the unexpected.* The mantra that had saved her life more times than she could count.

She'd drop her idea that she knew what to expect from Michael and treat him as a potential threat like everyone else. And do her research when she could. What was that investigation Cora had fawned over Michael about?

Devereux. Amalia pulled her smartphone from her pocket as Raksa lay down next to the emptied water bowl. She typed the name into the search box. Results popped up on the screen. She scrolled down and chose the first legitimate source she saw.

Four articles in, she had to allow a slight shift in her view of Michael, from annoyance to a fraction of respect. His work was impressive. He had the tenacity and brains to bring down a nasty criminal who had successfully masqueraded as an upstanding citizen for twenty-five years.

Michael hadn't only exposed the man's money laundering, he'd dug up all the dirty secrets—affairs, harassment charges, youthful indiscretions, and payoffs.

He'd probably done society a service bringing down Devereux. One more criminal she wouldn't have to deal with.

But Michael's relentless quest to find and expose every last secret the man had, the articles Michael wrote that revealed his dogged determination, spiraled a chill through Amalia's veins.

Good thing she never let her guard down with anyone. Because if Michael thought he was going to get anywhere near her and her secrets, he could think again.

Michael Barrett was a menace.

# SEVEN

He'd messed up. Michael shoved his hand through his hair, pulling it back from his face as he sat on the edge of yet another new bed in another new place. The quilt underneath him was a nice, homey touch to the safe house that was much more down-to-earth than the last one. The old, two-story house with small, cozy rooms reminded him a little of home back in Dallas.

He was overdue for his weekly call to *Papi* and *Mami*. But what could he say to Sofia's parents? *I found your daughter, but she says she doesn't exist anymore? Everything she told us was a lie?*

Neither of those options would fly. And if he just stopped at telling them Sofia was here, they'd probably jump in their unreliable van and make the long drive from Texas to Minnesota to see their daughter.

He grabbed his notebook computer from beside him on the bed and moved it to his lap. He typed a quick email, letting Papi and Mami know he'd call them in a day or two.

*Things are very hectic here right now*, he typed before signing off. That was certainly true.

He set the computer aside and stood, needing to pace. He'd have to see if he could make more headway with Sofia—Amalia—before telling her parents anything. If he could get her to come around, maybe she could talk to them herself.

Which brought him back, face-to-face with his error in judgment last night. He chalked it up to complete and total exhaustion with all that had happened during the day. Finding his best friend, but not really finding her, dealing with the lies of the past and present as well as multiple attempts on his life. Not exactly a run-of-the-mill day.

Even so, that didn't excuse how negative he'd come off when talking to Amalia last night. He shouldn't have challenged her so much, been so critical.

Honestly, the frustration had just slipped out when he'd seen how completely different Amalia really was from Sofia. An overwhelming sense of despair had hit him for the first time since Sofia had disappeared. The fear that, maybe, he would never find Sofia again. That she was lost forever.

He did not want to try to live with that reality. He wanted his best friend back. Her parents deserved to have their beloved daughter in their lives again. He couldn't give up when there was the slightest chance it might be possible.

But he wouldn't make any headway in finding out what happened to Sofia and bringing her back if he continued to seem judgmental of Amalia. Even if it gutted him to see what Sofia had become, he needed to befriend Amalia to have any hope of getting her to open up and share the truth. To let him see Sofia again.

And maybe his assessment of Amalia had been wrong. His frustration could've led him to inaccurate assumptions. If he was right the Phoenix K-9 Agency wasn't what it seemed, that didn't have to mean Amalia was willingly involved in anything criminal.

Michael stopped pacing, the possibility halting his breath.

Maybe she was caught up in something she'd never intended to be part of and couldn't find a way out. She could have had to change her identity because of something she'd been forced to become involved in. She could be in trouble, a victim.

And he could help her get out.

To do that, he'd need to figure out what was really going on at Phoenix K-9.

He grabbed his computer and dropped to sit on the bed, resting the laptop on his thighs. His gaze locked on the screen as he accessed his favorite database for searching criminal records.

He plugged in *Phoenix Gray* first.

Nothing.

*Bristol Jones.* Wait, she'd mentioned not being used to her new last name when she'd introduced him to Rem at Phoenix K-9 headquarters. She said Bachmann was her maiden name. He tried *Bristol Bachmann* instead.

No record.

He typed in all the Phoenix K-9 employees, one at a time, but came up blank. They were all clean.

Wouldn't be the first time people involved in shady dealings had managed to avoid ever getting caught. Devereux and most of his people involved in money laundering had escaped having criminal records until Michael found them out.

He'd go with a more general search and see what turned up. He navigated to a different search engine and started with Phoenix Gray again.

The woman was all over the news with her achievements at the Phoenix K-9 Security and Detection Agency. Judging from her praises sung by everyone from the police to the FBI, she sounded like she should be nominated for sainthood. The work she and her employees did through the agency clearly had a positive impact on the community. They'd rescued adults and children, brought down criminal organizations, protected celebrities and politicians, and stopped an environmental terrorist from flooding the Twin Cities. An impressive resume to say the least.

The internet search also revealed that Phoenix herself was involved in several charitable endeavors, including volunteer work and financial support of a no-kill animal shelter and training center called Forever Home. She even led free self-defense seminars for young girls.

Phoenix Gray was a good person and ideal citizen. Or so it seemed. Devereux had managed to cultivate the same kind of reputation, and he was evil as they came.

Blowing out a sigh, Michael moved on to Bristol Bachmann. Maybe he'd find something more obviously suspicious about her.

Nope. She was apparently a former Minneapolis Police Department officer, once a member of the MPD Bomb Unit, and was responsible for stopping the bomber who'd targeted river dams last year. Cops could be dirty, but her record definitely lowered her on his list of suspects.

Then there was Jazz Lamont, the former Army Military Working Dog handler that Phoenix had reunited with her K-9 partner.

Nevaeh Williams was apparently a correctional officer at a local prison, then quit and became an Emergency Medical Technician. Her association with the jail could give her connections with the criminal set, but the internet wasn't helping him find evidence of anything suspicious tied to her.

Cora Isaksson was seemingly as squeaky clean as she looked. She showed up in some online church videos and articles connected to church-related events. Church involvement was sometimes used by criminals to disguise their true activities. But Cora could also be an innocent party to what may be happening at Phoenix K-9.

Or the whole agency could be exactly what it appeared to be—a security and detection agency that protected people and fought crime. But then why was Amalia so secretive about her past if she'd simply been doing good at Phoenix K-9? And why had she changed her identity and lied to Michael and her parents?

He shoved a hand through his hair, pulling it away from his eyes as frustration churned his stomach.

Maybe the only way to find out for sure was going to be through Amalia herself.

He looked at the clock on his computer.

*Oh, man.* Almost eleven, the time Amalia's shift ended and

Nevaeh took over. He'd gotten up late, thanks to not hitting the sack until two a.m. And he hadn't felt up to facing Amalia until he had his head on straight.

Muffled voices carried through the vent into his bedroom.

Amalia? Maybe she was still downstairs.

He left the bedroom, hurried through the hallway and down the creaky stairs.

The sound of female voices carried to him. As soon as he got low enough for his head to clear the ceiling, he spotted the person he was looking for.

*Sofia.* His heart surged at the sight of her, standing with Raksa near the door. Her black hair flowed in soft waves, swinging past her face as she bent to pet the dog.

And in a split second he was seeing Sofia, bending to pick up her duffel bag to return to college, even though he wasn't going back with her. Sofia, about to leave him.

She straightened and gazed at him with big, dark eyes. Empty eyes. Amalia's eyes.

He blinked and cleared his throat, becoming aware that Nevaeh was there, too. And both women had stopped speaking as they turned their heads to look at him. Even Raksa and Alvarez stared.

He mustered a smile. "Why do I get the feeling my ears should've been burning?"

Amalia flashed that grin he was beginning to despise. "I assure you we don't discuss clients in any capacity other than their safety."

Almost icy cold this morning, despite her showy smile.

If she was angry with him, she didn't have to hide it behind her fake persona. Irritation sparked behind his ribs. But he thought before he spoke this time. "Thanks for the protection overnight. I never should've doubted you."

Nevaeh glanced from Michael to Amalia, her thick eyebrows lifted.

"We work hard to uphold our reputation at Phoenix K-9." Even Amalia's eyes squinted slightly, as if her smile was genuine. She was good enough to be an actress. "If you ever feel unsafe, let us know." Her grin angled as she moved her gaze to Nevaeh. "Later."

Nevaeh returned the grin and re-armed the security system as soon as she closed the door behind Amalia and Raksa.

At least Amalia hadn't given any hints she wasn't coming back this time. He'd have another chance. As cool and unemotional as Amalia Pérez seemed, she apparently wasn't impervious to irritation and anger. He was ninety percent sure some such emotion had been driving her heightened impersonal performance just now.

"Somebody's in the doghouse." Nevaeh's eyes glittered with amusement as her lips angled in a barely repressed smile.

"Is that what that was?"

Nevaeh shrugged, the humor escaping in a show of white teeth. "The last time I saw her with that particular smile was when—" She stopped herself. "Well, let's just say it wasn't good for the guys on the receiving end."

So he'd been right. He'd have to learn the nuances to these unfamiliar smiles of Amalia's. Or maybe, he could find Sofia under the mirage and not have to learn the pattern of deception Amalia had used to construct her new identity.

He had to find a way to do that, especially if she was trapped in something she hadn't wanted to be. He had to help her.

"By the way," Nevaeh's words drew his attention out of his thoughts, "I wanted to say…" She looked away. "Well… Thanks." She brought her dark brown eyes back to his face. "For helping me out yesterday. Getting me into the car."

A smile found Michael's face. Clearly, this wasn't easy for her. But he admired her courage in being humble enough to say thanks. "Happy I could help. Thank you for taking that bullet for me."

"I was going to grab some coffee." She thumbed over her shoulder in the direction of the kitchen. "You want some?"

Hope warmed his chest. A friendly opening. Could Nevaeh help him get the information he needed about the agency or Amalia? He nodded. "I never turn down coffee." He grinned.

Ten minutes later, he'd only learned bits of information from Nevaeh, even though she'd been downright chatty. For a talker, she was awfully careful about privacy and keeping information to herself.

He smiled at her over the mug of coffee in his hand as he leaned his hip against the kitchen counter. "So you're really not going to satisfy my curiosity about Phoenix K-9, are you?"

She leaned back in the chair she occupied by the square breakfast table. "We're a private little family." She shrugged with a mischievous smile. "I'll just say this, the one thing I've learned about PK-9 is that nothing is as it seems when it comes to the ladies on the team."

Was that a hint? Her way of telling him there were secrets?

He needed to dig deeper. Expand his search.

"Well, thanks for the coffee." He crossed the room with his mug in hand. "I have some work to do, so I'll take mine upstairs."

"Right." She shoved to her feet, Alavarez slowly getting up from the floor beside her. "We're off to make the rounds outside."

"Thanks." The thrill of a lead buzzed in his veins as he left the kitchen, trying to keep his pace casual. What had she meant by—

The ring of his phone in his pocket halted his thoughts.

He paused and pulled it out.

*Unknown number.*

Could be a result of one of the feelers he'd put out on the human trafficking investigation he was working. The best leads often came from unknown sources.

He pressed the phone to his ear as he reached the stairs and started up them. "Hello?"

"Who is this?" A woman's voice. With an edge of fear, if he wasn't mistaken.

"Michael Barrett." He didn't ask who she was. Never add pressure or a reason for a source to hang up before disclosing what they knew.

"I got your number from my uncle, Paul Bischoff."

The assassinated witness. Michael halted at the top of the stairs, his pulse picking up speed.

"Do you know who I am?"

Paul had told him about his niece, Vicki Wilson. She'd snagged the well-paid position as Rottier's personal secretary thanks to her uncle's recommendation before Paul knew what was going on at Rottier Furnishings. He'd hoped she'd testify at the trial, but she'd been too afraid to take the risk. At least according to Paul. Though he hadn't given up hope. Even asked Michael for the number of Michael's new FBI phone so he could give it to Vicki, just in case she changed her mind. That was the day Paul died. Michael swallowed. "Yes, Paul mentioned you."

"I think he killed my uncle." Her voice lowered to a barely perceptible whisper. Even in those soft tones, he heard her pain. The press hadn't gotten ahold of the news of her uncle's killing yet, and he doubted the FBI had even notified next of kin. But since Rottier was behind the killing, that must be how she'd heard.

"I'm so sorry." He meant every word, the burden of convincing Paul to testify weighing on his shoulders. It was the right thing. But not the outcome Michael had intended.

Her long silence ended with a muffled sound. A sniff? "Thank you."

"How can I help?" A much better question to ask, he'd learned, than questioning what she could do for him.

"You can make sure he pays for it."

"I'd love to. Rottier belongs behind bars, and I'll do everything I can to make sure that happens."

"I can help."

His breath quickened, but he kept his tone even. Didn't want to scare her away. "That would be great."

"I'll give you evidence so strong no jury will ever let him off."

"What evidence do you have?"

"I'll get a recording." Her volume dipped again to an almost-whisper. "Of him admitting the weapons trafficking."

"If you can do that, it would sink him for sure. He would go away for a long time."

"I have to go." The fear in her voice doubled.

"Are you okay? Are you safe?"

"I'll call you late—" Her whisper cut short, and the background noise shifted to silence.

He pulled the phone away from his ear to verify she'd disconnected.

He couldn't help her physically, but he could pray. He breathed a prayer for Vicki's safety and for success in her mission to expose Rottier.

With Michael's testimony and Brenda Nixon's, as well as the evidence Michael had compiled against Rottier, they should get a conviction. Which was apparently why Rottier was nervous enough to start bumping off witnesses.

But he could also afford the best lawyers in the country. Michael had seen money and power imbalance the scales of justice more often than he'd like to remember.

If Vicki obtained recorded evidence of the trafficker admitting his involvement, there'd be no way even slick lawyers could enable Rottier to walk.

They'd have him dead to rights, hopefully before his hired killer, or killers, managed to make Michael dead first.

---

"Did you find out who those guys were who attacked us at Phoenix K-9 yesterday?"

Amalia kept her eyes on the road as she considered how much to tell Michael. Phoenix seemed to be in favor of giving him more information, so she supposed she could answer the question.

"Were they related to Cora's narcotics case?"

Or that question. The man was way too inquisitive. Couldn't even wait for the answer to one question before asking another. And he apparently paid attention, too. Knew about Cora's case even though they'd only mentioned it once in front of him, at a time when he'd been obviously exhausted.

"Seems they were there for you, not her." She angled her lips in a smile as she slid on her sunglasses, the rising sun just bright enough to make them necessary.

"That makes you happy?"

She tossed him a sidelong glance as she slowed at a four-way stop on the quiet suburban road. "Makes me happy we were able to protect you. So efficiently."

"How did you figure out they were after me? Could someone ID them?"

"Process of elimination. They weren't associated with the DEA's case."

"I see." He tapped his long fingers against the curve of the passenger door where he rested his arm along the window.

The cold air from the air conditioning blasted into the silence.

"Are they still off the streets?"

Was he worried for his safety? She checked his expression out of the corner of her eye. His profile showcased a strong jawline, his stubble trimmed back to the controlled highlight that gave him an undeniable added appeal. But his body language communicated he was relaxed, not nervous.

No tension flexed the muscles in his forearms beneath the rolled-up sleeves of the vibrant blue button-down he wore. He'd tucked the shirt into his straight-cut jeans today. Must be his way of dressing up for his meeting with the U. S. Attorney at the courthouse for prepping his testimony. He was looking pretty good, actually.

She yanked her gaze back to scan the road, the

surrounding area. Checked for any surprises. Other than the one seated beside her.

The sporadic sleep he'd been getting shouldn't have made anyone look that good. Not that she cared.

"Not going to tell me?"

"They were bailed out by a cheap public defender. No one's been able to trace who sent the attorney." She mentally thrashed herself for getting distracted. By a guy. That hadn't happened since...Jacob. She didn't allow it. And now Michael of all people? She'd never found him attractive. Not like that. Apparently, being in the ninth hour of her twelve-hour shift was taking more of a toll than usual.

"Great." Sarcasm flatlined his tone. "But we can probably assume Rottier was behind it, right?"

"Looks likely."

"So he hired these guys because the other assassin failed?"

She slowed and turned the car onto another street. "If he did, it was a stupid move. Those thugs are bumbling amateurs compared to Verdugo."

"Even though you beat him?"

She glanced at him. Flashed a smile. "Didn't say we aren't better."

His mouth opened in a grin, crinkling his eyes at the corners. Eyes that looked so much bluer thanks to his shirt.

She jerked her attention to where it should be—the road. The surroundings.

"So is Verdugo gone now? Replaced by the bumblers?" Humor infused his tone with something warm and familiar.

She narrowed her eyes as she reached another intersection and feigned suspicion about the empty crossroad. "He doesn't like interference. Wants to be a solo hire. Likely he took what he was owed and left."

"That'd be a relief. An answer to prayer."

Surprise made her want to look his way, but she resisted the urge. That was a new phrase for Michael to use. Though she heard it often enough from Cora and even Bristol these days.

"I have to call your parents."

She swung her head toward him, smile dropped.

"I call them every week when I'm away." He held her gaze. "I have to tell them about you."

She broke contact. "No, you don't." She fought to keep her hands from tightening on the wheel, a tell she didn't need him to see.

"What do you want me to tell them about you?"

"Nothing." She kept her tone light. But her shoulders tensed.

"I won't lie. You know that."

"You don't have to." Her gut clenched. "Just don't bring it up."

"Same thing."

"No, it isn't."

"How would you know?" His tone picked up a sharp edge.

She threw him a glance. Without a smile.

"You clearly have no problem lying all the time."

She silently released a calming breath through her nose before responding to his bait. She didn't care what he thought. She just needed to manage his threat to tell her parents anything. "Only when it's helpful."

"You know it's always wrong. Remember that important little thing called the Ninth Commandment? 'You shall not lie'?" Michael dropped his arm away from the window and angled toward her. "You know lying is always wrong in God's eyes."

She laughed. "I know the whole idea of God is one of the biggest lies invented."

Silence charged the air between them.

"You can't mean that." The hurt in his voice was so thick she could've sliced it with a knife.

Might've made her feel something if she could still feel. But she'd done an excellent job ensuring she couldn't.

She just needed him to back off. This was a fast way to achieve that.

"So now you're telling me you aren't a Christian either?"

A low growl from the back seat seized Amalia's attention. Raksa sat up, stared out the rear window.

Where a black SUV barreled toward them.

# EIGHT

"Hold on." Amalia barked the order as she hit the accelerator.

Michael gripped the handle of the passenger door as the car surged. He looked over his shoulder. "The guys from last night?"

"If the vehicle gets close, you duck. Got it?"

"Got it." He glanced back again, over the head of Raksa, who watched the pursuing vehicle. "I think you're putting more distance between us."

He rotated forward in time to see her gaze dart to the rearview mirror, then to the road ahead.

"Were they following us the whole time?"

"No." The one word carried both afront and confidence. "They were on a cross street. Smart enough to wait until we were out of sight to begin pursuit."

"You mean they were parked there, waiting for us?"

She jerked a terse nod, intense gaze hopping to the mirrors and the road.

"That would mean they had to know we were going to the courthouse this morning, wouldn't it? Or at least that we were going into the city."

She suddenly swung the car to the right, taking a side street without slowing much at all.

90

"Whoa." He braced his other hand against the dash as his body swayed sideways.

"Told you to hang on." She darted the car around three vehicles at a standstill.

At an intersection.

With a red light.

She zoomed through, narrowly missing an oncoming pickup. On his side of the car.

He let out a breath, took in another. Forgetting to breathe wouldn't help his swirling belly.

"There." Her mouth widened with a grin. "That should do it." She turned onto another street and slowed to a healthier speed.

"You lost them?" He reached for the bottled water he'd stuffed in the door's cupholder earlier. Maybe the liquid would calm his nausea.

She aimed her smile at him. "I dare—"

A navy blue two-door appeared out of nowhere, charged at the passenger side.

Amalia yanked the wheel hard and launched her car into a spin.

Water from the bottle splashed onto Michael's shirt as he gripped the door for dear life.

The pursuer missed his target, braking just past them as Amalia straightened her car and gunned it forward.

The navy blue car zoomed up beside them on the two-lane road. A window on the passenger side rolled down. The barrel of a weapon stuck out the opening.

"Is that a rifle?"

Amalia snorted a laugh. Slammed on the breaks so hard Michael's breakfast lurched up his throat.

She spun the car around as the two-door unintentionally sped far beyond them. She floored it the other direction. Reached the intersection they'd narrowly escaped last time.

*Lord, help us.* The prayer calmed the tension that clutched Michael's throat as they hit the higher-traffic intersection.

Amalia didn't stop. She swung into a turn in front of a green truck that didn't have time to slow.

A honk blared behind them as Amalia darted her car around a red SUV ahead of them, then past a minivan.

Michael swallowed, desperately trying to keep the contents of his stomach from ending up on the floor of Amalia's car.

She turned onto a side street, then another.

Michael closed his eyes, but that only made the motion more nauseating. "Any chance we could stop now?"

"In a second."

He opened his eyes.

Just in time to see the navy blue two-door, ahead of them this time.

Amalia zoomed toward its bumper.

An oncoming car passed in the other lane.

She darted out the moment it was clear.

Was she going to pass the same people who'd just tried to shoot at them with a rifle?

She angled her car slightly.

Michael sucked in a breath.

She was going to hit them. She bumped the front corner of her car into the rear side of the two-door.

It flung into an out-of-control spin as Amalia surged ahead, out of the way.

Michael didn't dare look back with his stomach heaving the way it was.

But Amalia's gleeful grin as she looked in the rearview mirror said it all.

She'd bested the bad guys once again.

"Mind if I join you?"

"Shouldn't you be resting?" Amalia gave Michael a once-over in answer to his request to tag along as she and Phoenix surveyed the new safe house Agent Nguyen had sent them to. At least the hue of his skin was no longer a shade of green.

"I'm fine." His lips curved in a smile that had that softening effect on his eyes.

Amalia pulled her gaze away from him two seconds later than she should have. She let her hand rest on Raksa's head as she turned to looked at Phoenix.

The shadow under the bill of Phoenix's gray baseball cap obscured her unreadable gaze. But there was no missing her nod.

Great. Amalia donned a smile. "Looks like you get to join the tour."

"Thanks." He stuffed his hands in his pockets in that way that made her think of the small boy she'd once known, hesitant and unsure about needing to eat at her parents' house another evening. That was before his presence for dinners became normal. Before they'd come up with excuses to explain why he couldn't eat at home.

"This house is really something." Michael's gaze traveled over the open floor plan of the kitchen and living room that opened onto a walk-out patio. "Do you know how the FBI got it?"

Leave it to Michael to wait only ten seconds before asking a question.

She wasn't going to satisfy his curiosity by telling him the FBI had been able to seize the house thanks to a multimillion-dollar fraud bust. "Too many windows." She focused on Phoenix. "Are any of them reinforced or bullet-proofed?"

"No." Phoenix passed the counter in the kitchen and stepped into the living room area, sparsely furnished with a white sofa and glass coffee table. Clean lines and modern décor pieces, including a random sculpture of three vertical metal rods that passed for art, gave the space a cool hardness that was a helpful backdrop for the job at hand.

"You'll need to stay out of this area most of the time." Phoenix turned her head toward Michael, who followed them like a curious puppy dog. "Especially when not with a K-9 team. The boys will likely warn us before anyone can get close enough to take a shot. But we can't guarantee it. Stay away from the windows come nightfall."

Michael nodded, seemingly subdued by Phoenix's commanding tone.

Phoenix led the way out of the living room and around the staircase that divided the first floor in the middle. They went midway down the short hall at the rear of the house and stepped into a smaller room with a desk and bookshelves.

Phoenix walked to another floor-length window along one wall. She suddenly turned, faced Michael. "Do you know why you're the only witness being targeted, Mr. Barrett?" She crossed her arms over her black armored vest and open PK-9 windbreaker.

His eyes widened slightly. Maybe just from getting caught in the center of Phoenix's fierce focus. Even though Michael's six-foot height beat Phoenix's five feet and seven inches, she had a way of intimidating everyone. And kept enough distance between her and the subject that she didn't have to tilt her head. "You think I'm the only witness Rottier is trying to kill now?"

"A distinct possibility. You've been the only target since the Bischoff killing."

"I see." Michael pushed a hand through his hair, pulling the waves to temporarily rest farther back from his forehead. "I guess that makes sense."

No hedging to cover up what he knew and no sign of fear at being the target of killers. Either Michael was one of the most open and naturally brave people Amalia had met or he was putting on an act.

"Paul was probably the most dangerous witness to take the stand from Rottier's point of view." Michael rubbed the stubble on his jaw between his fingers and thumb. "He had been party to some of the trafficking, managed a go-between drop-off point for the weapons on their way through the U. S.

to and from Mexico. After Paul, I'd be Rottier's next worst nightmare."

"Doesn't the FBI already have all the documentation of the evidence you collected?"

Michael shifted his gaze to Amalia at her question. "They have some. But I can also deliver accounts of oral testimony from witnesses who wanted to remain anonymous. And I can personally testify to witnessing a transfer of weapons and some hidden stock at a warehouse that I wasn't able to get pictures of."

"What does Brenda Nixon know?" Phoenix delivered the question as Dagian sat down at her side.

"She can testify to notes and phone calls that she witnessed passing through the Texas office when she was a secretary there. Her testimony is helpful, but wouldn't be enough to convict, maybe even with the other evidence the U. S. Attorney would have if something happened to me."

An odd twinge pinged beneath Amalia's breastbone at Michael's words. Weird.

Raksa nudged her hand, drew her attention away from the oddly timed sensation.

Maybe a muscle cramp from the manhandling of the car she'd had to do during the road chase.

"The challenge has always been to tie the activities to Rottier, not just his business. That's where our case may fall short."

Phoenix abruptly started moving again, walking past Amalia to leave the office and head for the staircase.

"Since we're on the subject of me being a target..."

Amalia rolled her eyes at Michael's segue as they halted at the base of the stairs. She braced for another question from the intrepid reporter.

"How did the attackers know where to find us on the road this morning?"

Phoenix looked at Amalia.

Apparently, she was supposed to field this one. "They had to have intel about your meeting with the U. S. Attorney."

"And where the safe house was, right? 'Cause it seemed like they were waiting for us."

"Correct."

"What about the second car? How did that driver know where we were, too?"

"I'd gotten us back en route to the courthouse in Minneapolis by then. They were parked farther along the route."

"Okay, but how could they have known about the safe house and my appointment?"

Amalia glanced at Jeffers, the FBI agent positioned at the house's front entry.

Michael turned his head in the direction of her gaze, then looked back at her. Stepped closer. "You think there's a leak in the FBI?" He kept his voice low and quiet.

She gave him a smile. "Let's see the rest of the house and figure out positions for the security team." She turned, allowing Raksa to lead the way as they followed Phoenix and Dag up the stairs.

A leak was the only explanation. Possibly even a mole, though there could be other ways the information had been unintentionally mishandled.

Phoenix would take care of looking into it. Talk to Nguyen.

In the meantime, Amalia would have her hands full keeping the inquisitive journalist quiet, away from windows, and away from a phone where he could call her parents and bring her life crashing in around her.

Though judging from today's events, the greatest challenge might simply be keeping him alive.

# NINE

Anticipation bounced around in Michael's stomach like he was a pinball machine as he sat on the bottom stair in the fancy safe house, listening. He hadn't felt like this since the time Sofia had gone to ask her parents if he could spend a month at their house. He'd broken into a sweat waiting what felt like an hour for her to come out of the house with their answer.

Her smile that beamed as warm as the sunshine on the hot summer day had told him all he needed to know as she'd run across the crunchy brown grass to throw her small arms around him in a hug.

They'd told her parents his mom was going to visit her sister who was sick. Another lie.

A frown pulled down the corners of Michael's mouth as the bouncing in his stomach slowed.

All those memories were so bittersweet now. Sweet because of Sofia. But so bitter in the end.

And now, even Sofia was tainted in his memories thanks to her denial of who she was and the deceptive, cold persona of Amalia Pérez.

But he wouldn't give up. Even if she didn't want to acknowledge how awful their lying had been. Even if she wanted to reject everything from their past together.

97

Sofia had never given up on him when he'd needed a friend and champion during those rough years of childhood. He wouldn't give up on her now.

"Hey, girl." Nevaeh's greeting to someone reached Michael's ears from behind the staircase.

The door that led to the garage. He probably should've known Amalia wouldn't enter from the front door for the start of her shift.

He stood and took his phone from his pocket to check the time. *10:55.* A few minutes early.

He nodded to the FBI agent at the front door, then rounded the staircase in time to see Neveah and her dog Alvarez walk into the kitchen and living room area. Amalia must be ahead of her.

"He's been pretty well-behaved so far. Kept to his room mostly and didn't pepper me with questions this time."

"Hey." Michael feigned offense at Nevaeh's assessment as he entered the kitchen.

Nevaeh and Alvarez cast him grinning looks that appeared equally lighthearted.

Michael narrowed his eyes. "You knew I'd hear that, didn't you?"

"I'm good at my job. Know where the wit is at all times." She laughed.

He couldn't help but smile in return. "That's comforting." He colored his tone with obvious sarcasm.

He walked farther into the kitchen, and his gaze finally landed on the person it had been seeking all along.

Amalia leaned back against the sleek marble countertop in the corner where the refrigerator and cabinets had blocked his view before. Her Amalia smile was fully in place, but warmth still filled his chest at the sight of her. His best friend was in there somewhere. She had to be.

Her gaze drifted to the phone he held in his hand. "Calling someone?"

Like her parents? He'd thought about calling them during the day while he'd counted the hours until she'd return at eleven p.m. He probably should have, but he still couldn't figure out what he was going to say. Amalia clearly wasn't going to give him any help. He'd instead focused on writing a couple of articles, as well as doing research and sending emails that he hoped would further his investigation into the human trafficking ring.

"Maybe." Letting her sweat a little might not be a bad idea.

But her smile didn't even falter.

He met her stare above her smile. Did he see a hint of worry in those dark eyes? Not—

A ringtone punctured the air. His ringtone.

He lifted the phone and checked the screen. Vicki. Or at least the number she'd used last time. "Excuse me."

He turned and left the room as he held the phone to his ear. "Michael here." He hurried up the staircase, taking the steps two at a time.

"I got it." Her voice was hushed and shaky.

Michael's breathing quickened as he reached the bedroom and quietly shut the door behind him. *Thank you, Lord.* If it was true, this could put Rottier away for a very long time. "He admitted the arms trafficking?"

"And more. I can't keep this. I need you to get it right away."

"Okay. Tell me what you want me to do." He kept his tone calm and steady. She was right to be scared. She held Rottier's future in her hands. If he found out...

"Can you come? To my apartment."

"Yes." Except for the fact he was under armed guard twenty-four-seven. He dismissed the obstacle. He'd figure it out. Right now, Vicki needed only confidence and reassurance from him. "When?"

"Tonight. Midnight. Come to the side door in the alley. I'll leave it unlocked so you don't have to go past the doorman."

"Okay." How in the world would he get out of the safe house to do this? He set his jaw. He'd have to. There was no other option.

"I'll give you the address."

He grabbed the tablet he'd been using for notes earlier and jotted down the street address and apartment number.

"You promise you'll be here?"

"Yes, ma'am. I will be there at midnight. I never break my word."

She breathed a little into the phone. "Okay. Good." She coughed quietly. "One more thing."

He waited. Was she trying to decide if she should say it?

"I know you have people protecting you. Don't tell them anything about this. They can't know. He has a source in the FBI."

Michael's breath froze in his lungs. He swallowed, worked to find air for his question. "Are you sure?"

"Yes. Someone from the FBI reports to one of our employees."

Unbelievable. And yet, given what had happened today, quite possible. "Okay."

"You won't tell them?" Her voice quaked. Poor woman was frightened to death.

"No. I won't tell the FBI. I promise." He softened his firm tone. "I'll see you soon, Vicki. You can count on me. Just be safe until I get there."

"Thank you." A shuddering sigh, as if from relief, passed across the line. She ended the call.

Now all he had to do was figure out how to escape the people who were trying to keep him safe.

---

"I need to talk to you." Michael stood just inside the back door. Had he been waiting for her to return to the house after patrolling the property with Raksa?

More questions. Probably about telling her parents he'd found her. She'd taken down five armed attackers at a time. She could handle Barrett and his questions. "Shoot."

He threw a pointed glance at Lawson, the FBI agent

guarding the front door who'd stepped back to let her in. What was with the sudden suspicion in Michael's eyes? "Can you come upstairs for a minute?"

"Sure, I've got nothing but time." She gave him a grin.

He ignored it, turned away to walk to the staircase. "After you." He swung his hand toward the stairs.

"I'm protecting you." She left her lips in the curve of an amused smile. "You go first."

"Okay." He took the stairs quickly, then turned to meet her and Raksa at the top. "Can I trust you?"

She almost dropped back onto the top stair. Hadn't seen that one coming. She should've spit out a *yes* or *of course* without hesitation. With anyone else, she would have. But she wasn't even sure Michael would believe her if she said the words. "What do you think?"

His eyes narrowed, darker and intense in the shadows of the unlit hallway. "I just learned Rottier has a mole in the FBI."

Interesting. And not wholly unexpected. But where would Michael have heard that?

His mouth pressed in a hard line. "I need to go do something important with life and death stakes. I need to know if I can trust you."

"I'll keep you and your secrets safe." As she always had.

He shifted, weight moving back to his heels. "It's not a secret, exactly. Just information Rottier can't find out." Michael turned away, walked a few feet farther into the hallway.

Amalia followed, Raksa moving with her. She could flick the light switch beside her on the wall, but the darkness was appropriate at the moment.

"I need to get out of here. Now."

Another surprise. Good thing she always expected the unexpected. She didn't blink. Just watched him.

His eyebrows drew together, thick vertical lines of skin bunching above his nose. A grown-up version of the expression he used to get every time he'd talk about his mother.

He was serious. Invested. Something big, something he cared about was at stake.

"Okay."

His shoulders relaxed a little. "Just like that?"

"Sure."

"You don't need more information?"

"No."

The furrows smoothed a fraction. Something softened in the eyes that watched her.

"But I'll need to clear it with Phoenix first. She'll want more information."

He crossed his arms over the chest that was so much broader than it used to be. "Do you think Phoenix can be trusted? Even with the mole in the FBI? She seems pretty chummy with Agent Nguyen."

"I trust Phoenix more than anyone I know." That was saying a lot, considering she didn't fully trust any human being.

He slowly nodded as he studied her face. "Okay." He lowered his voice. "Rottier's personal secretary contacted me. She's the niece of Paul Bischoff and doesn't like what Rottier did to him. She says she got a recording of Rottier admitting his involvement in the arms trafficking and more."

"Do you believe her?" She could be leading him into a trap for Rottier.

He nodded. "I do. Her emotion was too raw, too real to be faked."

Not necessarily. But Michael was right that the average person lacked the ability to deceive so convincingly.

"I have to meet her at her apartment at midnight to get the recording." He pulled out his phone. Looked at the screen. "That only leaves thirty minutes. She lives in a different suburb. Black Bear River. My phone says it'll take twenty-seven minutes, so we'd better hurry."

"Hang on." Amalia slipped her phone from her pocket and selected Phoenix's number.

"Problem?" Phoenix answered halfway into the first ring, her voice curt.

"Our wit wants to sneak out."

Phoenix remained silent as Amalia quickly summed up the situation, including the source's claim about the FBI mole.

"Supposed to meet her at midnight."

"Take him."

Amalia smiled. Loved Phoenix's efficiency. "Care how I do it?"

"No one gets injured."

"Got it."

"If there is a mole, it isn't Katherine. Trust her, but no one else at the FBI right now."

As if Amalia could trust anyone even if she wanted to. But she knew what Phoenix meant. "Roger."

"Could be a trap."

Amalia's thoughts exactly. "Yes."

"Be on your guard. I'll send backup. Nevaeh and Jazz will meet you there, out of sight unless needed."

Good idea. Amalia kept the thought to herself. Phoenix didn't need anyone's reassurance.

"Wear your coms when you arrive and report back to me as soon as you get the recording."

The call ended before Amalia could respond. Her lips tugged into a slight smile at Phoenix's abruptness as she slid the phone back into her jeans pocket.

"We're okay to go?" Michael dipped his head toward her, the furrows on his forehead returning.

"Yep."

"How will we get away without the FBI agents noticing?"

She grinned. "Follow me."

"Wait." Gentle pressure on her arm stopped her progress.

She looked at his hand on her forearm, so large and masculine. His warmth permeated the sleeve of her black Henley that she'd pushed up to her elbow.

"You aren't going to hurt them, are you?"

She yanked her gaze from the distracting hand. Laughed as she pulled away, moved toward the stairs. "It'll be bloodless, I promise." She paused and shot him a grin over her shoulder. "But you might have to cover your ears because I'm planning to lie."

He narrowed his eyes, clearly not amused.

She chuckled as she traipsed down the stairs, Raksa thudding down behind her and reaching the bottom as she did. She headed for the garage door. Jeffers was away from the garage as he made rounds through the other rooms on the ground floor and then would be posted at the rear door for a time.

She activated her radio. "Team Leader, F1, and F2, this is PT1. Just heard from Agent in Charge I need to move package." Citing fake orders from Agent Nguyen should make the escape a walk in the park. "Location may be compromised. I need front coverage as we move."

"PT1, Team Leader, Roger."

Amalia angled back to give Michael a thumb's up as the responses from the other two FBI agents followed Lawson's. She stopped at the door to the garage. "Stay here."

"We really have to go. We're already late."

"If you want to get killed when you reach the garage and not make your meeting, go right ahead. Don't bother waiting for me to clear it." She gave him one of her sweetest smiles.

She patted his bare forearm and instantly regretted the action when a tingle shot through her fingers. Static electricity in the middle of summer? "I'll clear it in thirty seconds and get you to your meeting with time to spare."

"How can you do that?" Skepticism laced his tone.

"You've seen me drive, right?" She chuckled at the lift of his eyebrows as she and Raksa entered the garage. Her smile faded as they quickly canvassed the shadowy space. No intruders. But a mole in the FBI and a clandestine meeting with a Rottier employee could mean trouble.

Michael could be walking into something far more dangerous than he expected. He could get hurt.

The thought pinched beneath her breastbone. Not that she cared. Not for herself. But her parents would be devastated if anything happened to the man who was practically their adopted son. Even more devastated than finding out their daughter was suspected as a traitor.

Amalia would have to make sure this meeting was bloodless, too. Or, at the very least, that none of the blood belonged to Michael.

# TEN

Weird. The two streetlamps along the sidewalk in front of the apartment building were burnt out. Or turned off.

Michael's heart rate picked up speed. He leaned closer to the passenger window as Amalia slowed her car.

Moonlight silhouetted the lines of something on the sidewalk.

"Is that a sweatshirt? Or..." A person? He couldn't voice the thought as it nearly choked him. Couldn't be. Not again.

Amalia swung the car into the alley where they were supposed to enter through the side door. "Stay here." Her command was steely as she popped out and got Raksa out of the back faster than he'd have thought possible.

The outline of the gun in her hand as she disappeared around the corner pounded his heart against his ribs.

If that was a body out there, if it was Vicki, he wasn't going to hide in safety here. He had to know.

Shoving his door open, he treaded carefully as he approached the corner where Amalia had vanished. He pressed his hands against the rough white stone of the apartment building as he peered out.

Amalia straightened, as if she'd been squatting down to check something on the...woman.

He could see more clearly now. No mistaking the

contours of the person who lay there. He was suddenly next to Amalia, his feet apparently having moved without conscious direction.

She put her hand on his chest, pushing him back. "I told you to stay put. It's not safe for you here."

He resisted without planning to, his feet rooted as he stared at the woman on the sidewalk.

Vicki Wilson.

Dark blood pooled around her on the ivory-colored concrete. But somehow her face was undamaged. She looked exactly like the staff picture on the Rottier Furnishings website. And like the photo Paul Bischoff had once shown Michael on his phone. Minus the huge smile she'd sported as she'd hugged her uncle.

A lump the size of a softball stuck in Michael's craw. *Rottier*. Vicki had been so determined to make him pay. But he'd made her pay instead.

*Lord, this isn't right.*

He bit back the desire to ask God why He'd let it happen. He'd learned a long time ago that God's reasons for such things were always good, even when Michael couldn't see it. That he had to trust God with that.

But that didn't mean Michael had to let evil and injustice go unpunished. Fury burned in his throat. This is where deceptions and lies led. Always. Didn't Amalia see that?

He lifted his gaze, opening his mouth to confront her with the righteous anger boiling in his soul.

But she was talking. Into the coms earpiece she'd switched to on the way there, apparently. She'd said Nevaeh and the other Phoenix K-9 team member, Jazz, were going to be there but out of sight.

"Looks like the fall killed her. No other obvious injuries." She slid her gaze up to the tenth floor of the building where Vicki lived.

*Had* lived. He blinked back the emotion threatening to spill from his eyes in a show of softness he knew would definitely not earn Amalia's respect.

"Stay at planned positions when you arrive. I'll check the apartment." Amalia scanned the shadowed sidewalk one direction, then the other. "Keep your eyes peeled for any observers or shooters."

She paused as if listening. "Roger that."

She shifted her gaze to Michael. "We need to check out the apartment before the FBI gets here." She started for the alley.

"You called them?" Michael hurried after her.

Raksa rumbled a growl beside her, and she stopped.

Michael braced his hands on her arms from behind, halting himself just before he would've crashed into her small body. Even her upper arms, toned and taut, felt tiny in his hands. He'd forgotten she was so petite. Only five feet and four inches, if he recalled correctly. Her bigger-than-life ferocity now never let the observation cross his mind. A strange warmth rolled through him.

"Stay behind me." She gave the order in a quiet, firm tone as she slipped from his loose hold. "All teams, movement by jewelry store. Doorway."

Michael's gaze shot over her head to the location she described on the radio.

The black shadow covering the door shifted.

A short, small form darted out, running. A child?

Almost before the thought reached his mind, Amalia sprinted ahead as she commanded Raksa to stay. She grabbed the child from behind and drew her in close, both arms wrapped around the small, struggling body. The backpack the kid had slung over his shoulder dropped to the ground.

Michael hurried toward them, Raksa suddenly staying with him the way the dog usually did with Amalia. The German shepherd wasn't growling. Must know a child wasn't a threat.

Though he wouldn't know it to look at this kid.

Beneath the child's purple baseball cap that sported the logo of the Minnesota football team, he kicked and fought against

108

Amalia's hold as if his life depended on it. Amalia had her arms looped under the child's armpits and over his shoulders in a firm grip the kid wasn't about to break no matter how hard he tried.

"Do you want me to sit on you?" Amalia bit out. "Just keep struggling, and I'll do that."

The kid tried a backward kick.

Amalia wrapped her leg around the kid's other one and took him to the ground. He landed on top of Amalia, his back against her front as she cushioned his fall but kept him from harm.

The child still struggled. The forceful approach didn't seem to be working.

Michael leaned closer and used a soft tone. "Hey, I'm Michael. You don't need to be afraid. We're here to help." The kid kicked again. The movement lurched his body and knocked the cap off his head.

*Her* head? The child, dressed in loose-fitting jeans and a football jersey T-shirt, had straight brown hair that fell just past the small chin of a girl's face. Her delicate features contrasted with the fight in her eyes.

"Let me go!" She grunted as she tried to break free.

"If you promise not to run off, I'm sure Amalia will let you go." Michael smiled. "We just want to talk to you."

The girl let out a whooshing breath as she stilled. Glared up at Michael. "No tricks?"

He dropped his smile and gave her a serious nod. "No tricks. I promise."

"Okay. Tell her to let me go."

He shifted his gaze over the girl's shoulder to Amalia, who sent him a glare that was a close match to the child's. His lips twitched, but this was hardly the time for laughter.

He reached toward the girl, holding out his hand.

Her eyes lowered to look at it, then she stuck out her own little hand to take his.

Amalia let the girl go as Michael hoisted her to her feet.

"So what's your name?" He released her hand.

"Outta here." The girl jerked to run, but Michael clamped a hand on her shoulder and held her in place.

He looked over her head at Amalia, who gripped the girl's other arm. She quirked an eyebrow, as if surprised he had known the girl would run. Fun to surprise her for a change. He smiled and lowered his gaze back to the girl.

"Now that's not very nice. I helped you." He released his hold on her shoulder since Amalia wasn't about to let the girl go. He squatted down in front of the child. Was she eight? Nine? Up close, he caught something in her eyes he'd missed before. A shadow of fear hid behind the anger. "For this to go the way you want, you have to trust me, and I have to be able to trust you."

She clenched her small jaw as her gaze dropped to the ground.

"What's your name, really?"

"Rocky." She scuffed the toe of her gray tennis shoe along the cement.

He looked at Amalia.

She rolled her eyes, still gripping the girl's arm.

"That's your real name?"

"Yeah." The girl's gaze swung up to Michael with a defiant glare.

"Okay. Well, Rocky, we were here to try to help the woman who fell. Did you see what happened to her?" He inwardly winced, hoping she hadn't. Horrible sight for a child to witness.

She jerked a small nod.

"What did you see?"

"She fell from up there." She pointed with her free hand at the apartment building. Her finger shook slightly.

"I'm sorry you had to see that, Rocky. But you're safe now, okay?"

Her eyes drifted back to him, no longer cloaked by anger.

"We'll keep you safe until we can get you home."

Defiance slammed back into place, hardening her features. As if *home* was some kind of trigger for her defensiveness. What was she doing out here alone at this time of night anyway? The explanation probably wasn't a happy one.

"Did you see or hear anything else?" Amalia broke the silence with her question, an edge to her voice. "Anyone coming or going? Any noises, like fighting, before she fell?"

Rocky looked up at Amalia behind her, then lowered her gaze as she shook her head, staring at the ground.

"I need to look at the apartment." Amalia's expression was devoid of the usual humor as her attention landed on Michael. "The other PK-9 teams are almost here. I'll leave you and the kid with one of them."

"No." Michael stood. "I'm going with you."

She lifted a dark eyebrow again.

"I mean, I want to go with you. I need to see her apartment."

Amalia's eyes narrowed.

"Please? I'm the one she called. I feel responsible. I want to see if we can figure out what happened."

She stood still a moment, staring at him. "Fine. But you'll both need to keep quiet and do as I say. We probably don't have long before the FBI gets here. Let's move."

"Yes, ma'am." He threw Rocky a conspiratorial grin.

Her small mouth sneaked up at one corner, her eyes full of curiosity until Amalia pulled her away.

Michael's smile for Rocky's sake faded as he followed their leader into the alley to the side door of the apartment building. He hoped whatever they found in the apartment wouldn't be too disturbing. The girl had already seen too much. Given the state of his own mind as it flashed with images of Paul, dead outside the mansion, maybe they both had.

---

Amalia shot another glance at the kid who stood near the door of the apartment where Amalia had told her to stay put. So far, she'd obeyed.

Probably helped that Amalia had Raksa lie in front of the girl and told him to hold her there.

She still fidgeted constantly, her gaze darting around the apartment like she was looking for an escape. Or searching for valuables she could snatch.

"Doing okay, Rocky?" Michael came out of the bedroom and sent the girl a gentle smile.

Good grief. He was determined to coddle the girl. He apparently had no idea what children were capable of.

*"Casho!" The boy hefted the rifle.*

Amalia slammed the door on the vault of memory before it got any farther.

She checked on the girl. Still looked ready to bolt. She was clearly hiding something. Obvious from her shifty response when they'd questioned her outside. But she had enough street smarts to keep her mouth shut.

Amalia knew the type well.

She pushed her focus back to surveying the apartment before memories could break free again.

A spacious apartment, expensive and in a pricey neighborhood. Vicki must have been paid well.

White walls boasted original artwork, none crooked or hanging askew.

The ornate coffee table in the living room, centered on an oriental rug, was devoid of any clutter, as were the bookshelves. The cushions of the light green sofa and armchairs were perfectly in place, no stains visible. The kitchen countertops were equally spotless. Everything was too clean. Too perfect.

Cool night air flowed through the open balcony doors, blowing inward the sheer white curtains that were drawn across the opening.

The chairs around the dining table near the doors stood upright, perfectly aligned.

She swung around the bar counter of the open kitchen and perused it. The stainless-steel sink was empty and clean.

She pulled a zip tie out of her pocket, looped it around the dishwasher handle and pulled to open it without leaving fingerprints.

Three wine glasses, probably not even dishwasher safe, were perched in the lower rack.

The sound of Michael's footsteps made Amalia look up.

He stopped on the other side of the counter, meeting her gaze. "There's something you should see in the bedroom." He kept his voice low and glanced at the girl. Probably afraid it'd damage what he thought was a still-intact innocence. How little he knew of the world and the children who had tasted it.

"Watch her." Amalia jerked her head toward the kid as she stalked across the open space of free-flowing rooms to the enclosed bedroom. She didn't really trust Michael to keep the girl from leaving, but Raksa would take care of it.

The overhead light was on when she entered the room. Hopefully, Michael had remembered her warning not to touch anything.

She stood near the door and scanned the space.

A tipped-over pill bottle lay on the nightstand next to a half-empty glass of water.

She walked closer. Leaned down to read the label.

*Hydrocodone.*

An addictive painkiller. Had Vicki had a drug problem? Or was this carefully placed evidence, meant to divert attention from what had really happened? Amalia's money was on the latter option. Murder.

She walked through the bathroom, then headed back out of the bedroom to the open area.

Michael stood next to Rocky by the door, his arms crossed over his chest as he faced the same direction as the girl, both of them watching Amalia. "So how old do you think I am?" Though he was clearly talking to the girl, he sent Amalia a wink across the living room.

A jolt shot through her, making her blink. She looked away. Static electricity again. Must've been dragging her feet on the bedroom carpet. Nevermind the humidity index made static electricity unlikely. Maybe impossible.

But it couldn't be more impossible than having physical attraction to Michael. Amalia never felt anything for men anymore. And even when she'd known Michael, he'd been a friend. A brother. She'd never thought of him as anything else, and she knew he'd felt the same about her.

"Team 1, this is Team 2." Jazz's voice over the coms ended the disturbing moment. "FBI arriving. Coming in quiet."

"Team 2, Roger."

Lights from outside slid across the curtains billowing by the balcony. Headlights.

"Let's move." She headed for the door. Released Raksa on the way. She reached for the girl's arm.

The kid jerked away. Darted around Amalia.

She let her move without preventing the dodge.

The girl ended up next to Michael. "I want to go with him."

Amalia looked at him.

He nodded, his lips tugging up slightly at the corners.

"How will I know you won't run?" Amalia narrowed her eyes at the girl.

The kid tilted her head back to look up at Michael, then slipped her hand into his.

Amalia drew her attention away from the sight of Michael's masculine hand engulfing the girl's. Ignored the way that made something squeeze in her chest. "Okay. Just know Raksa here will be able to catch you if you try to bolt."

Raksa panted, practically grinned at the girl, belying the scary image he was supposed to project when Amalia was trying to make him sound ferocious. At least the girl hadn't tried to pet the German shepherd yet. Maybe she was afraid of dogs. Which could be helpful.

"Raksa, let's go." Amalia led the way as they left the apartment building, exiting into the dark alley.

Michael and Rocky came alongside Amalia in the alley, Raksa between them.

Michael looked down at the girl, drawing Amalia's gaze.

The kid pressed closer to his leg, her eyes growing bigger under her cap as they neared the sidewalk where agents in FBI jackets and T-shirts with armored vests swarmed.

An agent Amalia didn't know approached them, shifting her hand toward her holster as they emerged from the alley.

"They're okay." Agent Nguyen's commanding voice carried just ahead of her as she marched around the other agent. "You contaminated my crime scene?" She stopped in front of Amalia and planted her hands on her hips.

Nguyen was only an inch taller than Amalia, but she knew how to magnify her persona to gain power. Had to admire that, even if they'd never hit it off well.

"Glad to hear you're seeing it as a crime scene."

"Instead of suicide? From what Phoenix told me you were doing here tonight, that doesn't seem likely."

That was for sure. "The apartment's spotless. No signs of struggle."

"I'd like to see that for myself."

"You'll find a..." Michael glanced down at the girl before lowering his voice. "A pill bottle in the bedroom. I'm guessing it was planted."

Nguyen gave him a look that bordered on a glare. "Thanks." Her gaze shifted down to the girl who still held Michael's hand. "Brought a friend?"

He chuckled. An unexpected sound at a time like this. Almost as unexpected as the roll of warmth it tumbled behind Amalia's rib cage.

"This is Rocky Hardwick." He looked down at the girl, who leaned her shoulder into his leg, not looking up. "She's nine years old and lives at the Helping Smiles Home."

When had he gotten all that information from her?

"Would've guessed seven or eight." Nguyen looked at the girl skeptically, as if she didn't trust her more than Amalia did. "You found her here?" She pulled out a notepad from her back pocket, a pencil attached to it.

Michael's smile tightened a little around the edges, as if

he didn't like Nguyen's suspicions. "She was here when we arrived."

"Over in the doorway at the jewelry store." Amalia nodded toward the location. "Says she saw the woman fall. Claims she doesn't know anything else."

Nguyen jotted something down in her notepad. "What were you doing here alone?"

The girl stayed silent, bill of her cap tilted toward the ground.

"Miss Hardwick?" Nguyen stared at the kid. Or at least her hat. She shifted her attention back to Michael. "She doesn't seem so talkative now."

He shrugged.

Nguyen sighed. Stuffed the notepad into her pocket. "Likely a runaway. The residential home gets a few of those, despite their attempts at security. We'll take her back." She looked over her shoulders. Waved her fingers at the woman agent who walked toward them.

The agent came close and reached for the kid. She shied away, clinging to Michael.

"Hey." He crouched by the girl, his voice soft and soothing. "It's okay. Tell you what. I'll visit you." He smiled. "Okay? As soon as I can, I'll come and see you there. You can show me the video game you were telling me about."

She stepped closer to him, whispered something in his ear. His smile faded as a grave expression slid in place instead. He nodded to her as she pulled back. "Yes. I promise. You have my word."

If he thought Amalia was going to escort him to a group home to visit this kid, he had another thing coming. She was a security specialist, not a chauffeur.

"Will you go with the nice agent now?"

The kid nodded, probably thrilled she'd successfully conned Michael into giving her what she wanted. At least she went with the agent without throwing a fit.

Amalia blew out a breath and turned to Nguyen as soon as the girl and agent were out of earshot. "Did Phoenix tell you the other information Vicki Wilson gave Barrett?" Meaning, the existence of a mole in the FBI.

"I told Phoenix it's impossible." The firm set of Nguyen's jaw indicated she'd caught Amalia's drift. "I know my team."

"I don't think Vicki would've made that up." Michael watched Nguyen, apparently keeping up with their conversation just fine.

"This isn't the time or place for this discussion. Take it up with Phoenix if you want to know more. I have a crime scene to investigate." Nguyen spun on her heel and marched back to the team she trusted so implicitly.

Trust could get a person killed. Or worse.

"What do we do now?" Michael stepped to Amalia's side, gaze on Nguyen.

His proximity made her insides tense. She shifted away.

"Go to the safe house." An ironic title if there ever was one.

If Vicki had been right that there was a mole in the FBI, the location they had to go back to was anything but safe.

117

# ELEVEN

"Katherine might not be wrong." Phoenix slipped her bottled water back into the knapsack she'd laid on the floor in the safe house dining room. Dagian occupied the wood floor on the opposite side of the chair where Phoenix sat. Alert and ready, though he was lying down.

"An unintentional leak?" Amalia rested her arms on the glossy tabletop and watched her boss from her seat at the side of the rectangular table. Or tried to watch her. With the dim lighting and Phoenix's ever-present baseball cap, Amalia couldn't see much above her boss's chin. Not that it would've helped if she could observe more of the expression-less face.

Raksa shifted and leaned his shoulder against Amalia's ankle. He seemed to be trying to mimic Dag's alert posture, but his body's desire to relax at two-thirty in the morning was winning out. Amalia wasn't worried. Raksa could sense danger even in his sleep if needed.

"It's possible." Phoenix maintained the low volume they'd been using to avoid being overheard by the two FBI agents posted at the front and back doors. "There could be bugs in an office, a tapped phone. Katherine is going to investigate and plug the leak if there is one."

Amalia smirked. "She didn't mention to me she was going to look into it."

Phoenix was quiet for a few seconds. "She takes a while to warm up to people."

Amalia somehow suppressed the snort of laughter that surged up her throat. An ironic statement for Phoenix to make, to say the least. But Amalia maintained the serious demeanor that worked best with her boss. "Okay. If she's that cautious, then why won't she consider there's a mole?"

"She says there are only two other agents directly reporting to her who would have access to the information that's been compromised—safe house locations, Michael's meeting with the U. S. Attorney." Phoenix's slim, tan hands rested on the table as she talked, unmoving. "One is Craig Taft, a twenty-year FBI veteran she's known for four years. Impeccable service record. The other agent is Becky Radcliffe, a woman she trained herself and trusts as a friend."

There was that trust again. Anyone could turn on friends, family, fiancées.

"We both know betrayal can come from surprising places." Phoenix's off-the-charts perception abilities weren't dimmed by the late hour. Uncanny how she seemed to be able to read minds. Even Amalia's. Sometimes.

"But Katherine could be right. She also pointed out we can't know if Michael's source was telling the truth. Vicki Wilson could have had other motives or been mistaken when she claimed there was a mole. Perhaps she thought it was a good way to protect herself from any kind of leak or the chance Michael would bring the FBI with him tonight."

"My money's on the mole." Amalia pulled her hands off the table and folded her arms over her Henley. "Unless Nguyen's team really is that careless."

"All we can do is wait to see what she finds out. Might be as simple as some agents telling other agents more info than necessary, and it's reaching the wrong people." Phoenix turned her wrist toward herself, likely checking the watch she wore. "In the meantime, we'll stay alert. Keep doing what we do." Phoenix pushed her chair back and got to her feet.

Dagian stood beside her instantly.

"Dag and I will stay until sunup. Go ahead and make the rounds outside. We'll check upstairs."

Where Michael should be safely sleeping in his room. Hopefully getting much-needed rest after all he'd been through in the last forty-eight hours. Why the thought popped into her head, Amalia didn't know. Could be the increasing fatigue she'd seen on his face. Or his serious, quiet demeanor on the drive to the safe house from Vicki Wilson's apartment. He hadn't asked a single question. A sure sign he wasn't in great shape.

Putting thoughts of Michael out of her head, Amalia stood. "Let's go, Raksa." She activated the coms in her ear, informed the two FBI agents she'd ditched earlier tonight that she was heading out for patrol.

She scanned the yard as she and Raksa stepped out into the darkness from the back door. She'd turned off the security light above the door just before leaving the house. The light was a deterrent to attackers trying to gain access. But there was no need to make herself a target when she left the house.

The coolness of the overnight air that had made light jackets comfortable was giving way to heavy humidity. The promise of a hot day ahead.

A low rumble beside her spiked every nerve to attention. Raksa tensed, erect ears aimed forward. He stared beyond the short grass of the backyard into the blackness that shrouded the tall hedge bordering the property line.

A dirt road cut through the woods just beyond, blocked from view by the hedge. FBI Special Agent O'Brien should be there in his parked car.

Amalia pulled her Glock from her holster. "Team Alpha and all teams, this is PT1."

"PT1, this is Alpha." Phoenix instantly responded over coms. "Go ahead."

"K-9 alert. Backyard. Possibly rear road or the foliage."

"PT1, Roger. Proceed with caution. Package secure."

Raksa growled again, still staring in the same direction.

Amalia turned to the left. Moved along the shadowed wall of the house with Raksa. "F2, this is PT1. Report."

"PT1, this is F2. In position. Clear." If O'Brien was still in place, the threat must not be on that part of the road.

Which left the hedges and the large tree at the back of the yard.

Amalia angled a glance high as she neared the tree along the fence, tried to see through the dark thickness of leaves. No movement or color other than black and green caught her eye.

Gaze dropped, she crouched as she and Raksa moved closer to the bushes.

Raksa stayed silent beside her, easily keeping pace. But he knew not to growl if they were too close to a suspect.

The threat could still be here.

She scanned the six-foot hedge as she neared it. A gate split the middle of the manicured plant wall.

An open gate. Should be closed.

She lifted her weapon. Inched closer to the gate.

Stopped. Listened.

Crickets chirped nearby. No other noise to indicate someone on the other side. A silent, stealthy attack was a Verdugo hallmark. Not the approach Rottier's other thugs had been using.

Maybe Verdugo hadn't left. And he was here. Now.

The hedge was too thick to clear the opening of the gateway from all angles. If Verdugo was on the other side, she wouldn't survive taking him head-on when he had the tactical advantage.

That shouldn't be possible since O'Brien had said things were clear. And he was positioned directly behind the gate on the road.

But Verdugo did the impossible for breakfast.

She lowered her weapon as she swung back around,

quickly headed back the way they'd come. Going around the hedge might tip the scales her way.

And so would Raksa.

They reached the house in a few seconds, and she darted around the gap where the hedge stopped two feet short of the brick corner wall. Glock raised, she cleared both directions before moving along the outside of the hedge, staying low.

Raksa trotted at her side and paused at the corner when she did.

If Verdugo or anyone was still there, rounding the corner to the side of the hedge along the road was tricky. But not for Raksa.

She squatted by the shepherd, gave him the hand signal to search in stealth mode. If anyone was there, Raksa would be able to take the suspect by surprise better than she could. And the armored vest he now wore, thanks to Cora, lowered the risks.

His tail disappeared as he rounded the hedge.

She straightened. Waited a second.

Nothing.

She crouched low. Pressed against the hedge, branches poking her back through her Henley.

She spun away from the hedge, around the corner. Feet planted, gun raised.

Raksa stood twenty feet away and looked back at her. He wagged his tail, relaxed.

She let out a breath. Lowered her weapon.

"Team Alpha, this is PT1. Area appears clear."

"PT1, Roger." Phoenix's reply was quick and terse.

Amalia walked to Raksa, waved at O'Brien in his black car still parked on the road.

She stopped by the shepherd and rested her hand on his warm head.

Her gaze went to the open gate. Someone had to have been there. Unless the latch was faulty, and it swung lose on its own.

"Let's go, boy." She stepped through the opening into the backyard as Raksa fell into step beside her. She turned around, swung the gate into the closed position and latched it. The mechanism seemed secure.

Raksa's nose went to the ground at the base of the gate. Probably found a worm or something he'd like to snack on. "Raksa, leave it."

His head came up as she looked to see what he might've eaten.

"Yes. Good boy…" The end of the last word trailed off as her gaze locked on the unevenness in the dirt by the gate.

She squatted down.

A partial footprint. The toe of a shoe. Pointed toward the house.

---

He couldn't put it off any longer. Michael ducked into the office at the safe house, the need to tell Sofia's parents the truth about their daughter weighing on him.

He'd barely slept last night. The image of Vicki Wilson kept appearing before his eyes. But then it'd been replaced by other thoughts almost as disturbing. The cold way Amalia took the horrible sight of the woman, bloody from her deadly fall, in stride. Her apparent callousness about a little girl having witnessed the gruesome scene, likely a murder.

Amalia's treatment of Rocky was especially troublesome. Sofia had always loved young kids, and they'd returned that love with pure adoration. She'd been their champion, friend, and protector. But tonight, she'd acted as if Rocky had committed the murder herself.

*"I know the whole idea of God is one of the biggest lies invented."*

Amalia's words sliced into his chest. Had she really lost her faith? Or had she…?

No, he couldn't believe her Christianity had been a lie when they were young. They'd lied to others, together. Never to each other.

He pushed back his hair and pulled the cell phone from his pocket. This room seemed like the most private one to make the call.

Amalia was gone, and Nevaeh was there with Alvarez doing the patrol survey, or whatever they called it, outside.

He took in a breath. Sofia was Mami's and Papi's daughter, and she'd lied to them these twelve years. He knew what that had done to them. He'd seen the tears and shared their heartache. They didn't deserve to have to spend another moment wondering what had happened to their precious daughter.

He pressed the button to make the call. His insides twisted as he waited for someone to pick up. Mami probably would.

"Hello?" Her familiar, gentle voice warmed him from the inside out, loosening his tension. Her landline wall phone without caller ID wouldn't have told her who was calling.

"*Hola*, Mami."

"Michael!" Her smile carried over the line, infusing the word with love and joy.

He couldn't help but smile in response. What a blessing that God had let him be loved by such a wonderful woman.

"Alejandro, come. Pick up. It's Michael. How are you, *hijito*? Are you safe?"

A clicking sound signaled Papi had picked up the phone in their bedroom. "Hola, Michael."

"Papi. So good to hear your voice."

Papi's gravelly, gruff voice and stern appearance had never scared Michael, even as a child. The man had made Michael feel safe and loved through his actions, from the first time he'd bandaged Michael's knee after a fall to the time he'd slipped a hammer in Michael's small hand and shown him how to build a shed.

"I was asking how he is. Are you safe?"

Michael smiled at the question he'd known Mami would want answered as her first priority. They knew he was a protected witness until he testified at the trial. "Yes, I am. They're keeping me safe."

His smile flipped as he tensed. Part of him didn't want to tell them. It was good news, in a way. But would also cause them more pain, the last thing he wanted to do.

*The truth will set you free.*

The Bible verse that had long been Michael's guiding light checked him now. Secrets always led to trouble. He'd tell the truth in love and be there for them in the pain. He took a breath. "I found Sofia."

"Sofia?"

"You found our *hijita*?"

Mami and Papi blurted out their responses at the same time, elation and shock giving the simple words heavy meaning.

"Yes." Though, perhaps in the most important way, he hadn't. Maybe he should've worded the news differently. "Kind of."

"Tell us, Michael." Mami's voice softened into the patient, understanding tone that always calmed his nerves. Even now, when he had to tell her Sofia didn't want to be her daughter anymore.

"She's different now." He slid his tongue across his lips and swallowed.

"You sound worried." Papi was still as observant as ever when it came to Michael's emotional state. "Is Sofia safe?" And he was always the protector of his family.

Michael scrambled to find the best words. "Physically, yes. She's here in Minneapolis. She's with a private agency that's providing some of the protection for the witnesses."

"Oh? With technologies?" Mami's confusion carried across the line.

"Not exactly." Michael explained Sofia's position at the Phoenix K-9 Security and Detection Agency, how she had amazing skills and a protection K-9.

"Why did she not tell us? And that she's here, in the

United States?" Papi's tone echoed Michael's when he'd first seen Sofia. Maybe with less anger.

"That's part of the problem. She…" Michael stared at the glow of light trying to break through around the edges of the blinds that covered the window. "She goes by a different name now."

"A nickname?" Papi seemed to be struggling to make sense out of the truth Michael still hadn't been able to come to terms with himself.

"No. She changed her name. She said she doesn't want me to call her Sofia anymore because she's Amalia Pérez."

"Pérez?" The r rolled off Papi's tongue. "That is not a family name."

"Did she say why she is doing this, Michael?" Poor Mami. Always quick to have compassion, to try to understand even when the truth caused her pain.

"No. She won't talk to me anymore. She won't tell me the truth. About anything." Not about anything that counted.

He turned away from the window and paced around the desk. "I'm hoping I can get her to open up to me and explain what happened. To tell me why she lied to us all those years about where she was and what she was doing. I don't know if she was here the whole time or what."

He paused and shoved his hand through his hair. "I'm going to find out, though." One way or another.

"There's more, Michael. Yes?" Mami's wise perception only increased with age.

"It's just that…" He pressed his lips together. He had to tell them. "She seems to be against God now, too. Like she doesn't believe in Him."

Silence pulsed on the line. The worst blow of all. His heart squeezed as he pictured Mami wiping tears from her cheeks as he'd seen her do once before when she'd thought no one was looking. Tears for Sofia, the daughter she wanted to come home.

"We will pray." Papi's tone was thicker than before, heavy with emotion.

"Yes." Mami's voice firmed, as if strengthened by the faith Michael knew she had in abundance. "God is good. He has brought you and Sofia together again. You will help her."

"I'll try, Mami."

"God will bring Sofia home, Michael." Confidence undergirded her statement. "We have always believed that."

Would they still if they could see Amalia? How unrecognizable she had become?

"Thanks for your prayers. I'll do my best."

"God will do it, *mijo*." Papi's words, capped with the endearment for *my son*, echoed in Michael's mind as he said his goodbyes. He hoped it was true, that God would bring Sofia back to them and Himself. And that Michael wouldn't fail the couple that had become his parents.

*"You will help her."* Mami was counting on his ability to help Sofia. They'd always helped each other before. He should be able to do it now, when she needed his help more than ever.

He would have to figure out what kind of trouble Amalia was in. It had to be trouble, or she wouldn't have lied to her family and felt the need to change her identity.

Nevaeh had said no one was as they seemed at Phoenix K-9. But his basic search had shown them to be exactly what they seemed to be—an elite security and detection agency comprised of experienced professionals with fitting backgrounds.

He needed to dig deeper if he was going to find out what Nevaeh meant and the reason Sofia had gone into hiding and changed her identity.

Michael hurried out of the office and waved at the FBI agent posted by the back door as he made his way to the staircase, trying to move at a casual pace.

His mind raced as he headed up the stairs. He'd look into Phoenix more first. The woman was by far the most obviously mysterious of the team, and she was the mind and power behind the agency. If anyone was up to no good at the agency, it'd have to start with her.

He already knew which databases he wanted to try first by the time he sat at the desk in the bedroom and opened his computer.

A half hour into the more extensive search, he started to wonder if he was wrong about the agency. Still nothing but positive accolades, volunteerism, and entrepreneurial endeavors in Phoenix's background.

Wait.

There should be something about her before ten years ago. He'd guess she would've been in her early twenties then. Maybe in college or working. But he couldn't find any documentation for that.

A hunch tickled the back of his neck. He navigated to the birth records database and entered the information he knew about Phoenix.

Nothing. He tried every state.

A chill tracked down his spine.

Unbelievable.

Before ten years ago, Phoenix Gray did not exist.

# TWELVE

Amalia hung back. Watched the old man sitting on the bench as he tossed bread crumbs to ducks.

She and Raksa had stood for fifteen minutes in the trees and foliage that circled the large park. No one else had lingered that long in the large grassy area smattered with park benches.

Only Ramone Benito had stayed on a bench the whole time, facing the trail and the lake beyond it. Because he waited for her.

She needed to make sure no one else waited with him. Tricky balance with a source. Had to trust, or at least pretend to, but not too much. Ramone had gained more of her trust than anyone else during her stint with the CIA, including all the operatives she'd known.

But his family members still dealt in illegal weapons, even if he was retired. They could decide they didn't like their patriarch giving Amalia information.

She scanned the area one more time. Some pedestrians paused on the paved trail now and then to look at the water or watch the ducks. But they moved on, following the walkers and joggers who couldn't be interrupted during their quick lunch-break exercise.

"Let's go." Raksa instantly went into motion as she

walked out from the trees. Poor guy never did like to wait around.

She took her time approaching Ramone, a meandering route with plenty of casual pauses.

When she reached the bench, she stood behind it. "Never took you for a duck lover."

"Retirement changes a person." Ramone's thick, familiar accent, a hint of humor in his tone, nearly made her smile. "You like dogs now. I like ducks."

Amalia allowed a small angle of her mouth at that and rounded the bench. She sat on the other end of the bench and had Raksa lie in front of her. She stared out at the water, calm and smooth as glass on the hot, sunny day.

"It's good to see you, Marita."

She glanced at Ramone, who looked at the ducks, not her.

Even in profile, she didn't miss the closed smile that curved his pale lips. Lines creased his cheek, the saddle brown skin spotted and worn. But no crow's feet highlighted the corner of his eye. He'd had little to laugh at in his life. Tendrils of white hair peaked out from beneath the broad-brimmed hat that topped his head. Time left more of a mark with each passing year.

She turned her attention back to the water before she'd stared long enough to suggest more than a brief interest a stranger might have.

"You have family now? A home?"

So he remembered their last conversation. A year ago, when she'd come to him for information and said she didn't have a home. He'd told her she should find one.

"I have my dog."

"A dog is good. But not enough."

"You're right. I could use some information, too."

He shook his head, a half-smile angling his mouth in profile again. "You are too much about work. Not enough about life."

"I'm very much interested in life. Yours, mine, and my client's. Which means we'd better speed this up."

"I have not heard more since I called you. I don't know who hired Verdugo."

"But you suspect someone, don't you?"

He plunged his vein-lined hand into the small paper bag he held on his lap. "Everyone knows Rottier wants the witnesses dead."

"Badly enough to hire more killers?" She crossed her arms over her black tank top, the dark color of it drawing hot rays of sunlight. "What do you know about six thugs who targeted our witness? They drove a black SUV."

He tossed crumbs, one small clump at a time to the eager ducks on the grass between him and the trail. "They work for Rottier."

Good. At least they could confirm that. "Not professionals."

"No. His muscle. They work at the warehouses. Sometimes."

"Know why he'd hire them when he already had Verdugo?"

"I hear Verdugo failed."

She allowed a wry smile to twist her lips. "Maybe so."

"He didn't expect you."

Or the K-9s. She kept the thought to herself. Waited for him to fill the silence.

"Verdugo doesn't share jobs."

Raksa sat up as a few people approached on the trail.

Two kids and a woman. Probably the kids that caught Raksa's interest. She put a hand on his head, his black fur hot from the sun. "Think he left when Rottier sent his thugs to do the job?"

"It's possible." Ramone rested his hands on his thighs. "He could be waiting. Watching. Setting up his hit."

"You haven't heard anything about him leaving."

"No. I hear more about Rottier. His desire for witnesses to be dead."

"All of them?"

He tossed crumbs to two gray and brown ducks that

ventured closer. Didn't answer. His usual cue he needed more explanation or motivation to share what he knew.

"I think he may be after only one of the witnesses now." She casually threw out the fishing statement.

The silence continued.

She stared at the equally-still water, weighing the balance between sharing too much and giving Ramone a reason to risk breaking a confidence he might have with someone else. "He's a...personal friend."

"Ah." Curiosity and pleasure filled the short sound. "Maybe you are ready for more than a dog."

"He's like a son to my parents." She kept her eyes on a runner as he came up the trail in their direction. "They would be devastated if I let anything happen to him."

"Perhaps not them only." Ramone always had a romantic side. One that had led him to launch a Colombian rebel group with an idealistic vision of overturning a corrupt government. Then others usurped his leadership and became terrorists instead of idealists. His romanticism should've died then.

She kept her mouth shut as the runner passed on. Let Ramone think she had romantic interest in Michael. It would get him to talk. And the parent angle would seal the deal, tapping into Ramone's strong belief in honoring elders.

"You are right. I was told Rottier wants only one witness now. The reporter with much to testify and much evidence. He is your friend?"

"Yes." The lie slipped easily off her tongue. Michael certainly wasn't a friend of Marita or Amalia.

"I'm sorry." The sadness in Ramone's tone sent an odd shiver through her. As if he'd just announced Michael's death. Though would it affect her if he had?

"He's well-protected." She steeled herself against any further emotional reactions.

"By you?"

She shot Ramone a glance. He was getting a little too

inquisitive. Like he was fishing now, feeling her out. She took a risk. "Yes."

"Good." He crumpled the empty paper bag in his hands. Stuffed it into the pocket of the navy blue jacket she had no idea how he could stand to wear in this heat. The corner of his mouth pinched as he sat in silence and supposedly watched the ducks as they began to waddle away.

But there was something he was holding back.

"You'd better tell me now."

He lifted his gaze slightly at her statement, seemed to watch the stretch of lake in front of them. "There is another target."

The other witness? She sat still. Waited.

"Your friend was the only one until today. Now, Rottier's men, they ask for information about a child. A girl."

A girl. The kid they'd found last night?

His head lowered as he looked down at his lap. "I wonder who protects her."

From what Amalia had seen, the girl was the kind who could take care of herself.

But not against an assassin. Or even a gang of thugs.

The thoughts came quickly. Unwelcome and irritating. She couldn't protect everyone. Especially a child who didn't want any help. She'd learned that the hard way.

She got to her feet. Raksa rose beside her, panting heavily. She'd have to give him plenty of water and cool down the car before she put him in it.

A hand gripped her forearm.

She would've broken the wrist of anyone else who tried that, but she instantly knew it was Ramone, though he'd never touched her before.

He tilted his head to see her from beneath the brim of his hat. His dark brown eyes peered at her with the wisdom and courage he'd earned through his hard years. "If Verdugo has not left, be careful. He will have much to prove."

She met his gaze. "You know me. Always careful." She quirked her lips at a sardonic angle.

Ramone relaxed his weak hold on her arm, let his hand slip to the bench. "I worry about you."

"I've faced killers before."

His gaze probed hers until her gut started to tense. What was he searching for?

"That's not why I worry. There is something you're afraid to face." He turned his head away, toward the water. But the absence of his focus didn't dull the foreboding punch of his final words. "That is the danger."

# THIRTEEN

Ramone's warning echoed in Amalia's head as she and Raksa approached the rear door of the safe house. The same one as last night since Agent Nguyen hadn't wanted to move Michael again so soon without more cause. They couldn't be sure the footprint was fresh and that the gate hadn't simply blown open in a breeze.

*"There is something you are afraid to face."*

The statement had to be one of the most untrue things anyone had ever said to her. And she'd been lied to more times than she could count. She wasn't afraid of anything.

But her mind couldn't stop returning to what her source had said. The concern in his gaze. Just what did he think she was scared of anyway?

A twinge of something, like an overactive nerve in her neck, tweaked every time her thoughts reached that question. Probably from irritation. She wasn't often accused of cowardice.

The back door swung open as soon as Amalia reached it. Nevaeh held it, her usual laughing grin shrunken to a pitiful attempt at a smile. "Hey." Her black eyebrows drew together as she forgot to step back to let Amalia in. "We have a visitor."

"Yeah. I saw Nguyen's car out front."

135

"Not just her." Nevaeh drew out each word seemingly as long as she could.

"Want to let me in so I can see for myself?"

"Oh." Nevaeh blinked and stepped back, a more genuine smile brightening her face. "Welcome. Please do come inside." She swept her arm in an exaggerated grand gesture as she moved aside and held the door wide.

Alvarez and Raksa greeted each other with smells and tail wags as Nevaeh closed the door.

"Pérez. Good." Nguyen stopped a few feet away, apparently having come from the open living room.

Where Michael sat on a sofa. Talking to someone.

A very short someone.

No way.

"I've brought Grace Hardwick here. The girl you found at the scene last night."

So her name wasn't actually Rocky. "I assume you have a reason for that?" Better be a good one.

Nguyen narrowed her eyes. Always seemed to see Amalia as a threat. Maybe she was one. Like any good FBI agent, Nguyen liked to know she could trust the people she worked with. Nguyen probably didn't think Amalia could be trusted. And the FBI agent couldn't be more right about that.

"Let's talk in the office. I don't want the child to hear." Nguyen shifted her attention to Nevaeh. "Would you send Barrett in and watch the girl?"

Nevaeh swung her gaze from Amalia to Nguyen and back again. "Happy to."

Amalia followed Nguyen to the office where they waited in silence for Michael.

As soon as he appeared, Nguyen told him to shut the door. The second he'd done so, Nguyen dropped her bombshell. "Someone tried to kidnap Grace Hardwick."

Michael's brow furrowed, his brown eyebrows dipping with the concerned curve of his mouth. "You're kidding."

"Afraid not." Nguyen placed her hands on her hips, legs planted in a stance she'd probably learned to project confidence and strength in the dangerous crime world she had to survive. "They tried to nab her on her way out of a community center after an event they'd held for kids."

"Who tried to kidnap her?" Michael was ready with questions, as always.

"She described two men. She was apparently able to run away and duck into an outdoor vent they couldn't fit into. They left when more people exited the center."

"But why in the world would someone want to kidnap her?"

Amalia gave him a look. He knew the answer to that one.

"Rottier wouldn't have a reason to grab her. She didn't see anything last night."

"Actually," Nguyen stepped in front of the window that was covered by closed blinds, "she did. At least that's what she told her social worker after the kidnapping attempt."

"That's why you brought her here, then." Michael crossed his arms over his chest. "To keep her safe from Rottier?"

"Not exactly." Nguyen walked away from the window and stood behind the desk. Annoyance pinched her features. "I believe the girl is being targeted by Rottier. But I brought her here primarily because she said she'll only tell us what she knows if she can stay with you two."

Two? Amalia glanced at Michael, then back to Nguyen. "As in, Barrett and me?"

Nguyen jerked a nod. "Seems she took a liking to you last night."

Michael maybe, with the way he'd babied the girl. Even now, his frown had changed into a little half smile, as if he was happy or even amused. But Amalia couldn't believe Rocky would've mentioned her, too. Hadn't she made it clear she didn't even like the kid?

"You realize she could be lying." Amalia stared at Nguyen. The agent couldn't be that gullible.

"Of course. But Rottier's actions back up her story. He clearly believes she saw something very important. Maybe something that could put him away longer and more assuredly than the arms trafficking charge. Why else would he have tried to grab her so fast?"

"So you've told her she can stay with us?" Michael's smile grew as he glanced at Amalia instead of the person he was talking to. Was he enjoying her irritation over this idea?

"Correct. I've given her a few days to tell you what she knows."

"I'll have to check with Phoenix on this. She may not want us to provide protection detail for a child." Amalia was counting on it.

"I already did." The angle of Nguyen's mouth was smug as she moved around the desk and brushed past Amalia. "She okayed it."

*Well-played.* Maybe Amalia hadn't given Nguyen enough credit for craftiness.

The agent paused at the door. Glanced back. "Try to get her to talk, and report to me as soon as you find out what she witnessed."

"And then what will happen to her?" Concern lined Michael's voice like the creases on his forehead.

She'd go back to where she belonged, hopefully. Amalia kept the thought to herself. Let Nguyen respond.

"Depends on what she knows."

A perfectly evasive answer worthy of Amalia herself. But being on the receiving end of it wasn't so great. The timeline for this babysitting gig wasn't any better. A *few* days was as imprecise as estimates could be.

Now she'd have an insatiably curious journalist and a sneaky, streetwise kid to keep in line and protected. And this was only the start of her twelve-hour shift.

It was going to be a long night.

---

"Hey, Rocky." Michael smiled at the girl as Nevaeh rose from the sofa where Rocky sat in the corner, her small legs pulled into her chest. Her pale knees poked through the holes in her jeans.

"Hey." She didn't look up, her chin propped on her skinny knees, light brown hair hanging forward so he couldn't see her eyes.

Raksa suddenly jogged to her, his leash missing from his harness.

Michael glanced around and found Amalia. She stood at the edge of the open kitchen, watching. Had she had a change of heart about Rocky?

The suspicious gaze she leveled at the back of the girl's head answered his question. Definitely no change of heart. Though why Amalia was so antagonistic toward a nine-year-old girl, Michael couldn't understand.

But, at the moment, Rocky was more important than trying to solve the mystery of Amalia. Poor girl had witnessed a murder and nearly been kidnapped by two thugs, all in less than twenty-four hours. A trauma counselor, he was not. But he could at least try to give her comfort if he could. Though it looked like Raksa was already doing that.

The girl's small hands reached behind the shepherd's upright ears and scratched.

"Mind if I sit here?"

She angled her head up at Michael, not taking her hands from the dog's head. Her hair fell away from her eyes, showing a jaw set in stone and hazel orbs that revealed more pain behind the defiance than she probably wanted him to see.

She shrugged her small shoulders, and his heart squeezed. This girl should have a dad, someone to protect her and make sure she knew how special she was. Someone to take the burden of survival and sadness off her shoulders that were too tiny to bear such a weight.

He knew. The weight had nearly broken him when he was her age. Would have. If not for...

His gaze drifted to Amalia, the woman who used to be

Sofia. The one who'd helped him do more than survive. She'd helped him live.

Could he return the favor for her now?

A question for another time.

He swung his attention back to Rocky as he dropped to the sofa. "I'm glad to hear you're going to stay with us for a while."

Her gaze jumped to his face, her eyes searching for hope and truth there. He could see what she sought plain as day in the seconds when her defensive mask slipped away. Then she drew her eyebrows together and looked at Raksa instead.

The big shepherd rested his head on her lap. She stroked his black and brown fur. Her hand was so small, so fragile.

"Are you okay, Rocky? The men didn't hurt you, did they?"

Her fingers paused on Raksa. She shook her head, straight locks brushing against her chin with the movement.

"Thank the Lord. I'm so sorry you had to go through that. I know it must have been scary."

Her hand moved again, smoothing the shepherd's fur.

"Agent Nguyen says you saw something." Amalia's voice startled Michael as she suddenly appeared in front of them and walked to the armchair that faced the sofa. She didn't sit, just stood there with her arms crossed over her black bullet-proof vest and stared at Rocky.

Makeshift curtains—brown bedsheets stapled to the wall —shrouded the patio doors and windows behind her, giving her a fittingly dark background. "You won't be safe from the men unless you tell us what you know, Grace."

A scare tactic. Really? Michael sent her a glare, but Amalia wouldn't look his way.

Rocky's hands drifted off the dog's head, and her fingers buried into the thicker fur at his neck as he leaned closer to her. Amalia's protection K-9 was a lot friendlier than she was.

"My name's Rocky." The girl's chin clenched, but she didn't look at Amalia.

"What did you see last night?"

"I told you." Rocky's answer pushed out in a reluctant mutter.

"You said you saw the woman fall and nothing else. But you lied about that." Amalia's voice was steely, no flashy smile used for this interrogation. "You saw something else that made those men want to grab you. What was it?"

Irritation sparked in Michael's chest. Couldn't she see the girl was already terrified? "You're calling her out for lying?" He refrained from emphasizing the *you* in his question, but Amalia didn't miss his meaning.

Her eyes jerked his way, flashed for a second. Then that smile, the one that covered all real emotion, splashed across her face. "Why not?" She lifted a sardonic eyebrow.

"I can't tell you."

Michael almost didn't catch Rocky's murmured words. "You don't have to be afraid of us, Rocky. We're on your side. You won't get in trouble for whatever you saw. And Amalia and Raksa, her dog—they can keep you safe." Despite Amalia treating Rocky like an enemy spy at the moment.

Rocky shook her head. Which part was she denying? "You'll send me back if I tell you."

"Send you back." Michael repeated the words as he tried to figure out what she really feared. "To the group home?"

Her head dipped in a nod.

"Of course we won't send you back." Amalia interjected the quick denial with a broad smile. "You can stay with us as long as you like."

The first part could be true. The FBI would likely take the girl into protective custody if she'd witnessed something important, rather than send her back to the home. The second statement was a bald-faced lie.

Michael narrowed his eyes at Amalia, indignation burning his throat. He opened his mouth to let it out—

"Do you use your gun?" Rocky looked at Amalia.

"What?" Amalia's relaxed stance didn't change.

"The gun in your pants. You took it out last night. Do you shoot people?"

141

"No." Amalia's answer was laidback and without hesitation. Not too quick either. She was so good now that even Michael wouldn't be able to tell when she was lying except in situations like this, when he already knew the truth. The truth that she'd just fibbed to Rocky again.

Rocky swung her head toward Michael and looked up at him with those angry-sad eyes that spawned an ache just below one of his ribs. "Is she your girlfriend?"

The ache washed away under the hot flush that flowed through him at the unexpected question. He darted a glance at Amalia.

She flashed the smile that was no help at all.

People had frequently asked him and Sofia if they were dating when they were still inseparable all the way through high school. They'd always laughed—genuine laughter—and shared a secret smile because they knew they were better than boyfriend and girlfriend. They were brother and sister. Best friends and family. Forever.

So why did the question leave him feeling so flustered and, well, embarrassed now? "No. We're just..." What were they, exactly? "She's protecting me. Just like she's protecting you." For all he knew, Amalia might have a boyfriend already. Someone she met for dinner before she came here to babysit him.

The thought sank to the pit of his stomach as comfortably as battery acid.

"Why do you protect people?" Rocky mercifully turned her attention to Amalia.

"Okay." Amalia lowered her arms. "Enough of the twenty questions. It's bedtime."

The incongruity of the word *bedtime* coming from Amalia's mouth nearly made Michael laugh, especially as she snapped the leash on her protection K-9 and straightened, sending Rocky a look that was anything but maternal.

The girl's lower lip protruded.

Oh, boy. Hopefully, she wouldn't put up a fight about it. Neither he nor Amalia were experienced in the parent department. Though Sofia could've sweet-talked a child into anything back in the day. Without lying.

"Can Raksa sleep with me?"

The shepherd looked up at her with adoring eyes, obviously keen on the idea.

"He has to work." Amalia's answer was curt and without sympathy. Though of course she did need the K-9 for security. Couldn't fault her for that.

But Rocky's crestfallen look returned the ache to Michael's torso.

"How about I tuck you in?" His offer drew Rocky's gaze. "I can tell you a story."

Her lips tugged into an adorable little half smile that turned the ache into a throb.

Great. Now he had two females he had to worry about.

143

# FOURTEEN

"All comfy?"

Michael's deep voice carried to the hallway where Amalia paused outside the door of Rocky's temporary bedroom. She silently signaled Raksa to sit.

"Uh-huh."

"Okay, here goes." Michael paused, as if thinking. "Once upon a time, there lived a boy and a girl who were best friends."

Amalia tensed. He wouldn't.

"They'd been best friends for as long as they could remember."

"What were their names?" Rocky's small voice sounded so innocent.

"Mikey and Sofia."

Apparently, he would. At least he hadn't announced that his story was true or identified the characters as Amalia and himself. Mikey had been a nickname that had only lasted until they were eight or nine, when he'd declared it was too babyish.

Good thing she had decided she better supervise the tucking in. She might have to step in to keep Michael from pouring out their whole history to a kid savvy enough to use it for leverage if she could.

"When they were eight years old, a mean bully at school started to pick on Mikey."

"What did he do?"

"He stole Mikey's lunch when he had one. And, one day, he pushed Mikey down to the ground and wiped mud all over his face in front of the other kids."

The image of Michael's boyish face lit her memory. Tracks through the mud revealed he'd cried on his way home. She'd been sick that day. Her parents kept her home, though she'd begged to go. Michael shouldn't have had to face Hale the Whale alone.

"I know a girl like that."

"You do?"

Silence. Maybe the kid nodded.

"I'm sorry." Michael's voice filled with compassion. "That's hard. Is she at the home where you live?"

"Yeah." Rocky sniffed. "What happened with the bully in the story?"

"Well, Sofia hadn't been able to come to school the day Hale, that's the bully's name, covered Mikey with mud. When Mikey told her what had happened, she was furious." A smile infused Michael's voice as he continued. "Sofia was the kindest, sweetest girl you could ever meet. But when anyone was mean to people who couldn't defend themselves or people she loved...well, you did not want to be the one she was mad at."

The wistfulness in his tone seeped past Amalia's body armor easier than a bullet and crawled somewhere behind her ribs where it lodged uncomfortably.

She spun away, silently left the hallway with Raksa at her side. They were doing fine. And she didn't need to hear the rest of the story she already knew. She'd borrowed a knife from an older student, without his knowledge, and gave Hale the Whale the biggest surprise of his life that night, when the kid took out the trash at his house. In the dark.

She had no intention of using the knife for anything beyond scaring the bully. All she'd had to do was flash the knife around and make sure Hale knew she wasn't afraid of him.

Coward that he was, he'd dashed back into the house faster than a jack rabbit. And never bothered Michael again.

Why Michael was dredging up that old story and telling it to a random kid was inexplicable.

She reached the bottom of the stairs with Raksa. Turned right to go to the kitchen.

It made sense in a way, given how obsessed Michael seemed to be with the past. How he couldn't let it go. Couldn't stop trying to figure out her secrets.

He may not have asked her any pointed questions in the last couple days, but she knew he was still on the trail. Saw it in his eyes when he watched her, thinking she didn't notice. Knew from Nevaeh relaying the questions he'd asked about PK-9. He was like a bloodhound with a scent to follow. He'd never stop until he uncovered all the secrets, exposed all the lies. But if he did that, he'd risk her freedom and her parents' peace and happiness.

She couldn't allow that.

"Hey." Michael's gentle, husky voice behind her almost startled her.

Inexcusable. He could've been anyone. She'd let herself be distracted. A deadly mistake in this business. And in her life.

She went to fill Raksa's dish with water, using the bottle she'd brought from her house and left by the sink earlier. "You're pretty good at that."

"At what?"

She finished pouring water into the dish and gave Michael a wide smile. "The daddy routine."

His mouth formed a harsh line in the stubble that surrounded it. "It wasn't a routine. I wanted to be nice to her. She's been through a lot."

"Well, I'm sure she'll feel much better knowing she has you wrapped around her little finger."

He scowled. "She'd probably really feel better if you'd stop treating her the way you have."

"Oh?" She quirked an eyebrow, braced her hands on the island between them. "And how is that?"

He stepped closer to the island on the other side, his blue eyes darkening. "Like a terrorist suspect."

She grinned.

"You think that's funny?" His frown deepened.

"A little, yeah."

"Well, I don't." He thunked his hands down on the countertop and leaned forward. "What happened to the girl who loved kids? The one who carried that lost, four-year-old boy eight blocks to his home even though he was almost as big as you were." He lifted a hand to the side then let it fall. "I don't get it. Even when we were teenagers, you always had a group of kids hanging on you at church every Sunday. Remember?"

*The AK-47 aimed at her.*

*She almost couldn't move.*

*The small face above the barrel was so familiar. Cherished. Loved.*

*He grinned.*

*Instinct drove her to cover as he fired.*

*Sent her hand to her weapon.*

She pushed back from the counter. Glared at Michael. "What I remember," she suppressed the anger he'd made her feel, harnessed it into tight, cold steel, "is that no one can be trusted." She didn't look to see if the bullet hit its mark. Just focused on her K-9 partner, done drinking. "Raksa, let's go."

She rounded the island, passed the protected witness without a glance.

"Is that why you lied to Rocky?" His question made her pause.

She was a professional. Couldn't be rude to a principal—the person she'd been hired to protect.

"You told her she can stay with us as long as she wants. You told her you don't shoot people."

She wasn't a coward. She could face him without it making a chink in her armor.

Amalia turned. Met his gaze. The blue eyes angry, pained. "She didn't need to know."

And neither did he.

*"She didn't need to know."*

Amalia's words bounced around in Michael's mind like a tennis ball. As if that made lying okay.

He pushed up from the mattress on one elbow and punched his pillow before letting his head fall back onto it.

She should know better. How could she forget what their lying had done? What it had cost him? She acted as if it never happened.

Michael yanked the sheet off and swung his feet to the floor. Trying to sleep was obviously pointless.

He checked his phone on the nightstand. *1:15 a. m.*

He pushed a hand through his hair, his thumb sticking on the sweat that gathered along his hairline. Cool air from the AC pumped through the vent across the room, but not enough for him. Tossing and turning for an hour didn't help.

There had to be a way to break through Amalia's barriers. To dismantle her lies. Trouble was, she didn't care that he knew she was lying. She'd apparently told herself a bigger lie —that truth didn't matter anymore. And she seemed to believe it.

He had to find out why. What had driven her to deny even who she was?

The possibility that she felt she didn't have a choice flared in his mind again. Tension gripped his stomach. She seemed so strong, so independent. But even the strongest could get ensnared. He'd seen it before.

He went to his computer at the large desk and opened it. The fact that he couldn't find evidence Phoenix Gray existed before ten years ago told him he was probably on the right track. Things were definitely not all they appeared to be at the Phoenix K-9 Agency. But he'd need help pulling back the curtain even more.

He opened his email program and typed in the address of

Special Agent Daniel Carter. The FBI agent based in D. C. should be able to help. Do some digging beyond what Michael could do. Carter always said he owed Michael for the two cases his investigations helped close. But they'd truthfully developed a friendship that meant Michael could be sure Carter would help him out now, no questions asked.

Michael typed the email, listing the names of the Phoenix K-9 Agency team members and what he'd already learned.

Gentle footfalls sounded from the hallway outside his closed door.

He paused his typing to listen. Probably Amalia and Raksa, checking the upstairs for any threats. She'd go to the end of the hall, clear the bathroom and the unoccupied bedroom. He'd heard Amalia make the same rounds before.

Amalia. Not Sofia. How could he find the woman he'd searched for, longed to see again more than he'd wanted anything, only to have her pretend to be someone else?

He closed his eyes against the pain that squeezed his heart.

*Please help me find the truth, Lord. Help me bring Sofia back.*

Maybe he should attempt to talk to Amalia again, in the quiet of the late hour. He grabbed the black T-shirt he'd left on the chair back and pulled it on, the hem dropping to rest past the waist of his charcoal lounge pants that doubled as pajamas.

As he shoved his feet into his moccasin slippers, he started to have second thoughts. His conversations with Amalia hadn't gone very well so far even in the light of day. He sat down at the desk again. The middle of the night probably wasn't—

A loud crash catapulted his heart to his throat. Sounded like it was upstairs. Where Amalia was?

He leaped up, knocking the chair to the floor as he dashed for the door.

# FIFTEEN

Amalia spun away from the tear gas canister that had flown through the window of the unused second-floor bedroom. Landed on the carpet.

Raksa barked and snarled at the broken window someone had used a launcher to penetrate.

"Raksa, here." Amalia snatched the unzipped front of the windbreaker she wore and pressed the nylon over her face as she darted for the open door, escaped the room with the shepherd scurrying out behind her. The gas that spewed from the cannister would soon fill the whole house, spread more quickly by the AC.

She shut the door behind her. Whipped off her windbreaker. "Tear gas canister," she reported over coms, suppressing her pain response to the fiery flames that burned through her lungs. "Front right bedroom upstairs." She squatted, stuffed her windbreaker under the door to slow the gas.

"F1, get to the basement and cut the AC. Everyone else, hold positions. Watch for raid or ambush. Somebody's trying to flush us out. I've got the packages."

The agents confirmed her directions as she straightened.

A man stood in front of her.

Michael. The realization came before she pulled her gun.

150

"What's going on?" His widened gaze scanned her face, probably saw her reddened eyes. "Are you hurt?"

She ignored the searing burn that tried to force her lids shut. "Tear gas. Follow me." She darted past him, Raksa easily keeping up. Good thing Phoenix had thought to have all the PK-9 protection dogs undergo tear gas training. Raksa had more resistance to the substance than Amalia did. He'd be able to lead her out if the swelling got so bad she couldn't see.

She leaned into Rocky's bedroom door.

The girl awoke, sat up in bed, her eyes big as she stared at Amalia and Michael.

"We need to leave. Now." Amalia couldn't risk picking the kid up herself. The castoff residue could expose her to symptoms. Amalia jerked her head toward Michael. "Carry her and stay close to me."

Pops sounded outside.

Michael glanced at her but wasted no time following her instructions, reached the bed in two strides and swung Rocky into his arms like she weighed nothing.

"PT1, hostiles out front." Lawson, the FBI agent posted outside at the front of the property tonight, spewed the terse words over coms. "150 yards from house. We'll keep them busy."

"Team leader, Roger." Amalia kept her eyes on the kid and Michael.

"It'll be okay." The girl didn't fight Michael as he murmured the words. She clung to his neck instead.

"Stay close." Amalia let Raksa lead the way, closing her eyes slightly as powerful flames seemed to devour her eyeballs. She'd been through this before. At The Farm and in the field. Nasty pain, but temporary.

They reached the bottom of the staircase. She forced her eyes to widen. Scanned her surroundings.

"PT1, this is F1. AC is off, but we've got company." Jeffers shot the words through her earpiece. "Two breaching the garage. Two more at the front door."

"Roger that," Amalia responded as she marched to the door where Agent O'Brien held his post. "We'll evacuate via garage."

"PT1, Roger. Need backup?"

Shots fired into the front door.

She darted to the side, looked around the staircase that had blocked her view of the front and made a wall to take bullets.

Jeffers squatted. Returned fire through the door.

As if he could offer backup right now. "F1, just keep the front secure."

She needed all the agents to hold off the intruders long enough to get to the car with the wits. Before the gas reached the ground floor. It'd be there in a few minutes. A kid wouldn't be able to handle its effects.

She turned to Michael and the girl, waiting by O'Brien, who had his Glock out and ready.

Michael pressed the girl's face into his shoulder, his large hand on her head. Protecting her.

She met O'Brien's gaze. "I'll clear out the garage. You stay with the wits. Keep them safe until I get back." She let her eyes, puffy and red as they probably were, send him the message he'd better not mess up.

The young kid jerked a nod. "Yes, ma'am."

"Bring the wits as soon as I tell you, then lay down cover when I drive them out of here."

"Yes, ma'am."

Not her favorite thing to be called, but no time to waste on the young agent.

She shot a glance at Michael. "Stay here. Out of sight of the front."

"Be careful."

She shut out Michael's words and the twinge that the softness in his voice caused somewhere under her ribs. Adrenaline erased the unwanted feeling as she crouched by the door, her hand on the knob. "Ready, boy?"

The gleam of excitement in Raksa's brown eyes mirrored her own.

She'd bet her life a Rottier thug waited just outside this door.

She glanced back. O'Brien had moved Michael and Rocky to crouch against the wall behind the agent's back.

Amalia slowly opened the door just enough to free it from the frame.

She popped up, kicked it wide. "Raksa, on it!"

The shepherd flew out the doorway, launched his body at the armed thug waiting to the right of the door. The man went down, Raksa latched onto his gun arm, forcing the thug to drop his weapon.

Amalia cleared the other angles while Raksa kept the gunman occupied.

Movement on the far side of her car's hood. An aimed gun.

Amalia fired before the shooter could get off a round.

He ducked away.

"Get him off me!" Raksa's captive screamed.

Not until she could be sure he wouldn't go inside and give O'Brien trouble. Had to deal with the loose cannon first.

She crouched, darted to the near side of her car. Listened.

Raksa's snarls and the captive's grunts made it difficult to hear.

Her heightened senses strained.

A footfall.

The shooter was trying to round the car. By the trunk.

She waited, weapon aimed as she watched the concrete past the rear wheel.

A black shoe appeared as the guy came out firing.

She rolled, landed upright, shot him clean to bring him down fast.

He dropped.

She leaped up, jogged to her partner. "Raksa, out. Here."

The shepherd instantly released his hold and went to Amalia's side.

The thug grimaced as he grasped his elbow, probably afraid to touch the rest of his damaged arm.

She held her weapon on the gunman, his face familiar. One of the intruders at Phoenix K-9 headquarters. "O'Brien, cuff this guy."

The agent hurried into the garage and secured the thug. "What about the other one?"

"Probably needs a coroner. You can check on him once we get the wits out."

She leaned through the doorway into the house. "Michael."

He rose from his squat, still holding Rocky against his chest.

"Come on. Hurry." She led the way to the car, opening the back door for Michael to set Rocky inside. He reached in to help her buckle her seatbelt.

"No." Amalia touched his arm. The warmth and taut muscle beneath her fingers sent a jolt through her system. She jerked back. Looked at the girl as Michael pulled away from her. "Get on the floor and stay there until I tell you."

Rocky blinked at her, face pale, grave.

"Now!"

The girl flinched but slid off the seat and lay on the floor.

Amalia glanced at Michael and pointed to the passenger side. "Get in the front and stay down."

She sent Raksa onto the back seat and shut the door.

Jumped in behind the wheel and fired up the engine.

O'Brien waited by the car to provide cover fire as she'd instructed.

"All teams, PT1 coming out with packages. Cover me."

Michael lifted his head from where he'd folded in half to do as she said, for once.

"Stay down and hang on." She jerked the car into reverse and floored it.

Smashed through the closed garage door.

Two thugs at the front door turned, unleashed a volley of rounds as she zoomed the car backward down the driveway.

One of them dropped, another gunman from the PK-9 headquarters invasion.

Jeffers crouched in the now-open doorway at the front, firing at the hostiles.

She hit the street, swung the car around.

Lawson held off more hostiles from behind the open door of his car, flashes from their weapons sparking the darkness.

She pressed the pedal to the floor, leaving the agents to do their jobs while she did hers. "Anyone injured?"

Michael slowly sat up. "I'm fine. Rocky?"

He looked toward the floor behind the driver's seat.

No response.

Amalia's heartbeat paused.

"Rocky?" Worry pitched Michael's voice as he unbuckled his seatbelt and leaned toward the back.

"Can I get up now?" The girl's muffled voice jumpstarted Amalia's heart.

Michael lowered into his seat and cast Amalia a smile bright enough to light up the darkness surrounding them.

Another sensation, just as unwelcome as the unwarranted concern she'd felt seconds ago, seeped through her body, warming her from within. "Yeah." She reached for a casual or harsh tone. Either one could help combat the soft feeling that oozed through her veins. "You can get up now."

---

"You're where?" The fact Phoenix wanted Amalia to repeat her location revealed her surprise more than her near monotone.

Amalia adjusted the Bluetooth earpiece connected to her phone as she answered. "Smart One gas station off 94. The girl had to use the bathroom."

Working through pain, facing danger, expecting the unexpected. Amalia was an expert in those and more. But travel with kids was not something she was used to.

Only a few minutes up the road, Rocky had made her announcement.

"I would've waited until we were farther away, but it was apparently...an emergency." Judging from the whining and scrunched facial features that had soon followed.

The FBI agents at the safe house should still have Rottier's thugs too pinned down to follow her. Hopefully, they'd captured the would-be hitmen by now.

"Was she exposed to the gas?"

"I don't think so." The mention of the substance brought the fiery pain in Amalia's throat and eyes to the front of her mind. Even her underarms burned where the gas leached onto the sweat there. "I got them out fast."

Rocky hadn't exhibited any symptoms. Michael had a slight cough, probably from when he'd met her outside the room with the gas cannister on the upper floor.

The man in question appeared in her peripheral, coming out of the men's bathroom. His hair laid a little smoother than before, darker streaks revealing he must have run damp fingers through the waves.

Her gaze lowered to find a smile waiting for her. A familiar smile. Like the one he'd given her after she'd scared off Hale the Whale for good.

Or when she'd convinced her parents that his mom had gone to spend the summer at his aunt's house when she'd actually checked into a treatment center.

"They should change clothes as soon as possible as a precaution." Phoenix's statement jolted Amalia's attention back just in time.

"Yes. They don't sell clothes at the convenience store here."

"I'll have Cora bring some when she meets you at the safe house. How are you and Raksa?"

That was the closest to a personal question Amalia had ever heard from Phoenix. At least aimed at her. She took a second to answer. "We're fine. Raksa seems unphased." She glanced at the shepherd who sat at her side, panting as he surveyed the people and shelves between them and the front of the gas station. Good thing his canine eyes flushed out the substance much faster than human ones.

"Excellent. What's your condition?"

"I'm fine."

Michael, apparently listening to her end of the conversation, leaned forward so his head was in her line of vision. He dipped one eyebrow and lifted the other in a skeptical expression that was almost cute.

"I'll have Cora bring you a change of clothes, too."

A change in brain or some much-needed sleep would be more helpful, given she'd just thought Michael was cute. She flashed the smile she knew he hated and angled slightly away, scanning the gas station store as she should be doing. A task that was getting harder thanks to the increased swelling of her eyelids. What was taking the girl so long in the bathroom?

Amalia held back an impatient sigh. "What about the leak? Another safe house won't do us any good if Rottier can keep finding out where we are."

"I talked to Katherine." Phoenix's no-nonsense tone was no doubt effective in that conversation. "She agrees there must be a leak, though she hasn't found any taps or other evidence of how Rottier is getting his information. She's assigning the full protection detail to us."

Katherine apparently trusted Phoenix even more than Amalia had realized. Good thing. Amalia didn't want another night like this one. For Michael and Rocky. Too hard on civilians to have to fear for their lives.

"We'll report where we have the witnesses only to Katherine via private communication." Phoenix continued with the confidence that made even Agent Nguyen trust her implicitly. "You'll take them to a safe house I've prepared for our own clients."

She hadn't told Amalia that PK-9 had its own safe house for protection jobs. But Phoenix operated on a need-to-know basis just as much as the CIA.

"Got it."

Phoenix told her the address as Rocky finally emerged from the bathroom.

Amalia grabbed the girl's shoulder to stop her from walking away.

The kid cast her a dark look. "I'm hungry. I want some chips."

"I could buy her some."

Amalia shook her head at Michael with a don't-you-dare glare.

"Bristol is on her way to do a bomb sweep with Toby."

Amalia wasn't surprised Phoenix would clear even a secret safe house of undisclosed location for bombs before bringing witnesses there. Phoenix prepared for everything.

"I'll meet you there with Dagian so you can take a break." Meaning, recover from the tear gas. Phoenix didn't miss a trick. "Could you identify the men in the attack?"

"Two of them were the ones who tried to take us at head-quarters. Rottier's men."

"They'd have easy access to weapons, including tear gas, from his merchandise. Katherine said her agents captured three tonight, two of them wounded."

With the one Amalia took out, that meant two escaped. At least the captured ones shouldn't make bail this time with the level of violence of their attack.

Rocky fidgeted under Amalia's grip, trying to tug away.

"The kid's back. I'll move them out."

The line went dead without a word in response. Typical for Phoenix.

"Your eyes look weird." Rocky peered up at Amalia with undamaged hazel eyes, her nose scrunching and mouth stretching downward with squeamishness.

"She's right."

Amalia swung her head toward Michael on her other side.

He smiled. "Not that you look weird. But you do look like you're in a lot of pain. Can we get you something here that would help?"

Time would help. That and the dry tissues she'd already used to dab away as much of the gas residue from her eyes and nose as she could. Nothing she could do for her fiery lungs but wait.

She squinted through swollen lids at the handsome face and blue eyes softened with concern.

Had she just thought Michael Barrett was handsome?

She stifled a groan, which would only sear her burning lungs even more. "Let's just get the kid's snacks and get out of here."

They hadn't told her at The Farm that tear gas could affect the brain. Or bring to life the emotions she'd locked away, determined never to let them loose again as long as she lived.

Four days. Only four more days, and she could leave Michael, the kid, and the problems this job had brought into her life behind forever.

# SIXTEEN

Michael held Rocky's hand in his as they followed Amalia and Raksa from the car parked in the driveway, through a short wooden gate, and to the back door of the new safe house. *New* being a relative term.

If the house they'd just fled had been the epitome of modern decadent living, this was an encyclopedia's photo of a 1980s middle-class dwelling. The single-story house looked a bit like a box with yellow siding. The box sat in the center of a small yard inserted between similar houses and lots in the residential neighborhood. A quiet, dark neighborhood at two thirty a.m.

The door swung open as soon as they neared it, revealing Cora's beaming smile and a happy golden retriever at her side. "Welcome. Praise the Lord you're all okay."

*Praise the Lord?* The statement perked Michael's ears. Could Cora be a Christian?

She beckoned them to enter the small hallway, shutting the door behind them and rapidly entering a code into the security system control pad on the wall.

Another reminder that they still weren't safe. That the weary days of waiting for more attacks weren't yet finished. It hadn't bothered him so much before. But now...

The gentle pressure of the small hand in his swelled his

throat. He coughed, but it didn't lessen the weight that pressed on his chest. Rocky shouldn't have to worry about being kidnapped or worse just because of something she might have seen.

"You must have gotten that cough from the gas." Cora shook her head in the way Sofia's mom used to when she or Michael came down with a cold or the flu. "I'm so sorry. I have some tea that might help with that, but first, we need to get you into different clothes. I had to guess your size since we couldn't remove your luggage from the house yet, thanks to the gas. But I put the clothes on your bed. You'll find your room just there on the right." She pointed up the hallway at an open door, then transferred her gaze to Rocky with a maternal smile. "I bought you some new PJs for tonight and a new outfit for tomorrow."

"Why?" Rocky stared at Cora as if she'd announced she purchased a spaceship for the child.

"Because you may have some gas residue on your clothes, and it could cause irritation if we don't get you into different clothes."

Rocky looked down at her tattered T-shirt with a photo from the original *Rocky* film on the front. "I don't want new clothes."

Cora knelt in front of Rocky, her smile unshaken. "Don't worry, sweetie. You can keep the clothes you have on now. I'm going to wash them very carefully and get them right back to you, okay?"

Rocky tilted her head, then nodded.

Cora straightened. "Wonderful." She held out her hand toward the girl. "How about we check out your new room? It's just in there." She nodded to a doorway on the left.

Rocky looked up at Michael, her eyes filled with an unspoken question, a thirst for approval.

His heart twisted a little. He smiled past the lump forming in his throat. "Go ahead. You'll have fun. And I bet Jana will go, too."

The golden retriever walked to Rocky as if on cue and nudged her nose into the girl's free hand.

Rocky smiled and let go of Michael to take Cora's hand as she petted Jana with the other.

"You need to change." Amalia's command drew his attention to her face. "Could help your throat if you're breathing in what's on your clothes."

It was almost laughable, the woman whose eyes were nearly swollen shut worrying about his mild exposure. "What about you?"

"This is my job, Mr. Barrett. I'll take care of myself once I've seen to your safety."

He stepped close, hiding a wince at the pain she must be experiencing not only from her eyes but the other symptoms he'd read tear gas could cause. He lowered his voice. "We take care of each other, remember?"

She didn't flinch, didn't move. And he couldn't make out what emotion might be behind her puffy eyelids.

"Amalia?" A woman's voice made him step back. Bristol walked toward them up the hallway, her black lab trotting beside her with an enthusiastic tail wag. "Thank God you're all okay."

Another reference to God? Could Bristol be a believer, too?

"Or are you?" She squinted as she reached Amalia.

"Looks worse than it is."

Bristol grinned at Amalia's response. "Exactly what I'd say. Though I doubt it's true." Her blue-gray gaze moved past Amalia to Michael. "Mr. Barrett, I'm glad to see you don't seem to have been badly exposed."

"Michael, please."

She tilted her chin in a nod. "Experiencing any symptoms?"

"Just a little cough."

"Thank God it isn't worse. We were praying for you all as soon as we heard you'd been exposed to tear gas. It's survivable, but a nasty experience for anyone. Especially a young girl."

Michael barely heard the words that followed Bristol's admission she'd prayed for all of them. She'd even said *we* prayed. Who was the *we*? Bristol and Cora?

"Still, you should change into the new clothes Cora bought you." Bristol's stare brought him back to what she was saying.

"Exactly what he was just going to do." Amalia's eyebrow quirked above her slitted eye.

He gave her a look, not quite able to keep his mouth from twitching into a smile. At least she wasn't in enough pain to have lost her sense of humor. Sofia had always loved nothing more than bossing him around, too.

Bristol chuckled. "If you want to crash for a few hours, go ahead. It's only about a quarter to three, and you haven't exactly had a restful night. I know Cora's going to try to get Rocky to sleep."

The mention of sleep prompted a wave of fatigue to wash over him. Probably his body's response to the adrenaline finally receding from his system. He must look as exhausted as he felt, judging from the pity in Bristol's gaze.

"All right, I'm going." He walked past the two women but turned to face them as he backed up the hallway. "Make her take care of herself, will you?" He pointed at Amalia.

Bristol laughed. "I'll do my best."

He turned off at the bedroom Cora had indicated. He found a light switch to the right of the doorway and flicked it on. Soft light illuminated a small room that boasted a double-bed with a plain, gray bedspread and brown paint on the walls. A pair of jeans and a navy blue T-shirt waited on the bed.

The pillows called to him. But as he took off his shirt and collapsed onto the surprisingly soft mattress, his mind didn't immediately follow the signals of exhaustion his body was sending.

*"Thank the Lord."*

*"Thank God."*

*"We prayed for you all."*

The unabashed, natural way both Cora and Bristol had referenced God and prayer at work, in front of a witness under their protection, suggested the boldness and authenticity of genuine Christian faith.

If they were truly Christians, he'd have to rethink his theory that the Phoenix K-9 Agency was a front for criminal activities. Cora and Bristol wouldn't be involved in something of that ilk. At least not knowingly. And with Cora as the office manager and technologies specialist, she was likely in a position to know all the goings-on at the agency.

But if Phoenix K-9 was as legitimate as it appeared on the outside, then he was back to square one. No explanation for Amalia's behavior, her deception, and identity change.

His eyelids drooped as his mind hopped from one possibility to another, then finally settled on a prayer. *Lord, help me find the truth. Help me find Sofia and bring her back.*

"Are you sure you're okay to meet right now?" Cora examined Amalia's face as she handed her a mug of tea. "I'm sure Phoenix wouldn't mind if you need to rest."

Amalia swallowed, ignored the throb in her throat, and accepted the mug even though she wouldn't be caught dead drinking the mild brew. But Cora insisted it would help soothe her pain. Amalia flashed a smile. "Your tea already did the trick. I feel loads better."

Cora gave her a knowing smile over her shoulder as she crossed to the loveseat that faced the one Amalia sat on with Bristol. "It only works if you drink it."

"You're underestimating the sme—" She grinned. "The steam."

Bristol laughed. "Not a fan of the tea aroma, huh?"

"Let me put it this way." Amalia sniffed the tea and made

a face. "When the doctor there clears me for coffee, I'll be happy." She sent Cora a teasing smile.

"I can only lead the horse to water." The mischief in Cora's eyes belied her angelic expression.

Amalia and Bristol laughed, a sound that attracted the attention of Toby and Raksa. The dogs lifted their heads from where they lay beneath the window air-conditioning unit they'd located. Raksa still looked tired, his skin sagging around his eyes. Big night for him.

"Did I tell you about Raksa's takedown?" A smile stretched Amalia's face as something that felt almost like pride expanded her rib cage. "Textbook. Kept the guy pinned for several minutes while I took out the other shooter."

"You both did your jobs well." The unusual praise from Phoenix drew Amalia's gaze to her boss.

Phoenix appeared to be watching the shepherd, who plopped over on his side again with a sigh. Hard to tell for sure where she was looking, given that she stood off from the small group, away from the light of the floor lamps. Dagian lay at her feet, lost in shadows.

The bill of her cap swung as she turned her head toward Amalia and the other women. "From now on, we'll aim to keep the risks lower."

"So we have full control of the security now?" Bristol leaned forward past Amalia to see Phoenix.

"Yes. Given the confirmation from Amalia's source that Barrett, and possibly Rocky, are Rottier's only targets, Katherine agreed she doesn't need us also protecting Ms. Nixon. FBI agents will stay with that witness, but we're to focus all our resources on the two with us now."

"How do you want to adjust the shift schedule?" Cora opened her notebook computer on her lap.

"Let Jazz and Nevaeh get a full rest tonight, and then have them join the team here by ten a.m." Phoenix's head angled away. Was she listening for something? Watching?

Amalia's senses went on alert. Michael and Rocky were in

their bedrooms right now, getting much-needed sleep. They didn't need more excitement.

Phoenix looked back at the women, not giving any signs of danger. "Amalia, Nevaeh, and Jazz will stay with Barrett and Rocky around the clock until he testifies."

"Around the clock?" Amalia peered through the shadows at her boss.

"We need two on protection at all times." Phoenix continued as if she hadn't noticed Amalia's surprise. "We'll put you on staggered eight-hour shifts. Anyone off will always be on call. Amalia, you'll be Team Leader."

"I can't stay 24/7." Amalia's mind raced. What if the CIA located Verdugo in this area? They could close in, find her instead. Visions of a treason trial, life behind bars, her parents' tears of shame, catapulted through her mind as her throat constricted. "I have to take care of Gaston, too."

"I can watch him for you." Bristol offered the unhelpful suggestion. "He's used to me since I've been letting him out and feeding him during your twelve-hour shifts. And Toby would love the company."

The black lab looked their way at the sound of his name and thumped his tail.

"No." If Gaston wasn't with Amalia when the CIA showed up, she wouldn't have time to go back and get him before running. But she couldn't leave him behind. "He needs to be with me." Would Phoenix demand more of an explanation?

"Bristol can bring Gaston here, and he'll travel with you until we finish this."

The tension that clenched Amalia's muscles loosened at Phoenix's definitive statement. But Phoenix's hidden message was clear—Amalia had promised to see this job through before leaving. To finish it.

"What about Cannenta?" Cora looked at their boss. "Do you think Nevaeh would like me to take care of her at my house?" Good question. Maybe Nevaeh couldn't spend that much time away from her PTSD service dog.

Phoenix dipped her head in a nod. "Yes. I'll talk to her about it."

"Okay." Cora looked at a slip of paper in her hand. Probably one of her to-do lists. "I'll get groceries and the luggage Michael and Rocky had to leave behind as soon as the house is ventilated. I should be able to bring all of that later this morning."

"Good." Phoenix's voice softened slightly as it often did when she spoke to Cora. "Be sure you and Bristol check your vehicles for tracking devices and watch for tails when coming and going to our safe house locations."

Amalia and the other protection team members already made a practice of that when coming on duty, but Bristol and Cora hadn't been so directly involved with the safe house locations until now. The reminder was a good one. Without the FBI leak to deal with, the threat against Michael and Rocky should be significantly lower. If the PK-9 team was smart and kept it that way.

"How long are we staying at this location?" If Amalia were in charge of the security strategy, she'd move them to a new one soon, just as a precaution.

"Today and overnight. You'll move to a new location tomorrow."

So Phoenix had another location already lined up. Amalia hadn't known PK-9 had one safe house, let alone two. But she shouldn't be surprised. It was Phoenix.

"Bristol and I will stay here tonight and cover security while you and Raksa recoup."

Amalia bristled, even though the statement came from her boss. "I've been through a lot worse. I'm fine."

Bristol snorted, apparently having spent too much time in Nevaeh's company. Even Cora laughed, a soft sound almost like a giggle.

Jana got up from lying at Cora's feet, her golden tail wagging as she gazed into her human's smiling face.

"You must not have looked in a mirror lately." Humor

filled Bristol's voice as she grinned at Amalia. "Your eyes are practically swollen shut. It's painful to look at."

"I really don't think Rocky should see you like this in the morning, Amalia." Cora's big, blue eyes twinkled above her innocent expression. "You might frighten the poor girl."

Amalia laughed. "Okay. Since you're all so concerned with appearances, Raksa and I will get our beauty rest." She pushed up from the sofa, ignoring how tired her limbs were starting to feel.

"Don't forget to change into the fresh clothes I brought for you."

Amalia waved a hand above her shoulder to acknowledge Cora's reminder without looking back as she walked up the short hallway. Wasn't the first time tonight someone told her she should get out of the gas-laden clothes.

*"We take care of each other, remember?"* The intensity in Michael's blue eyes as he'd leaned close appeared in front of her, real enough to block her path.

She pushed forward, missing only a step. Didn't look at the closed door of Michael's room as she passed it and turned into the bedroom she was to use tonight.

Didn't think about the twisting sensation behind her ribs, more painful than tear gas, and spreading much, much deeper.

# SEVENTEEN

Shuffling. Bumping. Voices.

Michael's eyelids slowly tugged partially open. Where was he? He scanned the small room, minimally furnished. Right. Another safe house. He'd never moved around so much in his life. He was starting to miss the stability of waking up in the same place with the same people in the house every day.

It was a gift—one he still couldn't believe God had given him—to share a home with Papi and Mami in his adult years. Somehow, not having a loving, nurturing family in his own house growing up had made him want to savor the family he'd found with the Sanchezes for as long as he could.

His eyes opened the rest of the way, and he sat up in the bed. Checked his phone, lying beside him on the sheets. *10:10 a.m.*

Fifty minutes until Amalia would leave and Nevaeh would come on for her shift. He flipped off the sheet and swung his feet to the carpeted floor, glancing around for the change of clothes Cora had brought last night.

Nothing against Nevaeh, but she wasn't the one his heart thumped in anticipation of seeing.

Wait a minute. He paused midway to reaching for the new T-shirt partially buried in the bedspread. His heart?

He slipped the cotton T-shirt over his head as he frowned.

169

Of course his heart was involved with Sofia. He'd loved her like a sister, his best friend, all his life.

But he'd never felt a sensation like the one that beat against his rib cage now at the mere thought of being able to see her this morning.

And she wasn't even Sofia. Not really.

He shook his head as he ran his fingers through his hair. Nonsense. He was just jittery from the near-death adventures of last night. And probably from insufficient sleep. That was all it could be.

He purposely slowed his movements as he changed into the jeans Cora had brought. Not an exact fit, but they'd stay up. She'd done a good job noticing he preferred straight-cut instead of the trendy skinny jeans he could never understand a man wearing.

He ran his hand over his jaw, his stubble scruffier than normal. Could do with a cleanup, but his trimmer was probably still in the tear-gassed house. Not like he needed to impress anyone anyway.

Striding to the door, he opened it before he could change his mind and try to find a mirror.

A flurry of activity beckoned him just beyond the short hallway. A tall redhead walked by with a striking dog in a bulletproof vest. Looked like the breed often used in the military.

And a giant, brown bear charged directly at Michael.

"Oops!"

The huge, furry dog buried its head into the hands Michael held in front of his body, as if to insist on the petting he was already willing to give.

"Well, it looks like you're okay with him." Bristol smiled as she came up behind the brown dog.

Michael let out a surprised *oof* as the giant beast turned sideways and leaned his whole heavy body into Michael's legs. "If I don't fall over, yeah." He laughed as he braced one leg behind himself to bear the dog's weight. "Newfoundland?"

"Yep." Bristol smiled as she watched the dog's friendly greeting. "His name's Gaston."

"So you have two dogs? What's this one do?"

"Oh, Gaston is Amalia's dog. He does water rescue."

"Really?" He never would've paired this jumbo, gregarious goofball with Amalia. Gaston seemed about as open and unreserved as a creature could get. "Well, I figured he wasn't a protection K-9."

Bristol laughed. "Good instincts."

"I guess drool must go with the territory, huh?" Michael held up his forearm to show her where Gaston had left a long streak of sticky saliva from elbow to wrist.

"Oh. Yeah, that's a Newfie thing. I'm always telling Amalia she should carry a towel when he's around." Bristol thumbed toward the kitchen. "I'm sure she has one in there if you want to wipe it off."

Michael didn't need any more of an invitation than that. He maneuvered around the big walking carpet, a trick and a half when the dog seemed determined to keep him there, and made his way to the kitchen.

Amalia stood in the small room, laughing at something Cora was saying as the blonde reached into a brown grocery bag on the counter. Amalia's black, glossy waves swung over her shoulder as she turned her head in his direction.

His heartbeat stopped. Then tripped forward with a sputter. He mustered a smile as he took in her beauty. For beautiful, she undeniably was. Nothing short of gorgeous, really. Had she always been, and he hadn't noticed? Either way, he wouldn't be a normal, healthy male if she didn't stir something in him. It couldn't be anything deeper than that. For so many reasons.

He pushed his hands into the pockets of his jeans. "You're looking better."

An understatement, to say the least. But he was relieved to see her stunning brown eyes showed little remnant of the swelling of last night. Hopefully meant she wasn't in so much discomfort now. He still couldn't fathom how she'd

171

dealt with what must have been horrible pain with such stoicism. Then again, Sofia had always been the toughest person he'd known, even as a kid.

"So are you." She flashed her smile.

It felt different this time. Almost like she meant it. At least a little. Or his wishful thinking was making him imagine things. He searched for something to say, at a rare loss for words, maybe because they'd bunched into a knot in his throat. He cleared it and grabbed at humor. "Especially with this decoration." He bent his arm up to show the saliva coating the skin.

Amalia laughed, her accompanying show of teeth definitely revealing more sincerity than usual.

His pulse skittered under the wrist he was holding up.

"That's Gaston's way of sharing his love."

Why did her mention of love make his pulse race even faster?

"Here." She dampened the corner of a towel in the sink and handed it to him.

His fingers brushed hers as he took the towel, and a jolt shot clear to his toes. Man, he needed to get more sleep or something. Amalia Peréz wasn't Sofia. And he'd never loved Sofia romantically anyway. *Eyes on the prize, buddy*. Find out her secrets, recover Sofia. For her parents.

"I'm glad the clothes fit." Cora looked at him as she paused by a cabinet with a box of cereal in her hand, apparently unaware she'd given him a distraction he desperately needed. "Though I brought your and Rocky's things if you want to change into your own clothes. We've been airing them out over there." She inclined her head in the direction of the living room, where his suitcase lay open on a chair.

"Thanks. I appreciate it."

Cora smiled graciously. "It's my pleasure. I've brought some basic groceries, but are there any specific items you'd like me to get?"

Amalia brushed past Michael to leave the kitchen without meeting his gaze. He turned, watching her walk into the living room and say something to the redhead. He didn't recall Sofia ever filling out a pair of jeans with such womanly curves. "Um. I'll think about it."

"Sounds good. Here's my card so you can call or text me if you think of something I should pick up." Cora's statement made him angle back to her, his gaze reluctant to leave Amalia. She held out a white business card with flowers edging the border. "Have you met Jazz and Flash yet?"

Must be referring to the tall woman and her dog. "No, I haven't."

"I'll introduce you." Nevaeh popped around the corner, seeming to appear from nowhere. The water beaded on her black windbreaker and the black fur of Alvarez at her side indicated she'd just come from the outdoors. Must be raining.

"Aren't you a little early today?" His gaze drifted back to Amalia. She wasn't leaving early, was she? He wouldn't have any chance to talk to her. To try to make progress in getting her to open up to him.

"Haven't you heard?" The leading question got Michael to turn his attention more fully on Nevaeh. "We're staying with you 24/7 from now on."

"We?"

"Yeah. Me, Jazz, Amalia." She smiled. "You're gettin' the VIP treatment."

Amalia was going to be with him all the time? Hope, and maybe something else, ballooned in his chest.

"I'm guessing that goofy grin ain't for me."

"What?" Heat crawled up the back of his neck as he yanked his gaze from Amalia.

A scary glint lit Nevaeh's brown eyes as she glanced behind him into the kitchen, then back to his face. "Hey, Cora. I think we've got a smitten kitten here."

Michael immediately turned away from the living room to see Cora fold the grocery bag flat. A sympathetic smile shaped her features. "Now, Nevaeh. That's no way to treat a client."

"Well, he isn't really the client. That's the FBI." Nevaeh's grin grew bigger as she eyed Michael as if he were her catch of the day, about to be filleted for dinner.

"Uh, weren't you going to introduce me?"

"Sure. Why don't we go over there by the other ladies?" She winked, her jovial expression all too knowing as she led him to Amalia and Jazz, who stood near a sofa in the living room.

"Hey, Jazz."

The woman turned to face Nevaeh and Michael.

"This is Michael Barrett. Our number-one witness everybody wants to get at." Amusement still thickened Nevaeh's tone. "Michael, this is Jazz Lamont, security specialist. And over there," Nevaeh pointed to the unfamiliar dog who drank water from a dish near where Raksa lay on the floor, "is Flash, her Belgian Malinois K-9 partner."

"Pleasure to meet you." Michael extended his hand, not surprised at the firm grip of the tall woman. She gave him a measured smile to match her assessing green eyes.

"Hey, Mals."

*Mals?* He blinked at Nevaeh. Amalia had a nickname?

"Mike here and I were just talking about you."

*Oh, man.* What was Nevaeh going to tell her?

"I think our—"

"Gaston!" Amalia's shout stung Michael's ears as she darted around him.

He spun to see the giant Newfoundland charging toward the girl who stood at the end of the hallway.

Rocky shrieked. Was she afraid?

Michael went toward her as the big dog screeched to a halt directly in front of her and plopped his back end to the floor. Amalia reached for the dog's collar, but Rocky's beaming smile and outstretched arms revealed she was excited, not scared.

The tension in Michael's stomach released as she reached her small hands to touch both sides of Gaston's enormous head.

"He's *so* big!" Her wide hazel eyes sparkled at Amalia and Michael as he came close. "What's his name?"

"Gaston." Amalia let her hand fall away from the dog's collar.

"Is he yours?"

"Yes."

Gaston slid a big tongue across Rocky's face. She giggled.

Something constricted in the middle of Michael's chest at the sound. How long had it been since Rocky had been able to giggle? To be a happy kid?

"I love him." She buried her smile and entire face into the dog's furry neck.

Judging from the grin on the dog's face, he was in heaven.

"I think the feeling might be mutual." Could Amalia really just have said that? No sarcasm, no flashy smile to dismiss the moment?

Michael angled to see her face.

A half-smile curved her closed lips as she watched the dog. And the look in her eyes was almost...soft. Caring. Like Sofia.

Until she shifted her gaze to him, and the coolness of Amalia slid into place.

But he'd seen a glimpse.

She'd given him hope. Whether she meant to or not.

---

Amalia couldn't help but enjoy seeing Gaston happy. The big goofball had always adored children more than anything, but he rarely got to interact with them.

She watched the scene from the edge of the kitchen. As Gaston lay on the sofa with Rocky, providing a giant pillow for the kid to lie on, the dog looked happier than she'd ever seen him. And the girl was obviously happier than usual, too. Less defensive. More real. Open.

Cultivating a bond between the kid and Gaston could be useful. Maybe she would soften enough to tell them what she knew about Rottier and the murder, and she could become Nguyen's problem again.

"Like a match made in heaven, aren't they?"

Amalia could hear the smile in Michael's voice, too close to her shoulder, without turning. She could tell when he'd seen her reaction to Gaston and the kid that he'd misinterpreted her expression. She shouldn't have let that much emotion show. Stupid lapse. But it had warmed her to see Gaston enjoying himself with someone who appreciated him the way he deserved.

"If a person believed in heaven, I suppose you might say that." Amalia didn't have to look at him to know her statement would hit the mark. "What I see is a girl with secrets she doesn't want to share." Amalia turned to Michael. "A girl who might share them if she keeps letting her guard down like she's doing now."

Michael's mouth firmed into a hard line, surrounded by the brown facial hair that was a bit thicker than before. "I guess you'd know a lot about that."

She lifted one shoulder and flashed a grin. "I suppose I would." She stepped closer to him, needing to show he didn't know her, didn't control her, didn't affect her emotions in the slightest. "On the other hand, maybe she didn't see anything incriminating and Rottier only thinks she did. Maybe she's just stringing us along to get what she wants."

"You mean like we did?" Michael stared down at her, anger mixing with pain in his eyes, matching the last glimpse of him locked away in her memory.

Was that really what he thought they'd been doing? What she'd done for him?

His gaze softened, and his eyes widened as he looked at something over Amalia's shoulder.

She jerked around.

Rocky stood there, hands clenched into fists at her side. "I'm telling the truth." Unshed tears glistened in her angry eyes. "I did see something."

Amalia calmly crossed her arms over her chest. "Prove it."

The kid jutted out her small jaw. "No. You'll send me back if I tell."

"We wouldn't do that, Rocky." Michael must really believe that somehow, or he wouldn't tell the kid. After all, he apparently never lied anymore, as he liked to keep reminding Amalia.

"She would." The kid thrust a finger toward Amalia's face. Her lips trembled as she spun away and ran to the hallway.

Gaston jumped off the loveseat and jogged after her.

"You know," tension edged Michael's voice behind Amalia, "if you'd be nicer and show you trust her a little, she'd tell us what she knows."

She hadn't remembered Michael being so naïve. No wonder he needed a team of experts to keep him alive. In the twelve years they'd been apart, Amalia had grown up in the real world, and Michael apparently hadn't.

She turned toward him. Didn't bother with a smile. "I know how to handle kids like her. And I know how to keep you alive. So how about this? I'll do my job, and you stay out of my way."

He blinked as she left him there and called Raksa to her to go on rounds outside that weren't on the schedule at the moment.

She needed to move, to outrun the memories of the boy with an assault rifle who'd taught her the lesson she'd never forget. Trust was deadly.

She wouldn't even trust a nine-year-old girl.

Michael shoved a hand through his hair and puffed out a frustrated breath in the privacy of the bedroom. He fiddled with the new smartphone Cora had given him, navigating the unfamiliar screen. It felt awkward in his hand. But so had the phone the FBI had provided when he'd gone into their protection four days ago. Apparently, Phoenix felt the FBI leak could extend to being able to track his FBI-provided phone. And she was probably right.

He tossed the phone onto the bed and glanced at the beige carpet under his feet. He dropped to the floor, planted his hands in the threads, and began a set of pushups. Exercise helped him think better, but he'd been told in no uncertain terms by Agent Nguyen at the first safe house that he wasn't allowed to run or do any outdoor exercising. Too dangerous.

Heat surging through his body from the exertion, Michael stopped and sat back on his heels.

What about the danger of losing his mind over the mess Sofia had become? He had to get her to open up or he may never find out what was driving all the lies and changes in her behavior. And never be able to help her become Sofia again. But how could he gain her trust when she wouldn't even trust a little girl?

She'd clearly been even more upset than he was after their fight about Rocky. She hadn't joined him and Rocky for dinner, even though he'd invited her to sit with them. She'd said she had to patrol, but Nevaeh had managed to take time to eat with them. Obviously, he'd struck a nerve with something he said in their conversation. But how was he supposed to know what that was or why Amalia was so upset when she wouldn't tell him anything about her past? When she wouldn't even be honest about who she was now?

Sofia used to trust him. With everything. They'd had no secrets between them, nothing they couldn't share. She'd seen him cry about his mom. He'd held her hand when she was twelve, and her dog had died. Tears had run down her cheeks, and he'd given his shoulder to press her wet face into.

They'd known the deep things about each other. She knew his greatest fear had been that someone would learn the truth about his mom, that he and his mom would be shamed. He knew her greatest fear was disappointing her parents. They'd trusted each other with those secrets, with the truth.

Michael got to his feet. Maybe that was the key. He needed to remind Amalia of how things used to be when they were kids. How *they* used to be. She used to trust him. Maybe if he could prompt her to relive some of their past together, she'd remember how much she had trusted him and want to again.

She was going to be here all the time now. That should give him plenty of opportunities. His mind scanned for shared memories, things they had both loved. *Changua*. The traditional Colombian breakfast food had been their favorite meal that her parents made every time Michael stayed overnight at their house.

He picked up the new phone, which Cora had said she'd programmed with all the numbers of the PK-9 team members. He also pulled Cora's business card from his pocket to verify the correct number was in the phone. Nine p.m. shouldn't be too late to text. He quickly typed a message, detailing the ingredients he'd need to make the Colombian breakfast that he hoped would remind Amalia of old times.

As he pocketed the phone, his mind searched for anything else he could do in case this plan failed, and she still refused to be honest with him. He'd never finished that email to Carter at the FBI. Probably for the best, now that he'd found out some of the Phoenix K-9 team members were Christians and unlikely to be engaged in secret criminal activities.

And, truthfully, he just couldn't wrap his mind around Amalia being involved in anything so wrong either. She was incredibly different from Sofia, but one important trait hadn't been lost.

The protective nature that had characterized Sofia all the years he'd known her defined Amalia, too. Amalia was just as brave and determined to help others at risk of her own life. Amalia had already saved his life four times in as many days. Or was it five?

As cynical as the years had made Michael, he couldn't believe the secrets Amalia hid were dirty ones. She had to be on the side of good, even if she was still convinced, as they'd both been in their childhood, that lies were an acceptable means of achieving a positive outcome.

But what could she have done legally in her past that would explain her need for a new identity? And could account for her exceptional training, skills, and experience.

What if she was running from someone who wanted to kill her?

The thought cinched his throat.

But no. He couldn't see Amalia or Sofia hiding like a normal person would. She'd probably confront the would-be killer instead. The way she'd confronted all the people Rottier kept sending to kill Michael.

Then where—

The FBI. A government agency like the FBI trained its agents in combat skills like Amalia had. And sometimes required secrecy for undercover assignments. Could Amalia be working undercover on something right now? No wonder she wouldn't want him telling people her true identity if that were the case.

He marched over to his computer on the bed and pulled it open. He found the unsent email to Carter and tweaked what he'd written. This time, he'd only include the information on Phoenix K-9 for context of where Amalia was now and what she was doing. But he'd ask his buddy to look for information on Amalia Pérez or Sofia Sanchez, especially looking to see if she was associated with the FBI.

He held his breath as he hit *Send*. This could be the break-through he'd been waiting for.

Loud barks burst through the closed door.

His stomach lurched. Another attack?

He swung open the door. He wouldn't let Amalia fight this one alone.

# EIGHTEEN

Raksa aimed his barks at the front door. He ended in a warning growl as Amalia slipped her phone from her pocket to check for a security alert.

Alvarez echoed the barks from where he and Nevaeh were posted at the back door.

"What've we got?" Nevaeh's question came through Amalia's coms earpiece.

Beeping and vibration shook the phone in her hand, a few seconds behind the dogs' keen senses. "Looks like a visitor, front walk."

A door opened in the hallway. Amalia swiveled to see Jazz and Flash fly out of the spare bedroom and hurry toward the living room where Amalia and Raksa watched the front. Jazz slipped her earpiece into place as she reached Amalia, instantly ready though she'd probably been sleeping on her off time.

"Come around from the rear. Surveillance unless we need containment."

Jazz nodded, headed back down the hallway where she'd pass Nevaeh to go out the back door.

A brown-haired head angled out from another room. Michael.

Amalia's pulse ramped up speed. "Get back in your room and stay there."

He stepped out farther instead.

"Nevaeh." Amalia said the one word through the coms in a tightly controlled tone.

"On it." Nevaeh came up the hallway toward Michael. "Hostiles?"

Amalia turned back to face the front, where her attention should be, and stared at her phone's screen. The dark movement slowly came into better focus on the camera, partially obscured by shadows. "Can only confirm one person. A woman..." Her eyes narrowed. No way. "A middle-aged woman carrying a casserole dish."

Nevaeh's snort of laughter carried through the house as easily as over the coms.

"Team 1, this is Team 3." Jazz must have reached her position out front. "Confirmation on your ID. Woman matches Amy Belvadere, next-door neighbor, south side."

"Team 3, Roger." Jazz was right, the woman did look like Mrs. Belvadere the closer she got to the front entry camera. Phoenix had given them details and photos of all the nearest neighbors last night.

"All teams, look alive. I'll handle but provide cover if needed. Could be a decoy or disguise." If Verdugo was still around, the visitor might not be at all as she, or he, appeared.

Amalia left her weapon in her concealed holster and moved toward the door.

Just as the visitor rang the bell.

Raksa let out a bark, echoed again by Alvarez.

"Raksa, wait." She signaled for him to hold his position a few feet back from the door as she reached to open it.

A woman's smile greeted Amalia as she held out the casserole dish. "Welcome to the neighborhood!"

Amalia took the pan, ready to drop it at the slightest unusual twitch from the woman who appeared to be in her mid-fifties. Her face was fully exposed in the security light above the door, her graying brown hair pulled back with a clip. Her skin looked real, not like a mask. Female disguises were nearly impossible for a man to pull off up close.

"I'm Mrs. Belvadere, your neighbor from the blue house over there." She pointed to the single-story house surrounded with flowering bushes and other plants.

Amalia smiled. "Oh, yes." She slipped into a light southern drawl. "Your flower beds are gorgeous."

The woman's face lit with happy pride. "Aren't you a sweetheart." She reached out to pat Amalia's hand. "What's your name, dear?"

"Oh." Amalia flashed another smile. "Where are my manners? I'm Jennifer Kline. We just moved in." She let a flush of embarrassment travel to her cheeks. "My husband and I."

"Aw, newlyweds, am I right?" Mrs. Belvadere's gaze lifted over Amalia's shoulder. "And this must be your husband." The twinkle in her eyes clashed with the surge of irritation that burned a path through Amalia.

She turned her head to see Michael step close with a smile. "Oh, yes. This is David." Amalia managed to keep her persona and cheerful tone intact as she swung back to Mrs. Belvadere. "David, this is Mrs. Belvadere, our new neighbor."

With his penchant for honesty, would Michael even go along with the little charade? "Delighted to meet you, Mrs. Belvadere." He reached to shake the woman's hand as he slipped his other arm around Amalia's waist.

She tensed. For a second. Then willed herself to relax. Not give anything away. Not think about the new kind of heat that spiraled through her body, the muscled arm that held her close, made her feel—

"And what a handsome husband you have." The woman gave Amalia a wink. "You two make such a lovely couple."

Amalia forced a laugh. "You're so kind." She had to end this. Fast. She lifted the casserole dish a little higher. "Thank you for this. We'd invite you in, but we've been unpacking all day and were just about to go to bed. David has to work early in the morning."

"Oh, of course, dear." Mrs. Belvadere glanced at Michael and Amalia, her smile indicating she thought she understood more than she did. "I hope you'll both consider coming to a barbecue on Saturday at my house. My husband, John, would love to meet you."

"We'll check our schedule and let you know." Amalia beamed another smile as she slid away from Michael and shoved the casserole dish into his chest to excuse the motion.

He took the pan as a grin widened his mouth.

"Have a good night." Amalia reached for the door.

Mrs. Belvadere took the hint and backed away with a wave. "You, too!"

Amalia shut the door, her smile dropping like expended bullet casings. She spun to Michael. "What were you doing?"

He shrugged, the casserole dish lifting with the movement. "Helping you out? Your fib was going to fall apart in about a minute."

"And that's about how fast you could've been dead if she hadn't been an unarmed neighbor." Amalia folded her arms over her T-shirt and glared at the infuriating man. "I told you to stay in your room."

"Yes, Mother. But I didn't want to." Mischief twinkled in those blue eyes. Irked her all the more. He thought this was funny?

He stepped closer until only the casserole dish separated them. "Besides, she said we make a lovely couple." His lips twitched.

Was he flirting with her? Or only teasing the way they used to when people thought they were dating as teens? A flush that confused her almost as much as his behavior climbed up her neck. Threatened to reach her face. Not contrived or faked this time.

She cooled it fast with a quick revisit to an image in her memory banks.

Jacob, dead in the getaway car. He'd like to flirt and tease, too.

She flashed a smile, met Michael's gaze head on. "Next time you choose not to follow my directions, you will likely end up dead. Focus on that *lovely* thought."

A small dose of satisfaction infused her as the amusement faded from his eyes, whether from her smile he disliked or a perceived threat in her words.

She walked to the back of the living room where Nevaeh stood at the edge of the hallway. Nevaeh's gaze bounced from Michael to Amalia as she holstered her gun. She'd probably seen the whole exchange with Michael and the way he'd come up to Amalia and put his arm around her like they were a couple.

Amalia gave Nevaeh an easy smile. "Looks like we survived the great casserole invasion."

Nevaeh laughed, seemed to buy the deflection without question.

Amalia went through the motions of checking with Jazz on coms, verifying no other threats were on the premises.

Amalia's smiles and jokes had to hide more than usual the rest of the night. Including fury at Michael for putting himself in harm's way when she'd explicitly told him to stay hidden.

But the anger that grew stronger every second was aimed at herself. For the way the skin at her waist still tingled where his muscled arm had held her so securely.

For the way her heart thumped, and her stomach felt like the bottle of fireflies she and Michael had collected as kids. As if her response to his simple, unexpected touch was a good thing.

But she knew the truth. Feelings like these were a death sentence.

Michael had never been so excited to see a bag of groceries.

"Good morning." Cora smiled as he entered the kitchen and her golden retriever came close to greet him.

"Morning." He petted the golden's soft head. "And you, too, Jana."

"You're looking chipper this morning."

He shrugged as he went to the sink to wash his hands, eagerness bubbling in his stomach. "Just can't wait for breakfast."

"Well, I've never had changua before, but it must be something special."

"It is." He went to the ingredients Cora took out of the bag and lined up on the counter. So many memories were wrapped up in just the sight of the milk, eggs, and cilantro. The *almojabanas*, the cheese-infused bread that would be a perfect side with the soup, had his mouth watering. Some of the brands for the ingredients were different than the ones Mami used in Texas, but the result should be similar enough. He couldn't wait for the aroma of cooking changua to fill the kitchen. If this didn't remind Amalia of her childhood, of who she really was, nothing would.

He rubbed his hands together. "Wait until you smell this. You can practically taste the flavor in the air."

"Sounds delicious." Cora stepped back to give him room to work. "But I'm afraid I won't be able to stay. I'm going to open up your next safe house and make sure everything is ready for you and Rocky."

"We're leaving so soon?" Michael found a pot in the corner cabinet and set it on the stove.

"Yes. You'll be staying at my aunt's cottage on the lake. It's a beautiful place. She doesn't need it while she's in Italy for the summer."

"Sounds great."

"I'm curious..."

He glanced at Cora when she paused.

"Is there a special reason for this rather Spanish-sounding dish this morning?"

A half-grin quirked his mouth before he could stop it. "It's a traditional Colombian breakfast. Sof—Amalia and I

grew up with it at her parents' house." He hoped she'd interpret his near slip of Amalia's real name as a simple *so*.

"That's right." Cora crossed her slim arms over her
lavender blouse as she watched him add milk and water to
the pot. "Nevaeh mentioned you'd said you spent your childhood together. What was Amalia like as a little girl?"

His smile faded as he turned up the heat to bring the
mixture to a boil. "Different." Very, very different.

"It's hard when people we love change in ways we don't
understand, isn't it?"

He jerked his gaze to Cora's face.

Empathy glowed in her blue eyes, the set of her mouth
sympathetic and understanding.

How much did she know? He swallowed. "Yeah." He
drew in a breath as he turned to the counter to prep the scallions. "I'm honestly not sure what to do about it."

"Prayer helps tremendously."

He nodded. "I'm doing that."

"I noticed the Bible among your things at the last safe
house. Are you a follower of Christ?"

He smiled at her unusual forthrightness. "I am."

"Wonderful. Then I'm especially glad God brought you
into Amalia's life again."

He checked a cabinet for a cutting board but didn't see
one. "Thanks. I'm not sure I'm making any difference,
though."

Cora opened a different, low cabinet door and pulled out a
cutting board. "Sometimes God is using us even when it
seems like we aren't getting anywhere. And what you're doing
here," she handed him the board with a meaningful look,
"that works, too. You're creating connection, showing you
care. You're speaking the truth in love through your actions."

Speaking the truth. That was something he needed to do
more of with Amalia. Between frequent attempts on his life
and constant moving, they'd hardly had any time to talk. And
when they had, they'd only argued.

"I'll pray for you, that God will show you what to do." Cora lightly touched Michael's forearm as he set the scallions on the cutting board. "Amalia's become precious to all of us at PK-9. And I can see she is to you, as well."

"My, my." Amalia's voice made Michael jump and nearly drop the knife he'd just reached for. "Cora, what would Kent say?"

He turned to see that unfamiliar, splashy grin on her face.

Cora smiled, though a touch of pink brushed her cheeks. "He would say he was glad to see me encouraging a brother in Christ."

"A brother in Christ, huh?" Amalia hiked a dark eyebrow. "Don't tell me you're going to start up one of your church club meetings right here. Bristol isn't even around."

"Nice try, Mals." Nevaeh's jolly laughter preceded her curly head of hair and broad grin. "We all know what's going on here." She fanned her fingers out, palm toward the floor, and waved her hand between him and Amalia. "And it ain't no church meeting."

Heat traveled up Michael's neck, and it had nothing to do with the heated stove he quickly turned toward. Funny. Suggestions that he and Sofia were a couple had never embarrassed him in high school. But back then, his pulse hadn't tripped and then taken off at a sprint when it restarted the way it did just now at Nevaeh's teasing.

"Okay…" The awkwardness in Cora's tone made Michael risk a glance her way. Her eyes widened as she darted a glance between Michael and Amalia. Her attention settled on Amalia. "I already told Phoenix this, but you should know I found a tracking device on my Beetle this morning before I left home."

"Where?" Amalia's tone turned serious.

"Between the windshield and the hood. I disabled it and reported it to Phoenix. I know there were no devices yesterday before I came here, so it had to be put in place after I left the safe house."

"Nobody should know about our location, then, right?"

Nevaeh put a hand on Alvarez's head as she looked at Cora, and the dog leaned into her leg.

Cora gently shook her head. "No, but it's a good thing you're all leaving here this morning, just in case."

"When do you think someone could've put the device on your car? And who?"

Amalia swung her gaze to Michael as soon as he asked the questions, her eyes narrowing slightly.

He shrugged. "I'm a reporter."

Cora smiled. "And a very good one. We think it had to be Rottier's men, and it could have happened when I had my car parked at the front of Phoenix K-9 headquarters."

"What's Phoenix K-9?" Rocky shuffled up beside Alvarez, rubbing her eyes. She blinked as she lowered her hands. "Is that breakfast?" She lifted her nose in the air just as Gaston did the same, the big brown bear coming to stand by Rocky in the crowded kitchen.

Michael smiled at the adorable pair before turning away to add the onions, salt, and pepper to the pot. "Yep. Better wash up and grab a seat at the table because it's almost ready." He glanced back and caught Amalia watching the girl and Gaston as they trudged to the sink. "Going to join us?"

Her lips slanted slightly, a glint in her eyes as if she knew what he was up to. She probably did. There was no way she hadn't recognized the dish he was making. But that didn't mean it couldn't work.

"Come on." He tried for a charming grin. "You know you love it."

She flashed that smile she used to deflect and hide everything. "Raksa and I have patrol duty this morning."

"Nah." Nevaeh nudged Amalia's arm with her shoulder. "You missed dinner last night, so Alvarez and I will cover patrol. Go on and enjoy."

Amalia cut Nevaeh a look that conveyed her disagreement.

Jazz appeared in the doorway and sniffed dramatically as Flash paused with her. "That smells divine."

Rocky hurried out of the kitchen, passing Jazz in an apparent rush to get to the table in the other room.

"Traditional Colombian breakfast." Amalia's smile broadened. "Have a seat. You'll love it."

"No, Jazz likes to get in her steps before breakfast, don't you, girl?" Nevaeh looped her arm through Jazz's and sent her a glance with eyebrows raised.

Michael held back a chuckle. He'd have to thank Nevaeh later for her not-so-subtle efforts to get Amalia to join him for breakfast.

"Oh, yeah." Jazz nodded, her expression innocent. "I always exercise before I eat. And Flash has to go out anyway. We'll take patrol."

Amalia narrowed her eyes at Nevaeh. "I thought you were covering patrol."

"Not since Jazz wants it." Nevaeh shrugged as if she hadn't been caught in a contradiction. "I'll cover the interior while you sit down and enjoy your breakfast. Besides, isn't your shift basically over?" She tapped the watch that encircled her wrist.

Amalia opened her mouth, clearly going to protest being pushed into the breakfast even though Nevaeh and Jazz made a hasty exit from the kitchen.

"Not afraid to taste it, are you?" The challenge escaped Michael's mouth before he'd planned to launch it. But it worked.

She faced him, and her gaze met his with a defiant glint in her dark orbs. "Of course not."

"Good. You'll have to tell me how bad it is. I know I won't be able to touch Mami's cooking."

"You know me. Always honest." She spun on her heels and left the kitchen before he could think of a response to her doubly sarcastic statements.

His stomach churned as he squeezed oranges for fresh juice and finished cooking the changua. He transferred the soup to bowls as quickly as possible before Amalia could change her mind.

He brought the juice out first in glasses and then rushed back to the kitchen, returning with the bowls he carefully set in front of Rocky and Amalia. A knot formed in his gut as he waited for them to take their first bites.

Rocky held a spoonful of changua and blew on it before tasting. She smiled around the spoon. "This is good!" She grabbed one of the almojabanas and bit into it. "Mmm." The sound was all she could get out at first as she chewed the bread. "Can I give some to Gaston?" Her voice was muffled as she spoke with her mouth full.

The Newfoundland sat a couple feet from her and stared at her with adoration in his eyes as he drooled.

"I don't think so, honey." Michael smiled, his gaze returning to Amalia.

She ran her spoon through the changua, stirring the soup with more hesitation and delicacy than he'd ever seen her have with food. She spooned a bit of the broth and brought it to her mouth.

He held his breath while she slowly tasted, then swallowed.

She met his gaze. And a smile suddenly appeared. Not an Amalia Pérez, cool and deceptive smile. No, this was his Sofia, looking up at him from the table with an expression full of warmth and memory and truth. And maybe even love —the love her parents had shared with them, and they'd shared with each other over this same breakfast so many times.

His heart surged. It was the most beautiful sight he'd ever seen.

———

How could one taste of changua take her right back? Memories rushed in as she ate another spoonful, unable to help herself.

Emotions washed over her, a tide of nostalgia and...longing? An ache began to throb deep beneath her ribs.

If only it were as simple as sampling food to go back. To find the camaraderie, the deep, abiding trust, the friendship she'd had with the boy who had changed into the man who stood in front of her now.

But that was before the lies blew up in their faces and obliterated their friendship in the explosion.

*"It's our fault, Sofie. It's all our fault."* The accusation in Michael's eyes as he'd said the unbelievable words stared her in the face, blocking her view of the food in front of her. All she could see was the torment that had contorted his features. The agony she hadn't been able to prevent.

She pushed back her chair and stood.

Raksa sprang up beside her.

"We need to leave."

## NINETEEN

Cora's aunt must be very well-off because the cottage Michael was staring at was no cottage. It was a three-story mansion complete with excessively large garage, an additional storage building, and a grand glass-door entrance that belonged in suburbia, not a remote location in the woods.

"Keep moving." Amalia gestured for him to walk in front of her toward the house.

Rocky and Gaston trotted along a few feet ahead with Nevaeh and Alvarez. Rocky's head was on a swivel as she gaped at the towering trees around them. Had she ever seen a forest before?

He'd been just as amazed the first time he'd seen a forest. He and Sofie had been so excited when their church youth group announced they were organizing an all-expense-paid camping trip for the teens. It was the first time he or Sofie had been able to go on something like that, given that neither his mom nor her parents had money for pleasure trips.

"Welcome!" Cora waved at them from the front porch. She knelt and said something to Rocky before the girl passed on with a smile and went inside.

Michael took the five steps up to the porch and scanned the large, furnished space. "This is some cottage."

Cora smiled. "All depends on one's point of view, I

193

suppose." She moved her gaze to Amalia, who came to stand parallel with Michael.

"Amalia, for example, is thoroughly unimpressed." A hint of mischief twinkled in Cora's normally angelic gaze.

Amalia's dark eyes darted around as she surveyed their surroundings. "Remote location is good. But too many windows."

"Don't worry." Cora met the criticism without a hint of offense. "Shades cover most of the windows with the touch of a button, and I've brought curtains for any that don't have that feature."

"Inside, please." Amalia pointed at the door, making Michael feel a bit like Raksa must when she told him to seek or attack or whatever it was. Though the dog actually seemed to enjoy obeying her commands.

Michael stepped through the door, even more impressed by the large entry with high ceilings and a dramatic double staircase that led to a balcony overlooking the great room beneath.

Amalia finally gave him some breathing room by walking away, apparently assuming he was safer now that he was indoors.

"How did it go?" Cora stepped closer and lowered her voice to a near whisper.

His confusion lasted only a second before he realized what she meant. The Colombian breakfast. "I'm not sure." His gaze drifted to Amalia, who checked the perimeter of the house's interior with Bristol and her black lab. "I thought it worked. For a second."

Before Sofia had abruptly reverted to Amalia and become just as cool and distant as ever.

"Take heart." Cora's soft gaze seemed to read what was driving him, how much he wanted to reach Amalia. "That moment you thought it worked, I'm guessing it did. God often brings His children to Himself through many small moments until the final one, when He makes it all come together. Just trust Him, my friend. And keep trying."

Renewed resolve strengthened with her encouragement. She was right. He couldn't give up, even if the first attempt to remind Sofia of the past hadn't worked to bring her back permanently.

But this place they were in now would provide a perfect opportunity to try again. "You know," he walked to one of the large spans of windows Amalia had criticized, "this forest reminds me of the time Amalia and I went on a camping trip with our youth group."

"You don't say." A knowing smile curved Cora's lips.

"Is that a rowboat on the lake?" He pointed through the window at the dock that jutted out into the water at the end of a path.

"Yes, it is."

"Hey, Amalia." He tossed Cora a grin and made his way to the woman who turned toward him with obvious reluctance. Well, obvious if he discounted the pointless smile she donned.

"Can Gaston and me go swimming?" Rocky beat him to the punch as she darted in front of him with the giant dog who bumped against Michael's legs in an effort to stay attached to Rocky.

Michael bit back the urge to correct her grammar. He wasn't her dad, after all. Why that thought sent a pang through his chest, he didn't want to decipher right now. Besides, he just wanted to enjoy how cute the little girl looked with her hands pressed together as if in prayer as she tilted her head toward Amalia.

"Please? Nevaeh said Gaston saves people in the water. So can we go swimming?"

Amalia stared down at the pleading girl. "No."

Disappointment sagged Rocky's whole body. "But why?"

"It's not safe for you to be outside."

Rocky's chin trembled, twisting Michael's heart. He stepped next to her and put a comforting hand on her shoulder.

"Does that mean you don't want to take the rowboat out

either?" He gave Amalia a look he meant to be both genuinely hopeful and a hint that she should go easier on poor Rocky. "I thought you might want to for old time's sake. Remember that time on our camping trip? When—"

"No." Amalia held up a hand to stop him. "You can't go outside either."

"You're no fun." Rocky crossed her arms over her too-small T-shirt with some cartoon character on the front. She leaned into Michael's leg, and he smoothed a hand over her glossy hair.

"Now, Rocky, just because Amalia says we can't go outside doesn't mean she isn't fun. She's watching out for us and keeping us safe. Right, Amalia?"

Amalia's eyes narrowed slightly as she watched him. "Sure."

"There, I knew it. And to show you how much fun Amalia is, Rocky, I know she'll say yes to my next idea."

The girl angled her head away to peer up at him. "What's that?"

"A campfire."

Amalia opened her mouth, but he held up a hand this time.

"Not outside. An indoor campfire." He gestured toward the large fireplace that the owners must use in the winter. "It's cold enough in here with the air-conditioning. We can roast hot dogs for lunch and maybe s'mores if Cora can scrounge up the ingredients for us."

"What's a suh-more?"

Michael's mouth twitched at Rocky's cute pronunciation. He tapped a finger gently against the little girl's wrinkled nose, even as his heart twisted a little with the knowledge she'd probably never had a s'more because she'd lost her family so young. "Only one of the sweetest things you ever tasted."

Her eyes widened, and she swung her attention to Amalia. "Can we?"

Amalia raised her gaze from the girl to Michael. Her full

196

lips held a steady line, and her eyes didn't let him see her thoughts within.

"What do you say? You're not afraid of a little s'more, right?" His heart thumped as he waited. Did she still love the marshmallow and chocolate treat like she used to? Would she take the risk that might allow him to remind her of who she used to be, of who *they* used to be together?

"Fine. I'm game." A spark lit her eyes and flared hope inside him.

Sofie had never been able to resist a dare either.

Rocky giggled and pointed at Michael's face.

He smiled broadly as he tried to wipe off the melted marshmallow and chocolate that dripped down his stubbled chin.

As they'd heated hotdogs over the fire and Michael had shown the girl how to roast marshmallows and build s'mores, Rocky's defensive demeanor had slowly melted away and let smiles peak out. Amalia had to admit, the girl looked better with a smile than the closed-off toughness she usually tried to project.

Rocky laughed harder, the first time Amalia had heard such a normal kid sound come from her.

No wonder. Michael was attempting to lick the marshmallow mess from his finger that was still mostly on his face anyway.

Amalia shook her head as she gave up resisting and grinned. "You're a mess." She snatched a napkin from the stack Cora had wisely provided when she'd set out the s'mores ingredients and rose from one of the chairs they'd lined up in front of the fireplace.

She passed Rocky in the middle to reach Michael. "Let me see."

He tilted his head up to her with a laugh.

She held his chin between her thumb and fingers as she

wiped at the sticky marshmallow and chocolate with the napkin in her other hand.

The set of his mouth slowly straightened, covering his teeth. Signaled a shift in his mood. And made her aware of the warmth beneath her thumb. The roughness of the small hairs on his chin. The soft lips that had never stood out to her so much before.

And the blue eyes that stared at her. Deeply. Darkened with a heat that rolled through her, tingling every nerve and muscle.

She jerked back. Covered the tell by swinging toward Rocky with a smile. "Messy kid, isn't he?"

The girl giggled as Amalia flopped back into her chair, stabbed another marshmallow with the roasting stick, and stuck it over the fire.

Michael watched Amalia. She felt his stare without looking.

But she focused madly on the marshmallow that browned above the flames. Shifted attention was the only way to ensure the heat didn't reach her face with a flush of color.

What was wrong with her? So Michael had grown up into a hot guy. Amalia was impervious to attraction. Dead to romance, emotion. And the idea she could be drawn to Michael in that way was ridiculous. He'd never been a boyfriend prospect to her.

"Remember when I accidentally stepped on that marshmallow by the campfire?"

Not another youth group camping story. He'd been trying to take her down memory lane ever since she'd joined him and Rocky for this pretend campfire lunch.

He leaned toward Rocky. "I didn't know about it when I took my shoes off that night to go to sleep in my sleeping bag."

Rocky's eyes widened as she finished off another s'more. "What happened?" Her stuffed mouth garbled the question.

"When I woke up in the morning, there were about a thousand ants all over my shoe."

"Eww!" Rocky slouched in her chair, scrunching her features. "What'd you do?"

"Well." Michael's gaze hopped to Amalia, then back to Rocky. "I'm a pretty brave guy, you know."

The image of teenage Michael popped instantly to Amalia's mind. Flailing his arms and screaming. A snicker escaped before she meant to let it out.

Rocky swung her head in Amalia's direction. "What?" She quirked a little smile, and amusement lit her hazel eyes in a way that made her prettier than usual.

Amalia shook her head. "He totally freaked out."

The girl giggled, a sound that started small, then grew into a full-on belly laugh when Michael joined in.

"You can't really blame me." He grinned between bouts of laughter. "It was like something out of a horror movie."

"Yeah." Amalia chuckled. "A comedy horror movie."

Rocky, bent forward and holding her stomach, let out a long, noisy breath as if she'd exhausted herself with laughing so hard.

"Plus, those were the only pair of shoes I had."

"That's why I cleaned them out for you." Amalia met his twinkling gaze with a grin.

His lips closed but pressed into a softer smile. "Always took good care of me, didn't you?"

Another memory surfaced with those words. Her arm around Michael as they'd sat on the front steps of her house, his head heavy on her shoulder, his body heaving with the sobs, the wrenching pain he wouldn't let anyone else see.

But that was Sofia who'd held him. Sofia who'd kept his secrets and done whatever she had to so he wouldn't suffer even more.

Sofia was gone. In the past. Amalia Pérez couldn't afford to care, to be vulnerable for Michael or anyone else.

"What is it, Rocky?" Michael's voice drew her attention to Rocky. He placed his large hand on the girl's back.

She'd leaned back in the chair and sunk low with a frown marring her face. "I only have these shoes now." She lifted her skinny legs straight out in front of her and glared at her tennis shoes. "I used to have three." Her jaw shifted in profile as if she swallowed. "Dad got me new flip-flops every summer."

Something uncomfortable lodged in Amalia's torso as the kid slipped back into anger, all humor and happiness gone.

Amalia's gaze went to the backpack propped against the wall by the fireplace. "Your dad must've been a Rocky fan."

The girl shifted her head toward Amalia, her eyebrows pinched together.

Amalia tipped her chin in the direction of the backpack with the large, iconic photo of the fictional boxer printed on the front. "The movie."

The kid looked that way, gave a slight nod.

Amalia's guess had been right. Her dad must've given her the backpack. "Did he give you your nickname?"

"It's my real name." Rocky gritted her jaw and clenched her fists on her lap.

"Okay." Amalia let a pause sit between them a moment. "One of your parents must've given it to you then."

The girl shrugged. "Dad did."

"It's a cool name." Michael interjected the comment as he looked at Amalia over the kid's head.

"He said I was a fighter." The words were almost imperceptible, nearly a whisper as Rocky shrank farther into the chair, farther into herself. "And I'd be okay."

The heavy, clogged feeling in Amalia's torso traveled upward, lodged in her throat. Her hand reached out before she willed it to. Touched the girl's hair, rested on her head. "He was right."

Michael's gaze found Amalia's. Approval and something else lit his eyes.

Something that could almost scare Amalia herself.

She dropped her hand. "Keep fighting, kid." She muttered the words as she stood and stepped behind her chair. Feigned a look at the clock that hung on the wall to the right of the fireplace chimney. "Got to get sleep while I can."

Michael shifted in his chair to watch her. A frown pulled his lips down in an expression she'd much rather see than the unnerving one he'd had moments ago.

She stalked away. Forced her mind to repeat a disciplined mantra she apparently needed. Protect the witness. Get out before the CIA arrived. Simple assignment. She apparently needed to add two more statements, or she'd never survive this job unscathed.

Don't feel. Don't care.

Not about the orphaned kid. Or the man who threatened the secrets that kept her safe and free.

# TWENTY

Michael left his bedroom and glanced over the balcony railing.

Amalia and Raksa stood at the security system control pad by the front door. Maybe they had just returned from patrolling outside. She turned and led the shepherd along the edge of the great room below Michael.

She paused. Looked up.

Even with the distance and dim nighttime lighting, he recognized the Amalia smile she gave him. Probably thought he was trying to spy on her without her notice. He'd seen enough of her skills in action to know he couldn't do that if he tried.

He waved and turned away, pretending the retreat to her Amalia persona didn't churn like a bad oyster in his stomach. That's what it was, too. A retreat. He was sure of it since he'd glimpsed more hints of Sofia during their indoor camp-fire lunch today.

He could've fallen off his chair when she'd comforted and encouraged Rocky with a few simple words. And a sweet, almost maternal gesture.

It was the kind of thing he'd seen Sofia do with many hurting kids in their neighborhood and at church. She'd even comforted him with that honest, compassionate strength more than once.

Michael inched quietly toward the partially open door of Rocky's bedroom. He'd finished telling her a bedtime story about fifteen minutes ago and thought he had better check that she'd been able to go to sleep afterward.

Her soft, small voice reached his ears as he leaned toward the opening, light from the lamp she'd insisted he leave on spilling into the hallway. Who was she talking to?

He shifted his angle and risked pushing the door an inch wider to see.

Rocky lay in bed with Gaston sprawled next to her on the covers. Her skinny arm was flung across the Newfoundland's furry, broad neck, his massive head nestled on the pillow beside Rocky's face.

A smile tugged Michael's mouth at the adorable pair.

"I wish I could stay with them forever."

His chest squeezed as Rocky's quiet words reached him. Did she mean him and Amalia?

"She could be my mommy and Michael could be my daddy." Rocky's breath fluttered the fur on Gaston's ear, both of them apparently unaware Michael was listening.

And that a rush of heat surged up from his chest, seeking his face. Had she read something into the moments he and Amalia had shared at lunch? Not that they required anything to be read into them. They'd been too real and potent to mistake as anything other than what he'd felt. An attraction so strong, it took his breath away.

When Amalia had touched his face, stood only inches away, his heart had thudded hard enough to break out of his ribcage. He couldn't breathe or think about anything other than the gorgeous woman looking down at him, her high cheekbones and perfectly shaped mouth. The black tendrils of hair that swung forward and brushed his neck. The dark eyes that suddenly lit with passion.

"I want to be just like Amalia when I grow up." Rocky's

murmured secret drew Michael out of the memory that had his blood rushing in his ears. "She's a fighter."

Michael braced his hand on the doorframe. Poor kid. Searching so hard for a way to please her dad who wasn't there anymore. Searching for meaning and love in her empty life. His gut clenched. If only he could help her more.

"She keeps people safe. Like Michael and me." Her tone was knowing and wise, as if Gaston needed to learn these details.

Her cuteness brought a smile to Michael's face again.

"But she'll send me back if I tell her my secret."

A frown flipped his mouth.

"Do you want to know my secret?" Her voice lowered to a whisper.

Michael leaned closer to the opening and held his breath as she slid her face closer to Gaston's head.

"I saw men come out of that building. They didn't see me 'cause I hid behind the garbage cans."

Michael's eyes squeezed shut. Poor, scared girl. She never should've been there alone.

"One guy was really mad. He said, 'Kill her tonight. Nobody betrays me like that.'"

Michael held back the shocked burst of air that tried to escape his lungs.

"Then he said to make it look like an accident, and the other man said, 'Okay, Mr. Rottier,' and then they left."

This was huge. She'd even heard them say Rottier's name. No wonder the arms trafficker wanted Rocky dead once he heard the FBI had found a girl at the scene. If he suspected she may have been in the alley to hear and see him...

"Then the lady fell."

Michael had to strain to hear her last words, tightened with fear. Everything in him wanted to go to her, tell her she was safe and it was going to be okay. To try to erase the horrible memory for her somehow.

But then she'd know he'd been listening to the secret she clearly meant only for Gaston's ears. He didn't want to destroy her trust in him or make her feel even more insecure and suspicious.

Amalia needed to know this. And they should tell Agent Nguyen. Rocky could have a bigger target on her back than Michael did.

He crept away from the door and made his way to the staircase on the right as quietly as he could.

A creak sounded on the second stair down. He winced, then kept going. Hopefully, Rocky would drift off now that she'd been able to tell someone her secret. Thank the Lord for dogs like Gaston. He'd heard about the amazing therapeutic abilities of dogs, but he hadn't seen one in action until now. Gaston was the only being Rocky trusted enough to tell her deepest secrets.

Michael scanned the great room at the bottom of the staircase. He walked around the wall that divided part of the entryway from the back of the great room where it opened into a massive kitchen with marble countertops and state-of-the-art, stainless-steel appliances.

Light from the kitchen's inset bulbs glinted off Amalia's black hair as she stepped into the kitchen through the open door that led to the basement.

His pulse picked up speed at the sight of her.

He barely registered that Raksa passed through behind her before she turned to close the door.

What was he going to do about this strange new response to Amalia? She wasn't someone he could become romantically involved with, thanks to her anti-God views and lack of principles. And if he succeeded in bringing Sofia back, he couldn't risk ruining their special friendship with romantic feelings, could he?

"Thought you were in bed." Her statement, touched with a hint of displeasure, brought his focus to where it should be.

Rocky. The news. The danger. "I just checked on Rocky, and she was talking to Gaston."

A quirked eyebrow was her only response, the movement somehow heightening her cheekbones and the dramatic symmetry of her features. Drawing his gaze to linger on her perfect, topaz skin and wonder what it would feel like to touch. *Oh, man.* He was in trouble.

He yanked his attention to the mental image of the scared little girl snuggled up to the Newfoundland upstairs. He closed half the distance between them so he could lower his voice. "She was telling Gaston secrets, and she told him what she saw the night Vicki Wilson died."

Amalia tensed and crossed her arms over her T-shirt as she listened to Michael recount what Rocky had said. When he finished, he braced for her to suggest Rocky had made up the whole story.

"That explains the kidnapping attempt. I'll tell Phoenix, and she can pass it along securely to Nguyen. They're communicating via burner phone right now."

Michael blinked. "You believe her?"

Amalia grinned. "Of course. Nobody lies to Gaston."

"You're kidding, right?"

"Not really. Rocky thought she was telling only a dog, not a person. She's not sophisticated enough to have planned and timed that to happen when you came by."

"Oh. Glad you see that." Relief that he didn't have to argue for Rocky's truthfulness was quickly replaced by irritation. Why hadn't Amalia just believed Rocky earlier when the girl was so hurt that Amalia didn't trust her?

Amalia pulled her phone from her back pocket. "The U. S. Attorney might want to charge Rottier with murder after the arms trafficking trial if they can get evidence to back up Rocky's testimony. It's crazy he was there in person. No wonder he wants the kid dead. There's no way he could know how much she saw or heard."

"Exactly." Michael folded his arms over his chest. "I figured it had to be something like that. Which is why I knew Rocky was telling the truth."

Amalia looked up from her phone. "Just because she told the truth once to my dog doesn't mean she can be trusted." She shoved the device back into her pocket, clearly rethinking phoning Phoenix in front of him. "She lied initially when she said she hadn't seen or heard anything. Then she later told Nguyen she had information, which she wouldn't share. The kid knows when to use a little bit of truth to get what she wants."

"Maybe you should try that."

Her chin tilted, questioning but defensive at the same time.

"Telling a bit of the truth. It'd be a nice change." He heard the frustration that edged his voice but didn't hold back. She needed to see real emotion, the damage she was doing with her lies and secrets.

"Maybe I am telling the truth." That exasperating Amalia smile stretched her mouth wide. "You just don't recognize it."

"And maybe you've told lies for so long you've lost track of what the truth even is."

She laughed, a sound that scraped across his raw nerves. "There is no one truth, Michael. Haven't you figured that out yet?"

"Oh, man." He dropped his arms. "Don't tell me you've bought into that mumbo-jumbo that truth doesn't exist."

A glint flashed in her eyes. "In the real world where I live, you learn pretty fast that everyone has their own idea of truth. It's whatever they choose to believe. That's their truth."

"Come on, Sof—" He barely stopped himself from saying her real name, his breaths coming hard. "You're smarter than that."

"Maybe you're not smart enough. You're living in a dreamworld, Michael."

He coughed a humorless laugh. "Yeah, a dreamworld where facts are facts, good is good, and evil is evil. A world where truth is truth, and nothing will ever change that."

"A world without grays and where you get to be the judge and condemn anyone who doesn't follow your rules, right?" She pushed on before he could answer. "Sometimes doing good requires living in the grays. And that's where you learn truth is a fluid tool, something that changes with each person and situation."

"Then what about the time you lit into Brent Jackson at school when he said your parents were stupid because they couldn't speak much English? Was that fine because he was speaking his truth?"

"Of course not. He was hurting people."

"There, you see?" He moistened his lips and stared at her with a force he hoped would knock some sense into her. "You know there's right from wrong, you know there's real truth. If there wasn't, how would you know what to fight for?"

She narrowed her eyes. "I fight for freedom and justice. The protection of this country and the people in it by whatever means I have to. And that requires knowing truth doesn't matter unless it serves the greater good."

"I thought you were arguing there isn't any truth at all. But then you said it's fluid, and now you're saying it just doesn't matter." He lifted an exasperated hand into the air. "The irony is those are all truth statements. No one can make any claim without simultaneously claiming it's the truth."

She glanced away, lips pressed into a straight line. Then she returned her gaze and shrugged one shoulder, her features relaxing slightly as her eyes cooled. "That's your truth. And you have a right to believe it because you want to." She was retreating into the Amalia persona again. To that person who didn't even exist but had somehow stolen Sofia from him.

"No." His pain thickened his voice. "I have to believe the truth because it's *true*. Just like I have to believe in God because *He* is true." Michael pushed a hand through his hair, letting his fingers linger at the back of his head. "You know the truth as well as I do, Sofie." He met her gaze, hoping she saw his hurt and conviction reflected in his eyes. "You're only lying to yourself now. And we both know where lies lead."

Her jaw clenched as she abruptly stalked past him

without another glance. "Phoenix? I have news about the kid."

Michael turned to see her march away with Raksa, her phone pressed to her ear.

She'd finally talked to him. Honestly, as far as he could tell. But he had the terrible feeling, sinking like a rock to the pit of his stomach, that after this heated conversation, he'd seen his last glimpse of Sofia.

---

*"You know the truth as well as I do, Sofie."*

Sofie.

Amalia reached the balcony and stopped there with Raksa.

That nickname. The one only Michael had ever used.

He'd flung so many words and claims at her during the heated debate earlier. Accused and judged. He'd tried to get to her by using arguments, emotion, and even her past as weapons. But she was impervious to such tactics. Trained to be invincible.

But that nickname. He'd found the crack in her armor and shot through, straight to the heart that still twinged with the pain of the hit.

And she didn't know why. How could a simple nickname carry so much weight?

Raksa fidgeted at her side, and she squatted down beside him, petted the bristly fur on his back.

She stared down at the great room where Nevaeh was posted near the front door with Alvarez. But her thoughts weren't on security.

The ache in her chest that had started when Michael called her Sofie kept growing in strength. Pressed against her breastbone until she reached to rub the spot. But it didn't help. The discomfort was too deep inside.

She didn't want to name it. Couldn't.

But it was a more intense version of the pang she'd felt when she'd tasted the changua Michael had made.

Longing. But for what? Her parents? She could call them. It wouldn't kill her to do that, would it? But she'd have to lie to them. A lot. She'd gotten tired of that. Emails were easier.

And what good would it do to talk to them? She couldn't go back to being who they'd want her to be. She couldn't ever be Sofia again.

The ache exploded into a stabbing pain.

No. That couldn't be the cause of the longing.

But there was no denying the visceral reaction inside her. And what prompted it.

Some small part of her wished she could go back, become Sofia again.

How would she do that? She didn't believe most of what Sofia had, except the importance of doing whatever it took to protect the people she cared about.

But that was just it. She didn't care about anyone anymore. Couldn't afford to.

She knew better now. She'd grown up and become the person she needed to be to protect herself and get the job done.

But who was that person? The rebellious thought twisted her insides.

She'd had so many false identities for so many years.

Who was she?

She stopped scratching Raksa's head and stood, her hand going to grip the railing as if she needed the support. Because she didn't know the answer to that question. If those were false identities, what was her real one?

"Mals, are you okay?" Nevaeh's voice in Amalia's ear nearly made her start.

But Amalia Pérez was never startled. At least she knew that much. Amalia clung to that small semblance of reality as she cleared her throat before responding on coms. "Yeah, fine. Checking on Package Two."

"Roger." Nevaeh waved from the great room below.

Great. Now Nevaeh might wonder why Amalia had been acting strange. Could even tell others on the team. Thanks to Michael.

As she started toward Rocky's room for the usual periodic check, this one at four a.m., she turned the accusation on herself. More her fault than Michael's. She knew better than to let anyone get under her skin. It was her own weakness that made her vulnerable.

She paused at Rocky's partially closed door and pushed it open as her mind rambled on. Maybe he was savvier than she thought and had intentionally used the nostalgia-charged nickname to bring down her guard. Either way, she needed to get her head back in the game and—

Her breath froze in her lungs.

Rocky's bed was empty.

# TWENTY-ONE

Pounding threatened the peace of Michael's dream—a walk with Sofia through the woods as a group of kids trailed behind them.

The pounding grew louder.

His eyes popped open.

"Jazz! Go time!" Amalia's voice, loud and grim, yanked Michael out of bed. He ran to his door and pulled it open.

Amalia and Raksa stepped back from the bedroom at the other end of the balcony as Jazz and Flash emerged.

Amalia and Jazz spoke in low voices he couldn't hear.

He hurried past Rocky's bedroom door, trying to be quiet in case the knocking hadn't already woken her. "What's wrong?" He whispered the question as he reached the women and their K-9s.

Amalia turned toward him. Her gaze dropped below his neck, then traveled back up.

Heat surged to his face as he realized he'd forgotten to pull on a shirt before running out of his room. At least he was already wearing pajama pants. But judging from Amalia dragging Jazz out of bed, there was something more serious at stake right now than a missing shirt.

"The kid is gone." Amalia brushed past him as if she hadn't just stopped his heart with those words.

"Rocky? She's missing?" He padded after her on bare feet.

Jazz and Flash crowded behind him as he followed Amalia's quick clip down the wide staircase.

"But I just saw her with Gaston. Just a few hours ago, I think. What time is it?"

"Five after four."

He glanced at Jazz over his shoulder as she responded, then looked at Amalia as they reached the bottom of the stairs. "So it was like four hours ago when I saw her." He moistened his lips. "Amalia."

She finally stopped moving. Angled partially toward him.

"Was she kidnapped?"

"No." Amalia met his gaze head-on. "Gaston was with her. He's not a guard dog, but he's extremely protective of children. He would never let anyone take her, especially not without a fight or a whole lot of barking and growling."

Michael nodded, clinging to her every word for comfort and hope that Rocky was safe somehow.

"You checked on her at one thirty?" Jazz stepped even with Michael as she asked Amalia the question.

"Yeah. She and Gaston were there. She appeared to be asleep."

"Phoenix is on her way." Nevaeh hurried to join the group, Alvarez panting as he trotted along with her. "She's bringing Bristol and Cora."

"Are their dogs the ones that also do search and rescue?"

"Yep." Nevaeh swung her attention to Michael. "Raksa and Flash..." Her voice drifted off as her gaze locked on his chest, eyes slightly widened.

"Nevaeh." Amalia's sharp tone jerked Nevaeh's focus to her.

A smile played on the woman's lips as she finished her thought. "I was just saying Raksa and Flash are SAR K-9s, too."

He rubbed at the heat on the back of his neck. He really should go upstairs and grab a shirt. But he didn't dare leave right now. "So are we going to start looking for her?"

"*We* aren't going anywhere." Amalia gave him only a cursory glance before she swung her attention to her Phoenix K-9 team. "I'm going to start searching with Raksa. You two stay here with him."

"Wait a minute—"

"I'll take the satellite phone." She continued as if she hadn't heard Michael's protest. "Let me know when Phoenix gets here." She turned away.

"Amalia, wait." He grabbed her arm.

She stopped, and her gaze dropped to glare at his hand.

He let go. "I want to come with you. I need to."

She raised her eyes but shook her head without looking at him. "Too dangerous."

"I'm not afraid of the danger. Rocky's out there alone somewhere. I don't care if I get shot."

She met his gaze then, her expression hard. "You would only slow me down."

Meaning, she'd get to Rocky faster if he let her go alone. At least she hadn't flashed that infernal smile when she said it.

He swallowed. Nodded. He only wanted Rocky found, safe and sound, as quickly as possible. If that meant staying out of the way, then that's what he'd do.

Nevaeh handed Amalia a knapsack he'd seen Amalia carry when she'd arrived at the safe houses before. "Looks like her footprints are outside the back door. Trail headed down to the water, at least initially."

"So she just walked out of the house by herself?" His mind tried to comprehend what had happened.

Nevaeh's mouth curved in a bemused smile. "Well, Gaston went with her. She used the code to disarm the alarm system herself."

Jazz's eyes widened. "She must've watched one of us do it earlier."

"Pretty smart, really."

Amalia sent Nevaeh a look that bordered on irritated as she slipped her arms through the straps of the knapsack.

"Not smart enough to follow her head instead of her emotions."

Ah. Not irritation with Nevaeh. Amalia was angry at Rocky. Did that mean she was starting to care about the girl?

Hope stirred within as he watched her. "You think she ran away? But why would she? She loved it here." She'd admitted to Gaston she wanted to stay with Michael and Amalia forever, though he figured it was best not to share that tidbit right now.

"You can ask her when we find her." Amalia spun away, and Raksa immediately matched her determined stride through the great room.

As she disappeared around the corner, Michael's gaze landed on the curtained wall of windows across the large room. His pulse pounded as he pictured Rocky, lost and alone except for a dog, somewhere in the dark woods.

More dangers than Rottier's hired killers could lurk there.

"Lord, please cover Rocky with your protection." The prayer spilled out, unabated by the presence of Nevaeh and Jazz. "Help Amalia find her quickly. Please, bring them both safely home."

A quiet snap.

Amalia jerked toward the sound. Stared into the darkness beyond the tree trunks.

Raksa kept moving just ahead of her, off leash so he had more freedom to work.

The soft glow of dawn's beginning lightened the thick forest only a fraction. In the hour she and Raksa had been searching, her eyes had adjusted to the darkness. Enough to be confident no movement accompanied the sound she'd heard in the trees to the left.

She continued on. A drop of water penetrated her hair and trailed down her neck. She hadn't put up the hood of her windbreaker when it had started to rain. The thick leaves of the trees above blocked much of it.

But more drops broke through now. Faster. The noise of a downpour reached her ears just before the deluge.

She yanked up her hood as the rain poured down, wetting the precious trail of footprints. Lucky Gaston had been with the girl. Her prints sometimes disappeared, but the big Newfie had four feet and 165 pounds of weight spread across them. His giant paws left deep and broad, bear-like imprints in the dirt and leaves.

But this rain could wash them away in a few minutes.

A sick feeling churned her gut. Had Rocky brought any weather protection? The nighttime temperature had dropped into the low sixties. If she'd left the house in only her pajama T-shirt and shorts, she could've gotten chilled. Especially if she was soaked.

Amalia shoved away the image of a shivering Rocky as she followed Raksa. Gaston would take care of the kid.

And since when had she started caring so much? She'd let Michael make her question her identity and want to be the person she could never be again. And now she was acting like a mother hen over a streetwise kid who'd turn on her in a second if it served the girl's interest.

Amalia would not make the mistake of caring again. This was a straight-forward SAR mission. Nothing more.

The ring of the satellite phone broke through the shower of rain.

"Raksa, here." The shepherd stopped sniffing the air and jogged back to her as she swung her knapsack to her front and pulled out the phone. "Pérez."

"We've started out." Phoenix's voice came through loud and clear. "Dag has a trail."

Must still have it even with the rain washing things away. Just the leg up they needed.

"We'll stay with the trail as long as we can. Bristol and Cora are following with their K-9s in the Jeep. If Dag loses the trail, we'll park and go on foot from there."

And join Raksa's efforts to find the girl's scent in the air. "Roger. I've been following visual trail, but it's washing away."

A sound reached Amalia's ears, carried on the rain instead of hushed by it.

A truck, whooshing by on a wet road.

Her heart rate accelerated. "The trail leads to a road. Or at least near it."

"Could be Blyly Road. If the trail leads there, follow it. Raksa might pick up a scent if you're getting closer to her. Keep me posted."

"Roger." Amalia shoved the phone back into the knapsack and pushed her arm through the other strap. "Raksa, search."

The shepherd happily loped away from her again, his nose in the air as he tried to find a scent.

The trees suddenly stopped, formed a wall-like line that bordered a ditch of tall grass. Past the grass and weeds, the soft light of dawn illuminated a paved road.

Tension cinched her muscles. Had Rocky followed the road? Crossed it?

Amalia jogged across the wet blacktop, keeping an eye on Raksa in case traffic suddenly appeared.

She stopped on the other side of the road. No tracks in the mud along the gravel shoulder. But the rain could've washed the tracks away by now, especially out in the open without leaves to slow its progress. Or Rocky could've crossed farther down.

"Where would you go, Rocky?"

A city kid, lost in the wilderness, intent on getting away. Why, Amalia didn't know yet. But she did know people and what made them tick. Rocky was a stranger to nature. She'd be scared out here. She'd want people and civilization—the familiar.

Closest town to the safe house's remote location was Trickle City. And they'd driven through it on their way to the house. Rocky had said something about the name being funny.

Certainty settled the swirling in Amalia's belly just as her gaze landed on Raksa, who jogged along the road. Already headed in the right direction.

A smile curved her mouth. All she had to do was trust her K-9. He didn't appear to have a scent yet, but his instincts were on the money.

If they followed the road north back to Trickle City, they'd likely find Rocky in no time.

Unless someone else already had.

# TWENTY-TWO

"Not sure Cora's aunt will be okay with you digging a ditch in her floor."

"What?" Michael paused and turned to see Nevaeh and Alvarez watching him from the kitchen.

"You've been pacing in the same spot for like twenty minutes." A half-smile softened her expression.

"Oh. Sorry." He stared out the massive windows at the sunset-bathed trees and the path down to the water that Rocky may have taken last night. And then gone where? Was she scared right now, wherever she was? Was she hurt?

He swallowed, maybe for the last time given how tightly his throat was closing with worry. What if Rottier's men had found her?

"Hey." Neveah came to stand beside him. "The PK-9 team is the best. We'll find her." Her eyes were soft with sympathy. For how he felt or because she wasn't sure what she said was true?

*Please, God. Give Amalia and the team wings of speed and guidance to find Rocky before Rottier does. Before anything can happen to her.*

"And she's got Gaston with her. He'll take good care of her." Nevaeh smiled.

He tried to return the smile but failed miserably. "I hope so. I wish I could be out there. Doing something. I feel so..."

"Helpless?" Her smile turned rueful as she finished the sentence he'd let trail off. "I know the feeling."

Michael looked at her. An elite security specialist at Phoenix K-9 knew how it felt to be helpless? "That's hard to believe."

She shrugged and moved her gaze to the window. "You'd be surprised." She stayed silent a few more seconds, then turned to walk away.

A moment later, her voice drifted to him. "I saw your Bible with your stuff."

Michael shifted to see Nevaeh, paused ten feet away.

"Cora says that helps. It's not for me, but maybe it'd help you."

"You're right." And Michael should've thought of seeking God's comfort, rather than only His intervention. But God would always find a way to get His child's attention. "Thanks."

Nevaeh gave a quick nod and continued on her way.

"Lord, forgive me for choosing fear and worry over the peace you offer." Michael pulled out his phone from his back pocket. Handy to have a digital Bible there, too.

He went to the sofa and sat as he brought up the Bible app and selected the Psalms. As he read, comfort and the peace that surpassed all understanding slowly started to rein in his erratic pulse and unwind the knots in his stomach.

An alert popped up on the phone's screen, blocking his view of the Scripture verses.

New email. From Agent Carter.

His heart rate sprinted again as he opened the message. He skimmed past the friendly greetings to see what information Carter had found about Sofia.

*Sorry to say I can't find any info on Amalia Pérez or Sofia Sanchez.*

Michael's heart thudded to a stop and dropped to his stomach. No. This couldn't be a dead end. How would he help her, get Sofia back, if he couldn't find out what had happened to her?

He continued to read. Maybe there was something useful farther on.

*Can't say anything regarding Phoenix Gray. It's classified.*

Classified? Why would information about Phoenix Gray be classified with the FBI? Why did she even have a file with the FBI?

His reporter's mind lit up, sorting through possibilities and theories.

*About Pérez or Sanchez, have you checked with the CIA?*

The CIA. That could fit. She would've received extensive training for the CIA. Including training in how to lie and deceive even better than she already could before. It would explain her secrecy, the multiple identities. But he didn't have any contacts with the CIA, and it wasn't as if a clandestine organization would tell him about one of their agents.

*Try emailing Kenneth Owens. He owes me a favor.*

A smile found Michael's lips. Carter had come through again. Or maybe he should say God had. Carter even gave Michael an email address and direct line to Owens at the CIA.

Probably not the kind of email he should send from his phone. He stood and went to the stairs, jogging up them two at a time.

He plunked down in the chair by the desk in his massive room and opened his computer to compose the email. He asked only about Sofia Sanchez this time. If she'd been with the CIA, maybe she had joined or been recruited right out of college.

Hopefully, he'd have his answers soon. And the key to bringing Sofia back, to freeing her from the web of secrets and lies that threatened to keep her trapped forever.

He may not know what had happened to her in the twelve years since she left him and her parents. But he knew, every time he looked into her eyes, that she was lost. As lost as Rocky. And just as much in need of rescue.

Raksa's body froze, nose in the air.

He had the scent.

Amalia's pulse took off at the same instant Raksa launched into a run and bolted up the quiet main street that cut through one side of the small town.

Amalia sprinted after him. Yanked the satellite phone from her knapsack. Managed to dial Phoenix's number as she ran, kept her breathing steady. "Raksa's got her scent."

"Where are you?" The sound of the same wind that swept through Amalia's hair backdropped Phoenix's voice.

"Trickle City."

Raksa veered hard right into someone's yard.

"We're close to there. Dag is still tracking."

"Roger." Amalia lowered the phone from her ear, gripped it in her hand as she pumped her arms, pushed to keep up. Through the yard, past the house, along the back fence.

Another yard.

A street.

Raksa barked as he turned left onto the road. Cut through another yard.

A different dog barked in response, but the shepherd didn't look, didn't slow.

Amalia's breath started to come hard. She pushed her legs faster.

Rocky had to be close.

The shepherd let out another bark as he veered right.

Amalia sucked in air, kept her pace. Reached the spot where he'd turned off. She followed onto the grassy area that opened up to clusters of trees and paths. A park.

Her gaze caught the sign that blurred as she raced past. She lifted the phone to her mouth. "Trickle Lake Park."

"Roger." Phoenix must have kept the line open on her end, too.

Raksa barked. Three times.

Amalia ran out from a group of trees. Spotted the shepherd.

He raced toward a long dock that stretched out from the shore onto a medium-sized lake.

A big, deep *woof* resounded.

Gaston.

Amalia's heart surged as her gaze jerked toward the sound.

The brown dog stood at the end of the dock, fifty feet out from the shore.

And a skinny girl in baggy jeans and a purple T-shirt stood beside him.

Energy pumped through Amalia's muscles as something warm and wonderful surged from her torso out to her fingertips. "Rocky!" The call exploded from her lips.

The girl spun her direction. Slipped.

Fell.

Off the dock. Into the water.

Disappeared.

# TWENTY-THREE

Ice shot through Amalia's veins as Rocky vanished from view.

A loud bark rang out. Gaston jumped off the dock, his huge body launching into the water just as Raksa reached where they had been.

"Raksa, wait!" Amalia shouted the command as she ran, kicking up sand on the shore. She hit the dock, lifted the phone to her mouth. "Package fell into lake. Rescue in progress."

She didn't wait for an answer as she jogged to the end of the dock, scanning the water. The wind created choppy waves that wouldn't slow Gaston. But who knew if Rocky could even swim?

Splashes yanked Amalia's attention farther from the dock than she'd been looking.

Rocky coughed, choked as she struggled to do a basic front crawl stroke twenty feet from the dock. But her body started to sink under. Her jeans and shoes were probably too heavy for her.

Gaston's head bobbed above the waves only a few feet from the girl.

"Rocky!" Amalia threw her voice as loudly as she could. "Gaston is coming to rescue you. Hug him around his neck."

The Newfoundland paddled up close and came alongside her exactly as he'd been trained.

Rocky splashed, flailed her arms.

"Rocky! Look at Gaston! Give him a big hug!"

He turned his head and nudged the girl under her arm.

The contact broke through her panic. Rocky looked at him, threw her arms around his neck.

"Good girl!"

Gaston automatically headed for shore. The strong dog paddled easily through the choppy water as Rocky held on.

Amalia dashed back up the dock, Raksa running with her. She kept checking on the swimmers as she reached the shore and turned to jog to where Gaston headed in.

"Come on, Gaston! Good boy." The encouragement was more for Amalia than the Newfoundland. He was born for this work. Adored it more than anything.

Amalia's pulse raced as she stepped into the water, shallow along the shore. Cold shocked her legs as the water soaked through her jeans. She kept her gaze locked on Gaston and Rocky.

Just a little closer.

She resisted the urge to jump in and swim to Gaston. He could bring Rocky in more easily than Amalia could. She needed to let him do his job.

A few more feet. She waded farther in, closed the remaining distance between them. She put her arms around Rocky's small waist and lifted her.

The girl swiveled, instantly threw her arms around Amalia's neck, and pressed her small wet body close.

Warmth swelled in Amalia's torso. Maybe to combat the cold of the water. Or maybe because Amalia was starting to care about the kid.

She shoved the thought from her mind as she wrapped her arms tighter around Rocky. Though with the way the girl squeezed Amalia, there was no way she was going to fall.

As Amalia trudged through the water, her gaze caught movement.

Two people walked toward the beach. A woman with a small white dog on a leash and a middle-aged man in a reflective jacket, probably both out for ill-timed morning walks.

"Is she okay?" The woman put her hand over her eyes to shield the sun that rose over the lake behind Amalia.

"Yes." Amalia flashed a smile as she walked onto dry land, Gaston in step beside her. "We're fine, thanks."

A black Jeep pulled into the parking lot, sunlight glinting off the silver bumper. Bristol's Jeep.

Good. The PK-9 team could deal with crowd control while Amalia focused on Rocky.

Gaston shook his entire body, splashing water everywhere, including Amalia's face.

She leaned over to set Rocky on her feet.

The girl cinched her legs around Amalia's waist and squeezed her neck harder.

"It's okay, Rocky." She stroked the girl's back gently. "You're safe now." That pinching sensation beneath her breastbone spread and pushed against her skeleton as if trying to get out. Fighting for release. Amalia leaned her head toward Rocky's, pressed to her shoulder. She touched her lips to the girl's wet hair as her voice lowered to a whisper. "I've got you."

Cora and Bristol jogged past the bystanders who had increased to four people now, thanks to the addition of an elderly male cyclist and a male runner who stopped to watch the show. Phoenix approached at a walk with Dag, her keen gaze no doubt perceiving there was no cause for alarm.

Cora's bright eyes glistened with concern as she reached Amalia and Rocky. "Is she all right?"

"I think so. Haven't been able to look at her yet."

"We called the ambulance just in case." Bristol glanced back to where Phoenix walked around the bystanders.

A siren wailed, not far away. The ambulance was probably dispatched from the fire station Amalia had run past on her way to the lake.

"Rocky, I need to put you down now. Okay?"

The girl's head slid in a nod on Amalia's shoulder.

She leaned down, and Rocky dropped her feet to the ground, finally releasing her choke hold.

Amalia scanned Rocky for any visible sign of injury as Cora squatted in front of the girl with a gentle smile. "I'm so sorry you fell in, sweetie."

A slash of something dark marred Rocky's forehead.

Amalia's chest squeezed. "Is that a cut?" She dipped her chin toward Rocky.

Cora looked closely. Touched the area around the wound. "Yes. But it's not as bad as it looks. I think there's some mud on it, too."

The siren blared as a white and red ambulance pulled into the parking lot.

It wasn't alone. A police squad followed quietly behind.

"Do you know where you got this cut, honey?" Cora's question drew Amalia's attention back to the girl.

Rocky nodded. "A branch."

"In the woods?" Cora examined the cut more.

Rocky shrugged. "It was dark."

Relief trickled through Amalia's muscles, relieving their tautness. The kid was back to acting tough. Protecting herself.

The best thing for both of them.

Two EMTs hurried over. "Hi, there. How's everyone doing?" The woman homed in on Rocky while the male EMT hung back and held their equipment bag. He glanced at Amalia's soaked jeans. "Did you pull her out?"

"He did." She tilted her head toward the Newfoundland who hovered close to Rocky, his wet, feathered tail swishing.

"Wow. A water rescue dog?" He peered at Gaston with a smile.

"Trained and certified."

"Awesome. Are you okay?" He glanced at her again.

"Fine."

"Are you her mother?" He looked toward Rocky.

"Yes."

Rocky's gaze jumped to Amalia. Then her small mouth curved upward.

Amalia winked.

Rocky's smile broke wider, showing her teeth as her eyes lit up.

That disturbing warmth ballooned inside and filled Amalia's body. "Jessica Banks." She gave the EMT a motherly smile as he jotted down her name.

"Cora." Phoenix's deep voice was much closer than Amalia realized her boss had come. Only Phoenix could manage to surprise her. Or maybe she was letting herself be too distracted by this situation.

Amalia pulled her gaze from watching the EMT clean Rocky's cut. Couldn't let anyone else catch her off guard.

Cora nodded to Phoenix and headed toward the bystanders. What was she—

A woman wearing a hat and clutching a small child's hand somehow still managed to hold up her smart phone. Recording.

Alarm spiked Amalia's nerves. She couldn't be in a video likely to end up online. The CIA would easily find Amalia with that kind of help. And Rocky couldn't appear online either. Rottier's people could see it.

Phoenix stepped in front of Amalia, her taller frame blocking Amalia's view. And blocking the woman's shot. "Cora will get her to delete the recording."

If anyone could do that, Cora could. Her persuasive talents were legendary at PK-9, even though her honest and empathetic technique was the opposite of Amalia's.

"I have to deal with the police." Meaning, Phoenix was going to step away.

"Got it." Amalia checked on Rocky. The EMTs had her sitting on the ground between them and the woman with the camera. Rocky also faced away from her. Should be safe. The woman better not be live streaming to her social media.

Phoenix turned back, whipped off her baseball cap and handed it to Amalia.

She stared at the cap. Phoenix rarely went without it. And Amalia had never seen her share any of her personal belongings with anyone. Wasn't her style. If Amalia's suspicions about the reasons for the mysterious aura her boss cultivated were right, Phoenix would want to avoid being recognized in a video as much as Amalia.

But Amalia snatched the cap before she irritated her boss with her delay.

Phoenix swiveled and strode with Dag toward the police officer that Bristol must have intercepted before he reached Rocky and Amalia. She stood talking to him. Maybe about being a former cop herself. Because she shouldn't be giving him more information than that given the security risks that would pose for Rocky and potentially Michael. Couldn't have their names transmitted over radios or included in police records where they could be easily heard or seen.

Phoenix would likely tell the cop to call the Minneapolis FBI field office and ask for Agent Nguyen with the clearance code she had for such situations.

"Okay." The lady EMT stood and smiled down at Rocky. "She's all good to go." The woman turned toward Amalia. "Nothing serious. Just a minor cut. No stiches needed."

"Great." Amalia extended her hand to the EMT. "Thanks for your help."

The woman returned the handshake. "No problem." She glanced at Rocky one more time. "Just try not to fall into any lakes again, okay?" She chuckled and walked away as the other EMT fell in step beside her.

The crowd beyond them was finally breaking up. The old man on the bicycle was already yards away, the runner must have left a while ago, and the woman who'd been recording walked away with her child. The woman with the white dog was nowhere to be seen. And the other random people Amalia had been too busy to take stock of also dispersed.

A light touch on her back drew her attention. Rocky had closed the distance between them and leaned against

Amalia's hip, her small hand a warm pressure through Amalia's windbreaker.

Amalia stiffened. Not good. She couldn't have the kid thinking she had meant anything by telling the EMT she was the girl's mom. It was a cover like everything else. This kid was not going to get Amalia to care. To be soft and vulnerable.

But her own hand rebelled against reason, drifted to Rocky's head, smoothed her damp hair.

Cora walked toward them, a gentle smile on her face. Good. Cora could take over the mothering. She was made for that kind of thing.

Amalia used Cora's approach as a reason to pull away from Rocky.

"Ready to go home, Rocky?" Home. Only in Cora's unstoppably positive thinking could one of many safe houses be considered a home.

"Did you get rid of the video?"

Cora switched her blue gaze to Amalia as she stopped in front of them. "Yes, praise the Lord. Tracy agreed to let me delete the video from her phone when she learned it could endanger our lovely girl here." She turned a smile on Rocky with the last statement.

Amalia couldn't help but grin at Cora's unbelievable personality. She was already on a first-name basis with the woman who'd wanted to capture a near-tragedy to boost her social media numbers.

"What?" Cora gave Amalia an innocent look.

"You're something else, Cora."

"So I've been told." Her eyes twinkled as she laughed.

Amalia chuckled as she glanced at her boys. "Raksa, Gaston, let's go."

The K-9s followed behind as they headed for the parking lot.

"I need my backpack." Rocky's unamused statement brought Amalia's attention back to the girl who walked at her side. She looked up at Amalia, sporting a cartoon-decorated bandage on her forehead that seemed an odd accessory for such a tough kid.

"Where is it?"

"Over there." Rocky pointed to a stand of trees beyond the parking lot. Looked like a picnic table stood near the trees with a lump beneath it. Probably the backpack. "I'll get it. Cora can take you and Gaston to the Jeep."

"Raksa, with me." The shepherd jogged with Amalia to the picnic table where Rocky had stashed her backpack.

Amalia looked at the flattened grass under the table. Had Rocky slept there part of the night?

The image of the small girl, alone and scared in the dark, twisted Amalia's stomach.

But by the time she and Raksa rejoined the PK-9 crew at Bristol's Jeep, Cora and Rocky were snuggled on the back seat together, the girl getting all the maternal comfort she needed from a woman much better suited to the job.

Perfect. Amalia clearly needed space and time to shut down the dangerous feelings she was having. Yes, feelings. The deadliest risk of all.

She volunteered to stay behind when Phoenix said someone would need to wait at the park since there wasn't room in Bristol's Jeep for the whole group. Especially with Toby's crate in the rear.

But Cora insisted Amalia get to the house to change out of her wet clothes.

Her pants had already half-dried in the warm sun, but Phoenix seemed to buy the reasoning. Told Bristol to stay and Amalia to get in.

She put Raksa in Toby's crate, abandoned by the black lab who would wait with Bristol. Gaston had already found a spot to squeeze in by Cora and Rocky.

Amalia sat in the front passenger seat as Phoenix drove the Jeep out of the parking lot. At least Phoenix wouldn't try to talk to her. Amalia needed the time to refocus. Get her emotions under the rigid control she'd had over them for three years. She stared out the window. Refused to relive the way her heart had frozen at the sight of Rocky falling into the water.

She forced her mind on the more important memory to keep close. The lesson learned.

*"You can be like my mother, Casho. Yes?"* Ahmed watched her with an adorable, crooked smile as he asked the question, hope in his dark eyes.

*"Yes. Just like that."* She wrapped him in a hug, and he giggled.

*Two days later, he stared at her over the barrel of his AK-47. Hate and victory blazed in the eyes of the homeless street kid she thought she'd befriended.*

*She'd been played.*

*Bullets spattered.*

*She dropped. Rolled.*

*Applied her years of training to outwit the enemy. Got around him.*

*He spun to face her. To kill her.*

*But she shot first.*

# TWENTY-FOUR

"No." Nevaeh held up a hand to block Michael's attempt to run out the front door of the safe house. "It's safer if you wait inside. They'll be here in a sec."

Considering she had a hefty rottweiler mix at her side who stared at Michael with caution in his eyes, Michael shifted back on his heels with a nod. Reined in the urge to push the slim woman aside and rush out to take Rocky and Amalia in his arms and—

*Whoa, boy.* He stepped away and angled so Nevaeh wouldn't see any giveaway of his thoughts on his face, though she'd turned back to the door. The image that flashed in his mind, the scene of those desires, showed him as the dad, the husband. Of a family that didn't exist.

He ran a hand down his face, ending on the scruff he needed to trim. Man, had he let himself get carried away. It was one thing to care about the well-being of an orphan girl who probably had a hit out on her. But he wasn't her dad. He couldn't be.

And he wasn't even going to let himself get into the part Amalia had in his brief, crazy vision. Sofia was his best friend. Amalia was...should be nothing to him. Their beliefs and world views were polar opposites. She saw him as a job to finish. He should only allow himself to entertain the feelings his imagination had conjured if she became Sofia again. Then, maybe... They were grown up now. Maybe something could change. Maybe a shift in their affections for each other wouldn't be a bad thing.

The door opened, cutting into his dangerous thoughts with the most joyous sight he'd seen in a long time.

Rocky and Gaston trudged through the door with Amalia just behind them.

"Rocky!" Michael crouched and opened his arms wide.

The little girl beamed a smile and ran into his embrace, nearly knocking him over with her enthusiasm.

His heart swelled until he thought it might crack as he hugged her through the towel wrapped around her shoulders. "I was so worried, Rocky. So worried about you."

Looked like Amalia's jeans were wet, too.

His gaze traveled up, found her face. Where a smile rested on her mouth as she watched him and Rocky. A smile so real, so Sofia, it took the air right out of his lungs. Oh, yes. He could learn to love her in a different way.

"Gaston saved me!" Rocky pulled back, that happy smile lighting her eyes as she rested her small hands on Michael's shoulders.

"Di—" Thickness stuck the word in his throat. He cleared it and chuckled. "Did he really?"

"Uh-huh." She twisted around to see the big dog who wagged his tail at her attention. She waved him over, and he wasted no time closing in, sharing the slobbery love with Michael. "I fell in the water, but Gaston got me out."

Michael laughed at the Newfoundland's friendly snuffles wetting his cheeks. He stroked the dog's ears. "Well, I guess I owe you a debt of gratitude, Gaston." He looked into the dog's bearish face and had to laugh again at the happy-go-lucky expression that stared back.

"What's a debt?"

Michael brushed Rocky's soft hair back from her face. "A debt of gratitude basically means that I'm very thankful to Gaston and to God for keeping you safe." He stood and transferred his gaze to Amalia. "And to you for bringing her back." He hadn't caught the change before the words were out of his mouth.

But she'd switched to the wide Amalia smile. Coolness took up residence in her eyes again. "Well, it wasn't exactly how I planned to spend my evening. But I would've been babysitting you if not her." She laughed.

Confusion and hurt swirled in Michael's stomach. What had happened? Softness and authenticity one second, and then a full Amalia disguise in place the next.

"So now that we're all safe and sound," Amalia locked her attention on Rocky, "I want to know why you ran off."

The girl clutched the towel, holding it closed in front of her chest. She avoided Amalia's gaze.

"Come on, Rocky. You just caused all of us a ton of trouble. Not to mention we're going to have to move to another location now, thanks to you."

"Now, hold on." Michael held up a hand to stop more accusations. "I'm sure Rocky didn't mean to cause you any problems." The girl stepped closer to him and pressed against his leg. "Things are hard enough for everyone as it is. She didn't ask to be in this situation."

"Actually," Amalia glared as she crossed her arms over her black T-shirt and open windbreaker, "she did. She asked to stay with us in exchange for information she still hasn't given us."

"But you already know." Rocky's small voice veered their attention to her.

"What do you mean?" Amalia's tone didn't lose its edge. Did she have to scare the girl after all she'd been through?

"I heard you." Rocky tipped her head up toward Michael. "You told her my secret."

A twinge of guilt pinged in his chest. But he'd done the right thing. "It's not good to keep secrets, Rocky. Especially dangerous ones. I heard you tell Gaston and knew I had to share it with Amalia, so we would be able to keep you safe and keep the bad men away from you."

"But now you know." A frown tugged Rocky's lips downward and pulled at his heart. "I was afraid you'd send me back to Helping Smiles."

"Of course we wouldn't do that. You should've talked to me about it instead of running off." Amalia lowered her arms and stepped closer. "You'll never have to go back there again."

Michael's gaze shot to Amalia's. Was that another lie? Sounded like the most blatant, hurtful one he'd heard from her yet.

"Really?" The hope that lifted Rocky's voice stabbed him in the gut.

He opened his mouth to say something, to challenge Amalia or see if there was any semblance of truth in her statement.

"We have to move them." Phoenix's deep tone cut him off before he could start. "Now."

Where had she come from? He vaguely recollected her and Cora entering behind Amalia and Rocky, but he'd been so focused on the first two that he hadn't noticed where they'd gone afterward.

Amalia jerked a nod. "A video?"

Cora looked up from her smartphone as she walked down the staircase, carrying Rocky's duffel bag in her other hand. "Nothing online yet. I deleted Tracy's on her phone, but I can't be positive no one else recorded or posted something. Everyone loves the online spotlight these days and everyone has camera phones at the ready."

"Yeah. We've gotten too much attention now thanks to the park scene." At least Amalia didn't look directly at Rocky this time with the insinuation.

"Rocky, how about you change into dry clothes in the bathroom down here? And then you'll be ready to go in a jiffy." Cora graced Rocky with a sweet smile as she approached the girl and put a gentle hand on her back to guide her away.

"Was that really necessary?" Michael kept his voice low as

he stepped closer to Amalia, her German shepherd between them.

"Careful, Barrett. That kid will eat you for lunch."

He bit back irritation at her switch to his last name. "She's a little girl. Not a shark."

"If you want to get hurt, that's your business. My business is keeping you both alive." She spun on her heel and stalked away, Raksa sticking close as if his owner wasn't the prickliest woman on earth.

"Get packed, Mr. Barrett." Phoenix's command made him startle and turn her way.

She stood in the shadow between the banister and the wall.

Okay. Maybe Amalia wasn't the prickliest. But she'd run a very close second.

"Cora brought a cot you can use for off times in the hallway upstairs." Phoenix marched down the narrow staircase of the next safe house with Dag ahead of Amalia and Raksa.

"Got it." Amalia scanned the living room where the staircase ended. Though this house was located in a remote, rural location like the lake house they'd just vacated, the structures couldn't be more opposite.

They'd exchanged a massive, open floor plan and modern amenities for a two-bedroom house sectioned into small rooms. The house showed it's sixty-plus years of wear and tear, but the plentiful walls and two floors could be helpful for security.

"I can take the cot." Michael looked up from the book he held in his lap on the wingback chair. The man had just had his fifth move in six days, but he looked as relaxed as ever. She had to give him points for resilience. And for his appearance. He looked especially good now that he'd had a chance to trim his stubble back to a light shadow framing his jaw and mouth. And the blue plaid shirt he'd changed into made his eyes pop.

"I'm sure the team won't mind the inconvenience." Phoenix's answer halted Amalia's disturbing train of thought.

"Of course not." She tightened her jaw. Glanced away from the handsome picture Michael made, looking like he'd arrived from work and was settled into an evening routine. At his home. With his family.

"I'm sure."

Her gaze drifted back to see him set the book aside on the small end table and stand, facing them.

"But I was raised to treat women better than that." His eyes flicked to Amalia with the statement. They both knew who had raised him, who taught him how to treat others. Amalia could still see Papi directing Michael to hold the door for Mami and Amalia herself when they went to church together.

He focused on Phoenix again. "I'll take the cot."

Amalia's gaze darted to her boss. Was he seriously going to contradict Phoenix Gray? The man was nuts. Maybe it was just ignorance. Didn't know who he was dealing with.

Phoenix crossed her arms over her black windbreaker. "When you're in charge of a security detail for the FBI, you can make that decision." Her tone remained as even and emotionless as usual. But steel always undergirded every ounce of her persona. Like an unspoken threat.

"Okay. Point taken." Michael's mouth twitched at the corner. Like he wanted to smile. "I'm sorry for overstepping. But I do feel strange taking a comfortable room and bed when the ladies are sleeping on a cot in the hallway."

A snort sounded from behind Amalia.

She turned as Nevaeh walked into the living room with Alvarez in tow.

"Have you seen your room yet?" Nevaeh snickered.

Michael finally got his chance to smile, the expression widening his mouth and sparkling his eyes.

The tingle in Amalia's stomach had nothing to do with how attractive that particular look was on him.

"It's not that bad." He chuckled.

"Not if you don't mind a 100-year-old mattress." Nevaeh's grin slanted. "I'll take the cot, thank you."

Since when had Nevaeh become so relaxed and friendly with Michael? She didn't even like men. She was more against them than Amalia was. Especially since they seemed to be the cause of her PTSD.

Come to think of it, Nevaeh had been acting differently with Michael for a while now.

Before Amalia could figure out why, Rocky ran down the stairs. Stopped when she saw Phoenix standing at the bottom. Her eyes widened slightly, then she pushed past the intimidating figure to reach Michael.

"Hey, Rocky." Amalia reached into the back pocket of her jeans for the burner phone Cora had brought to the house. "This is for you." Amalia stepped around Phoenix to hand Rocky the flip phone.

"A phone?" A smile brightened the kid's face as she looked up from the device to Amalia. "For me?"

Amalia ignored the lump sliding into her throat and donned a broad grin. "Sure. Every kid should have one, right?"

"Michael!" Rocky dashed around her and nearly crashed into Michael as she held the phone high. "Look what Amalia gave me!"

"I see." His smile looked as forced as the words sounded. "That's really nice." His gaze cut to Amalia. The suspicion in his eyes contradicted his words.

"Bomb sweep is done." Bristol and Toby walked into the living room—luckily the largest room in the house—and joined the growing crowd. "We're all clear." She looked at Phoenix. "Need me for anything else?"

"Stay on call as needed." Phoenix gave the terse response as she turned and walked from the room.

"Will do. Have a good night, everyone." Bristol waved and

smiled, nearly as friendly as the black lab at her side. Amalia would never get used to the new, chipper Bristol. She and Cora would claim it was because she'd become a Christian. Amalia suspected it had more to do with getting married to the charmer, Rem Jones. He seemed to be one of the few good guys. But only time would tell.

"I have to show Cora my phone." Rocky still smiled as she dashed to the open doorway that led to the dining room, beating Bristol and Toby by inches.

Bristol tossed a grin over her shoulder as Nevaeh laughed.

Nevaeh swiveled toward Amalia. "I'm going to tell Jazz she can knock off and get some sleep. I'll finish her rounds outside."

"Don't get run over by a kid on your way." Amalia flashed a smile.

"Gettin' too dangerous around here." Nevaeh laughed again as she and Alvarez left the room.

Amalia felt Michael's approach without looking.

His warmth buzzed awareness through her body, even though she'd guess he stood two feet away. "That wasn't just a gift, was it?"

She turned toward him. Her arms wanted to fold in front of her body, but she forced them to stay lowered. Kept her stance relaxed. She wasn't on trial. Didn't have to justify her actions. To him or anyone.

She kept silent. Let him fill the emptiness.

Michael's arms crossed over his broad chest instead. His forearm muscles bulged beneath his rolled-up sleeves. "You gave her the phone so you could track her, am I right?"

"Your point?"

"You tricked her. She thought it was a gift. Because you *care* about her." A muscle in his jaw clenched, pulsing the bristles of hair there.

"Can you think of a better way to keep her safe?"

He didn't look away. Didn't answer either.

"If she runs again, we need to be able to find her." Amalia didn't reach for her smile. Opted to just meet his gaze head-on. "Sometimes lies are needed to keep people safe from themselves."

His eyes narrowed. He took two slow steps, closed the gap between them. "You know what I think?" His head dipped down as his gaze skimmed her face. "I think you use lies to keep yourself safe."

She refused the urge to swallow. Ignored the cinch of her ribs. The scarcity of air supply. "Everyone does."

He didn't react to her defense. Stepped closer yet. "Like the lie that you're not Sofia." Had to be only an inch between them. His breath fanned her cheeks. "And the lie that you don't care about your family anymore. That you don't care about *me* anymore." His eyes darkened. Gaze flicked to her lips.

She tensed. What was he doing?

His head lowered toward hers.

Why didn't she move? Why didn't she want to?

"Cora says she likes my new phone!" Rocky's voice burst into the room a split second before she did.

They jerked apart.

Amalia glanced at the clueless kid. Never wanted to hug her more than at that moment.

But Amalia couldn't do that. And she sure couldn't let Michael Barrett kiss her. Never mind her rapid heartbeat that still hadn't slowed and the oxygen deficit she focused on satiating without letting her chest rise and fall.

She left the room without a word, Raksa padding behind her through the dining room and into the small kitchen at the back of the house.

Michael was right about one thing. She used lies to protect herself. They were all that kept her free and kept her from hurting her parents beyond belief if the CIA were to catch her, brand her a traitor.

And right now, she had to tell herself more lies. That she didn't care about Michael at all. That her response to his almost-kiss was purely an instinctive chemical reaction.

She'd made the mistake of trusting someone enough to love him before.

The image of Jacob, shot dead in his car, flashed before her eyes.

She needed the lies about Michael more than any of the others. Because another wound to her most vital organ—that soft, vulnerable thing beating erratically inside her chest—would kill her.

"It's still there." Nevaeh's voice drifted up to Michael as he walked softly down the staircase, trying not to wake Rocky. The girl's bedroom door upstairs was closed, but the house was small with thin walls.

He smiled as he pictured Rocky's sleeping, peaceful face. She'd fallen asleep before he'd finished his story tonight, her cheek resting on Gaston's furry head on the pillow.

"I don't see the technician on the pole anymore."

Michael paused partway down when Amalia came into view as she spoke. She stood with Raksa about ten feet from the picture window that looked out onto the driveway and a road backdropped by a cornfield where green stalks stretched at least six feet high.

But the scenic view outside only drew his glance for a second. His heart thumped against his ribs as his attention returned to the raven-haired beauty in the living room. Heaven help him. He couldn't be stupid enough to fall in love with her, could he? Then again, he'd been stupid enough to try to kiss her just a matter of hours ago.

He'd wanted to kick himself as soon as Rocky had interrupted them. It'd been the wrong move for so many reasons. But his heart didn't want to listen. And his head kept wanting to think about what it would feel like to kiss Sofia. If she were Sofia.

What a crazy mess. He shoved a hand through his hair as he walked down the remaining three stairs.

Nevaeh stood closer to the window, slightly off to one side. Alvarez lay next to her feet on the brown carpeting.

Michael came up beside Amalia, carefully leaving a good five feet between them. "What are we looking at?"

She cut him a glare. At least it wasn't that ingratiating smile defense. "The security team is assessing a potential threat."

His lips tugged with a grin that wanted to show itself. Using anger to hide her true feelings was very Sofia. Not that he wanted her to feel something for him. She wasn't a Christian, so he couldn't have a romantic relationship with her. He quashed his hopeful reaction and cleared his throat. "A threat?"

Nevaeh nodded, looking out the window again.

He followed her gaze and spotted what must be the concern—a white van was parked on the far side of the road that ran in front of the house. He squinted to read the words printed on the side. "Looks like the power company."

"Supposedly." Nevaeh glanced at him.

In the movies, the power company guy with the van was always someone else. Usually, FBI or the police. But this was real life. "Why do you think it isn't the power company?"

Amalia rolled her eyes. "You ever heard the saying, 'curiosity killed the cat'?"

His mouth twitched again. "Yes. I find it very offensive to cats." He let his grin loose.

Amusement lit her eyes, surging warmth through him from his chest to his toes.

The light quickly vanished from her irises, and she returned her attention to the vehicle outside. "The van arrived at seven thirty and hasn't left since."

Michael pulled out his phone from his pocket to check the time. "It's eight forty-five now."

"Exactly. How many power company employees do you know who would stay that long past business hours?"

"Maybe there's an outage somewhere?"

"There is."

Michael raised his eyebrows at Nevaeh, hoping she'd fill him in.

"We called the power company when the van first showed up. They said they sent a tech out to this area because some of the houses lost their power at seven."

"But..." he looked at the two women who stared out the window, "you don't believe them?"

Amalia ignored his question and turned a determined gaze on Nevaeh instead. "Wake Jazz."

Nevaeh hurried away with Alvarez and headed for the back of the house where Jazz had opted to set up the cot near the back door instead of the hallway upstairs.

"Are you going to check it out?" He looked out the window. The smoky light of dusk cast the country scene with a romantic glow, but his muscles tensed. Though he didn't know what he suspected or feared. More of Rottier's men? Someone come for Rocky?

"Jazz will. We won't leave you and Rocky unprotected in the house."

"That's not what I'm afraid of." In that moment, he realized with a jolt of alarm what did have his chest knotted up in a ball.

Her jawline firmed as she stared outside. "Don't go caring about me, Barrett."

How did she know he was worried about her safety when he'd just figured it out himself?

"Won't do either of us any good."

He watched her, the beauty of her profile undeniable even when it screamed she wanted him to stay away. "Maybe it will."

She jerked toward him. Fire lit her eyes, making them more entrancing than usual.

"I hear we have a visitor."

Amalia spun to face Jazz as she walked through the doorway to the living room, her Belgian Malinois pulling at his leash in front of her. "Possible hostile. He was on the pole for a while after he arrived. Appeared to be working. Nevaeh saw him last, getting in the van, at eight thirty."

The woman with the head of abundant black curls appeared just then. "Checked the back door. We're still clear." She looked at Jazz. "The yard patrol showed us clear, too. And no one should know where we are now that Phoenix is calling the shots." The glance Nevaeh sent Amalia seemed to seek reassurance.

"You know what I always say."

Nevaeh's lips curved into a much smaller smile than normal, stress pinching the corners of her eyes. "Expect the unexpected."

Jazz nodded as she slipped on her earpiece. "Always better safe than sorry. I'll check it out. Coms check."

Nevaeh gave her a thumbs-up, which Jazz returned before she turned away and left through the dining room and kitchen. Must be intending to start at the back of the house.

Michael fell silent with Amalia and Nevaeh as they watched out the picture window. Their edginess was getting to him. Or maybe it was just the waiting.

*Lord, please keep Jazz and Flash safe. And please let there not be a real threat in that van. Or anywhere else. I don't matter much, Lord, but there's a little girl involved now. And Sofia.*

It felt like ten minutes of his heart beating in his ears until Jazz finally appeared, somehow already on the road, approaching the back of the van. She must have gotten there by way of China.

"Team 3, Roger. Use caution." Amalia's voice broke through the tension thick enough to slice. Jazz must've said something through the coms.

Nevaeh stepped closer to the window, her fingers clenched into fists at her side as she watched.

Alvarez growled—from Nevaeh's apprehension or a real threat? The K-9 stared out the window, too.

Raksa tensed in response and walked closer to the window with a low rumble.

"Team 3," Amalia's tone was level and calm, "are you picking up on any threat?"

Jazz and Flash disappeared behind the driver's side of the van.

"Roger."

Seconds ticked off as Michael held his breath. He couldn't stand the suspense any longer. "What's happening?"

Nevaeh glanced at him before springing her gaze back to Jazz. "She said there's no driver. The van looks empty. She's going to try the driver's door to get to the ID that's on the sea—"

A burst of light yanked his attention to the window.

*Boom.*

The ground beneath his feet trembled as the van exploded in a ball of fire.

# TWENTY-FIVE

"Jazz!" Nevaeh's scream rent the air, sharper than the explosive cacophony that still shook the atmosphere.

"Nevaeh don—"

Too late. She'd already yanked open the front door and sprinted toward the van.

Amalia held back the urge to order her to come back. The woman's best friend could be dead. "Slow down, Nevaeh." She kept her voice even and solid as she tried to inject some sense into Nevaeh's coms earpiece. "This was deliberate. Be careful."

Nevaeh cut down her pace, and Alvarez caught up to her side as she moved her head from side to side. She still marched quickly in the direction of the van, consumed by flames, but at least she had more situational awareness.

Amalia whipped out her phone, texted an SOS to Phoenix.

"I'm going out there." Michael's announcement clenched every fiber in her chest and instantly banished her unemotional control of the situation.

She couldn't afford distractions or emotion right now. She braced herself against the image that flew to her mind—Michael, caught in the explosion or barrage of bullets someone could be waiting to unleash if he went out there.

"No." She injected the word with steel.

He pressed his cell phone to his ear. Was he calling 911? "I might be able to help. Hello?" His gaze fell away from hers as he talked to someone on the other end. Reported the explosion and possible casualty with an efficiency that would've impressed her under different circumstances.

"Okay. Thank you." He walked toward the front door as he finished the call.

"Get away from the door, Michael."

"I want to see if I can—"

The lights went out, a single beep sounding from a carbon monoxide detector, AC abruptly shutting down. The power was cut.

"What—"

"Shh." Amalia motioned with her hand for Michael to be quiet. The house was darker than she'd expected, thanks to the ending twilight. She pulled her Glock from its holster.

Raksa growled.

But not toward the front of the house. The K-9 stiffened, gaze locked on the rear, something past the dining room and kitchen.

"Michael?" Rocky's small voice on the staircase spiked alarm through Amalia.

She sidestepped to the stairs, gaze on the doorway that led from the living room to the rear of the house. "Go to your room until I come for you." The intense hiss of her order seemed to do the trick.

The girl's footsteps padded quickly back up the stairs.

"Team 2, this is Team 1. Hostile inside." She kept her voice low, almost a whisper as she crept back toward the doorway but stayed off to the side.

Raksa let out another low rumble. "Hold it." The command told the shepherd his warning was heard, and he now needed to be silent. Didn't need to alert the intruder to the K-9's presence or their exact location.

"I'm taking Jazz's vitals." Nevaeh's reply was thick with emotion. Maybe tears. Near panic. "She's unconscious.

Blood, but I can't see how bad the injuries are yet. I have to check."

"No." Amalia kept her tone firm. "She knew the risks. You're needed to protect the wits."

A second of silence. "Fine." Iron edged Nevaeh's voice. "But let's take out the creep who did this fast. Jazz needs me."

Amalia's lips tugged into a smile at the return of Nevaeh's humor and toughness. "You got it."

"Coming in at the rear."

Good. They could flank the intruder. Or intruders. Rottier's men always seemed to move in packs. "Roger that. Look alive." Amalia swiveled her head to check for Michael.

He stood out in the open by the sofas.

"Flip that coffee table on its side and get behind it."

He nodded, for once not arguing as he grabbed the table and did as she said.

She crouched, weapon ready as she listened. Best to hold off the intruder until—

Pops cracked the air.

"Down!"

Raksa dropped beside her as she hit the floor.

Bullets sprayed through the wall above her head.

She twisted to see Michael, carpet rubbing her cheek.

He'd hunkered down behind the table.

She signaled with a push of her hand to the floor that he should lie down instead.

He quickly flattened, keeping his head and upper vitals behind the cover of the table.

The shooting paused.

A short China cabinet lined the wall on the dining room side. Should keep the shooter from being able to target them on the floor.

Single attacker. Sophisticated set up. Planned and expertly executed.

Her nerves twitched.

Verdugo was back.

He'd have night vision goggles to see better than she could in the increasing darkness of the house. Knew he could hit his target through the wall or rush the room with his AK-47 or the precision weapons he was sure to have on his person. He'd try to pin them down, then breach the room.

Adrenaline kicked through her veins. She and Raksa had foiled him once. They could do it again.

Raksa. She looked at the shepherd, lying by her side, as ready for action as she was. A plan clicked into place in her mind.

She pointed her Glock at the wall pockmarked by bullets. Aimed high, just below the ceiling. Couldn't risk a bullet cutting through multiple walls and hitting Nevaeh or Alvarez at the back of the house. She fired.

Return bullets smattered the plaster, sliced through the air above her head. He'd be busy for a few seconds.

"In position at back door." Nevaeh's whisper came over coms. "Entering now." She'd be in the kitchen when she entered. One room away from Verdugo on the opposite side. Perfect.

"Send Alvarez, stealth attack, thirty seconds."

"Roger that. Thirty seconds. Commencing now."

Amalia checked her watch, eye on the second hand as Verdugo continued his barrage of bullets.

"I need to give myself up." Michael's deep whisper came from her left side.

She swallowed a curse as she turned her head to glare at him.

His face was close, too close, as he lay on the floor less than a foot away.

"Get back behind the table." She shot off another round.

More return fire from Verdugo cut through the wall.

Michael cast a glance to the open doorway as bullets whizzed above his head. "If I give myself up, he'll leave you alone." He turned his blue eyes on her. "I can't watch you get killed for me."

250

The words, the emotion in his eyes pierced her chest, punctured her heart more painfully than a bullet.

"I'm going." His statement jolted her into action.

"You do, and I'll shoot you myself." She let her straight face show how serious she was.

His eyes widened, but she didn't have time to enjoy the moment.

She jerked her attention to her watch. Show time. She angled her body toward the K-9 on her other side. "Raksa." She whispered his name and gave him the hand signal for a stealth attack.

Eagerness lit the shepherd's eyes as he crawled forward.

She fired off more rounds, kept the bullets high.

Pops signaled Nevaeh was doing the same from the other side.

Raksa reached the doorway just as Verdugo opened fire again. The assassin wouldn't like taking this long to get out. He could've made his move this time, charged the living room if Nevaeh hadn't been on his other side. Now he'd be pinned until he figured out which of them to take out first.

Amalia belly crawled to the doorway, swung her legs to the side, body pressed along the base of the wall with her head by the opening.

Snarls reached her ears, cut Verdugo's firing short.

She popped her feet under her, squatted.

Sirens blared outside. Maybe a mile away.

She swung around the corner, weapon ready.

Raksa and Alvarez each held an arm in their mouths. They snarled as the assassin, night goggles covering his face, tried to shake them off. He swung at them with the rifle, but they hung on, close enough to his body to miss his blows.

Nevaeh appeared from the kitchen, gun leveled at Verdugo.

But they couldn't shoot. Verdugo and the dogs jerked and turned as they fought. Any bullets could hit the K-9s instead of the assassin.

The sirens wailed, closer. Probably out front.

Verdugo dragged himself toward the window, Alvarez and Raksa hanging from his arms. He jabbed the butt of his rifle through the window, shattered the glass.

Amalia glanced at Nevaeh. All they needed to communicate.

"Raksa, out!"

Nevaeh shouted the same command to Alvarez simultaneously.

The K-9s let go, pulled back from Verdugo.

Amalia and Nevaeh fired, but he was already through the window. Dropped out of sight.

Amalia dashed to the wall by the window, angled to peer outside.

Nothing.

She leaned closer to the opening. Looked at the ground beneath.

The grass was flattened below the window. He must've rolled away. Made it to the tall grasses and bushes twelve feet away.

She could still catch him. She put her foot up on the windowsill.

"Mals, no."

Amalia paused, glanced back at Nevaeh.

Her dark eyes pooled with concern. "Jazz. I've got to help her."

Which would leave the witnesses alone if Amalia pursued Verdugo.

She lowered her foot back to the floor. Jerked a nod. "Go."

Nevaeh dashed for the back door as Amalia took one last look outside.

This attack had come way too close. Verdugo surprised them, got within range of Michael. Injured, maybe even killed one of their own. And he was still out there.

Next time, he might get what he came for.

But it'd have to be over her dead body.

Michael cautiously rose to his feet. The silence that had descended over the house was almost eerie.

He looked out the front window. An ambulance and police car had parked on the road by the van, their emergency lights flashing. Flames still ate at the vehicle, but they had shrunk considerably from the initial explosion.

Headlights glared into his face as another van swung into the driveway and pulled close to the house. Another *white* van. His stomach clenched. Until Phoenix dropped out the driver's door. Of course. She drove a white van.

He spun away, the tightness in his belly increasing as he walked toward the doorway that led to the dining room. Where the shooter had been.

Shouldn't Amalia have come back now? Or Nevaeh. Were they injured?

He hesitated at the doorway, then stepped through.

Glass covered the floor where Raksa was, wagging his tail at Michael.

Amalia stood by the shattered window.

No visible bullet wounds that he could see, though her back was turned. She was all right. Relief washed through him from his chest out to his fingertips. *Thank you, Lord.* He opened his mouth to tell her he was glad she was okay, but she smacked the wall with her palm, then turned around.

She paused when she saw him. Fire lit her eyes, whether because of him or the attacker, Michael couldn't tell.

"Don't ever do that again." She bit out the words, her tone low and sharp.

Guess that answered his question who had caused her anger. "Do what, exactly?" Though he had an inkling he knew.

"Try to 'sacrifice,'" she bounced her fingers in the air for quotation marks, "yourself for me." She stalked up to him and stopped about a foot away. "My job is to keep *you* safe. Not the other way around."

He looked down at her gorgeous, unharmed face. Those eyes full of the passion he hadn't seen for twelve years, not since Sofia had stood in front of him, claiming they'd been right, telling him she was leaving. "Is it really still just a job to you?" The words slipped from his throat, thick and quiet.

She stared up at him. Her chest rose and fell with emotion he knew she felt, too. But was it the same emotion that gripped his heart in a vise? The kind he didn't want to na—

She grabbed his arm and swung him to the side, knocking him off-balance as she pulled out her gun.

Phoenix stood with her dog in the doorway from the living room.

Michael righted himself and took in a much-needed breath. He hadn't even heard her approach. But Amalia apparently had.

She lowered her Glock as Phoenix glanced around the room. "You'll need to check Raksa's paws for cuts."

Michael stared at the woman in the gray baseball cap. She sounded more like a professor telling a student how to improve an essay than someone who'd just come on the scene of an assassination attempt.

She turned and went back to the living room.

"Let's go." Amalia talked to her dog instead of Michael as she followed Phoenix.

"Verdugo?" Phoenix crossed her arms over her windbreaker and looked at Amalia.

"Yes. The boys pinned him. We couldn't take a shot without risking them."

"So he got away."

Amalia dipped her head in a short nod. "Now that you're here, I could try to track him. I know the direction he went."

"I'll go with Dag."

From what Michael had gathered when Nevaeh had kept him abreast of the search for Rocky, Phoenix's dog was the tracking expert. Though Nevaeh had mentioned Flash could track, as well.

"He went out the dining room window, south into the grass."

Phoenix headed for the front door.

"Any news on Jazz?" Amalia took a few steps toward her boss as if she'd just remembered to ask.

Phoenix paused. "Alive and conscious. Paramedics and Nevaeh are with her."

Amalia gave a cool nod as if she didn't care very much. But Michael spotted the way her fingers opened, relaxing with the good news. Maybe she cared about more things than he'd been able to see at first. Or, maybe, she was starting to change.

A hopeful smile fought to find his face, but he held it back. Amalia was probably about to light into him again, and he didn't want to invite more of her wrath.

She withdrew her attention from the door Phoenix had closed as she left but didn't look at him. "You better go up and see to the kid."

His momentary relief that she wasn't going to scold him again ended abruptly with a twist to his stomach as he thought of Rocky. Poor girl was probably scared to death. "You told her you'd come for her."

"I have work to do." Amalia crouched down by Raksa and lifted one of his paws for inspection. "If you want to leave her up there alone, that's up to you."

He knew what she was doing. Maneuvering out of another relationship she didn't want to deal with. But at least she'd remembered about Rocky. That meant something, didn't it?

He went to the stairs and took them two at a time. "Rocky? You can come out now." He headed for her closed bedroom door. He reached for the knob just as the door flew open and a small body launched at him.

His heart warmed as she squeezed his legs with her arms. He reached down and slipped his hands under her shoulders.

She loosened her grip and let him lift her into his arms. Her hazel eyes latched onto his face. Moist tracks streaked down her cheeks.

The sight surged a pang behind his ribs. "Oh, honey." He

shifted her so that he could hold her with one arm and gently wipe away the wet trails with his thumb. "I'm sorry."

She sniffed. "I'm a fighter." Her chin trembled as she said the words.

His heart cracked, rattling in his chest like it might break entirely. "Yes." He didn't know how he got the word past the knot lodged in his throat. But he managed to nod. "You are."

"Like Amalia." Rocky turned her head and pressed her cheek against his chest. "She scared away the bad guys, didn't she?" Her question was muffled in his shirt.

"Yes, honey." He stroked her small back with his hand. "She did."

"She's really brave."

"Yes. She is." But not brave enough to let him in or tell him the truth. Even if her life depended on it.

# TWENTY-SIX

"Hey, Mals." Nevaeh's mouth pressed into a close-lipped smile that lacked her usual humor.

"Hey." Amalia opened the door to the hotel suite wider and held up her fist.

Nevaeh bumped it with her own fist as she passed by with Alvarez, headed for the PK-9 team assembled on the sofas. "Nice digs." She scanned the large suite, complete with a living room area, full kitchen, and three bedrooms—one of which was located up a flight of stairs. Michael should be resting there now, and Rocky was in one of the lower rooms.

Cora had somehow secured the suite immediately after Verdugo's invasion. Located about an hour and a half from the Twin Cities, the luxury hotel should be an ideal place to stay inconspicuous for one night. The hotel manager had allowed them to bring Michael and Rocky in the back door to avoid being seen. Paid to have connections in high places, apparently. Or maybe Cora had just talked the hotel manager into it.

The angelic blonde with the golden tongue rose from the white sofa, a mug of the coffee she'd brewed for the group cupped in her hands. As she went to the kitchen, Jana got up to greet Nevaeh and Alvarez, swishing her tail.

Toby rushed over to do the same, accidentally pushing

Jana out of the way to reach Alvarez with enthusiastic whole-body wags.

Raksa stayed where he was, lying as close to the air-conditioning unit as possible as he recouped his energy following the evening's events. Amalia swung wide to scratch behind his ears before she returned to her seat on the other end of the sofa she shared with Bristol.

Nevaeh plopped down on the sofa Phoenix occupied. She let out a whoosh of air.

"How are Jazz and Flash?" Cora went to Nevaeh and bent to hand her a steaming mug of coffee.

Nevaeh took the mug, stared at the liquid inside. "Mild concussion, bruised ribs. Needed stiches for the cut on her head. But she'll be okay." Nevaeh lifted her gaze, weariness in her brown eyes. "Girl is tough."

"Thank the Lord." Cora breathed the words into the silence.

"That's for sure." Bristol seconded the opinion. "What a praise."

Amalia looked at the brunette who used to be as against the idea of God as Amalia herself. Bristol met Amalia's scrutiny with an open, serious expression that signaled she meant what she'd said. Amalia glanced away. Still wasn't used to having two Bible-thumpers on the team.

"Flash?" Phoenix asked the question they were all wondering.

"A small scratch on his face. Must've taken some shrapnel. No other injuries."

"That's incredible." Cora shifted her gaze to Amalia. "From your description of the explosion and seeing the aftermath, it's a miracle their injuries weren't more extensive."

Nevaeh shot Amalia a look as she shifted on the cushion. "Jazz said Flash warned her just before the bomb went off. He barked, and she pulled back and dove into the ditch as the van exploded."

"Lucky break. They could've been killed." Amalia's jaw clenched at the thought. Never liked anyone to be killed on her watch. And somehow, she'd allowed herself to care—just a little—about the women on this team. Another weak spot she'd have to eliminate. One more day, and this job she'd promised to do for Phoenix would be over. She would move on and soon forget about the PK-9 team. Cut out all the vulnerabilities she'd mistakenly let in.

"Yes." Phoenix's firm tone cut through Amalia's inner lecture. Her gaze, shadowed under the bill of her cap, aimed at Amalia. "This was too close."

Amalia's thoughts exactly.

"It's awful that he killed the power company technician to take his van and impersonate him." Lines crossed Cora's pale forehead as she took a hesitant breath. "What I've been trying to understand, besides Verdugo's need to kill everyone he perceives to be in his way, is how he located us at the safe house." Her thin eyebrows drew together. "And so quickly."

Amalia paused a beat before sharing the bad news. "I found a tracking device in Rocky's backpack." Something she kicked herself for not finding earlier.

"No way." Nevaeh stared at Amalia, her brow furrowed.

"But how could Verdugo have gotten to her backpack?" Cora leaned forward, cupping the black mug in her hands. "It's always been with her since she came into our protection."

"Was the tracker there the whole time?" Bristol turned her head toward Amalia.

"No. I searched the backpack when she first arrived."

"There's no way the dude could've gotten into one of the safe houses and left the tracker without us knowing." Nevaeh set her mug on the table in front of her and leaned back against the cushions. "No way."

"He didn't have to." Phoenix interjected the comment, clearly aware of what Amalia had also concluded.

"The park."

Cora sucked in a sharp intake of breath. "When Rocky ran away?"

"Oh, man." Nevaeh groaned. "He was in the crowd?"

"Somewhere at the park at least." Amalia mentally reviewed the bystanders she'd spotted. He could've been any of them, except for the children. The elderly man on the bicycle was the most likely.

"But to find us with Rocky at the park," Bristol rested her head on her hand, fingers stabbing into the hair on her scalp, "he would've had to know we were in the area, at least."

Amalia nodded. "Only thing I can think of is he must've tailed someone to one of our earlier safe houses. He could've then put a tracker on that person's vehicle or followed them to the next house."

"Oh, no. I hope not." Cora pressed her palms to her cheeks. "I took all the precautions and checked for tracking devices."

"I know." Amalia was confident Cora and Bristol had done just that. "Verdugo is that good." She glanced at Phoenix. "He showed that tonight with his misdirection setup. It was brilliant. And it almost worked." With Michael and Rocky in the house. Amalia ignored the way her throat tightened at the thought. She concentrated on what Bristol was saying.

"I thought Verdugo wouldn't work for Rottier after he brought in those other thugs."

Phoenix looked at Amalia, apparently letting her answer.

"I'm going to reach out to Ramone. He might have heard more by now."

"Maybe Rottier paid triple Verdugo's usual rate to get him to come back." Nevaeh watched Amalia over the mug she brought to her lips.

"Could be. If he did that and agreed to pull off his thugs, Verdugo might have taken the job again. Or maybe just stayed. He may never have left."

"You mean he could've been here the whole time. Watching." Bristol lifted her head as she looked at Amalia. "Biding his time until the opportunity was right."

"Fits his style." Which usually worked for Verdugo, every time. He couldn't be happy with how things went down tonight.

"Barrett testifies tomorrow morning." Phoenix's statement drew everyone's attention to her. "Rottier won't give up without another try at the witness."

"But will he send Verdugo or the other men?" Cora's wide eyes echoed her question.

"No way of knowing." Phoenix's tone stayed steady, resolved. "We'll be ready for anything."

"I'll see you in a little bit." Michael squatted in front of Rocky just inside the door to their hotel suite, trying to think of a way to change her frown into a smile. "How about after I testify, we go to the IPF Tower you were telling me about?"

Her eyes brightened. "Daddy said you can see for miles and miles."

"Then we absolutely must go." He smiled, and his heart swelled when her mouth curved to reflect the expression back to him. "Not afraid of heights, are you?" He gave her a teasing squint.

She lifted her chin. "Nope."

He chuckled. "Then we'll go as high as they let us." He held up his fist for a bump. "Deal?"

"Deal." She knocked her small fist against his with a giggle that made his heart do a flip. There was something special about this girl.

"But why can't I just go with you and Amalia?" Her lower lip protruded again.

"Bristol and Rem will take good care of you and bring you for our visit to the tower once I'm done. You don't want to sit outside a courtroom for an hour, do you? It'd be super boring. You can hang out with Toby and Gaston here at the hotel longer, and then come to see me after it's all over." And after the danger had passed.

He'd been relieved to learn this morning that Phoenix had decided Rocky should stay behind at the hotel for thirty minutes after he and the others went ahead to the courthouse. She'd travel in a separate vehicle with Bristol and her private investigator husband, Remington Jones. Both would be capable of protecting Rocky, from what he'd heard. Bringing her to the courthouse after the danger had passed, at least for Michael, would allow her to go back into FBI or Phoenix K-9 protection immediately after they didn't need to protect Michael anymore.

Rocky shrugged. "I guess that'd be more fun."

He smiled. Thought she'd like the prospect of hanging out with the dogs.

"But only 'til you're done."

"Right." He nodded and stood. "See you then, kiddo."

She threw her arms around his legs and squeezed, melting his heart into a puddle at his feet.

He reached down to gently press his hands against her back. "I'll see you soon."

She nodded against his thigh.

"Hey, Rocky." Bristol approached from the kitchen area with Toby by her side. The dog's black body wagged as he watched Rocky. "Want to see Toby do some tricks?"

Rocky instantly spun away from Michael. "He does tricks?"

"Yep." Bristol held out her hand to Rocky. "Come and see."

The girl went to take Bristol's hand and eagerly left with her, leaving Michael bereft with a slight ache in his chest.

"Let's go." Amalia appeared at his elbow. Intensity reflected in her gaze. The same mood that seemed to emanate from most of the Phoenix K-9 team today. Not fear. Just alert readiness.

Even Raksa looked up at Michael with the same expression in his eyes.

"Yeah." He followed Amalia and Raksa out the door into the hallway. Jazz and Flash waited at a corner up ahead. Apparently, she and Flash had already recovered enough to join the protection detail. Michael mustered a half-smile, and Jazz nodded in return, her features marked with determination beneath the bandage on her forehead as she fell into step behind him.

Weird feeling, bodyguards sandwiching him like he was the President or something. The strangeness only increased when Nevaeh and Alvarez flanked him in the hotel lobby as they moved toward the front doors.

A line-up of vehicles waited for him under the awning outside the entrance, which made him feel even more like a dignitary.

Amalia's car waited at the end of the four-vehicle line, behind Phoenix's white van, but she didn't head that direction. She went to a dark green sedan directly in front of them instead.

It was parked so the passenger door faced them, but she went to the back door instead and pulled it open. "Raksa, in."

The shepherd jumped onto the back seat.

Amalia looked at Michael next. She was putting him in the back today? He tried to read her expression to determine the reason for it. Security concerns or leftover anger from last night? The anger he was sure she was using to mask her true feelings.

At least she wasn't sporting that Amalia smile. But she wasn't letting him see in either. Nothing besides grim preparedness reflected back at him. Like the expression he'd seen in soldiers' eyes when he'd interviewed them in war zones.

His stomach clenched as he ducked to sit on the back seat next to Raksa without a word. On a day like today, when the team seemed convinced another attempt on his life was imminent, he wouldn't make Amalia's job harder by insisting he ride in the front. As much as he'd like to be nearer to her, maybe one last time.

If they made it to the courthouse in one piece, and he testified against Rottier, her job would be done. What would happen then?

She shut the door behind him, and Raksa's face suddenly moved in close to Michael's. He chuckled as he scratched

Raksa's ears, the dog's nose wiggling as he smelled Michael's features.

Michael turned his head away in time to see Nevaeh talk to Amalia a few feet from the car. Looked like a serious conversation, judging from the frown that shaped Amalia's lips. She rounded the front of the vehicle, her expression becoming grimmer by the minute.

"Bad news?" He asked the question as she slipped into the driver's seat. He hid a wince when she didn't answer. Probably should've given her a few seconds. She didn't like his questions in the first place.

She adjusted the review mirror, and her dark eyes found him in the glass. "Not yet." The engine already idling, she shifted into drive and pulled away from the hotel, her gaze constantly moving, scanning everything.

"Are you sure Rottier will try again? Maybe he's given up after what happened last night." She and Nevaeh had foiled Verdugo. That could've daunted Rottier, couldn't it?

She turned onto the street in front of the hotel. "If you were Rottier, and the witness who could put the nail in your coffin was about to take the stand, wouldn't you try to stop him? It's not like Rottier has anything to lose."

"Yeah." The truth sank in his gut. "I guess you're right." He pulled his cell phone from the pocket of his dress pants that squeezed the device against his leg. It didn't fit in the pocket very well when he was standing, let alone sitting.

"Glad to hear you say it for once." The sarcastic humor in the remark drew his gaze to the rearview mirror just in time to catch the glimmer in her eyes before they darted away.

Hope squeezed his chest. Another glimpse of Sofia? It seemed like she was beginning to peek through more every day.

*Please, Lord. If it's your will, let us both live through today so I can have a chance to bring Sofia back.*

He cleared his throat, eager to engage with her, to see if he could cajole more of Sofia out of the persona she was trying to hide behind. "Who do you think Rottier will send this time?" He tried for the casual tone she and the Phoenix K-9 team adopted when it came to discussing danger that would frighten the wits out of normal human beings. Like himself. "Verdugo or the gang of those other guys?"

Amalia turned the car around a corner onto another street, traveling at an unusually sedate speed for her. At least in his recent experiences as her passenger.

His stomach floundered just from the memories of her stunt driving. Now that he thought of it, he should've protested riding in the back seat. If they got into another of those situations, the motion sickness would be a hundred times worse in the back.

"Verdugo, most likely. Rottier would've had to drop the other crew to get Verdugo to do the job again. He doesn't share hits or money."

Michael swallowed. He'd probably never get used to being an assassin's *hit*. Hopefully, it wasn't something he'd need to become accustomed to.

His smartphone vibrated in his hand. He glanced down at the notification. New email.

From the CIA agent, Kenneth Owens.

Air stuck in Michael's shrinking throat as he glanced at Amalia in the mirror. Her gaze skimmed their surroundings at a one-way stop before she started the car forward again.

He looked at his phone and navigated to the email, forgetting to breathe.

*Interested in discussing the person in question with you. Meet me at Dacre Park at noon today, 7/13. I'll find you.*

He checked on Amalia again as his pulse reverberated in his ears. A CIA agent knew who Amalia was and wanted to talk about her. That confirmed it. She must be associated with the CIA somehow. Had she been one of their agents? Or could they be after her because of something she'd done illegally?

No. He wouldn't let his suspicions go that direction anymore. She was obviously still intent on doing the right thing and helping people, even if he didn't approve of her methods.

But the CIA agent was coming here, probably from Washington, D. C., just to talk to Michael about Amalia. She must be more important to the CIA than he'd imagined.

"You don't need to get nervous yet." Amalia's voice jerked his attention to the rearview mirror, where her steady gaze watched him.

He resisted the urge to swallow. Did she suspect what he'd been doing? Still investigating her? Not that there was anything wrong with it. She was the one who refused to tell him why she was pretending to be someone else and why she'd lied to her parents for twelve years. But he still found it hard to meet her eyes.

"Verdugo will have to attack near the courthouse since he can't know where we're coming from."

Rottier and his assassin. Right. Michael let out a slow breath through his nostrils. She must've seen his stunned expression and thought it was prompted by anxiety over the probable attempt on his life. She didn't know how much more important it was to him to recover Sofia, to enable her to be herself again and free her to live in the truth instead of lies. "I'm not worried." Not about his life.

She quirked an eyebrow he saw in the mirror.

"Not very worried, anyway. I know I'm in good hands."

She lifted the other eyebrow and cast him a glance over her shoulder.

"God's and Phoenix K-9."

"There it is." She rolled her eyes. "Knew Michael had to still be in there somewhere."

He grinned. "Well, I assume you have a plan for handling whatever Verdugo has in mind. Starting with driving a different car?"

"It's a rental Cora picked up this morning. In case Verdugo figured out which car I've been transporting you in."

He chuckled. "'Transporting.' Makes me sound like a load of goods."

"Better than contraband."

His chest warmed at her teasing. A definite improvement from the cold shoulder she'd given him since Verdugo's latest invasion. "So where's the rest of the team?" He stretched his neck to look out the rear window, the small city already fading into the background as they drove through green countryside on a quiet two-lane road.

A semi they had passed a bit ago seemed to be the only vehicle behind them, unless it blocked others from view. "I thought you'd be doing a caravan type of setup."

"Too conspicuous." Amalia checked the mirrors. "We're traveling on parallel routes, and Cora is tracking us with GPS. They'll be able to come to us quickly if anything goes wrong. But it's not likely this far from the Cities. Agent Nguyen has her people staking out the courthouse and checking for any suspicious vehicles and people there. She might c—"

Raksa growled beside Michael, his gaze locked forward.

An oncoming pickup truck swerved into their lane, charging head-on.

A man's head appeared above the cab. Along with—

Wait, was that—

"Hang on!" Amalia jerked the wheel, flinging the car into a spin.

# TWENTY-SEVEN

A rocket launched from the bazooka as Amalia swung into an evasive maneuver. Braced for impact at the rear of the car. Better than the windshield where the thug had aimed.

The rocket hit hard, jolted the car with an explosive crack.

She pressed the gas, tried to surge forward, angled across the opposite lane.

The car listed to one side, wouldn't turn. Could be a broken axel.

She slammed the brakes, jammed into park. "Get out, now!"

She grabbed her knapsack and scrambled from the car. Yanked open the back door for Raksa to leap out. "This way!" She whipped out her Glock.

Michael hesitated just before exiting on the right side— putting himself in the pickup's line of fire.

The truck swung back their way just as a black SUV appeared on the horizon, zoomed toward them.

She could hold out on her own with only the immobile car for cover but couldn't chance Michael. Not when Rottier's people already had reinforcements.

Michael's feet hit the pavement.

"The salvage yard. Move!" Her shout urged Michael into a run ahead of her. She spun back, fired a round at the bazooka shooter as he jumped down from the bed of the truck.

He squealed, went down as she turned away and sprinted after Michael.

Raksa easily kept pace at her side as they ran down the steep incline, long grass slapping her legs.

A salvage yard stood about sixty yards away. A potential refuge.

But fenced.

She scanned for a weak spot as she raced toward the huge gravel lot occupied by hundreds of parked cars.

Michael reached it first, glanced back at her. "Climb it?"

"Yes!" She mustered the extra oxygen to shout as she neared the yard. "Go!"

He started to climb as she reached the chain link fence. She'd have to find another way in that Raksa could make. He was a good jumper, but the ten-foot fence ruled out that option.

Michael grunted as he climbed. At least he'd be over. Could hide in the maze of cars. Maybe she could hold them off from here.

She glanced at the uncut grass that surrounded her. Not exactly concealment or cover. Needed to get past the fence.

"Raksa, with me." She darted along the fence.

"Where are you...?" Michael breathed hard as he pushed out the words.

"Keep climbing." She shot the order over her shoulder. Scanned the links for an opening as she jogged.

Raksa surged ahead of her. Paused and looked back with a bark.

Had he—

She hurried to the shepherd and looked.

A damaged fence post leaned outward, leaving a gap she could widen for them both to slip through.

She grinned and gave the shepherd's ears a quick scratch. "Good boy, Raksa."

A shot cracked the air.

She dropped to the grass. "Raksa, down."

Silhouettes of five men lined the top of the hill.

Easy targets.

She fired at one.

He yelled. Dropped. The others hit the ground.

She glanced behind her at Michael.

He landed inside the fence and jogged her way.

"Get behind the cars!"

He ignored her, as usual. Reached the opening behind her while she fired a couple more rounds to keep the enemy pinned.

"Come on." He pushed at the pole and the fence panel, easily widening the opening.

She shoved up from the ground and ducked through under his arms. "I could've done that myself."

He shrugged and sent her a grin as he held the fence for Raksa to dart through. "Makes me feel useful."

A man who could joke in the midst of a firefight? Her heart knocked against her ribs as she grinned back at him.

*Pop-pop-pop.*

"Go." She grabbed his arm to usher him ahead of her. They crouched low, kicked up gravel as they scrambled behind the nearest row of cars. She peered around the hollowed-out automobile at the end.

Men ran and tripped their way down the hill toward the same fence she and Michael had conquered. She squinted at movement above them, the road at the top. Four more men. And unless her count was off, either the silhouette she'd nailed or the bazooka shooter wasn't too badly injured to join in the fun.

"Are Phoenix and the others coming?" Michael's breath found her neck where her hair was flipped away to the opposite shoulder.

"Yeah." She didn't have to check in with them to be sure. Phoenix would be here in minutes. But she, Jazz, and Nevaeh would have to find a way in or set up an offensive perimeter to box in Rottier's thugs, which could take a bit.

At least it wasn't Verdugo. These thugs would be a cakewalk compared with him. She'd try to keep one alive to find out how they knew where Michael would be, the route they were taking to the courthouse.

She swung her knapsack off her shoulder and plunged her hand inside for the box of cartridges. Glanced at their surroundings as she reloaded her Glock.

The automobile skeletons of various colors and sizes were stacked higher in the next row over. Better cover.

"Whoa." Michael's eyes widened as she pulled out her secondary weapon from the knapsack. "You don't mess around."

"Never know when I'll need backup." She released the safety on the second gun. "You should take this one." She handed it to him, grip first. "Just in case."

He shook his head. "Never had much use for guns."

Figured. She stifled an eye roll. "Could save your life."

He quirked a smile that did odd things to her pulse. "Isn't that what I have you for?"

He had a point. And she wasn't about to let him get killed on her watch. "Okay. Then you'll have to start doing exactly what I say, when I say it. Got it?"

"As long as I agree, I promise."

She puffed out a breath and shoved the secondary weapon into her waistband behind her back. "You might not know why it's a good idea, so just do it."

A rumble at her elbow yanked her gaze to Raksa. His ears angled as he growled at something he could hear or smell.

She peered around the car skeleton.

Two men walked toward the rows of parked vehicles. Inside the fence.

"Follow me." She whispered the command as she spun on her heels, stayed crouched as she led them to the opposite end of the row. Pressing her shoulder blades against the shell of a black Jeep, she angled to see around the corner. The graveled, car-width path between rows was empty.

She looked over her shoulder. Gaze hit Michael's, his face

close as he squatted behind her. "We're going two rows down. Now."

She darted out from the row, turned to the right.

A man walked into the path. Twenty feet away.

"Hey!" His gun hand didn't get halfway up before she pulled the trigger. He dropped.

She jogged two rows up. Paused by the triple stack of car frames. Something was missing.

Michael.

She swiveled.

He stood where she'd been when she took the shot. Stared at the fallen thug.

"Michael. Now." She hissed the words.

He blinked, then lurched to follow her.

She ducked around the pile of cars. Waved Michael past her as she crouched. Listened.

The gravel was good. Should let her hear anyone coming. Unless they were stealthier than she guessed.

Barks pierced the air.

Her chest swelled as Raksa let out one bark, a response to his pals.

"Is that...?" Michael's whisper tickled her ear.

"Yep." A grin stretched her mouth. The K-9s barks were the team's calling card for Amalia to know they'd arrived and for Rottier's men to shake in their boots. The cakewalk just turned into a picnic.

She reached in her knapsack and grabbed the coms earpiece she'd brought for use at the courthouse.

Pops cracked as she slipped the earpiece in place. Target practice for the PK-9 team? Hoped so. Amalia's fingers itched for her to jump out there and engage the enemy with them. But her priority had to be Michael.

She looked over her shoulder, checked behind. Clear.

"This is Team 1, checking in." Amalia kept her voice quiet as she spoke into the coms. "Glad you finally joined the party."

"Can't believe you started without us." Nevaeh's humor-filled voice needed no identification.

"Team 1, this is Team Alpha." Phoenix's serious tone cut through the coms. "What's your status?"

"Team Alpha, package is safe. No injuries. Positioned in west quadrant of lot."

"Roger that. How many hostiles?"

"Not sure. At least ten. One down, two injured or down."

"Team 1, Roger. Stay with package while we clean up."

Amalia grinned at Phoenix's choice of words.

*Crunch.*

The sound came from the other side of the row of stacked cars.

Amalia rose, toe-heeled her way to a small gap between two piles of cars. She looked down at Raksa.

He stared up at her, tail wagging, desperate for action.

She smiled as she gave him a hand signal and pointed him through the opening.

He surged through the small space.

The attacker yelled as Raksa hit his mark.

Amalia dashed around the row.

The man faced away from her, Raksa gripping his arm.

She jumped onto the thug's back to reach his neck, wrapped him in a chokehold, counted seconds 'til he'd be unconscious.

"Raksa, out." She gave the command as the attacker slouched, fell forward. She climbed off his back, grabbed his gun, and scanned the area as she hurried back to Michael. The yelling and growls had likely drawn too much attention to their position. They had to move.

She paused at the end of the row where Michael waited, Raksa by her side. "Follow me."

Michael's eyes grew large as Raksa whirled around with a snarl. "Watch out!"

She spun before he finished the warning.

But Raksa already had the bearded man's gun hand clutched

in his mouth. "I'll take that." Amalia pulled the weapon from the attacker's fingers as he grimaced and tried to shake Raksa loose. "Hey, be gentle with the K-9 or he won't be gentle with you."

A grunt from behind made her jerk toward Michael.

A tall man lunged at Michael, his gun already on the ground. Had Michael knocked it away? She moved to intercept the attack, but Michael dodged with perfect timing. He grabbed the man from behind, wrenched the guy's arm behind his back and forced him to the ground.

Amalia tilted her head as Michael looked up. "Thanks."

He gave her what could be the cutest smile she'd ever seen, even if it was over the head of a would-be killer. "We take care of each other."

She whipped a zip tie from her knapsack on the ground and stepped behind Michael to wrap the man's wrists. "Didn't know you had any moves."

His mouth broadened the smile to a big grin, and he turned his head toward her, inches away as he helped hold the thug in place. "Oh, I have a lot of moves." Heat fired the mischief in his blue eyes.

Amalia's pulse skittered. His mouth was close enough to—

"I was gonna ask if you need help," Nevaeh's voice made them both spin in her direction, "but it looks like you have things under control. Whatever you're actually doing here." She winked at Amalia, her grin wide.

More shots sounded.

"That'll be the boss and Jazz." Nevaeh thumbed over her shoulder. "They boxed in four of those dudes. Don't know how many are left." She glanced beyond Amalia. "Want to do something with him?"

Amalia turned toward the thug Raksa still had under control. She aimed her gun at him. "Raksa, out."

The shepherd immediately released the attacker, and the guy lifted his hands above his head. "Take care of him, Nevaeh, will you?"

"My pleasure." Weapon drawn, Nevaeh walked toward

the man with Alvarez, who delivered a menacing growl at her side.

Amalia holstered her Glock and looked up at the tall stack of cars.

"Give you a boost?" Michael appeared at her elbow, a half-smile on his face. Weird how he was on the same page with what she was thinking.

She didn't really need his help, but the hopeful glint in his eyes made her nod.

He cupped his hands, and she put her foot in them. He easily pushed her up, giving her a head start on the second car.

She found holds on the partially gutted skeletons of the cars and clambered up the stack. She planted her feet on the crushed white roof of the top car as she scanned the yard from her nearly bird's-eye view.

Spotted Phoenix's gray cap and flying braid as she kicked a thug, darted around him, then downed him with her favored mix of Krav Maga and Brazilian jiu-jitsu techniques.

Jazz and Flash passed through an empty row between cars, headed for the middle path. Where a thug waited.

"Team 4, this is Team 1. Hostile ahead on your right."

"Team 1, Roger." Jazz's answer came a second before Flash charged, sprinted around the corner, and took down the thug before he could get off a shot.

Movement caught her eye. Another man about to walk out of a row farther down, twenty feet from Jazz.

"Team 4, behind you."

Jazz whirled as the man emerged. Swung her hand.

He yelled as his back slammed against the truck behind him.

Jazz must've thrown her knife. Pinned the guy's arm or sleeve to the truck.

Amalia grinned as she checked on Phoenix. The PK-9 boss had a nice collection of four bound and unconscious thugs on the ground around her.

Scanning the yard, no movement caught Amalia's gaze. "All teams, this is Team 1. I think our work here is done."

Sirens drew her focus to the road east of the salvage yard. Police squads with flashing lights sped toward their location. "And transportation for Rottier's hired guns is almost here."

Nevaeh let out a whoop from below as Amalia climbed back down. She swiveled to Nevaeh as soon as her feet hit the gravel and grinned as they smacked hands in a high five.

She turned to check on Michael.

His soft blue eyes crinkled at the corners with his smile. Almost before she knew what was happening, he reached for her and engulfed her in a hug.

With her honed reflexes, she could've prevented the hug in a heartbeat. But she didn't.

And as his strong arms held her close, his breath heating her ear when he whispered, "Thank you," she was glad she hadn't.

# TWENTY-EIGHT

"Heard you're responsible for getting our witness here alive." Agent Nguyen stopped a few feet from Amalia in the wide hallway of the courthouse and crossed her arms over her white shirt and black suit jacket.

Amalia met Nguyen's dark gaze. First time Amalia had ever gotten anything that close to credit or praise from the FBI agent. "It was a team effort." She scanned the people passing in the hall behind Nguyen. A familiar figure in a gray cap, walking with a sandy-colored K-9, caught her eye.

"He in there?" Nguyen tipped her chin to indicate the door to the men's room behind Amalia.

She nodded. She'd cleared the bathroom before Michael had entered it to clean off the dust and grime of the salvage yard. And now she would make sure no one went in until he came out.

"Katherine." Phoenix and Dag approached as Nguyen angled to see them and Amalia at the same time. "What happened?"

"It was Taft."

The twenty-year veteran with the perfect record. Who apparently wasn't so perfect after all.

"I didn't want to think it, but..." The usual sharp edge to Nguyen's tone dulled as she looked at Phoenix.

"You were driving when I told you the route we were taking this morning."

Nguyen nodded at Phoenix's statement. "He bugged my car after the last sweep I had done. Heard the route you told me on speaker."

"And you're positive he's the leak?"

"No doubt about it. I'd bugged his office and Radcliffe's, though I didn't believe either of them was the leak. Not intentionally. I didn't have time to monitor the bugs around the clock, of course, so I'd check their recordings twice a day. Nothing incriminating until today. Taft called one of Rottier's people, apparently." She shifted her gaze toward Amalia but stopped short of meeting her eyes. "He told them where you were coming from with Barrett and when. By the time I heard the recording, the attack was already happening."

Phoenix watched Nguyen with her unreadable gaze. "You have him in custody?"

"Yes." The agent's confident air returned, stiffening her spine. "He's not talking yet, but he will. Now that I've stopped the leak, we'll take over the protection of Grace Hardwick."

Rocky? Amalia blinked as Nguyen's announcement sparked an odd twinge in her chest.

"The U. S. Attorney wants us to put her in WITSEC with the U. S. Marshals as soon as we can since she'll have to be protected for an extended period before the murder trial can take place."

The twinge intensified to a sharp pain under Amalia's breastbone.

"The girl is on the way here?" Nguyen looked at Phoenix.

"Yes. ETA forty-five minutes."

Who would tell Rocky the news that she was being handed off to the FBI? And then the marshals?

Amalia clenched her hand into a fist at her side to keep from rubbing at the throb that pushed against her breastbone. She couldn't care. Not about a kid. Not again.

She'd known protecting Rocky was only temporary. A job

like any of the others. A job that was only for a few days and then Amalia would never see the girl again. She hadn't even wanted to protect the kid in the first place.

And this was one of the reasons why. Children were wilier than adults. They could wriggle past defenses that were impenetrable to everyone else.

It seemed Rocky had done just that. Found a way to make Amalia care when she shouldn't. With her rare smiles, her friendship with Gaston, her vulnerability. She had no one. Not even a home.

*Not your problem.* But for one, crazy, irrational moment, Amalia wondered if she should make it her problem.

Michael smoothed his tie and checked his suit jacket in the mirror of the men's bathroom one last time. Looked like he'd finally managed to wipe off all the gravel dust and dirt. The knees of his suit pants were still stretched and puckered a bit, but, thankfully, no one would see that once he was in the witness-box.

He should've brought a comb for his hair, but he'd done what he could to smooth it with water and his fingers.

He checked the time on his cell phone that he'd set on the counter. A few more minutes to see Amalia before he went into the courtroom. He hurried to exit the bathroom and scanned the hallway for the black-haired beauty.

"Nervous?" Her voice jerked his gaze behind him to the left. She leaned back against the wood-paneled wall. Probably been there the whole time, watching him look for her.

He grinned. "Nah. After what we just survived, this'll be a walk in the park."

She straightened, her gaze locked somewhere above his eyes. She closed the gap between them, suddenly standing only inches away from his chest.

His breath caught. Heart thudded in his ears.

She reached up. Her hand went past his face as she raised

on tiptoe. Her fingers curled through his hair, ratcheting the thump of his pulse to a dull roar as heat fired his chest.

"There." She lowered to her usual petite height but didn't back away. "Can't have you looking like you just tangled with a gang of hired killers in a junkyard." Her mouth curved in a grin that was nothing like Amalia's. And everything like Sofia's.

His hands went to her upper arms before he could stop them. Everything in him yearned to pull her to his chest and hold her close. To kiss her full, upturned lips. "I meant what I said." His thumbs caressed the skin beneath the short sleeves of her black T-shirt. "Thank you for saving my life. Again."

Her dark brown eyes were soft and warm as she looked up at him. "You turned out to be pretty handy yourself."

A lump wedged in his throat as he stared at the woman who was becoming so much more like Sofia. Was this it? Was Sofia returning to him?

"Not bad for a last hurrah."

*Last hurrah.* He lowered his hands as the reminder sank like a rock in his stomach. She'd kept him alive for his testimony. Once he went in the courtroom, her job was done. She'd have no reason to stay. Would she disappear again? He had to know. "Will you be leaving now?"

Her eyes cooled as she took a step back and darted her gaze elsewhere. "You should probably go in."

But he couldn't. Not without one more try to find out the truth from her, to recover Sofia. "Will you tell me now?"

She met his gaze, her eyebrows dipped low.

"Once I testify, will you tell me about Sofia? You promised you would, remember?"

"Mr. Barrett?" The female voice called for Michael's attention, but he couldn't look away from Amalia. Not until she answered. "Mr. Barrett, we need you in the courtroom."

Amalia broke contact and glanced at the woman a few feet away. "You better go."

He looked to see one of the U. S. Attorney's assistants

he'd met once before. Her smile was strained, something bordering on panic in her eyes.

He knew how she felt. But he didn't want to put a burden on anyone else. And his testimony was what all this had been for. He couldn't let the deaths of Paul and Vicki, as well as the sacrifices of the Phoenix K-9 Team and the FBI, have been for nothing. He had to go.

"See you after?" His gaze found Amalia, hope probably obvious in his eyes.

She nodded, no Amalia smile but also no hint of Sofia in her dark irises.

Apparently, it was still a good thing he had that meeting with the CIA agent right after this. He followed the assistant into the courtroom, his jaw firming with the resolution that formed in his mind.

He'd have to learn the truth about Amalia and Sofia from the CIA agent even if he had to squeeze it out of him with his own two hands. He needed that information to free Sofia and get her to stay with him, to keep her from disappearing again.

Because the twelve-year-old, nearly fatal wounds in his heart meant there was one thing he could not do. He couldn't come this close to finding Sofia only to lose her forever.

# TWENTY-NINE

Amalia scanned the hallway outside the courtroom. Watched a man in a suit as he walked by with a briefcase. She could hardly believe this was her last time on duty, protecting Michael as he testified on the other side of the big oak doors behind her.

Maybe she should try harder to protect herself from the dangerous thoughts spinning in her head. The warm feelings that were softening her heart, making it pliable beneath her rib cage.

She shouldn't have stepped so close to Michael to fix his hair. Should have resisted the urge to touch the soft waves. To be close one last time.

Ever since she'd made the dumb move, Nevaeh's words from when they'd left the hotel that morning echoed in Amalia's mind, bouncing all the way down into her chest where they ricocheted against her heart.

"You trusted Michael when you were kids, right?" Nevaeh had angled her curly head, her eyes unusually serious as she'd studied Amalia's face. "Has he really changed so much? I don't trust men, but...even I'd trust him." She'd shrugged and walked away.

Amalia had pushed the moment aside and focused on her job—transporting Michael to the courthouse unharmed.

But now, the job was almost done. Nevaeh stood at the end of the hallway, posted for security within Amalia's sight-line. She hadn't said another word about Michael, but her surprising questions wouldn't leave Amalia alone.

Because Nevaeh was right. Michael hadn't changed much. Not in the ways that counted. He was still the good guy she'd known when they were kids. Kind, courageous, protective, loyal. And downright sweet.

He'd been the person she could trust more than any other back then. With every secret and every thought.

Maybe, despite her own cynicism inflicted by her experiences, he was the same in that way, too. Maybe she could trust him.

The dangerous idea sent a tremor down her spine.

Raksa looked up at her, as if he knew she'd just felt a warning. But it wasn't the kind he thought.

"Good boy." She rubbed him behind the ears as she watched the people passing by and checked for threats.

But something surged through her, something like hope. Or was it more than that? Something stronger?

She'd seen the look in Michael's eyes before he'd gone into the courtroom. The way his intense gaze had flicked to her lips and back up when he'd gently caressed her arms, sending shivers through her body.

And, for a crazy second, she'd wanted to lean in and make the decision for him. After all, she'd already considered kissing him when she'd fixed his hair, the softness of the waves and scent of his cologne nearly overcoming her professionalism.

If she chose to trust him again now, she'd risk more than the vulnerability of friendship. She'd be betting the whole pot —friendship and romantic attachment. All of her heart. Could she do that?

If things went south, it would be even worse than what had happened with Jacob. Because she had never felt for Jacob what she did for Michael. She'd thought she loved Jacob. They'd been attracted to each other and rushed into a commitment because the CIA wanted them engaged and married quickly. Eliminate all security risks. A lesson she'd learned well.

Michael was different. Their history, her love for him in the past, and the way her heart reacted to him now—this thing with Michael was stronger, deeper, and powerful enough to nearly scare even her.

But fear had never been her weakness. Caring, softness. Those were her downfalls. Until she'd rid herself of them.

Could it be she'd lost something important when she did that? Lost herself somewhere along the way?

Bristol appeared at the end of the hallway with Rem and Rocky.

Warmth swelled in Amalia's chest as her gaze fell on the small girl. Couldn't deny she felt something for Rocky, too. And that it didn't seem like such a bad thing.

Was this new ability to care again, without letting the risks stop her, thanks to Michael? She took in a strengthening breath. Maybe it was time she trusted him again. Really trusted him. Told him the truth he wanted to know. Her history with the CIA, her three years of running from them. The treason accusation. Why she'd had to hide.

Maybe, if she told him, he could help her find herself. Sofia Sanchez.

"Amalia!" Rocky ran toward Amalia, a smile beaming on her pretty face.

Without thinking, Amalia squatted down and opened her arms to welcome the girl in a hug.

Rocky giggled as Raksa pushed in and licked her ear.

"Can I join the party?" Michael's deep voice sent Amalia's pulse skidding.

She stood and turned to see him step away from the courthouse doors, now closed behind him.

His lips curled in a smile that shot a thrill to her fingers and toes.

"Michael! Are you all done?" Rocky bounced on her toes like she wanted to jump into his arms.

He scooped her up and held her against his chest with a grin, looking every bit like he could be Rocky's dad. An image that did more crazy things to Amalia's heart. "Yep, I'm all done."

"So now we can go to the IPF Tower?"

Michael laughed, his eyes twinkling as he looked at Amalia, including her in the moment. A moment that gripped her with a longing she didn't know she'd had. To take this family-like scene from illusion to reality. To make it come true. To make it hers.

Agent Nguyen approached in Amalia's peripheral, plummeting her fantasies.

Her stomach clenched. Bad timing. But it had to happen sometime. Rocky had to leave, and so did Amalia. "We can ask Agent Nguyen if you have time to visit the observation deck before you go with her."

Rocky frowned, her expression matched by Michael's as they both looked down at Amalia. "What?" Rocky's voice shrunk from the boisterous girl of seconds ago as caution stiffened her body.

Amalia reached for a smile to cover the pang in her gut. This was life. Rocky would have to learn to deal with it. "Agent Nguyen and the FBI are going to watch over you now, to keep you safe."

"But you said I can stay with you and Michael as long as I want." Her words dropped to a whisper.

Amalia's throat closed, but she kept her smile on. "I didn't mean forever, kiddo. That's impossible. I just meant you didn't have to go back to the group home."

"No!" The shout exploded from Rocky's mouth, and she squirmed in Michael's arms. Pushed against his chest.

He shot Amalia a grim glance as he hung on. "Rocky—"

"No. I won't go." She paused her struggle to glare at Amalia. "You lied! You always lie!" She kicked, knocked Michael's arm loose, and he let her slide to the floor.

Amalia grabbed her shoulder.

Rocky tilted her head up. Tears pooled in her hazel eyes. "Why did you have to lie?"

Amalia's stomach twisted.

The girl wrenched away. Amalia let her go.

A touch on her arm jerked her gaze to the left. Bristol's gray-blue eyes reflected concern. "I'll go after her."

Amalia jerked a nod.

"You didn't have to lie to her at all."

Steel slid through her body at Michael's accusation, hardened every muscle as she turned to face him.

"You could've avoided all this." His eyes were stormy, his brows pulled low.

She crossed her arms over her T-shirt. "I told her what I did so she wouldn't run off. So she'd feel protected and safe."

"So you could get more information out of her, you mean."

She raised her shoulders slightly. "So we could keep her even safer. It was all for her."

"Oh, that's so sweet." He chuckled, a sound devoid of humor. "You lied to her about the thing she wants most in life—a family, people to love her and care for her. Not because she's a witness to a crime but because of who she is."

Amalia clenched her jaw against the guilty response he wanted to see. "Her physical safety is more important than her emotional happiness. In your world, that may not be the case, but in the real world, my job was to keep her alive. I did that."

"Right." His lips pressed into a flat line. "You know, at first I wasn't sure I'd need to keep my meeting today, but now I see it's very necessary."

Amalia's fingers twitched at the hint of a threat in his tone.

"I heard back this morning on an inquiry I made." He glanced away. His mouth closed, then opened to deliver what her senses warned her was going to be a blow. "A CIA agent is going to meet me at Dacre Park."

286

*Operative.* The correction to his terminology popped into her mind as if that were the most important point at this moment. As if Michael hadn't just plunged a knife into her heart. As if he hadn't betrayed her like Jacob.

No, far worse than Jacob. Because this came from Michael, the man who once knew and loved her better than she knew or loved herself. Pain seared through her chest as her heart crumbled into pieces around Michael's blade.

Amalia's highly trained brain reminded her to check her surroundings, make sure Bristol was still outside the door of the bathroom Rocky had run into. Verify the witness was safe. Good thing her training didn't require her emotions or her heart. Because both were dead now. Destroyed. Permanently.

"Amalia—"

She jerked her attention to his traitorous face. "Goodbye, Michael." She spun, stalked to the exit door at the end of the hall they'd intended to use for Michael—her betrayer—in an emergency. Hadn't thought she'd be the one getting attacked.

"Amalia, wait."

She ignored his quick steps behind her, slammed into the steel door to the emergency stairwell. Held it open just long enough for Raksa to scurry through behind her.

"So that's it?" Michael's frustrated voice echoed in the empty stairwell as he entered behind her.

She marched down the staircase.

"Mission accomplished, goodbye?"

She didn't hear any footsteps following as she continued, putting distance between them.

"So this really was just another job to you." His tone twisted with emotion. "It was more than that for me. I care about you."

The words hit her as she reached the first landing. Quiet filled the stairwell—all concrete and metal pieces as cold and hard as the insides of her heart. Thanks to people like Jacob. Like Ahmed. Like Michael.

287

She spun to face him, glared up the stairs. "I wouldn't have thought you could sink so low."

"What?" His eyebrows pinched together.

"You told the CIA where I am. You brought them here."

"Amalia, no. That's not—"

"What'd they offer you? Or did you do it just to feed your obsession with exposing the truth to the world?"

"I would never take money for something like that." He started down the steps toward her, his hand on the metal rail. "I don't even know what you're talking about. I asked them about you. I didn't give them any information. Well," he paused on the steps, and tell-tale guilt glinted in his eyes before he looked away, "not intentionally."

"Right, you *accidentally* told them exactly where to find me, and now you're meeting to help them some more. Let me guess, you want me to go with you to make it easier for everyone?"

"Amalia, what are you—" He stopped on the landing as she shifted out of the way, kept distance between them. "Are you in trouble with the CIA?" He reached for her arm.

She jerked back, stared at the innocent surprise, sprinkled with a dash of worry, in his eyes. She wasn't buying it this time. How had she ever thought for a moment she could trust him? He was a better conman than Jacob, even without CIA training. Maybe because he had more reason to want to hurt her.

Amalia's heart froze into a block of ice behind her ribs. "Oh, man." She let out a sardonic laugh. "I get it now."

"Get what?" Michael lifted his hands out from the sides of his body, holding them in the air.

"This isn't for money or truth. It's payback." The realization squeezed her throat, nearly choked her.

"Payback." He blinked as if clueless. He'd become an amazing actor. Maybe better than she was.

"You can't get over what happened with your mom. You still blame me."

Darkness slid from his eyes to cloak every feature of his

face as he straightened, staring at her. "I blame *us*. It was our fault. Denying it won't change the truth."

"You want the truth?" Disgust pushed through Amalia's tightened throat. "*She* got drunk. *She* got in the car. And *she* drove into a tree. That wasn't us, Michael." Amalia pointed to her chest and then to him. "It was her. Her decision, her choice."

"Oh, come on, Sofie." He yanked his fingers through his hair. "You know she needed help. And our lies prevented her from getting that."

"You know what our lies did? They kept her happy. They kept you happy. She told you not to tell anyone about her addiction. And you..." Amalia let her lips curl with the mixture of irony and pain that tore through her insides like a cyclone. "You begged me to keep it a secret. To *help* you so no one would ever know."

"Because I was a kid, and I didn't know our secrets and lies would end up hurting her."

"Exactly!" Amalia threw her hand up into the air. "We were *kids*, Michael. Kids, just trying to make the best of the bad cards you were dealt."

"But we knew lying was wrong. We weren't ignorant of that."

She shook her head. "It's never that simple. We were doing the right thing protecting your mom and protecting you. She would've been humiliated if people had known. She would've been an outcast, ridiculed." Amalia moistened her lips with her tongue. "And you would've been destroyed by that."

The memory of what had driven her to tell the lies and keep Michael's secrets cinched her ribs. She would do it all over again to protect him from watching his mom suffer more than he'd already had to. From enduring more humiliation and pain himself. He'd loved his mom more than anything. Always had a sensitive heart, a protective nature that made him more the parent than his mother. So Amalia had to protect him.

"But she died, Sofie." Michael's voice dropped to a whisper that carried in the cavernous stairwell. "If we'd told your parents, the guidance counselor at school, or Pastor Abasolo—if we'd told any of them, she wouldn't have been alone in her fight. They'd have come alongside her and gotten her the help she needed." Moisture pooled in his blue eyes. "She could've been set free, she could've lived, if we'd only told the truth."

Amalia gritted her teeth and looked away. But she still saw the tears that had coursed down Michael's cheeks at the funeral and the tear he hadn't meant to let escape as he'd yelled at her before she'd left. The evidence that she hadn't been able to protect him from the greatest pain he'd ever felt.

But she'd tried. Used every means in her power to help him, to keep him from getting hurt. And she'd kept trying after his mom's death. She'd left everything she knew and loved behind for him. Went back to college and stayed away so he could have her parents as his own, knowing he wouldn't have wanted her around after what had happened if she'd tried to visit on breaks. She couldn't force him to leave the only real home he'd ever known. The home he might've lost if she'd tried to return.

So what if he didn't know that either, if he blamed her for leaving and never coming back. When all the while, she was still protecting him the best she could. That was all she could have done. All she could ever do.

She pushed back her shoulders and lifted her chin to meet his accusing gaze. "That truth you love so much? It will only lead to trouble. You're going to hurt Papi and Mami more than I ever did. You have no idea what you're getting into."

"Then tell me, Sofie. Remember what Jesus said? 'If you abide in my word, you are truly my disciples, and you will know the truth, and the truth will set you free.'"

She scoffed. "That same verse is carved into the wall at CIA headquarters. The world is a more complicated place than you realize, Michael. If you don't get that soon, it's going to take more than Phoenix K-9 and the FBI to keep you out of the danger you'll put yourself in. I just hope you don't keep hitting others with your collateral damage."

She took a step toward him, popping her smile into place and locking it there as she tapped into Amalia's callous and carefree mentality. "You're using your idea of truth like a weapon. But there is no truth. There's only whatever it takes to get what you want. Just like you pretended to be trustworthy and to care when you were selling me out."

His eyes flashed. "I never did that."

She didn't break contact, didn't drop her smile. "Right now, that's my truth. Whether you like it or not."

"You don't believe that lie any more than I do." He held up his index finger, angled it toward her. "You were obviously with the CIA, so answer me this—how could you know anything you did for them was right? How could you know who were enemies and who were friends?" He lowered his hand, his mouth pulled into a sad line. "If there's no truth, then there's no right and wrong, and you can't justify anything you did for the CIA or Phoenix K-9. If there's no truth, none of us could get up in the morning."

He was throwing a philosophical argument at her to distract from what he'd done. From his betrayal and the deception he refused to admit. Clearly, she'd underestimated him. Michael had changed a lot.

But she knew from personal experience that arguing with someone who was set on deception only garnered more lies. That was the only defense he'd have.

"Have fun at your meeting." She swiveled away with a quick, "Let's go," to Raksa.

"Sofia!"

She didn't look back when Michael shouted the name as she pushed on down the four flights of stairs.

Sofia was gone forever. He'd believe that someday. Because he'd never see her or Amalia again.

# THIRTY

One question reverberated through Michael's mind as he walked along the paved path at Dacre Park.

Would he ever see her again?

Before the Amalia mask had clanged into place like the barred door of a prison cell, he'd seen the truth in her eyes. Pain, hurt, grief. All because she couldn't, or wouldn't, trust him.

How could she honestly believe he would betray her? That he would pretend to be something he wasn't, all the while planning to trick and hurt her?

Maybe because that's what she did. She probably couldn't fathom that anyone didn't do the same things—bend the truth and lie with abandon to get what they wanted.

But he wasn't like that. He'd fallen into a pattern of lies as a child for the sake of his mom and himself, but Sofia knew he didn't lie about anything else. And she should know better than anyone that he wouldn't lie now. Since he'd had to identify his mother in the morgue, had to look on her damaged, lifeless form and know he might've prevented her death by telling the truth—Michael had promised God he wouldn't lie again. And he'd kept that promise for twelve years and counting.

Amalia ironically claimed the truth would lead to trouble

for Michael. But lies, secrets, and deception—those were the dangerous elements that could derail a life. That could imprison a person the way they'd imprisoned Sofia in a false identity, locking her into a web of deception that held her captive. She might not be aware she was trapped, aware she needed help.

But Michael couldn't leave her there. Not while there was still hope, a chance he could free her to live in the truth, to not have to hide behind lies anymore.

He pulled out his phone to check the time. *12:00 p. m.*

The humidity in the air made his suit jacket start to cling, heavy and stifling. He pulled it off as a jogger passed on his left.

Owens had said he'd find Michael. Did that mean he should stop in one place instead of continuing to walk? The path led him into a clearing where benches were paired back-to-back. Just like in the spy movies. His mouth pulled into a wry grin.

He didn't exactly want a CIA agent to suddenly appear directly behind him, and he didn't want to talk to the back of someone's head. He looked for a single bench instead.

None were nearby, but a picnic table stood in the shade of the trees. He made his way there, carrying his suit jacket hooked on a finger over his shoulder as he glanced at the people who peppered the more open area.

He sat on the wooden bench attached to the table. At least there was a slight breeze that pushed through the clearing.

*"You're going to hurt Papi and Mami more than I ever did. You have no idea what you're getting into."*

He tapped his fingers on the tabletop as the words Amalia had thrown at him continued to bounce around in his head. What did she mean? Nerves clustered in his stomach. He couldn't see how meeting with a CIA agent would lead to hurting her parents. Certainly not more than she already had by not even visiting them for twelve years. And lying to them about everything. And rejecting the name they'd given her, rejecting her true identity.

Irritation pumped into his chest as he ticked off the list of her grievances against her parents. The kindest, most loving people he'd ever—

A tall, muscled guy in jeans and a gray T-shirt with a football team emblem on the front sat on the bench at the opposite side of the table. Sunglasses shaded his eyes from view, allowing Michael to see only his closely shaved black hair and dark brown skin. "Glad you could meet with me, Mr. Barrett."

"You're Agent Owens?" Michael had expected a suit and tie like in the movies.

Owens dipped his chin in a quick nod. "You have information about Sofia Sanchez. Is she in Minneapolis now?"

A trickle of warning slipped down Michael's spine. "Why are you so interested in her?"

"We're interested in everyone associated with the CIA."

Michael watched the man who clearly wasn't going to give anything away unless he thought Michael already knew the information. "I know she was a CIA agent."

"Operative." The man's mouth shaped into a smile that looked more genuine than Michael would've expected.

"Okay. I know she was an operative. But I need to know what happened while she was there." Though the CIA would never give him that kind of information. Michael scrambled for what they might share. "I need to know what happened when things ended. Why she's changed her name now."

"Yes, thanks for giving us her current name. She's been a challenge to track down."

Why did guilt slide down his throat as he swallowed? He'd only been seeking the truth she wouldn't tell him. He hadn't meant to reveal her new name or location, though why that would be a bad thing, he didn't understand.

"If you can tell us where she is right now, you'd be doing a service to your country."

"A service to my country?" Michael tilted his head as he

tried to peer through the guy's sunglasses. "You can't think she did anything wrong." Michael had seen her do plenty of things wrong in recent days, at least when it came to lying. He rephrased the statement. "She wouldn't do anything against the United States. Nothing that would hurt our country."

"So you know her well?" Owens smiled again.

"Yes. Well, I used to."

"People change, Mr. Barrett. In our line of business, people change faster than you can say 'patriotism.'"

Interesting choice of words. Michael narrowed his eyes. "I'm loyal to my country, Agent Owens."

"Glad to hear it. Then you won't mind telling me where Sanchez, alias Pérez, is at this moment."

"I don't know where she is." That was the truth, considering she'd left the courthouse stairwell so fast he couldn't even find her when he'd tried to follow.

Owens rested an arm on the picnic table and slouched to one side, looking every bit like a laidback park visitor rather than a clandestine government operative. "She's a threat to United States security, Mr. Barrett."

Michael's stomach clenched. Sofia? "I don't believe it."

"It's true. She was involved in a conspiracy with another operative to betray our country's interests. Their actions led to the assassination of an official and a compromise of national security."

"You mean treason?" Michael's jaw clenched at the accusations. Sofia might be mostly hidden behind the Amalia persona now, but there was no way she'd become a traitor.

He slowly shook his head. "You don't understand. Sofia's parents are the most patriotic people I've ever known. They immigrated to this country from Colombia when Sofia was three years old. They raised her to love and respect the United States for the freedom and opportunities the country gave them. Sofia would never betray the U. S."

Michael's heart raced as his mind finished with the thought he chose not to voice. Even if Sofia had somehow strayed from her loyalty to the U. S., she wouldn't, couldn't do such a thing to her parents. It would kill them if they learned she was a traitor, and Sofia knew that.

*"You're going to hurt Papi and Mami more than I ever did."*

Is this what she had meant? That the CIA had accused her of treason, and she didn't want her parents to find out?

Suspicions melded into facts as details he hadn't made sense of before clicked into place. Owens had been so careful with his wording when accusing Sofia of causing, not actually performing, an assassination. "Did Verdugo assassinate the official?" That would explain why Sofia knew so much about the hired killer.

Owens put his other arm on the table, squaring his body toward Michael. "Where did you get that information?"

"Not from Sofia, if that's what you're worried about. She hasn't told me anything." Michael leaned forward. "But you should know she's fighting *against* Verdugo, not with him. He was hired to kill me, but she protected me from his attempts."

"Yes, we know he's here. We have a team coming in to apprehend him today."

"Probably too late." Had they brought in a *team* for Sofia, too? Michael glanced around but couldn't see anyone noticeably suspicious. "Thanks to Sofia, he failed to kill me before I could testify at a trial to put away Leland Rottier, the man who hired Verdugo. I just testified, so he's out of a job now."

"Our intel says Rottier didn't hire Verdugo."

Michael blinked. "What do you mean?"

"He was hired by Minerva Harris."

"Minerva Harris? Who is—" Michael's mind latched onto the forgotten detail. "Minnie Devereux." The daughter of Wayne Devereux, the man he'd helped bring to justice and put away for twenty-five years.

"She's married now."

"And you're saying *she's* the one who hired Verdugo? Just because I helped put her father away?"

"Things are not always as they seem, my friend." Owens's

296

tone was casual, as if they were discussing the weather. "You may think you know Sofia Sanchez, but she's different now. She can make anyone believe whatever she wants them to believe. She's a highly trained and skilled operative. No one knows her."

Michael frowned, the operative's words smarting because they bordered on the truth. He didn't know Amalia Pérez, but he knew Sofia. And she was still there, underneath all the lies. She had to be.

He looked at Owens and tried to meet his gaze through the sunglasses. "I know her well enough to know she's not a traitor. She would never betray this country or anyone else she loved."

"I admire your loyalty." Owens slowly rose to his feet.

Michael stood and faced him across the table.

"Minerva Harris didn't hire Verdugo because of her father." Owens seemed to watch Michael through his sunglasses. "Her mother apparently loved her husband and didn't know he was unfaithful until you exposed his many affairs. She killed herself because of it. Minerva thinks you should die for that."

Shock slammed into Michael's chest, halting his breathing. That's why Leila Devereux had committed suicide? He'd known she killed herself two weeks after her husband was put in prison. Because of her husband's conviction, he'd thought.

Owens's hand appeared in front of Michael, a white business card dangling from his fingers.

"Things aren't what they seem, Mr. Barrett. But believe me when I say I have the country's best interests in mind. Give me a call when you're willing to share Sofia Sanchez's location."

Michael took the card on autopilot, and Owens disappeared from view.

The truth reverberated through Michael like a tidal wave. Verdugo was still hunting for him, and he had only himself to blame.

*Rocky's missing.*

Phoenix's terse text message banged Amalia's heart against her ribcage as she ran up the emergency stairs with Raksa, faster than the elevator could've carried them.

She hit the landing where she and Michael had fought only forty minutes ago. Pushed aside the vision of the hurt in his eyes when she'd called him out for betraying her. For being the reason she suddenly had to leave, had to run again.

Even if Michael honestly believed he'd set up a simple meeting with a CIA operative, the operative wouldn't have come alone. Not with a rogue agent, a fugitive traitor, in the area. And the CIA team sure wouldn't leave without scouring the Cities for her. Might've pinpointed her already if Michael told them where she was.

She could've been headed out of the Cities by now if not for needing to pick up Gaston from Rem, who'd apparently taken the Newfie to a public wading pool. Still, she could've gotten him and been on her way, if only she'd resisted the urge to look at Phoenix's text message. Ignoring her boss's two phone calls had been easier. Amalia couldn't risk that Phoenix would convince her to stay again.

The game was up this time. The CIA had found her, thanks to Michael, and she was not going to prison for a crime she didn't commit.

She slammed into the heavy stairwell door and emerged in the hallway outside the courtroom where Michael had testified.

Jazz and Bristol hurried toward her, Flash and Toby tight at their sides.

"She said she wanted to see the view from a higher floor of the building." Bristol's mouth pinched at the corners. "She was so upset. I wanted to give her one last happy memory. We were going to go up in the elevator. She was standing next to Toby as the doors started to close."

"And she darted out just before they shut." Amalia

pressed her lips together as Bristol nodded. "Any trace of where she went?"

"Phoenix and Agent Nguyen are in with the security guard, looking at footage from the cameras." Concern pooled in Jazz's green eyes. "Poor girl. She kept going on about how you'd said she could stay with you. She says you lied to her."

Bristol joined Jazz in looking at Amalia, a hint of condemnation in her gray-blue eyes.

Amalia met their gazes without flinching. "I told her what I had to so she wouldn't run off again while we were protecting her."

"Well, she ran now."

Yep, definitely condemnation and more than a little disappointment written all over Bristol's face. Since she'd become as much of a blind believer as Cora of the fiction that was God and Christianity, of course Bristol would judge Amalia for creating her own illusions. Never mind that the lies had been for a good cause.

But Amalia knew how to get the job done better than anyone. And right now, the job was to find Rocky before anyone else did. Rottier might be about to be convicted for arms trafficking, but as soon as he could gather more henchmen, Rocky could still be in danger for having witnessed the murder Rottier had directed. Adding a murder sentence would ensure Rottier spent the rest of his life in prison.

A vibration in her back pocket signaled a text message. Amalia pulled out her phone, checked the screen.

Ramone.

Hadn't heard from him since she'd texted for more intel on Verdugo. She'd wanted to know why Verdugo was back and if that meant Rottier had pulled his other men off the hit on Michael. But she'd already learned the answer to that question when Rottier's thugs attacked this morning. Verdugo had to be gone since Rottier had put other henchman on the job again.

She opened the message.

*Rottier not hire V. Job came from out of state. Word is V still here.*

Gunning for Michael. Amalia's fingers squeezed the phone as her breaths shallowed.

"Amalia? Are you okay?" Bristol's voice pierced through the fluid rushing in her ears.

"Verdugo is still after Michael."

"What?" Jazz's eyes widened.

"How do you know?"

Amalia lifted her phone in answer to Bristol's question. "Ramone. He says Rottier didn't hire Verdugo."

"You're kidding." Bristol's eyebrows drew together. "Who did?"

"He doesn't know. Someone out of state. Somebody who still wants Michael dead."

Bristol's eyes lit with realization.

Amalia's pulse sped up. "What?"

"When Rocky ran out of the elevator, she shouted something." Bristol moistened her lips. "She said she was going to Michael because he doesn't lie to her."

"But if she finds Michael..." Jazz let her sentence hang. They all knew how it ended.

Rocky would find Verdugo, too.

# THIRTY-ONE

This couldn't be happening. Horror slid up Michael's throat and stuck there in a clump that kept him from breathing as he re-read the text message he'd just received. It hadn't changed.

*Rocky is waiting for you at IPF Tower observation deck. Come now if you want to see her. Alive.*

The phone shook in Michael's hand. *Dear God, please, no.*

He pushed up from the park bench and clumsily navigated to Phoenix's number, grateful Cora had programmed all the PK-9 team members' numbers into the phone. He'd call Amalia, but she probably wouldn't pick up. Not after their fight.

Phoenix would know what to do. He pressed the call button and started across the clearing.

She picked up instantly. "Phoenix."

"It's Michael. I just got a text message that says Rocky's at the IPF Tower. It's threatening, says to come now if I want to see her alive." The tightening of his throat was the only thing that kept his voice from trembling.

"We'll take care of it." Phoenix's tone didn't change—as solid and matter-of-fact as usual.

"Phoenix, I think it's Verdugo. I just found out..." The

explanation that he was to blame for Verdugo's attacks stuck in his shrinking larynx. "He's still after me."

"We know."

They knew? How could they?

But the dead silence in his ear told him she'd already ended the call.

He lowered the phone and kept walking as he tried to select a rideshare app on the screen. The phone slipped from his sweaty hands. He stopped and bent to pick it up.

*Breathe.* He wouldn't be any good to Rocky if he passed out from lack of oxygen.

Grit from the well-used path stuck to the phone, but he didn't bother to brush it off as he summoned a rideshare through the app.

Five minutes was the fastest option. He started off again. People on the path blurred as he focused only on getting to the street outside the park where the car would pick him up.

*Please, Lord. Keep Rocky safe. Let me get there on time. Or send the Phoenix K-9 team. Please, just save her.*

She couldn't die for him. Because of him.

The possibility gripped his throat, choking him. He had to stop. Couldn't breathe.

He stepped off the path, bent double, hands braced above his knees.

How could he have done this to Rocky? And to Amalia?

Owens's words rushed back to him in a terrifying onslaught.

*"Her mother apparently loved her husband and didn't know he was unfaithful until you exposed his many affairs. She killed herself because of it. Minerva thinks you should die for that."*

He remembered Leila Devereux, how she'd hung on her husband's every word in public and sung his praises in the one interview Michael had scored with her. He'd thought it was an act. Especially when he'd uncovered the evidence of Wayne Devereux's philandering ways. How could his wife not have known about the affairs, even if she hadn't been party to his criminal activities?

But, evidently, she'd been in the dark. And thanks to Michael, she found out the truth in a way that was too much for her to bear.

The truth was always good, though. There was no doubt about that. God's Word made that clear.

But a realization struck Michael for the first time, blindsiding him as he straightened, just in time to absorb the blow. He hadn't needed to publicly expose the affairs to ensure Devereux would be brought up on charges and convicted for money laundering. Devereux wasn't convicted for the affairs but rather for his criminal operation. Michael had included the information about the affairs in his articles to expose the complete and whole truth about a man who'd masqueraded as a pillar of society. To leave no skeleton unknown to the public. To eliminate every secret.

Had he been wrong to do that? Had he gotten carried away? Leila Devereux had deserved to know the truth, and it was far better for her to know than to continue being deceived. The truth needed to be told and known even when it hurt. But always told in love. Mrs. Devereux shouldn't have had to learn it from the press. Shouldn't have had her husband's betrayal of her and their marriage publicly exposed for the world to see.

If Michael hadn't done that, Rocky wouldn't be with a killer right now. Rocky and Sofia wouldn't have been in danger from Verdugo this whole time.

Verdugo's attacks at the safe houses, the near-misses when Michael had feared Sofia would be hurt or killed for his sake—none of that would have happened.

"Dear Lord, I'm so sorry. Please...forgive me." His murmured plea didn't relieve the terror that gripped his chest as he returned to the path and brushed past people, pushing his weakened legs to keep moving. Forgiveness wouldn't save Rocky or Sofia from losing their lives because of him.

Sofia would be on her way to help Rocky now. He knew it in his soul. Even if she'd left after their fight, even if she hated him now, she could no more leave Rocky to die than slit her own throat.

But she'd said it herself—Verdugo was the best. She could get killed, along with Rocky.

The thought wrenched his heart so hard he nearly cried out from the pain. But that would only be a fraction of the devastation if Verdugo hurt Sofia or Rocky. If he killed them.

Michael loved them both more than life itself. The realization that dropped his stomach to his toes wasn't a happy one.

Because his mistake caused this—put their lives on the line. And if they died now, because of him, he would never be able to go on.

*Dear God, what have I done?*

---

Amalia kept her eyes moving as she drove through sluggish traffic downtown. Just as well, given she had to scan the sidewalks as she went. This was the most likely route Rocky would have taken on foot to make her way to the IPF Tower. If the girl even knew how to get there at all.

Amalia's hands clenched the wheel. This couldn't be a fool's errand. If Rocky was out here alone, she could be vulnerable to more than Rottier's men. The city itself held plenty of dangers for a young girl.

Her phone vibrated in the holder mounted on the dash. Phoenix.

Amalia pressed the receive button. "Pérez."

"Verdugo has Rocky."

Shock dropped into Amalia's stomach, exploded into a frisson of nerves and alarm that ricocheted through her system.

She was prepared for anything, but not this.

"IDS Tower." Phoenix continued as if Amalia hadn't taken a crippling hit. "He texted Barrett with a threat he'd kill her and told Barrett to come to the observation deck."

And he would, no doubt about that. Michael would sacrifice himself without hesitation for Rocky.

But he'd be going in alone. To meet a professional hit man.

Thanks to her. Amalia's gut wrenched, lurched bile up her throat.

"We're on our way, but you'll arrive first."

Yes. She was already partway there. Amalia swallowed the bitter taste that surged into her mouth and focused on the road. Pressed the gas as she jerked her car around a slow-moving truck. "I'm fifteen minutes away."

Phoenix didn't say a word.

Amalia grit her teeth. "I'll make it ten."

"Rocky is our priority."

If it came down to a choice between the victims. Amalia's mind filled in the subtext of Phoenix's statement. "Roger."

But could she let Michael die?

The phone's screen showed Phoenix had ended the call.

Tension gripped Amalia's muscles as she darted into the opposite lane to pass more traffic.

She had to stay loose, had to think clearly. Training and intelligence had to be in control. Not emotion.

But her pulse thundered in her ears. Horror coursed through her. How could she have let this happen?

*"She said she was going to Michael because he doesn't lie to her."* The memory of Bristol's words slammed against the walls that shielded her heart.

She saw Rocky's face. The tears in her sweet hazel eyes, waiting to overflow. *"Why did you have to lie?"*

Amalia blinked hard against the burn at the back of her eyes. Jerked the car into a turn. The shortcut should shave off time.

But not enough. Rocky was already with Verdugo. Had he killed her? Or was he keeping her alive for leverage?

The image of Rocky, crumpled on a floor, dead, blocked Amalia's view.

A vise gripped her ribs, squished them so hard she had to consciously suck in air, squeeze her eyes to banish the image.

She'd done this. Left Rocky unprotected. The girl had only run off this time for one reason—because of Amalia's lies.

*"You didn't have to lie."* Michael's accusation flew at her like an unexpected bullet.

He was right. She didn't have to lie. And if she hadn't, Rocky would still be safe. Not in the hands of a ruthless assassin.

And Michael was about to join her.

Amalia strangled the wheel.

Why had she run off and left him alone? If she had stayed, maybe taken Rocky to meet Michael at the tower, she'd be there to protect them both from Verdugo.

But no one had protected them from her.

The thought hit her like a kick to the face. Nearly made her miss the car stopped in front of her.

She slammed on the brakes, screeched to a stop just behind the car's bumper.

A line of traffic stood still in front of the car she'd almost hit.

Construction zone. One lane.

A man held a rotating sign at the front of the line that had *Stop* faced her way.

She craned her neck to find a way around. Had to be a way out.

Oncoming traffic in the single opposite lane meant she'd crash if she tried that route. The sidewalks were fully occupied by construction workers, blockades, and pedestrians. She'd kill innocent bystanders if she blew through there. Vehicles already gathered behind her and boxed her in.

She let out a guttural grunt of frustration.

Raksa pressed his chin onto her shoulder from the back.

"Sorry, boy." Her hand went automatically to his head, scratched behind his ears.

She let the other hand drop from the wheel as her dying heart plummeted.

*"This isn't for money or truth. It's payback."* The accusation she'd thrown at Michael echoed back at her.

He'd denied it. If she'd believed him, she'd be with him now. Protecting him. Keeping him out of harm's way like she should. Like she'd always done. Or tried to do.

She pressed her fingers into her forehead, tried to push out the stupidity housed there. He hadn't betrayed her. He wouldn't do that. He was Michael. Her Michael.

Why hadn't she believed him? Had he been right, that she'd told lies for so long she couldn't even recognize the truth when it was right in front of her?

Sofia had known the truth. Even when lying to help Michael and his mom. She'd never felt great about it. Always hoped it was temporary. Especially lying to her parents.

But Amalia didn't even know how to find Sofia within herself anymore. She didn't know who she really was. She'd drifted in a world of deception for so long, she couldn't get out.

Which meant she'd lied to a little girl, sending her to her death. And she didn't believe the one man who would never lie to her, didn't trust him when he told the truth. Left him alone and in danger. Even at this moment, he could be facing a trained killer. Because she no longer knew what truth was.

Their blood would be on her hands.

Her heart, at the worst possible moment, screamed a truth she couldn't deny any longer. She loved Michael. Not as a brother anymore. Not only as a friend.

And despite doing her best not to care about Rocky, she'd begun to love her, too.

God help her.

# THIRTY-TWO

Michael stared out the window from the back seat of the white sedan and willed the rideshare driver to go faster, praying the traffic would clear.

But would he still be too late? Or what if Verdugo wouldn't take Michael as a trade and decided to kill Rocky anyway?

*God, please. Don't let her be hurt. And don't let Sofia get in harm's way either. Not for me.*

He should be the only one to die. This was all his fault.

He'd only wanted to tell the truth. Since his mother had died thanks to his lies, he'd made it his life's mission to save others from the danger of secrets and deception. To end their imprisoning, deadly effects wherever he could.

But had he gone too far?

*"I just hope you don't keep hitting others with your collateral damage."*

Michael winced as Amalia's angry words singed his conscience. She'd accused him of using truth as a weapon. In a way, truth was a weapon to defeat evil. But had he wielded that weapon the wrong way? Misused it to cause harm instead of victory?

Like when he decided he had to know all of Amalia's secrets, whether she wanted to share them or not. Secrets could be dangerous, as he'd told Rocky. And he was sure Amalia's were since they'd made her hide her identity and stay away from her parents.

But hadn't he created more danger for her now that he'd uncovered her secret and exposed her location to the CIA? That operative, Owens, was no dummy. He would be able to find her quickly now that Michael had led him to the Twin Cities. Practically pointed her out.

Michael tried to swallow, barely able to get past the knot in his throat.

Turned out, she had a good reason for her secret. She couldn't exactly go around telling everyone she was suspected of treason. She'd have no place to hide if she did that. And if she'd tried to face the charge? He wasn't naïve enough to be certain she would've been cleared. And he knew her parents, knew how much it would hurt them to learn their daughter was suspected of treason.

Sofia was in a terrible position, and he'd made it worse. All because he had to know the whole truth. Because he had to know her secrets.

For himself.

He coughed, struck hard with the truth he'd never seen before. Sure, he wanted to save others from the dangers of lies and deception. From secrets. But even more so, his passion for uncovering them all, for hunting down every last morsel of truth, was a drive to satisfy himself.

He had to know everything—all the secrets and all the facts. He thought everyone needed that to be safe. For right to be done.

But look where that had gotten him. Sofia thought he'd betrayed her and sold her out to the CIA for revenge. Rocky and Sofia were in danger of losing their very lives because of his insatiable thirst to uncover every secret.

But wasn't it true that no truth should remain hidden, that it became like a lie when cloaked in secrecy?

He awakened the phone in his hand, desperate for

answers. Opening his Bible app, he searched for verses about secrets.

His gaze locked on a result he hadn't expected to find.

*Whoever goes about slandering reveals secrets, but he who is trustworthy in spirit keeps a thing covered.*

Is that what he had done with Devereux and Sofia? He shivered as conviction coursed through him.

He'd gotten so caught up in the righteous work of exposing the truth where people lied and deceived that, somewhere along the way, he'd swallowed a lie just as dangerous. The lie that everything hidden was a deception and every secret needed to be exposed.

He shook his head as he set his phone on the seat beside him. How could he have forgotten that even God kept some truths as mysteries, secrets to be revealed in His timing?

Michael had become so accustomed to uncovering truth and tearing down lies that he'd started to think he needed to know all truth personally, right now, and that he was the one to make that happen.

But falling for that lie had put him at the center, placed Michael Barrett in charge. Somewhere along the way, he'd stopped trusting God, stopped believing that even with secrets, God would let Michael know what he needed to at the right time.

Michael closed his eyes. *Forgive me, Lord.*

And Michael knew He would. Just like he knew without a shadow of doubt that he could trust God with the truth.

He only hoped, and desperately prayed in his heart, that he'd have a chance to tell Sofia he was sorry. For condemning her for secrets he had no business exposing. For making her think he'd betray her. And for believing she would betray her parents or him. All along, she'd been trying to protect them by staying away and keeping her secrets.

If only he could tell her he knew that now. And tell her he'd rather die for her than ever hurt her.

"Here we are." The rideshare driver's voice prompted Michael to open his eyes.

The massive IPF Tower stood just ahead, the front entrance crowded with people and blocked by heavy traffic.

"I'll get out here." Glad he'd already paid the driver on his app, Michael opened his door and jogged between slow-moving cars to reach the sidewalk.

Adrenaline pumped into his veins but mixed with something else. A different kind of energy. A confidence.

The God of truth wouldn't let lies, deception, and evil win. Not in the end.

And if Michael had to die to bring Sofia to know the God of truth, to know how much Michael and God loved her, he was ready.

He only hoped he wasn't too late.

*God help her.* Amalia's own thoughts tormented her as she stared blankly out the windshield at the blockades and traffic that held her prisoner.

But her own plea, to the God she claimed she no longer believed existed, cut through that lie along with the others with the precision of a laser beam.

*"You know the truth as well as I do, Sofie."*

She could still see the hurt that had filled Michael's eyes that night.

*"You're only lying to yourself now."*

A humorless laugh pushed past her lips as the memory twisted her heart.

Even before he'd discovered she was in the CIA, Michael had somehow known exactly where to aim to hit her weak points.

*"You know there's right from wrong, you know there's real truth. If there wasn't, how would you know what to fight for?"*

The words had bounced off her hardened conscience when he'd said them, but now they easily pierced her weakened armor.

She thought she had known what to fight for. She'd been

311

so sure. If she hadn't, she couldn't have done the many things she'd been assigned to do. Lived lies, deceived and manipulated, fought the enemy—clandestine attacks, lethal action.

It couldn't have been wrong. She'd done all that for the best of reasons. To protect her country, but most of all, to protect the people who lived there. To save others. That's all she'd wanted to do, why she'd joined the CIA in the first place.

But Michael was right. If there wasn't any truth, she couldn't know that the terrorists, the murderers, the assassins were wrong. She couldn't know what she had done was right.

*"I have to believe the truth because it's true."*

Michael's words, searing her memory, launched the final strike. Shattered the armor around the heart and conscience she'd worked so hard to gird with steel.

Phoenix had said it before this whole messy protection job began—Amalia was running.

But she hadn't been running from the CIA. She'd been running from the truth.

The truth she'd known all along. The truth that chased her everywhere, clinging like a shadow. A shadow with the power to destroy her.

She couldn't try to ignore or deny it anymore as the weight of the truth crushed her.

She'd pretended she'd left home and stayed away because Michael was wrong. Because she'd done the right thing in lying for him about his mom, and he'd refused to see that. Because she didn't want to go back home and ruin what he had with her parents.

More lies. She had fled and never looked back because she couldn't. Because doing so would undo her. She would have had to face the truth that she was at fault for lying to cover up his mom's problem. That she had failed to protect Michael from his greatest pain.

And she was responsible for everything she'd done since,

including the life of deception she built around herself to justify every action she'd taken. Whether the end goal of those actions was wrong or right didn't matter. What she did made her guilty, regardless.

A car honked. She jumped, more unaware of her surroundings than she'd ever been.

But she couldn't escape the strangling clutch of guilt that gripped her soul, tormented her mind.

Another memory nudged at the darkness that closed in. What else had Michael said that day?

*"Just like I have to believe in God because He is true."*

The statement rang in her ears, echoing as she tried to grab hold of the words. Because they suddenly sounded like hope instead of the reason for guilt she'd been running from all these years.

The God she'd learned about from her parents as a child was not only a God of judgment but of forgiveness. She'd been taught in college and by the school of life to dismiss Him as another deception. But what if that had been the lie?

What if she'd been running from God when He was the only One worthy of her trust?

A feeling, the one she'd probably tried to squelch most of all, rose from somewhere within her. Or maybe it was put there. Whatever the source, it was a conviction so strong she couldn't deny it any longer.

*And ye shall know the truth and the truth shall make you free.*

The words inscribed on the wall of CIA headquarters blazed through her, filled her soul with the truth.

Those words were from the Bible, God's Word. And He'd made sure she had seen them at headquarters, heard them from Michael, and remembered them now.

She recalled enough of her Sunday School lessons and what her parents had taught her to know He offered her protection, safety, and love. That He offered forgiveness.

Her head full of lies had created a web of deception that made her lose her way. But her soul knew.

There was real truth. His name was God. And she could trust Him because He was the Truth itself.

"God." Her voice drew Raksa back to her shoulder. She touched her hand to the side of his face. "It's me." Her mind floundered through her identities, trying to choose which name to use.

She swallowed. "Sofia." Moisture sprang to her eyes as she voiced the truth, her own name, for the first time in so many years. She blinked rapidly, not sure what she'd do if the tears fell.

"I'm sorry I ran from You." Totally inadequate. It wasn't like God didn't know the whole truth even if she tried to mask it. She moistened her lips and tried again. "I'm sorry I denied You. That I didn't trust you and didn't believe the truth about You. Mami and Papi raised me better than that. They taught me that You'll forgive anyone who repents and asks for Your forgiveness."

She raised her hands to the wheel. Gripped it though she wasn't going anywhere.

"I'm asking you for that forgiveness now, God. I don't want to live in a world of lies anymore. I want to be free to know and live by the truth. Like You said we can. Please, God. Please, let the Truth set me free."

Raksa nudged his wet nose into her neck.

She drew in a shaky breath and chuckled, not sure where the sudden surge of joy that infused her body was coming from. She stretched away from Raksa's moist affection and caught a glimpse of herself in the rearview mirror.

Sofia smiled back.

She stared at the reflection. Was that her? Yes. The brightness, the passion in the eyes. It was Sofia. *She* was Sofia. But better. Because the face that stared back at her had assets Sofia never used to have. Truth, forgiveness, hope.

Energy infused her as she became aware of the sensations within that seemed to be showing on the outside. It was if a fog of confusion in her mind had been cleared away, and the vulnerable, grounded, powerful parts of her that she'd closed off now flexed and breathed, shaking off dust and readying for action.

Action.

Rocky and Michael were still in danger.

And she was still trapped.

Or was she?

Another smile stretched her mouth. "Raksa, let's get out of here. Michael and Rocky need us."

She grabbed her knapsack, opened the door, and sprang out. She freed Raksa from the back, and he barked in an echo of her excitement.

"Let's go!" Sofia took off at a sprint, darted with Raksa past barriers and obstacles, flying on wings of trust that God would protect her loved ones better than she ever could.

# THIRTY-THREE

Michael sucked in a breath as the elevator doors opened and allowed a gush of fresh air into the crowded space. Thank the Lord he wasn't claustrophobic. But being stuffed into the elevator like sardines with all the other tourists eager to see the view from the IPF Tower didn't do a thing to calm his pulse.

He stepped off the elevator and moved to the side, letting tourists brush past him as he checked the time on his phone. Twenty-five minutes since Verdugo's threatening text.

Was he too late to save Rocky?

No. He couldn't be. Verdugo wanted Michael, not Rocky. The assassin would keep her alive to be sure Michael came, wouldn't he?

The Phoenix K-9 team would come soon. And Sofia. He was sure of that. But it would take them longer to get there from the courthouse than it'd taken him from the park.

He was Rocky's first and best chance to be rescued. After all, he was the only one who could offer Verdugo a trade.

Michael scanned the space in front of him, far more interested in the people than the views from floor-to-ceiling windows of the observation deck.

Gift items were sold in a store-like kiosk in the center of the space, surrounded by a wide path that edged the perimeter of windows. Most of the people pressed toward the windows, but some browsed the gift options.

No one seemed to watch him suspiciously. Would he even know if he saw Verdugo? Sofia had said the assassin could disguise himself as anyone.

Could be the middle-aged woman who glanced his way by the spinner rack of postcards.

Or the man who held a guidebook in front of his face? Probably too obvious.

This wasn't getting Michael any closer to finding Rocky or getting her away from the assassin. He started to walk, following the open path behind visitors that lined the windows.

*Lord, please help me find her.*

Would Verdugo have Rocky with him right now? He wouldn't be able to disguise her very well. But that likely meant he wouldn't risk having her out in the open like this.

Michael's pulse ticked off seconds as he kept moving, checking the people he passed, homing in on any children Rocky's size.

He lifted his phone again and pulled up the text message. *Rocky is waiting for you at IPF Tower observation deck.*

He had remembered correctly. But no Rocky. Now what?

Verdugo wouldn't have left her here somewhere, would he?

Michael's gazed landed on an information desk toward the center of the space. No employees were there right now. He walked toward it, his breath shallowing. Could Rocky be hidden behind it? He gripped the smooth brown finish of the countertop and stretched to see behind the desk.

Empty.

He straightened. "Where are you, Rocky?"

Something hard and cold jammed into his ribs. "Glad you asked." The man's voice muttered from behind as his breath hit the skin of Michael's neck just above his collar.

Michael held still, though adrenaline filtered into his

veins. The man was shorter than he was. Good to know. "Verdugo?"

"Not many people get a chance to speak my name in front of me." A foreign accent Michael couldn't place sharpened the assassin's consonants and colored his vowels.

He must have his weapon concealed somehow or panic would've already taken hold of the bystanders. This could be the best chance Michael would have to disarm him. In public, when Verdugo didn't want to draw attention.

"Don't think of trying anything. You would be dead before you could move. And then I will kill the child."

She was alive. Michael's eyes slid shut as relief coursed through him. *Thank you, Jesus.* "Where is Rocky? Is she all right?" He risked angling his head toward the man but couldn't twist far enough to see him with the gun digging into his ribs.

"All your questions will be answered if you cooperate."

"You have my word." He would cooperate all the way to Rocky. But after that, all bets were off.

He might not be able to defeat a world-class assassin like Verdugo, but if it meant saving Rocky, he'd die trying.

---

"I'm in."

Sofia pressed the earpiece farther into place just in time to hear Cora's voice. Didn't know if it was meant for her or not, but she responded anyway. "Base, this is Team 1." As first on scene, she assumed the designation for her and Raksa. "We're onsite. Repeat communication."

She breathed deeply and evenly, tried to come down from the long sprint as she and Raksa crossed the IPF Center's main lobby to reach the elevator bank. Thanks to two years of living in the Cities and constant awareness of all escape routes, she'd been able to cut through alleys and shortcuts to reach the IPF Tower faster than she could've by car.

"Team 1, this is Base. I'm in the location's security cameras."

Cora had hacked into the IPF Center's security feed? Sweet. One of the many benefits to working for an agency that wasn't confined by the same restrictions as law enforcement. Agent Nguyen would be able to get legal access and was probably working on that, but red tape took way too long. Rocky and Michael could be dead by then.

"Michael and another man just went into the emergency stairwell from the observation deck."

Sofia's pulse surged. Michael was still alive.

"Could you ID the other guy?" Sofia darted with Raksa through the crowds gathered by the fleet of elevators she bypassed in favor of the emergency stairwell access door at the end of the wide hall.

"Team 1, that's a negative. Medium height, brown hair, full beard. Tan jacket and blue jeans. No noticeable weapon or use of force."

Always so bold. Verdugo didn't have to dodge cameras when he knew his disguise made him unrecognizable, and he had control over his hostage without having to touch him or have a weapon in sight. Threatening Michael with Rocky's life would be enough to get complete cooperation in this case.

Sofia gritted her teeth as she reached for the door to the stairs.

"Team 1, hold it." Cora's voice stopped her cold. "Running up fifty flights will take too long."

"What floor did they go to?"

"No cameras in the stairwell, so I can't be positive."

Sofia could tell from Cora's tone that she was about to drop one of her hesitant, yet incredibly helpful insights. "But I didn't see them get off. There are no cameras on the fifty-first floor. It's closed, awaiting office renovations for a new renter."

Sofia turned back toward the elevator bank. "There are

319

too many people waiting for elevators here. It'd take forever to reach the fifty-first floor."

"Team 1, head back to the elevators. I have an idea."

Sofia walked with Raksa toward the crowds. Three of the elevator doors opened, and a third of the people waiting piled into them.

"Got it." Cora's voice carried a lilt of triumph. "Team 1, go to the farthest elevator on your left."

Sofia weaved through the people just as those near the elevator Cora had directed her to looked above the doors and shook their heads. They stepped away, allowing Sofia and Raksa close to the suddenly unpopular elevator.

She glanced up. The digital sign above the doors flashed three words: *OUT OF ORDER.*

Sofia grinned. "Nice one, Base."

"It's all yours, Team 1."

Sofia punched the button, her grin widening as the doors instantly slid open. She stepped onto the diamond tile with Raksa and pressed the button to shut the doors before another opportunist decided to join her. "Fifty-first floor, here we come."

"Team 1, all PK-9 teams en route to you. Alpha Team ETA is ten minutes."

Good. Phoenix and Dagian would be the best assets to have in a fight with Verdugo. But Sofia couldn't wait ten minutes. Rocky and Michael wouldn't have that much time.

Michael was already in Verdugo's hands. He was the assassin's mission. Unless Sofia could reach them in the next minute, maybe seconds, there was nothing to stop Verdugo from completing the job.

# THIRTY-FOUR

Verdugo exited the stairwell behind Michael without a word.

Michael's breaths came shallow and fast, whether from the climb up four flights or the adrenaline pumping through him as he'd tried to think ahead. Think of some action to take that could save Rocky's life and maybe his own.

He scanned the expanse in front of him and stepped farther into the room. Nearly the whole floor was open, no furniture and few walls standing. Clean, white walls appeared to box in one corner with a glass door as the entry point. Perhaps where the elevator opened onto this floor?

Gray carpet squares covering the floor suggested the space waited to be partitioned into offices.

Where was Rocky?

The hairs on the back of Michael's neck stood on end. Had Verdugo led him here without intending to let him see Rocky at all?

He turned toward the assassin, using the movement to angle his body and increase the distance between them. "Where's the girl?"

Verdugo's face, what little of it Michael could see past his bushy beard, remained expressionless.

Except for his eyes. A coldness tinged the brown orbs, probably not even the guy's natural eye color.

He was at least four inches shorter than Michael. On the heavier side. Not in great shape. But that could be part of his disguise. And Michael knew enough about martial arts and weapons to know smaller size didn't mean Verdugo was any less dangerous. If Michael hadn't believed that before, he would now after seeing Sofia in action against bigger opponents.

"Where's your bodyguard?"

Michael blinked at Verdugo's sudden question, then wished he hadn't shown a reaction. Did he mean Sofia? Michael moistened his lips. Crossed his arms in a movement he hoped looked casual despite the way his heart crashed into his ribs. "I have a lot of bodyguards."

Verdugo didn't move, didn't go closer to Michael. Yet a subtle shift of his features—or was it his stance—slid a chill down Michael's spine. "You would have been dead minutes ago if I desired. Don't tempt me now."

Michael's throat dried to gravel. Afraid his voice would crack if he spoke, he swallowed first, hoping Verdugo didn't notice the sign of fear. "So you aren't going to kill me?" Of course he was going to. But he hadn't even tried to yet. Was that a good sign or a bad sign? What was he waiting for?

"I'll ask you one more time. Where is your bodyguard? Long, black hair with a German shepherd."

Michael's mind raced, searching for the right answer. Hard to know when he couldn't figure out why Verdugo was asking. Why he hadn't tried to kill him yet like the other times he'd attacked the safe houses. "She's always nearby." Maybe that would scare the assassin a bit. Make him nervous. If a man like him could worry about anything, he should be worried about Sofia and Raksa.

"I'm counting on it."

Another chill trembled through Michael at Verdugo's deadly tone. He wanted to see Sofia? Dismay twisted Michael's gut. "I thought you were hired to kill me."

Verdugo chuckled. A hard sound devoid of humor. "Don't worry. I will get to you."

"What do you want with my bodyguard?"

"Sometimes I work for myself."

"You—" Michael's voice stuck on his incredulous question. He tried again. "You want to…kill her?"

He flinched as Verdugo finally moved.

In quick, precise movements, the assassin jerked up both sleeves of the tan jacket he wore open over a navy blue T-shirt. Red, swollen wounds pierced the sandy-colored skin of his arms. Marks in half-round shapes. The shape of the teeth in a dog's mouth.

If he'd been looking at anyone else's wounds, Michael would've felt sorry for him. But those bites had saved Sofia's life, Rocky's and Nevaeh's, not to mention his own.

"These cannot be erased. Difficult to disguise. They always will be." Verdugo snapped his sleeves back in place, covering the wounds. "Anyone who interferes with my work must be eliminated."

Eliminated. The word pierced Michael's chest and tumbled downward, into his stomach.

And Sofia was sure to be coming here now. To save Rocky. To save him.

*Lord, please help.*

She had beaten Verdugo before. Could she do it again? This time to protect herself?

———

Sofia stared at the numbers on the elevator screen as they counted up. *49, 50.*

She hunkered down with Raksa in the back corner.

Not ideal to arrive blind on the floor where Verdugo likely was. But speed was top priority now. She could deal with an ambush. Couldn't deal with Michael or Rocky, dead.

She shoved away the emotion that clenched her insides.

*51.* The elevator slowed. Stopped.

She breathed in. Out. Glock aimed.

The doors shifted, loosened. Opened.

A blank white wall greeted them.

She stood, cleared the opening from all angles.

Empty.

"Raksa, with me." She gave the quiet command. Wasted no time leaving the elevator to find Michael.

Back against the wall, she sidestepped toward the glass door that was centered in a glass wall at the end of the partitioned entryway.

Open, carpeted floor lay beyond the door, running uninterrupted until the far wall.

A rumble stopped her.

Raksa stood still as he emitted a low growl, head angled toward the wall, just in front of her to the left.

Was Verdugo on the other side?

She dropped. Lay flat on her belly. She gave Raksa the hand signal to do the same.

Pops cracked the air. A shower of bullets punctured the wall above her.

Verdugo must've packed his AK-47 again.

The shots suddenly tracked upward. Out of control?

The pops stopped, allowed grunts to reach her ears.

A crack. Then a thud.

Michael? Her heart seized. Had he tried to make a move on Verdugo? He should know better than to attack a trained assassin. But he couldn't stand by while someone shot at her. That wasn't Michael.

Her pulse throbbed in her throat. She had to distract Verdugo before he decided to kill Michael and be done with it. Unless Michael was already dead, and the noises were from something else. Maybe Rocky?

"That trick is getting old, don't you think?" She shouted loud enough to be heard through what was evidently a thin wall.

"What would you prefer? Explosives?"

"And blow yourself up along with me and the building?" She tinted her voice with haughty challenge. "You're supposed to be the best, Verdugo." Her heart pounded against her smooshed ribcage, belying her bluff. If Verdugo was here, ready for her, had he already killed Michael?

"Don't worry about me." Michael's voice, though weaker than normal, reached her through the wall with the force of a sunbeam shooting to her soul. "Go ahead and finish him."

A smile stretched her mouth, and she didn't try to hold back the laugh that tumbled out. She was suddenly eight years old again, eager to give Hale the Whale a pounding for Michael's sake.

"Would you like to see him die or should I finish you first?" Verdugo's icy threat cooled Sofia's joy.

And layered steel in her veins.

"What's your escape plan, Verdugo?" She paused. Let the question sink in. "I've got my team and the FBI hot on my heels. Oh, and your CIA buddies." Might as well use them for something helpful. "You know, the ones you're always running from? They know you're here, too."

And they would arrive shortly, no doubt. Sofia's jaw clenched. But she didn't think of running. Not until Michael and Rocky were safe.

"Every second we spend here is helping me. Hurting you." Wasn't like him to have delayed this long. Almost seemed like a miracle he hadn't killed Michael before she got here. Unless...

"Oh, I get it." She let her smile infuse her voice. "You wanted to see me. Aw, that's sweet."

"You won't think so when I end you and that mutt."

The confirmation of her suspicion sparked hope in her chest. He was mad she'd beat him, she and Raksa. Verdugo finally had a weakness. She could use that.

"Then forget the hostages. If you're as good as your reputation, you don't need the leverage. Just you and me. The best wins, and winner takes all."

Seconds ticked as she waited for his reply.

"Or I could send my K-9 after you. That went well last

time." Even a cold assassin like Verdugo might've fallen prey to the common fear of dog attacks. Especially when his wounds—to his skin and his pride—were probably still fresh.

"Rooftop. One minute." His curt reply surged energy through her veins.

She kept her voice even, as if she couldn't care less. "Agreed."

"You welsh, I'll finish Barrett and the girl. Slowly. And I'll let you watch."

That meant Rocky was still alive, too. Sofia breathed easier and ignored Verdugo's threats, though she knew he would do his best to make good on them.

"One minute and counting. You first." She pulled her feet under her.

He spattered the wall with bullets.

She ducked. Looked through the glass door to see him move backward to the emergency stairwell with the AK-47 aimed her direction.

She waited until he reached the stairwell door and disappeared behind it. She straightened and dashed for the glass door, pushed through and jogged around the corner with Raksa.

Michael was slowly getting up from the floor, shoving up onto his knees.

She bent and took his arm, pulled to help him up.

"I could've decked him, you know." His mouth angled in an adorable grin as he straightened. He swayed slightly.

She tightened her grip on his arm and smiled. "Oh, I know." She scanned his handsome face, the features she'd thought she might never see again.

Blood slashed across his forehead where Verdugo had probably rammed the butt of his rifle into Michael's skull.

Her fingers went to the wound, stopped short of touching it. Her hand drifted lower, made contact with the rough stubble coating his jaw. Lingered there.

Everything in her yearned to slip her arms around him

and hold him close. But he might not stay alive if she didn't meet Verdugo. And end this.

She dropped her hand. "Gotta run."

Michael caught her wrist in a gentle hold as she passed him. "Don't go. You can stay. Help me find Rocky. The others will come, and we'll be safe."

She shook her head. Met the storm of emotion in his amazing blue eyes. "You'd never be safe. You or Rocky. He'll always come back until he finishes the job."

"Then let me go with you. I can help."

She gave in then. Slid her arms around his waist and touched her cheek to his chest, ever so briefly, as his strong hands went to her back, holding her like he didn't want to let go. "Rocky needs you more." Sofia pulled back. "Find her."

His eyebrows drew together as he gave a slow, grim nod.

Raksa whined. She looked down at her partner. Her friend. Strategy said to keep him with her. He would be an asset against Verdugo, tip the scales in her favor.

But Rocky could be hurt right now. She was for sure scared and alone. And if Sofia failed and Verdugo returned for Michael, he'd need Raksa's protection more than she did.

"Raksa, wait." She stepped back from Michael as she gave the shepherd a quick scratch behind the ears. "You're with Michael now, buddy."

She returned her gaze to Michael. "As soon as I'm gone, tell him to 'Search,' and he'll help you find Rocky." She backed away as she continued the instructions. "He'll look for human scent anywhere on this floor or wherever you take him."

"Sofie," Michael took a step toward her, his hand outstretched, "you don't have to do this. We can hide together if we need to."

"No. I'm not hiding anymore."

His eyes brightened around the edges of the pain and worry.

"Besides, I do have to do this." She let a small smile play on her closed lips. "We take care of each other, remember?"

The warm, surprised smile that curved his mouth and the love in his eyes were the last things she saw as she turned and ran.

Toward the most dangerous fight of her life.

For the first time, she didn't know if she could win.

# THIRTY-FIVE

Expect the unexpected.

The mantra had never served her better than at this moment—an appointment with an assassin.

She paused in front of the door at the top of the emergency stairwell marked, *NO ENTRANCE. AUTHORIZED PERSONNEL ONLY.*

Verdugo had blown the lock with a small explosive. And now he waited for her on the other side.

He wouldn't play fair. Wouldn't follow any rules.

Just the way she liked it. She rolled back her shoulders and took in a deep breath. Let it out. And grinned.

She ducked low, shoved the door open, and rolled onto the concrete.

Shots cracked, whizzed past her as she slid out of the somersault into a side spin. She came up and lunged behind a tangle of metal antennae and satellite discs. Patchy concealment at best.

The bullets had come from the east.

A shed stood that direction, in the middle of the roof.

Best place for cover. And Verdugo had gotten there first.

She'd just have to get around him.

She stayed low, wove through the web of crisscrossed grids that supported a network of antennae and receivers.

Movement by the shed.

She flattened. Bullets pinged off the metal bars between her and Verdugo.

She aimed her Glock at his head, just past the north wall of the shed. Fired.

He jerked back.

She couldn't stay long here. Too exposed. His next shot could find her through her spotty concealment.

She reached for her ankle. Slipped her small backup gun from the holster there.

He shot off another round.

She returned fire. Pushed him into cover.

*Now.* She leaped up. A gun in each hand, she fired both, one after the other, as she ran through the powerful wind to the west end of the shed.

She hit the wall with her back. Enough bullets left in both guns to finish him if she played it smart.

All she had to do now was get around the shed to Verdugo without him expecting her.

Simple. She grinned at her inner sarcasm as she bent and returned her secondary weapon to the ankle holster.

She straightened and inched toward the southern corner of the shed. An attempt to get behind him. Though he'd expect that just as much as a head-on attack.

She peered around the corner.

Nothing.

A gust of wind blew strands of hair across her eyes. She pulled her hair back, tucked it behind her ears. She took in a breath and inched soundlessly to the south wall.

A slight scraping sound jerked her head to the roof.

Just as Verdugo crashed down on her.

Michael's heartbeat thudded in his ears as he followed Raksa across the large space of the fifty-first floor. Would they find Rocky? Would she be hurt...or worse?

And what about Sofia? Right now, fighting an assassin on the roof.

She was Sofia now. He'd seen it in the brief moments before she'd left to battle Verdugo. In her eyes, in the very real smile she'd given him. He'd felt it in her gentle touch, in her unexpected embrace. But would being more like Sofia make her vulnerable? Maybe she needed the coldness of Amalia to defeat a cruel killer like Verdugo.

He gulped down the worry. *God, you're not surprised by any of these things. Please, help me to trust you. I don't have to know what's going on with Sofie, so long as you know. Keep her safe, Lord. And help us find Rocky soon. Let her be okay.*

Raksa darted behind a wall, and Michael jogged to follow. As his adrenaline had subsided a bit after Verdugo and Sofia left, Michael had seen the floor wasn't as completely open and unfinished as he'd first thought.

Two of the corner sections were partitioned into office spaces enclosed by white walls that he'd thought were the outer walls from a distance.

Michael lurched to keep up with Raksa as he darted around another wall to a second square-sized room. The shepherd's determination and focus infused Michael with hope. The moment he'd given the *Search* command, the K-9 had launched into action, nose in the air as he seemed to look for a scent.

Of course, Verdugo had already been there. Probably with Rocky. Would the dog be able to distinguish the scent from wherever they had walked before and any scent of Rocky still there, now?

The shepherd went to a closed wooden door in the wall. He sniffed at a small gap between the door and the carpet. Then he lifted his head and barked.

Michael's heart jumped in his chest. Was Rocky inside?

"Rocky?" Her name burst from his lips as he lunged for the door and yanked it open.

A lump lay on the floor in the dark closet. He reached for it as Raksa leaned in to smell the object.

The *Rocky* film backpack her dad had given her.

She had been here. But did that mean she was gone now?

A vise crunched around his rib cage. *Lord, please let her still be here. Or somewhere we can find her.*

Raksa reversed suddenly, nearly knocking into Michael's legs as he dashed by.

The K-9 wasn't done yet.

Michael's pulse surged, rushing at a faster clip than he could chase after Raksa.

The shepherd sprinted out of the walled-in section and bolted for the opposite corner, where another office area was divided by walls.

Had finding the backpack helped Raksa distinguish between multiple scents? Or maybe he'd heard something?

Raksa barked as he reached the other section well ahead of Michael.

Pumping his arms, Michael sprinted to catch up. He swung around the first wall.

Raksa's tail disappeared through the next doorway.

Michael surged forward again. Rounded the corner.

Raksa barked as he paused by a large desk that stood against a wall. The only piece of furniture Michael had seen on the whole floor.

Could Rocky be in the desk somehow?

A small sound reached his ears in a brief pause between Raksa's barks. Thudding?

Energy pumped through Michael's muscles as he gripped the heavy desk and pulled it away from the wall.

A steel, square plate covered part of the wall, secured with screws.

Raksa rushed forward and barked at the plate.

What did Sofia tell him when she wanted the barks to stop?

"Okay, boy. Enough barking, Raksa."

Something in what he said must have been right because the shepherd instantly stopped and panted as he stared at Michael.

A quiet thump came from behind the plate. Twice.

"Rocky?" He leaned his ear against the steel.

A moan responded.

*Rocky.* Desperation and joy crashed together in his soul. "It's okay, Rocky! I'm here. I'm going to get you out of there."

He reached for the plate as he shouted reassurances. He tried to push his fingers between the plate and the wall.

There was no gap.

He pushed harder. Winced as the edge sliced the skin under his short nails.

He kept pressing his fingertips in until he finally felt the plate give. He slipped his fingers into the gap and pulled. Then harder. Grunted as he pulled again.

The plate popped free, sending him backward.

He clambered up to the balls of his feet and reached for Rocky.

His sweet girl was crunched with her knees up, touching her chin, in the small space Verdugo must have cut out of the new wall.

She stretched her hands toward him, but her little wrists were bound with duct tape. The same tape that covered her mouth.

Anger fired his blood. He'd like to go up to the roof and take care of Verdugo himself right now.

But his girl needed him. "It's okay, baby girl. I'm here." He engulfed Rocky in his arms, lifting her as he stood. He touched the edge of the tape over her mouth. "This might sting a little, okay?"

She nodded, her hazel eyes rimmed in red from crying.

His gut clenched at the evidence of her tears. He pulled the tape off quickly.

She closed her eyes, then popped them open again, just before she buried her head into his chest.

Raksa barked, making Michael jump.

Another dog answered, barking from somewhere close.

"Raksa!"

Was that Nevaeh's shout?

"In here!" Michael walked quickly to get out of the office area.

The Phoenix K-9 team hurried across the open floor to meet him and Rocky.

Relief washed over Michael in a wave of praise. *Thank you, Lord.*

But would they be in time to help Sofia?

# THIRTY-SIX

Sofia grappled with Verdugo, her Glock knocked away on the ground by the shed.

She'd gotten an arm inside the rear chokehold he'd tried to lock on her when he dropped from the roof and took her to the ground from behind. Kept him from choking her out.

But she wasn't free. Yet.

She gripped his arm with her other hand at the same time she twisted one of her legs backward to trap his. She rolled, pushing him off-balance so he had to tumble with her or let go.

He rolled with her. As he rotated to the bottom position under her back, she thrust her elbow hard into the flesh where his liver should be.

Verdugo only grunted as they continued to roll. But loosened his hold on her neck.

All she needed.

She slammed her head backward into his nose.

He jerked away, opening his grip even more.

She slipped her arms around his, flipped her body to face him and let go to smack his ear with an open hand. Struck hard enough to possibly rupture his ear drum.

An ordinary man might've screamed. Verdugo's dark eyes,

close to hers, turned fiercer. He pushed her away with his legs. Launched a kick to her stomach.

Her breath left in a pained whoosh as he got to his feet.

She scrambled up, reaching for her ankle holster.

He dashed away, zig-zagged behind poles as she aimed.

He jumped over the parapet. Dropped out of sight.

No way he would've jumped off the building. Must be a ledge there. Probably buying time to get out the gun he must've put away to tackle her.

She took an angled approach, ready to hit the concrete if he appeared.

Movement.

She dropped. Too late.

Fire seared her shoulder as she rolled under his other bullets.

She twisted. Aimed at the parapet he'd disappeared behind again.

She was out in the open. An easy mark.

But she was never an easy mark.

She waited. Breathed.

The curve of his head, a fraction of movement.

She unleashed one round.

He jerked as he fired, shot wild.

Her second plug hit his low shoulder, sent him back, out of view.

The boom of the shot faded. Silence answered.

She pulled her feet up under her. Listened.

Nothing but wind.

Crouched, she quickly moved toward the parapet, crossed over tracks that must be used for some kind of heavy equipment. She reached the parapet, looked over it.

Five feet down, jagged platforms jutted out—a topside view of the tower's famous sawtooth design.

Fingers clung to one of the angled teeth.

Verdugo.

She froze. Should she help him? Letting him die would guarantee he would never kill anyone again.

She knew what Amalia would do. But she remembered what Sofia would do, too.

Sofia climbed over the parapet and dropped to the triangular space of roof. Tucked her gun behind her back. Reached for the assassin's hands. "Grab on."

Blood trickled down from where her bullet had nicked his head, the red drop nearly touching his narrowed eyes. His hairline was fractured, revealing a touch of blond hair beneath the wig. "You were the one..." He grunted out the words. "In Colombia."

She moved closer to the edge and reached lower. "Take my hand."

"You had..." he puffed out air, his face reddening, "brown hair then."

Her gaze rested on the bullet hole in his tan jacket where his shoulder connected to his chest. Dark blood soaked through. He couldn't hang on much longer. "Game's up, Verdugo. Let me help you."

"Never." He grimaced. Fingers slipped.

She reached for them, tried to grab.

He fell.

Seconds passed.

Then screams rose from the street below.

She looked over the edge. A crowd parted around his body. At least he hadn't hit anyone.

"Amalia!" Nevaeh's shout made her spin away from the edge.

She hefted herself over the parapet and waved at Nevaeh and Alvarez, Jazz and Flash. A sight for sore eyes.

She walked toward them as they approached her, stopping near the shed.

"Cora's beside herself." Jazz's smile matched Nevaeh's. "Apparently, our coms don't work up here." She glanced in the direction of the many antennae. "Too much interference, I guess."

Movement caught Sofia's attention at the east end of the rooftop. She reached for her weapon.

Phoenix and Dag emerged from behind a large satellite dish.

Sofia let out a long breath. Phoenix would be in the most strategic position to handle Verdugo if he wasn't contained. Always prepared.

"Looks like somebody finally got you." Nevaeh's remark drew Sofia to notice the direction of her friend's gaze. The wound to her shoulder that Sofia became aware was oozing blood through her short T-shirt sleeve and down her arm.

"We all thought you were invincible." Nevaeh tilted her curly-haired head with a grin.

Sofia smiled. "You mean this red stuff? I don't think it's even real."

Nevaeh and Jazz laughed as Phoenix and Dag reached their little gathering.

The slight hint of satisfaction in Phoenix's gaze, a rare glimpse of emotion, answered the question that kept Sofia from joining the laughter.

"Rocky's okay." Sofia made the statement, and Phoenix's nod confirmed.

"And so is Michael." Nevaeh's mouth curved in a gentle smile, her brown eyes softened as if she could detect the love bursting Sofia's heart. "Go on, girl. Go see your people."

Sofia didn't need any more encouragement than that. She bolted for the door to the stairwell, a grateful prayer on her lips for the truth she no longer wanted to deny. She, Sofia Sanchez, loved Michael and Rocky more than anything. And she wanted nothing more than to look into their eyes and tell them that truth.

---

Michael frowned from his sitting position on the floor next to Rocky as Owens appeared with what must be some of his CIA buddies and stopped to say something to the nearest FBI agent. She pointed toward Agent Nguyen, and Owens strode her way with his cohorts.

The previously empty fifty-first floor suddenly felt as crowded as Times Square thanks to the various agencies represented, along with the two EMTs who examined Rocky and Michael in the corner.

Bristol and Toby gave them a line of protection from all the chaos, standing a few feet away. Raksa lay protectively at Rocky's other side, and Cora, also standing nearby, was doing a good job mothering the girl when the EMTs weren't examining her.

Bristol kept a vigilant watch on the door to the stairwell where FBI agents had recently disappeared to join the rest of the Phoenix K-9 team on the roof. And Sofia. He hoped.

*Lord, please let her be all right.*

"There." The male EMT who bandaged Michael's forehead backed away, giving Michael a clearer line of sight to the stairwell door. "You just missed needing stiches. Keep it bandaged and clean until the wound seals."

"Thanks." Michael couldn't pull his gaze away from the door as he responded. If it was possible to will things into being, Sofia would be here by now.

Maybe he should go up to the roof himself.

He put a hand on Rocky's shoulder through the blanket the EMT had wrapped around her. "I'll be right back, baby girl."

The door opened just as he stood.

Raksa barked and jumped to his feet.

Sofia appeared, walking toward him like a breathtaking vision out of a dream.

Raksa ran to her, earning a laugh—a glorious sound that trickled joy into Michael's soul.

He couldn't hold still any longer. He hurried toward her, brushing past uniformed agents until he stood in front of her.

She straightened from petting Raksa.

Her dark, brown eyes—Sofia's passion-filled eyes—locked on his.

He opened his arms, and she went into them, fitting against his chest as naturally and easily as if they'd been doing this their whole lives. As if they'd been made for each other.

And he knew it was true. She was his past and his future.

"Amalia!" Rocky, bouncing back from the trauma as quickly as only a child could, put her small hands on Michael's leg and Sofia's hip.

"Rocky." Love infused the word and lit Sofia's face as she squatted down by the girl and pulled her into a fierce hug.

Only then did Michael notice the red streak on Sofia's arm.

"You're hurt."

She glanced up at him, then followed the direction of his gaze to her shoulder where the blood seemed to originate. "Just a scratch." She set Rocky away from her but took the girl's hand as she stood. "I have something to tell you both." She included Michael with her warm gaze.

"I hate to interrupt this reunion." A deep male voice halted the anticipation building in Michael's chest.

Owens stood to Michael's right and stared at Sofia with dark eyes that were finally devoid of sunglasses. "Sofia Sanchez. We've been looking for you."

She stiffened but kept Rocky's hand in hers. "I know."

"You gave us quite a chase. I'm impressed."

She dipped her chin slightly, an acknowledgement of the backhanded compliment.

"Look, you can't believe she's guilty of treason." Michael stepped closer to Owens. "She just captured an assassin the CIA has been after and couldn't apprehend."

"Michael." Sofia's cautionary tone drew his gaze to hers.

"What? Didn't you capture him?"

"He's dead. But—"

"There." Michael swung his head to Owens. "See? She took care of him for you. For our country."

"Michael, you can't fix this." Her eyes softened even as she stopped him. "I'll have to go with them."

No. She couldn't. Not when he'd just found her. He glared

at the man who threatened to take her away. "Have I mentioned I'm an investigative journalist? What if I—"

"Relax, Barrett." A woman's low-pitched tone cut through his desperate attempt to stop the inevitable.

Phoenix Gray stood with her silent dog to Michael's left, her gaze shooting between him and Sofia to fix on Owens. "You haven't checked your messages in the last ten minutes." It was a statement, not a question, said with enough confidence that the operative pulled out his phone and tapped the screen a couple times.

After a few seconds, Owens looked to Phoenix, then glanced at Sofia before he swiftly turned and walked away as he lifted the phone to his ear.

Michael and Sofia turned to Phoenix.

"He won't be bothering you again." She watched Sofia as she said the words in the even tone she always seemed to use. Even though her statement jumpstarted Michael's hopeful pulse. Did she mean what he thought she did?

"He's contacting his superior, who has seen reason concerning the suspicion about you."

Even Sofia looked puzzled, her black eyebrows gathering. "How?"

"It seems Ramone's testimony about you when he was debriefed and allowed to immigrate was overlooked. He had given a complete account of your role in the Colombian assassination—your attempt to stop it and your betrayal by the same agent who turned on the CIA. That, combined with testimony from another key source, cleared you in their eyes."

Michael had a feeling from the smile that shaped Sofia's closed lips that the other key source and the impetus behind the clearing of Sofia's name was Phoenix.

"Thank you." Sofia looked at her boss, who met her gaze with one Michael couldn't read.

Phoenix dipped her head in a half-nod, then left as silently as she'd appeared.

"Does that mean...?" Michael swung his attention to Sofia.

"I'm free!" The words burst from her in something like a squeal as she threw her arms around his neck and crashed into his chest.

Rocky's giggles blended with their laughter as he caught Sofia in his arms.

"I love you, Michael Barrett." She whispered the words in his ear as her laughter subsided.

Surprise jolted through him.

She pulled back slightly and looked at his face, letting out a laugh at what she must have seen there.

"Did you just say what I think you said?" He felt his mouth angle into a stupid grin as his heart turned to jelly.

She smiled—a passionate, Sofia smile. "I love you, Michael Barrett." She delivered the declaration at full volume this time. And there was no mistaking the truth of the words mirrored in her eyes.

He couldn't wait another moment to show her the answer swelling in his heart. He lowered his head and pressed his lips to her smile.

She returned the kiss with passion as his hands drifted up from her back to her neck where his fingers plunged into her lush hair.

A touch on his leg reminded him they had a young observer. He reluctantly ended the kiss, but his gaze lingered on the woman who'd stolen his heart. "I love you, Sofia Sanchez."

She tilted her head as her smile shifted to the teasing grin he knew by heart. "I know."

"Does this mean you could be my new mommy and daddy?" Rocky's small, hopeful voice drew their attention to the sweet girl, her head tilted up to see them.

Sofia shot him a sly wink before redirecting her gaze to Rocky. "I'll tell you one thing it does mean." She gently caressed Rocky's chin with her curved knuckles. "I love you, too, kiddo."

"Me, too." A smile lit Rocky's face.

Sofia bent to scoop the girl into her arms, Rocky's legs dangling to Sofia's knees.

Michael stepped close and encircled his girls in an embrace he wanted to last forever.

He hadn't found Sofia. God had. And He'd given her to Michael in a way he never could have imagined—to love and to cherish for the rest of his days.

COVERT DANGER

# EPILOGUE

*One month later*

"I think you got more out of the surprise in this party than even Grace did." Nevaeh grinned at Sofia as she approached, a paper plate with birthday cake and a plastic fork in one hand and Cannenta's leash in the other. Although the calm corgi-mix service dog didn't seem to need a leash to stay with Nevaeh. "I've never seen anybody who likes surprises as much as you."

"Guilty as charged." Sofia returned the grin as Nevaeh stopped beside her and turned to face the gathering in the banquet hall. The huge room was decked out in streamers, balloons, and every kind of birthday decoration Sofia, Michael, and the Phoenix K-9 crew could find for Grace's surprise birthday party.

"Good thing Michael knows that about you." The humor in Nevaeh's voice kept the smile fixed on Sofia's face. "Not every girl would appreciate finding an engagement ring in her ammo box."

Sofia laughed. "The even better part was seeing Michael pop up from behind the barricade. I still can't believe Phoenix allowed him to interrupt our drills for a proposal."

Nevaeh shrugged, her grin still intact. "Boss is full of surprises, Sof."

Sofia rolled her eyes at Nevaeh's new nickname for her. She'd wasted no time coming up with one, switching easily and without judgment to using Sofia's real name along with the rest of the PK-9 team.

Gratitude swelled in her chest as she spotted her PK-9 family spread out in the large party venue. Cora and Jana were among the kids at tables in the middle of the room. Grace laughed with the new friends she'd made at Cora's church, which Michael, Sofia, and Grace had started to attend.

With more than a little influence from Phoenix, and even Agent Nguyen, Sofia had managed to gain temporary custody of Grace. By the time Sofia and Michael were married, they should be able to settle the paperwork to officially adopt her. Her heart squeezed at the memory of the day she and Michael had told Grace they wanted to make her their daughter.

"Can I be called Grace again when my last name changes to yours?" Her small features had scrunched as she asked the unexpected question.

Sofia had glanced at Michael before she asked, "Do you want to be called Grace?"

The girl nodded. "It's what mom and dad used to call me. Before..."

She didn't have to finish for them to know what she meant. Before her life had begun to change, starting with her mother's death. Before she'd had to become a fighter to survive.

They and everyone else had switched to calling her Grace from that day forward. And Sofia and Michael couldn't wait to add Barrett as her surname.

But there was a lot to be done before then. Including something that had been pressing on Sofia's heart, growing weightier with every day. She had to see her parents. She wanted to, now that there was no need to hide or run anymore. But she only hoped they'd be happy to see her.

Michael had told them everything that had happened via phone calls. But Sofia hadn't been able to bring herself to talk to them that way. After twelve years without seeing their faces, she had to see them in person the next time they spoke. Had to look into their eyes when she told them she was sorry. Said she loved them, even though she'd done a terrible job of showing it.

But there'd been one delay after another to the plan she and Michael had to travel together to Texas to see her parents.

After Verdugo's death, she'd had to stay with Grace, especially since she initially thought she'd have to go with the girl into witness protection.

Rottier was put behind bars for his arms trafficking conviction, but he could still have a long reach and might try anything to avoid the additional conviction for the murder of Vicki Wilson. Grace's eyewitness testimony was still a threat to him, since it could potentially give him an additional sentence of life imprisonment.

Sofia would never forget her relief when Agent Nguyen had called to tell her the good news. They'd found a recording device hidden behind a vent in Vicki Wilson's apartment that had recorded the events of her murder. Rottier's voice and name were captured for posterity.

One of Rottier's henchmen who had committed the murder on Rottier's orders also agreed to cop a plea and became an eyewitness that could replace the need for Grace to testify. They had Rottier dead to rights without Grace, which meant she was out of danger and free to start a happy and safe new life with Sofia and Michael.

The intrepid reporter had returned to Texas for a couple weeks to put things in order at his old job, but he'd just finished moving into his new apartment in Minneapolis, about five miles from Sofia and Rocky. It turned out that more than one Twin Cities newspaper wanted Michael's journalistic talents, and he had only to choose between offers.

Sofia smiled as she recalled one of the final articles Michael had written for the Houston Chronicle. The piece was a beautiful tribute to Paul Bischoff and Vicki Wilson. Though Paul had been murdered because he accidentally got in the way of Verdugo's attempt to kill Michael, he had died a hero's death. He and Vicki had put their lives on the line for the sake of truth and justice, to expose a treacherous individual and stop him from hurting others. Michael's powerful article had given them the honor due for their bravery and sacrifice.

"Earth to Sof." Nevaeh nudged her arm with an elbow. "You're looking dreamy again." Nevaeh shook her head. "Oh, man. Another of the mighty has fallen."

Sofia gave her a grin. "I wouldn't say fallen, exactly." Though *fallen in love* would exactly describe the fluttery feeling that somersaulted in her belly.

"First Bristol, then Cora. Now you." Nevaeh narrowed her eyes at Sofia, though her mouth pursed like she could barely hold back a smile. "You were the one I would've bet would never give in. Well, after me, that is."

"Careful, Nevaeh." Sofia returned the nudge with a grin. "If it can happen to me, it can happen to anyone. The man of your dreams might be waiting for you, just around the next corner."

Something like fear flashed in Nevaeh's eyes, and Cannenta leaned into her leg.

"You okay?"

"Of course." Nevaeh's smile was forced this time. "Speaking of men, where is Michael, anyway?"

"I'm not sure." Sofia pulled her gaze from Nevaeh to scan the partygoers, reluctant to take Nevaeh's obvious hint that she didn't want any attention drawn to whatever had just bothered her. Frightened her.

Bristol and Jazz had joined Cora to help herd kids as they lined up to pin the tail on the bear—a twist on the classic party game that put Gaston at the center of the kids' attention where he most wanted to be. Raksa and the other Phoenix K-9s joined in the fun as much as they could, nudging kids for attention and letting their off-duty personalities shine.

Phoenix and Dag stood near one of the two exits. Never off duty.

Sofia pressed her lips together. Someday, maybe she'd learn Phoenix's secrets. But for now, she was just grateful her boss had helped her out of the biggest mess of her life. Sofia would look for a chance to return the favor one day.

She scanned the rest of the attendees, Bristol's and Cora's significant others, Rem and Kent, among the people she knew. Others were people Cora had invited from church for a bigger turnout.

No Michael.

"You're right. I don't see him. He was just here a few minutes ago."

"That's strange." The note of humor had returned to Nevaeh's voice and drew Sofia's gaze to her friend's face.

"What are you up to?" Sofia narrowed her eyes.

"Oh, it's not me. It's Michael."

A smile lifted Sofia's mouth. "Another surprise?" Though after his perfect proposal, what could be left?

"You and surprises." Nevaeh shook her head with a chuckle. She glanced toward the open double-doorway. "Okay, you can look now."

Sofia jerked her head in that direction, anticipation skipping her pulse.

Michael stepped through the doorway, handsome enough in his light blue blazer and jeans to take her breath away every time she looked at him.

But the petite woman on his arm drew her gaze.

"Mami?" The whisper fell from her lips as her feet moved.

She wove through the people to cross the room as a man, shorter than Michael and exactly the size of Papi, stopped next to him.

Then she was jogging, joy and sorrow and hope jammed together in her throat. But she stopped short of the two people she most wanted to see, her heart twisting like it might break.

Mami and Papi. But she couldn't touch them, couldn't hug them. She didn't deserve even to be their daughter anymore. She'd tried to reject them, their name and all they held most dear.

"I'm sorry." The murmur was all she could get out. All she could say.

"Oh, Sofia. *Mi* hijita." Papi closed the gap between them as he called her his little daughter. His arms opened wide, and Mami came close, too.

They gathered her in their embrace, crying and laughing.

"Oh, Sofia." Mami, her tearful eyes so near, stared into Sofia's face. "Is it really you?"

Tears tumbled down Sofia's cheeks as she nodded and looked at Michael behind them. "Yes, Mami. It's me."

And Sofia knew, held in the arms of her parents and the gaze of the man who loved her, under the watchful Providence of the God Who made her and called her His own, that truer words had never been spoken.

Turn the Page for a Special Sneak Peek of

GUARDIANS UNLEASHED, BOOK 3

- - - - - - - - - - -

# UNSEEN DANGER

- - - - - - - - - - -

COMING 2023

# EXCERPT OF UNSEEN DANGER

"Branson!"

He swung his head to the source of the urgent call.

B-Puff hurried toward him, the man's bling—two long and clunky silver necklaces—catching the light from the arena's overhead fixtures that were powered on for the evacuation.

"Kicker's hurt." The widened whites of B-Puff's eyes showed his panic. "He got burned up."

Branson put his hand on B-Puff's shoulder. "It'll be okay, man. There's an ambulance on the way. Where is he?"

"With the chick." B-Puff nearly stumbled as he turned away. "Over there."

Branson spotted a person kneeling in the area B-Puff pointed to. Even from behind, there was no missing the womanly curves, but his gaze locked on her red jacket with *Phoenix K-9* printed on the back. She must belong to the K-9 unit the PowerSource Center's head of security had boasted they'd added for D-Chop's concert.

He started in her direction.

"She saved his life." B-Puff's gruff voice at Branson's shoulder made him pause and look at the shorter man. "He was burning up, and she came out of nowhere and was just there. And she put out the flames. It was..." He slid a hand over his bald head and shook it slowly back and forth as he blew out a breath.

"Okay. You better sit down, B-Puff." Branson gently thumped the man's bicep. "Why don't you sit on Pinky's stool until I see how Kicker's doing. Then we'll get out of here, so long as the police don't need to talk to you guys, all right?"

B-Puff wandered toward Pinky in a daze.

Branson swung back toward the woman who was apparently some kind of heroine, if the DJ's drug-fogged account could be trusted.

As he continued her way, Branson assessed the scene. Kicker lay still on the stage floor in front of her.

Movement on the far side of the woman caught his eye.

Was that a dog? A square black and brown head came into view. The stocky dog Branson guessed was a rottweiler watched him with a pink tongue hanging from its mouth.

The woman's voice, husky and rich, floated to Branson as he came up behind her. "I know it hurts, Eddie."

Eddie? Kicker had let this woman call him by his real name?

Maybe he'd been charmed by her mesmerizing voice.

Or maybe it was the hair. Branson's gaze locked on the black bounty as he paused a few feet away. He'd never seen such an abundance of curls as those surrounding her head. A crazy urge to touch the black spirals to see if they were as soft as they looked twitched his fingers.

A pained groan yanked him out of his temporary insanity. Kicker must be hurt badly, but at least he was alive.

"I just need you to breathe for me, okay, Eddie?" The woman's tone stayed even and calm. "The ambulance will be here soon, and we'll get you help with the pain."

Branson stepped to her side, where he could see she held Kicker's wrist in her slim fingers, apparently checking his pulse. Was she a medic instead? Her bounty of curls blocked her face from view.

He crouched beside her. "How's he doing?"

The woman started and leaped away faster than the pond frogs back home.

His heart jumped as he stood and reached for her in case she toppled as she landed five feet from him.

But she jerked back before he could touch her. Her eyes were wide, and her nostrils flared as she stared up at him as if he'd tried to attack her.

A hot zing blazed through his chest as he took in her deep brown eyes, flawless skin, and full lips. Ironic to say the least. D-Chop had given Branson an unsavory nickname because of his disinterest in the female groupies in the hip-hop star's entourage. Now here he was, attracted to a girl for the first time since high school.

And he'd clearly just scared her to death.

Want to be the first to know when you can get *Unseen Danger,*
Book 3 in the *Guardians Unleashed Series?*
Subscribe to Jerusha's newsletter at
www.FearWarriorSuspense.com
and get a free suspense story to read while you wait!

**She never invites visitors. But visitors sometimes invite themselves.**

When a winter storm brings more than snow, May Denver is forced to flee from her home and fight for her life. Can she trust an unwanted neighbor and risk her greatest fear in order to survive?

GRAB THIS ROMANTIC SUSPENSE STORY FOR FREE
WHEN YOU SIGN UP FOR JERUSHA'S NEWSLETTER
www.FearWarriorSuspense.com

# ABOUT JERUSHA

Jerusha Agen imagines danger around every corner, but knows God is there, too. So naturally, she writes romantic suspense infused with the hope of salvation in Jesus Christ.

Jerusha loves to hang out with her big furry dogs and little furry cats, often while reading or watching movies.

Find more of Jerusha's thrilling, fear-fighting stories at www.JerushaAgen.com.

facebook.com/JerushaAgenAuthor

instagram.com/jerushaagen